HEAT STORM

RICHARD CASTLE

HEAT STORM

Paperback edition ISBN: 9781785654930
E-book edition ISBN: 9781785654923

Published by Titan Books
A division of Titan Publishing Group Ltd.
144 Southwark Street, London SE1 0UP

First paperback edition: January 2018

1 3 5 7 9 10 8 6 4 2

A CIP catalogue record for this title is available from the British Library.

Printed and bound in Great Britain by CPI Group UK Ltd.

Did you enjoy this book? We love to hear from our readers.
Please email us at readerfeedback@titanemail.com or write to us at
Reader Feedback at the above address.

To receive advance information, news, competitions, and exclusive offers
online,
please sign up for the Titan newsletter on our website:
WWW.TITANBOOKS.COM

Every writer needs an inspiration.
And I found mine.
Always.

ONE

The foreigner's chest was broad and powerful, and the arms that hung on either side had a solid, useful look about them. His torso tapered to his trim waist, underneath which his thighs bulged back out again. Crowning this impressive example of the human male was a square-shaped head, atop which sat a thick thatch of wavy, dark hair.

In truth, it all might have been too much, too action adventure–hero clichéd: this stunning physique with the square jaw and the perfect teeth, this man who seemed to have been ripped from the cover of a Victoria St. Clair romance novel.

Except of course there were the eyes. They were eyes that teased and danced and loved even when the rest of the foreigner's demeanor was serious. They were eyes that had seen much. They were eyes that missed little.

So, yes, he was handsome. Some would say ruggedly so.

The foreigner was dressed in black tactical gear, a bulletproof vest providing a comforting embrace. Standing next to him, a head shorter and half his weight, was a man wearing the squared-off green uniform of the People's Armed Police, the largest branch of China's Ministry of Public Security. His shirt was tucked neatly into his belt in a way that suggested a perfectly flat

7

stomach. His insignia marked him as a colonel. His name strip contained Chinese characters that are commonly translated into the Roman alphabet as "Feng."

He smoked an unfiltered cigarette, its lit end glowing orange in the predawn dark. When he exhaled, the smell of cloves filled the air.

The men stood side by side on a small bluff. The foreigner's binoculars were trained on a warehouse below them, a two-story painted steel structure with a flat roof and no windows. The only points of egress were the front door and a small hatch in the roof.

The building was almost conspicuously spare, like its owners had worked so hard to make it seem unremarkable that it actually stood out. There was no signage, no attempt at landscaping in the weed-choked lot that surrounded it. The parking area, which was covered in crumbling asphalt, contained a smattering of vehicles, mostly older. It was illuminated by a single floodlight on a pole. There was no sign of movement outside. Most days, very little happened there.

But every once in a while, something did. And on those days, the activity in that spare little building had come to the attention of the highest reaches of the United States government, half a planet away.

"Amazing, an operation like this being able to establish itself and yet going completely undetected," the foreigner said, barely bothering to hide his irony. He spoke in smooth Mandarin, one of the nine languages he had mastered.

"Sometimes the best place to hide is in plain sight," Colonel Feng said, his voice raspy. A wry grin barely formed on his thin lips before he stanched it.

"You would have thought someone would have noticed and started asking questions," the foreigner said.

"You are assuming there is something worth noticing," Colonel Feng said, then switched to English. "I believe there is an American saying about those who assume."

"Yeah, I think it's, 'Keep your friends close and your enemies closer,'" the foreigner said.

Colonel Feng narrowed his eyes and took another drag on his cigarette. Beyond the warehouse, the Huangpu River rolled silently by. Beyond that—and all around them—was the city of Shanghai.

The foreigner did not need to be told that what is today the world's second largest economy—number two with a bullet, some would say—really started in this historic city in east central China. Long ago, it was the first Chinese port opened to trade with the West after China's defeat in the Opium Wars. More recently, it was where the Chinese Communist Party decided to begin loosening the reins on its economy, allowing the tight strictures of Marxism to slough away and be supplanted by the ruthless efficiencies of capitalism.

American financial success had a lot to do with that decision. So did China's long-standing and ingrained sense of exceptionalism.

What has developed since that time is a complicated, delicate relationship between what are essentially the world's only two superpowers. Each country is the other's largest trading partner. Each country is heavily invested in the other. Each country's economy would collapse if the other were to vanish. And yet each country perpetually thinks the other is trying to screw it over.

So there was symbolism there: a Chinese man and an Amercan, standing side by side, at once inextricably aligned and yet at cross-purposes.

"Should be any time now, wouldn't you say?" the foreigner said.

"I'm sure I don't know," Colonel Feng replied. "May I remind you that I am merely here in an oversight capacity, and that this unusual . . . collaboration, shall we call it? . . . is only occurring because of your government's continued insistence about the nature of this operation. But my government categorically denies any knowledge of what you allege is transpiring here."

"Oh, yes, of course," the foreigner said. His face was impassive. But his expressive eyes had sparked. "And that's why you're here completely and totally alone, with no backup whatsoever. To provide oversight."

"It seems we understand each other perfectly," Colonel Feng said.

The clove cigarette glowed again. For a short while, neither man spoke.

What was about to occur had been set in motion two weeks earlier, with a single phone call between two powerful people.

The initiator of that phone call was a mystery to the foreigner. The receiver of it was a man named Jedediah Jones. He worked for the CIA's National Clandestine Service, where his title was head of internal division enforcement. Sometimes he just used the acronym. Spy humor.

Just as the relationship between the United States and China was complex, so was the dance between the foreigner and Jones. The foreigner worked for Jones on a temporary, ad hoc, totally unconfirmed basis. If you were to look at only certain small sample sizes of the men's interactions, you'd draw the conclusion that Jones valued the foreigner like a disposable coffee cup, and, likewise, that the foreigner trusted Jones about as much as a savvy consumer trusted the claims of late night infomercials.

Yet the truth was that they needed each other as much as their nation needed their service. And each had come to rely on the other for his unique set of skills, traits, and resources, many of which had already been called on to arrange this raid.

His cigarette now extinguished, Colonel Feng coughed twice. They were loud, barking coughs, and the foreigner briefly wondered if they were meant as a signal of some sort.

"You know, it's very strange," Feng said when his throat was clear. "You look a great deal like an American intelligence operative by the name of Derrick Storm, a man who freelances for a part of the CIA that supposedly doesn't exist."

"He must be a very good-looking man," the foreigner said.

"We have a full complement of pictures of him, many of them quite explicit, owing to his romantic involvement with an agent of ours a few years back. Perhaps you'd like to accompany me back to my precinct and have a look at them?"

"Who doesn't love looking at someone else's explicit photos?" the foreigner said. "I'll absolutely have a look. As soon as we're done here."

"It would, of course, be illegal for him to be in this country without having properly notified the authorities," Feng said. "He would spend a long time in prison if he was caught."

"Which is why I'm sure he's not here," the foreigner said. "I'm sure a man that attractive and intelligent wouldn't risk a—"

Any further conversation was cut off when, from within the building, there came a low rumbling. It could be both heard in the air and felt in the ground below, which now shook gently.

"Excuse me. That's my cue," the foreigner said. Then he pressed a button to activate an open channel on his communication system and said one word into the microphone attached to his earpiece:

"Go."

The first bullet sprang out of a muzzle that had an Alpha Dog 9 silencer affixed to the end of it, lowering the sound output by more than fifty decibels. What should have been a loud crack was reduced to more of a thump.

The target—the bulb in that single floodlight—stood no chance. Its shattering could not possibly be heard by any of the men inside. Not over the roar of the machines.

With the parking lot now plunged into darkness, the foreigner moved out, sprinting along the bluff then cutting down a path that had been carved into its side. He approached from the south.

Two other men, including the one that had put the lightbulb out of business, were coming from the east. Two more came from the north, where they had been hiding by the banks of the river.

These four were also foreigners, in China on tourist visas, officially unofficial. It was illegal for them to possess firearms. Everything they were about to do was probably illegal.

If anything went wrong, every single bureaucrat at the US Embassy would be able to claim ignorance without a trace of deceit. The ambassador himself was similarly in the dark. At that point, with no diplomatic protection, the men would be left to fend for themselves in the Chinese legal system.

Which was why nothing could go wrong.

And nothing would. The foreigner's intelligence was solid. There was no sign the facility was guarded. He had been training his men for two weeks, so they knew its layout perfectly, having set up a mock version of it during their repeated dry runs. They would have it secured before the men inside were even aware what was happening.

Or at least that's what the foreigner hoped.

Then a gunshot—this one loud, without a silencer to soften it—echoed off the bluff.

"Man down," the foreigner heard in his earpiece. The voice was not panicked. More matter-of-fact. These were professionals.

The foreigner rolled before coming up into a low crouch, pausing midway down the path. They had decided to eschew night-vision goggles, which were bulky and had been deemed unnecessary to achieve their objective. The foreigner now cursed that decision.

Another shot. It had the distinct sound of a rifle. The velocity of its projectile was unmistakable.

"Fall back, fall back, find cover," the foreigner heard one of his men saying. "Where the hell is this coming from?"

The foreigner held his position. He was brutally exposed against the side of the bluff. Only his dark clothing kept him hidden in the night.

The rifle went off again. This time, the foreigner was able to locate the muzzle flash. The prone form behind it was a dark smudge.

"Sniper on the roof," the foreigner said into his watch. "Just hold tight for a second. I've got him."

The foreigner quickly centered the crosshairs of his Swarovski Z6 scope on the part of the smudge that was shaped like the gunman's head. It wasn't much of a target, but it was the only one the foreigner really had.

The night was windless. And he was fifty yards away, roughly at the same elevation as the height of the roof. In daylight, the foreigner could have decided which eye socket he wanted to shoot out. In darkness, it was still an easy enough shot.

The foreigner squeezed the trigger. Through the scope, he could see the prone body go lifeless.

"Got him," the foreigner said into his watch. "What's our medical report?"

"Hit in the vest," came a wheezing voice. "Hurts like hell"—large gasp—"and I can't goddamn breathe"—large gasp—"but I'll be fine."

"Can you still do your job?" the foreigner asked.

"Hell yes, sir."

"Good," the foreigner said. "We're running out of what little time we had to begin with. Let's move in."

"What if there's another sniper up there?" one of the men asked.

"Pray he has lousy aim," the foreigner replied.

Without further delay, he descended the bluff, arriving at the lone door to the warehouse at the same time as the men from the north, one of whom was carrying a two-man battering ram.

Only one man came from the east. The other, the one who had been shot, was still out there somewhere.

Wordlessly, two of them gripped the handles of the battering ram.

"One, two," the foreigner said.

The "three" came out as a grunt. The men strained at the handles. The steel door dented, but did not give.

"Again," the foreigner said. "Aim a little closer to the handle."

He resumed the count. This time, the word three was followed shortly thereafter by the sound of metal breaking.

"One more time," the foreigner said.

What little further resistance the door could offer was almost gone. The foreigner gave it one final kick, and it gave way.

They entered a large space with their guns raised. It was brilliantly lit from above by rows of fluorescent lights protected by cages. But the light was less impressive than the sound: When operating at full speed, Heidelberg offset printing presses make a hell of a racket.

It was loud enough that the half dozen men inside, who had earmuffs to protect them from the roar, had not heard the melee outside. They were too focused on the paper running through the press in a speedy blur, staying hyper-attuned to any miniscule adjustments they needed to make in ink levels or paper alignment.

They were not, in fact, aware anything was amiss until the foreigner located one of the red emergency cutoff switches on the far wall and yanked it up, immediately severing power to the press.

As it rolled to a stop, its output came into better focus. It was sheet after sheet of US twenty-dollar bills faked to absolute perfection, with the signature 75/25 cotton-linen blended paper, the raised feeling of the green ink, the security ribbon threaded inside, the tinting that only appeared at an angle. These were no slipshod knockoffs sliding out of some hack's Hewlett Packard. These were totally indistinguishable from the genuine item, created in almost precisely the same way the US Mint printed legal tender, with metal plates created by a forger of exceptional skill.

Arrayed around the side of the warehouse were other tools of the counterfeiter's trade: a platen press for embossing, an industrial paper cutter, a counting and banding machine.

It was an extraordinary operation, the largest of its kind in the world. Once the press was calibrated properly and running at top capacity, it could spew out fifty million dollars an hour. There were shrink-wrapped stacks of faux greenbacks sitting on a pallet in one corner. In another, massive rolls of blank paper awaited ink. The only real logistical issue for the crooks behind it was finding ways to spend the money.

The foreigner would have been forgiven for stopping and gawking. It's not very often you see a fortune in cash being created in front of you.

But the foreigner was not there to sightsee. As his men subdued the printing press operators, who were dutifully raising their hands and then allowing themselves to be zip-tied, the foreigner moved quickly to a small hutchlike office that had been built in the back corner of the rectangular building.

Covering his fist with his sleeve, he punched one of the windows. Its single pane shattered immediately, allowing him to reach around and unlock the door.

He threw open the door, but when he took his first step in, he heard a loud hiss, then felt a stinging somewhere below his waist. He looked down to see a dart sticking ominously out of the side of his buttock. Three more darts had just missed and buried themselves in the far wall.

Booby-trapped. The office had been booby-trapped. Their intelligence had not indicated any such threat. And, really, who used a dart? A dart wouldn't hurt anyone, unless it was . . .

Poisonous. The foreigner grabbed the dart and yanked, hoping he had extracted it before the toxins could enter his bloodstream. He examined the tip quickly and found, to his surprise, only his own blood. There did not appear to be any other substance.

Which explained everything. It must have been meant merely as a nonlethal deterrent to prevent lower-level employees from snooping where they didn't belong—and punish them if they tried.

The foreigner put those thoughts aside and entered the office. This was the real focus of his raid. It was not enough to merely destroy the printing plates and disable the presses. Jedediah Jones had been quite explicit that the foreigner also needed to find evidence of who was behind it.

The belief, as widespread as it was unsubstantiated, was that this was one of the many offshoots of a group of Chinese businessmen known as the Shanghai Seven. If the story of modern Chinese economic might starts in Shanghai, the story of Shanghai itself cannot be told without the seven members of the Chinese Communist Party who were given the seed money, freedom, and directive to begin assembling a massive corporate conglomerate. The Shanghai Seven were supposed to propel China in its drive to overtake the United States and to show other Chinese how Western business was done.

The first part was a work in progress. The second part had not gone quite as well. Other Chinese entrepreneurs, the ones who had been self-selected and had succeeded because of their good ideas and hard work, turned out to be far more profitable. The Shanghai Seven, forever fat and lazy, turned out to be middling moguls, with more failed ventures than successful ones. They also had a certain penchant for criminality. Raised in the rampantly corrupt culture of the CCP, they slipped rather easily between legitimate enterprises and the underworld.

But knowing that and proving it were two very different things. And they had been too slippery—with the blessing and backing of the CCP—to have ever been caught at anything big enough that the Chinese authorities would have been pressured, by force of embarrassment or complaints from legitimate businessmen, to act.

Until now.

Perhaps.

The foreigner was moving quickly, knowing his time was short and getting shorter. The office was nicely—though not extravagantly—furnished and had a well-inhabited feel to it. This was an office that got frequent use, though the foreigner could guess it was not the base of operations for one of the Shanghai Seven. They would never allow themselves to get so close to an operation of this sort.

No, this was the workplace of a high-level lieutenant, someone trusted enough to run this operation and yet be deemed ultimately expendable should a scapegoat be needed.

The foreigner went to the desk in the middle of the room first. The side drawers contained a teapot, a liquor flask, and a variety of snacks. The lieutenant apparently liked to be well provisioned. The top drawer was a mess of pens, pencils, paper clips, and sticky notes—criminals needed office supplies too, it seemed. The foreigner was about to move on when a rainbowlike glint caught his eye.

It was a compact disc, nestled in a transparent jewel case. The foreigner grabbed it and stuffed it inside his bulletproof vest.

Then he moved on to a filing cabinet against the far wall. The first file folder contained not papers but cassette tapes. He pocketed those, too. Then he moved to the next file folder, which contained documents that the foreigner began photographing.

He was clicking as fast as he could, not bothering to look before he shot. There would be time later to determine whether any of this was useful or whether he was copying a criminal enterprise's equivalent of a grocery list.

Then, suddenly, his time was up.

From outside, there was a new round of shouting. Through the office windows he could see a swarm of People's Armed Police, in their green uniforms, pouring into the facility. They were yelling, though their agitation did not seem to be directed at the six pressmen who were sitting mutely in a row on the floor by their idle machinery; no, the orders were being shouted at the four men in bulletproof vests who were in the midst of destroying as much of the counterfeiting apparatus as they could.

The foreigner came out of the office just as Colonel Feng entered the warehouse, his lit cigarette leading the way. He was grinning broadly, deeply satisfied with himself, as he approached the foreigner.

"Colonel Feng," the foreigner said. "I see you had company after all."

"The sound of gunfire must have alerted this squadron," he replied. "Aren't we fortunate they happened to be in the area on a training mission?"

"Quite," the foreigner said. He was moving closer to his men, who had formed into a small clump.

"But now that they are here, they are certainly capable of assuming jurisdiction over what turns out to be, much to our surprise, a crime scene," Feng said. "On behalf of my government, I thank you for discovering this illicit enterprise."

"Oh, you're very welcome."

"Now, I believe your work here is done. You will now turn over any evidence you have collected, including the phone you have been using to take pictures. We will make sure it is handled by the proper authorities and that the wrongdoers are prosecuted."

"I'm sure you will," the foreigner said.

He was, by now, next to his men. One of them had reached under his bulletproof vest to produce an object roughly the size of a shoe. Or at least it was until the man pressed two buttons and it instantly expanded to form a six-foot-by-four-foot barrier. The men crouched behind it, with their fingers jammed in their ears and their eyes screwed shut, as Feng looked on, more curious than threatened.

Then the foreigner said, "Deploy."

Three things happened in quick succession.

First the lights went out.

Next there was a tremendous explosion, one with enough force to tear a large jagged hole in the side of the warehouse.

Finally, the blast wave reached Feng, knocking him off his feet and extinguishing his cigarette in the process.

By the time the dust cleared, the foreigners were long gone— and they had taken the evidence with them.

TWO

HEAT
ONE WEEK LATER

We need to talk about your mother," Derrick Storm said.

New York Police Department captain Nikki Heat holstered her 9mm and studied the man whom, moments earlier, she had mistaken for an intruder.

It was Thursday evening at the end of a very long day, which was itself at the end of several other very long days in Nikki Heat's life.

But she had a sense, from the deep circles under her visitor's eyes, that he had also been getting a lot of recent experience with sleep deprivation.

"How did you get in?" she asked, stalling while she tried to make sense of the intrusion.

"Your doorman is not very good," he said.

"Which doorman? Bob Aaronson?"

"Is he built like a bowling pin, with a face full of childlike freckles that go very poorly with male-pattern baldness?"

"Yes."

"Then you should inform your co-op board that Bob Aaronson is completely incompetent."

Storm was sitting in a chair that had once been a favorite of

Heat's mother's, in the corner of a Manhattan apartment that had once belonged to her mother. And now he wanted to talk about her mother.

Did he know? Did he know that after seventeen years of being presumed dead, Cynthia Heat had surfaced in a bus shelter two days earlier—dressed as a homeless woman—and then vanished so quickly Nikki was left doubting what she had seen? Did he know that the ashes Nikki had venerated for seventeen years as being her mother's remains turned out, upon laboratory testing, to be nothing more than cremated roadkill? Did he understand the circumstances that led to Cynthia's disappearance and then sudden reappearance, a set of facts Nikki herself didn't begin to understand?

"So, my mother," Heat said, still standing at the ready. "What do we need to talk about?"

Storm appeared troubled. "Look, you should know, I almost didn't come here. It's selfish of me to even bring this to you. But you're the only person alive who might be able to help me decipher some potentially important evidence I've found. It's a recording of your mother. Would it be too painful for you to listen to it?"

"I'm beyond feeling pain about my mother," Heat said.

That was a lie. And Heat suspected Derrick Storm could tell. But he let it pass.

"This is all classified, of course, so I'd appreciate your discretion, Captain Heat."

"And of course you'll have it."

"Thank you," he said. "So, first, some background. I think you know from our little jam-up involving that dead currency trader a few years back that I work for a part of the government that likes to operate on the hush-hush."

"I remember a CIA station agent calling me in the middle

of the night, insisting that if I didn't let you go, not only would he be fired, but the world as we knew it would come to an end."

"That is a testament to the power of the man I work for. His name is Jedediah Jones. He operates a strictly off-the-books unit deep within the CIA. He has solved enough problems for enough important people that he has an essentially unlimited budget. And he works with limited oversight, because people in Washington understand it's in their best interests not to ask too many questions about his methods. I think he last corresponded with his morality in the third grade, though he certainly gets things done."

"I can think of a few people at the NYPD who would love to meet him," Heat said.

"I'm sure. Anyhow, the latest insect to capture the attention of Jones's flyswatter is a group of Chinese businessmen known as the Shanghai Seven. Are you familiar with them?"

"Not really."

Storm told Heat about the Shanghai Seven, the counterfeiting operation he believed them to be behind, his raid, and how his evidence collection ran into interference from the corrupt Colonel Feng.

"And he just stood there the whole time, smoking cloves, denying that anything was happening . . . until suddenly he showed up with a squadron of troops," Storm finished.

"Which means he was working for the Shanghai Seven, yes?"

"Well, yes. Except we can't really prove his ties to them, any more than we can prove the Shanghai Seven is really behind the counterfeiting. And until we can—and more or less shame the Chinese into doing something about it—we fear the Shanghai Seven will just start it up somewhere else," Storm said. "They have the supply lines and technical know-how, and we would have very little ability to stop them. Beyond counterfeiting, they've also been tied to human trafficking, drug smuggling, and a whole host of other nasty businesses over the years. Suffice to say, you should not confuse the Shanghai Seven with the seven dwarfs."

"Understood."

"Most of the evidence I found during the raid was disappointingly inconclusive. But there were two items that may be able to help us. The first is a compact disc that seems to contain some kind of data."

"A CD? Who still uses those things?"

"I have no idea. It's very possible this was made in 1999."

That was the year Heat's mother had been murdered. Or, rather, the year Cynthia Heat had faked her own death, taking a drug that plunged her heartbeat to almost nothing, then hiring actors to pose as EMTs and take her body away.

"But why . . . why don't you know for sure?" Heat asked.

"The data is encrypted at such a level that you can't even copy it to another computer without running into more encryption. And I haven't been able to crack it yet."

"I thought your boss has people who can do that," Heat said.

"He does. But, frankly, I don't trust him. I've known him for too long. The way he's been acting around this entire assignment has been strange, even for him. There's something he's not telling me, something else at play, something big. And until I better understand what the game is, I'm not going to hand him a baseball bat he might use to bash me over the head. He doesn't even know about the CD. I'm guessing a person in your position understands the importance of being able to manage up."

"I do," Heat said, offering him a knowing smile.

She sat down, choosing the chair closest to his. For reasons she didn't entirely understand, she felt instantly comfortable with him. Anyone looking at the two of them without the benefit of being able to hear the topic of their conversation might have even thought this rendezvous could soon turn into romance. They certainly would make an amazing couple. She was a striking brunette, long-legged and dark-eyed, with cheekbones that modeling agencies scoured the globe to find. He was the kind of handsome that writers felt compelled to begin a book with. Their children would not only be beautiful but also cunning, brilliant, and strong.

Yet that was not the dynamic at play here. For as hunky as he was, for as gorgeous as she was, there was not a whiff of attraction between them. It was almost like a long-lost brother and sister meeting for the first time.

Storm continued: "The other evidence I found is this recording of your mother, and that's where I need you. Are you . . . are you sure you really want to listen to it?"

"I'm sure," Heat said. She had spent years of her life dredging up every morsel she could about her mother's life. It was ingrained in Nikki—both as a daughter and as a detective—to want to know more. Her heart was already hammering from some combination of anxiety and anticipation.

Storm reached down to a small bag that was resting by his chair. He pulled out a circa 1984 cassette player, then the tape itself, which he held out for Heat to look at.

"Can you read simplified Chinese?" Storm asked.

"Not a bit."

"If you could, you'd know that this is an approximation of your mother's name, spelled phonetically. Mandarin lacks the *ess* sound, so they did the best they could. And it's dated November 1999."

Storm hit the eject button on the cassette player to open its small door, then gently slid the tape inside. For a pair of thirtysomethings like Heat and Storm, it was rather nostalgic to be operating such outdated technology.

"Whoever produced this recording had tapped your mother's home phone. Most of the conversations were ordinary run-of-the-mill stuff. You're even on there a couple of times, calling in from college."

Heat shook her head. "My dorm had a bank of pay phones in the basement," she said. "A few people were starting to get cell phones, but they were still considered a luxury item. I used a phone card every time I called her. Remember those?"

Storm grinned. "I'll leave the cassette and player with you, in case you'd like to listen to all of it later. I've already made a copy of the important parts for myself. But I've got it cued up to the pertinent part right now. You ready?"

Heat bobbed her head. Storm depressed the plastic play button and, for the first time in seventeen years, the voice of Cynthia Heat filled the Gramercy Park apartment she had once called home.

"Hello?" Cynthia Heat said.

"Hey, it's Nicole," a female voice said.

Nikki reached over and jabbed the pause button. "That's Nicole Bernardin, my mother's best friend and fellow operative. They were part of a network of domestic workers and high-end tutors who spied on the rich and connected—"

"The Nanny Network," Storm said. "I know all about them. They're legendary."

"Anyway, Nicole . . . she . . . she died a few years ago. She was killed by some people who tossed her in a suitcase and then put her in a deep freeze. It was the same people who killed my mother. Or at least I used to think it was the same people who killed my mother. . . ."

Heat realized she didn't know what she thought anymore. As a way of stopping Storm from asking questions, she hit the play button again.

"Thanks for calling back," Cynthia said. "I just wanted you to know I've dealt with those phony bills. I found a place to hide them."

"Where?" Bernardin asked.

"You don't want to know. It's for your own good."

"Right."

"They definitely have fingerprints on them. I dusted them. They're faint, but they're there."

"So . . . I guess that makes those bills your insurance policy? As long as they're out there, somewhere, you've got some leverage."

"Exactly," Cynthia said.

This time it was Storm pressing the pause button. "It's my belief that the fingerprints on the fake money belong to one of the Shanghai Seven," he said. "That would make the bills powerful evidence against them."

He resumed playing the tape.

"And you're sure they're in a safe place?" Bernardin asked.

"Let me put it this way: I'd not only trust this spot with my life, I'd trust it with my best Scotch."

Storm pressed the pause button again. "Does this apartment have a liquor cabinet by any chance?"

"Yeah, and you're welcome to take it apart. But, believe me, I've been over, around, under, and through every nook and cranny of this apartment a hundred times looking for hiding spots, false fronts, concealed compartments. There's nothing here. Besides, she wouldn't have hidden them here. My mother was incredibly careful about not bringing her work—and by that, I mean her *real* work, not her cover job as a piano teacher—home with her."

Heat pressed PLAY.

"But I don't understand," Nicole said. "If the bills have those prints on them, why don't you just come forward with them?"

"Because the fingerprints by themselves don't prove anything," Cynthia said. "If it's in a court of law, a good lawyer could come up with a million reasons how those prints got there. I need to really nail this thing down. I can't go halfway with something like this. I'd get buried. Besides, they're—"

Cynthia's voice trailed off, like she was suddenly overcome with emotion.

"Honey, what's wrong?" Bernardin asked.

"It's . . . They're not even bothering to threaten me. It's like they know they can't get to me. They're saying they'll go after Nikki."

"Oh, Cyn . . . I'm so sorry. Do you want me to go up to school and get her? I'll keep her safe. You know I will."

"Yeah, but what are you going to say to her? 'Hey, you know your mom, the one you think is just a kindly piano teacher? Yeah, she's really a spy and she's gotten herself in some serious trouble, so you need to come with me.'"

"It's better than them getting to her first," Nicole said.

"I know, I know. I just . . . I keep thinking there *has* to be a way to prove what's really going on with these fake bills."

"Be careful, Cyn. Be careful. If it's who you think it is—"

"I know. I know. Look, I'll call you if I need you. You know that."

"I know. Love you. Be careful."

"Okay. You too."

Storm hit the stop button. "The next call is your mother ringing what I now know is a pay phone in your dorm. She talked to a girl who knew you and asked her to leave a note for you to call."

"She was trying to convince me to come home from school

early for Thanksgiving. I told her no, I couldn't, because I didn't want to fall behind in my classes," Nikki said, so momentarily transfixed by the memory that she sighed without meaning to.

"Sorry," Storm said. "I know this can't be easy. But, look, I need to know: what was your mother up to in 1999? What was she doing that she might have been tussling with the Shanghai Seven?"

Nikki Heat was flummoxed. She had been over the final months of her mother's life backwards and forwards for years. She had come across evidence that her mother was trying to expose her former handler, Nanny Network chief Tyler Wynn, as a traitor who was selling American secrets. For a time, Nikki thought Wynn even killed her mother because of it. Now she thought it more likely that Wynn—who in his own twisted way loved Nikki like a niece—helped Cynthia fake her own death.

But what did any of that have to do with the Shanghai Seven?

"I'm sorry," Heat said. "If I knew the answer to that, I'd give it to you. I'm tempted to tell you she had nothing to do with the Shanghai Seven. But she . . . Let's just say the things I've learned about her life have surprised me more than once over the years."

"Still, take me back to 1999. There has to be something that . . ."

Storm began restating the question, doing his investigator's best to try to extract some bit of thread that would help him put a neat bow on an otherwise untidy package. But Heat wasn't really listening to him as much as she was assessing him.

Up until now, she had only told one person about her mother's dramatic reappearance: her husband, two-time Pulitzer Prize–winning journalist Jameson Rook. She knew she could trust Rook, that Rook wouldn't dismiss her mother's sighting as some stress-induced delirium. She also knew that Rook wouldn't have some hidden agenda that would place some other need ahead of her mother.

Could she trust this man the same way? Nikki Heat had spent her professional life reading people, many of whom were criminals who lied whenever their lips moved. And a man in Derrick Storm's line of work had surely worked his share of deceptions and run his share of cons.

Yet Heat recognized that Storm had a deeply embedded moral compass, that he would never allow it to point him anywhere but true north. He was legitimately trying to turn out the lights on some bad actors who, it seemed, really did have something to do with her mother. Therefore, he needed to know the full truth.

She rejoined the conversation just as Storm was saying ". . . and I think I've lost you."

"I'm sorry," Heat said. "Look, there's something you need to know. You're asking these questions about 1999, and I'm not saying we shouldn't look there. But it seems my mother's story didn't end in 1999."

"What do you mean?"

Heat told him about the bus shelter and about her mother's counterfeit ashes.

"So she's really still alive?" Storm said when she was through.

"I don't know, really. I mean, it's still possible I was just mistaken. I saw her for maybe half a second."

"But in that half a second you were sure?"

Heat nodded. "And there's more. The man who ordered the hit on her is a crooked former FBI and Department of Homeland Security agent by the name of Bart Callan. He was later connected with a plot to unleash massive quantities of the smallpox virus in New York City."

"Yeah, he was never going to be able to pull it off, though. I know you guys got to it first, but you weren't the only ones who figured out the true purpose of that antique fire truck," Storm said, adding a quick wink.

"Well, then you know that Callan was bought off by Carey Maggs."

"The brewery magnate who also owned the pharmaceutical company that was going to get rich selling the smallpox vaccine? Yes."

"But did you know that Maggs was found murdered in his jail cell two days ago? Someone got him with a garotte wire."

Heat drew a line across her throat. Storm showed no reaction to the death of a man who would have happily murdered thousands in the name of profit.

"And there's more," Heat continued. "Callan had been incarcerated at a supermax prison out in Colorado until about three weeks ago. Then he was mysteriously transferred to a medium security facility in Cumberland, Maryland."

"Medium security? For a former federal agent who killed multiple people and was tied to a mass murder plot?"

"Well, exactly. And then, of course, he escaped while on a work detail. He's still at large."

"Let me guess: This happened within the last week," Storm said.

"Yes. On Tuesday. Also two days ago."

The skin around Storm's eyes squeezed as he squinted in concentration, giving him a pensive look.

"I'm not saying this is going to fit perfectly, but let's try it on for size," Storm said. "My raid on the Shanghai Seven happened a week ago. My team made a bit of a mess on our way out, so it took them a little while to sort things out. They didn't think they were going to lose any of the evidence I took. They've been scrambling a bit since then. When they did an inventory, they noticed that this cassette tape was among the missing items. They would know your mother is on the tape, talking about her hiding these bills. Where? No one knows.

"But what if the Shanghai Seven knew about Bart Callan's connection to your mother? I know this may sound odd, but in order to kill someone, especially a pro like your mother, you really do need to learn a lot about them—their patterns, their hideouts, their peccadilloes. There would be no one more qualified to go on a scavenger hunt for those bills than Callan."

Heat asked, "So they helped him escape from prison with the understanding he would then work for them?"

"The Shanghai Seven was betting he could find the bills before I did."

"But then why did the transfer happen three weeks ago?"

"Well, I don't know for sure, of course," Storm said. "But that's when my team and I started training. That must have also been when the Shanghai Seven were tipped off that the raid was coming. So they began making contingency plans, getting Callan into a place where they could access him if they needed him."

"Okay. I understand. Now explain Maggs's death for me."

"Part of the escape. Maggs and Callan were, quite literally, thick as thieves at one point. Callan would know the authorities' first step would be to go to Maggs to learn where Callan was likely hiding. And at that point, after all those years in prison, Maggs would give it up in exchange for a Big Mac and a new pillow. Maggs had to be silenced."

Heat felt her head bobbing up and down. She didn't know if, in fact, Storm had everything lined up right. But there was no denying the timeline. The Shanghai Seven learned their counterfeiting operation had come to the attention of the US government, and they started making plans to eliminate any potential evidence that tied them to it. At the top of that list were the fake bills—with the damning fingerprints—that Cynthia Heat had stashed away long ago.

The bills also explained why she felt she had to vanish. In the Shanghai Seven, Cynthia Heat knew she had made a powerful enemy—an enemy with global reach, an enemy that would have no compunction about killing her daughter. And yet Cynthia didn't have quite enough substantiation to be able to get the Shanghai Seven shut down for good, especially not with the Chinese legal system stacked against her.

So she faked her own death. It was the only way to make the Shanghai Seven think she was no longer a threat, the only way to save her daughter.

Nikki Heat breathed deeply. Having—perhaps—finally put together the narrative that explained one of the most agonizing chapters in her life did not give her satisfaction.

Not until she could prove it.

And then use what she learned to put the Shanghai Seven in such a deep hole they could smell the middle of the earth.

Which, in turn, would allow her mother to rejoin the living world.

"All right. Then just to restate things, Bart Callan is working for the Shanghai Seven, looking for the counterfeit bills my mother hid," Heat said.

"Check."

"In return for which the Shanghai Seven sprung him from prison."

"Check."

"And your mission is to put the Shanghai Seven out of business."

"Check."

"Then Callan's escape is our hot lead," Heat said. "There

has to be some kind of paper trail at the Bureau of Prisons that explains how a serial killer got transferred to a medium security prison. Someone signed that order."

"Probably someone who was either threatened or bribed into doing it," Storm said.

"Exactly. If we can prove who applied that pressure and/or gave that incentive, maybe we can start building a chain of evidence that ultimately leads us to one of the Shanghai Seven."

"Agreed."

"So we're going to partner on this thing," Heat said.

"Agreed."

She stood. He stood. He reached out his hand. She took it in her own with a firm grip and gave it a hearty shake.

Nikki Heat and Derrick Storm as partners.

Something about it just felt right.

THREE

HEAT

Nikki Heat squeezed her phone so hard she was fairly certain she was going to grind its silicon microchips back into sand.

"I'm *not* going," she said through gritted teeth.

"Oh, but you are," the man on the other end informed her. "And you will wear dress blues. And you will smile pretty for the cameras. And you will wave to the crowd and look very, very happy to be there. And that, in turn, will make the commissioner very happy."

There was perhaps no worse way to start a morning than with a phone call from Zach "The Hammer" Hamner. His official title was senior administrative aide to the NYPD's deputy commissioner for legal matters, but Heat had often thought they should simplify it by changing it to senior vice deputy prick. No, actually, make that chief executive prick. The only thing worse than having to listen to his unctuous voice over the phone would have been having to look at his pallid face, which only left the office and saw the sun for approximately two hours on the Fourth of July every other year.

But the fact was, when he dropped the c-word—commissioner—Heat knew her personal feelings no longer mattered. And when he called, he was seldom expressing his own opinion. He didn't get the nickname The Hammer because of some fondness for home improvement.

Still, to preserve some sense of self-respect, Heat felt she had to put up the good fight.

"It's a ridiculous political dog and pony show," she said. "Look, I did my job and caught the bad guy. That's what—"

"Yes, except Legs Kline just happened to be a bad guy who was three weeks away from being elected president of the United States until you tied him to that ISIS-wannabe video," Hamner inserted.

"Right, right. But, as I was saying, that's what cops are supposed to do. Put bad guys in jail. We don't need to hold a press conference every time we do it."

"May I point out that 'we' are not holding this press conference," Hamner said. "This press conference is being held by the senior senator from the state of New York, Lindsy Gardner, who is now, because of your efforts, very likely also three weeks away from being elected president of the United States. There will be a number of other dignitaries from One PP in attendance, including the commissioner—did I mention the commissioner yet?—but in case that's not enough for you, the mayor will also be there. Even with all that, the Gardner campaign was quite explicit about your attendance. In fact, you were personally invited by her campaign manager and likely future chief of staff John Null. Now, the NYPD can either be on the future president's good side or the future president's bad side. Which one do you think the commissioner prefers?"

"She's a former librarian," Heat said. "She doesn't have a bad side."

"You obviously haven't known enough librarians. I wouldn't

wish a pissed-off librarian on the worst cretin at Rikers Island.

"Now," Hamner concluded, "in case I haven't made it clear enough, this is not a request. This is an order."

That was what led, two hours later, to Nikki Heat standing on a hastily constructed stage in Central Park, wearing a forced grin as the now seemingly inevitable future president of the United States addressed a collection of New York's most well-used cameras and microphones, with a large crowd of curiosity seekers assembled behind them.

"Thank you, thank you. Thank you, New York," Gardner was saying, having just been introduced by the mayor. Her distinctive voice was part of her charm. It was strong and authoritative, yet somehow still quiet. Like a good librarian should be. She had resisted all efforts from political consultants who told her she ought to adopt a more forceful tone when speaking in public. A variety of comediennes had tried to imitate it. None could.

She waited for the crowd to settle down, her mere look the mild rebuke they needed to come to order.

"Thank you again," she said. "I have to say, I'm very pleased to be here with you on this occasion, because after fifteen months of campaigning, I'm tired of talking about myself. My opponent doesn't seem to have that problem."

The crowd chuckled. Her opponent, Caleb Brown, was what Shakespeare had in mind when he coined the phrase "ass hat."

"But today," Gardner continued, "I don't have to talk about myself. I get to talk about a true New York hero, Captain Nikki Heat."

Gardner paused and the crowd roared. Heat waved, because she was too embarrassed not to; because that's what she had been told to do; and because the commissioner and a half dozen of the NYPD's other top brass were onstage next to her, jostling for position in front of the cameras and evaluating her every move. She tried to distract herself by thinking about things that were more pleasant than this. Like dental surgery.

The candidate went on about Heat for a while, telling how she had exposed that Kline Industries was supplying bullets to ISIS and then prevented Kline and his daughter from escaping to a foreign country that did not have an extradition treaty. Heat kept the tight smile on her face the entire time, dreamed of root canals and Novocain-free extractions, and was trying to stay good, but drifted off until Gardner managed to catch her attention again.

"It's not very often on the campaign trail that I get to tell personal stories," Gardner said. "And I'm not sure Captain Heat would even know this. But my children were once among the least distinguished of her mother's piano students. I'm afraid Louisa and Ben inherited their total lack of musicality from their mother. Still, they tried hard and I think Mrs. Heat tolerated them because of their dedication. So we made it all the way to the end-of-year recital, except my Ben . . . Well, we were going back and forth between New York and Washington quite a bit back then, and Ben left his music in Washington. But who ran out to a local music store and found the last copy of Beethoven's 'Fur Elise'? It was Mrs. Heat's teenage daughter, Nikki. So it seems she's been saving the day for a long time now."

Heat had no memory of this long-ago event, but she smiled as if she did, if only to keep up the show.

"And now it's time for me to repay that favor. I don't mean to put Captain Heat on the spot with what I'm about to say next," Gardner said, "but it's very important to me that I enter this plea into the public record. And, Captain Heat, you should know I've run it by your very fine commissioner, and he was very graciously enthusiastic about this proposal. I've said from the outset of this campaign that my administration will be about bringing in the best possible people from a great variety of backgrounds, many of them from outside of Washington and outside the political realm, and giving them roles where their talents will benefit America. With that in mind, I hope that if I am elected, Captain Heat will accept my invitation to be my director of Homeland Security."

There was a murmur from the crowd. Heat immediately looked toward the commissioner, who was nodding his approval—probably thinking of all the antiterrorism money that would pour into his budget if a New Yorker were in the job.

"Don't worry," Gardner added. "I'm not looking for an answer right now."

Now the crowd was laughing and Heat mouthed the words "thank you."

Except, already, her brain was whirring. The director of Homeland Security? Her? The thing she liked least about running the Twentieth Precinct was the bureaucratic nonsense that came with the job. Imagine being in the red tape capital of the country, running what was, at its core, nothing more than a large bureaucracy.

Besides, she wanted her energies to stay focused on her mother, on learning more about the Shanghai Seven, on making the world safe for her return.

But maybe as director of Homeland Security she'd have an easier time accomplishing that. Surely if she had the entire weight of a new president's administration behind her, she'd have the juice to get the Shanghai Seven decommissioned?

She realized, much to her surprise, she was intrigued. More than she would have admitted.

***

Ten minutes later, having provided enough sound bites to feed the cable news networks until dinnertime, Gardner announced her departure to a cheering crowd.

After the Secret Service ushered her away, it was everyone else's turn to leave the stage. As Heat descended the steps, her head felt like it had been put through a blender without a top on it, and her thoughts had been sprayed all over the place. She had to concentrate on making sure her foot hit every tread on the stairs, so she didn't become an instant YouTube sensation by falling off the stage.

She was so focused on that task she didn't pay much attention to the tall dark-haired man who was approaching her until he stuck out a hand in her direction.

"Hi," he said. "I'm John Null. I'm Lindsy's campaign manager."

He was wearing a tailored suit that he filled out nicely. Null was a former army helicopter pilot who had served two overseas tours in Iraq and Afghanistan before going into civilian life. It was a background that played well with veterans' groups. And he had clearly managed to maintain his physique from his days as a serviceman.

"Nice to meet you," Heat said.

"Just so you know, Lindsy is really serious about this. This isn't a presidential candidate just trying to win a news cycle and get some reflected glory from the hero of the day. The campaign is already vetting you, and we're impressed with what we've found. We think you've got what it takes to do this job. I know the management side of it might be a bit much at first, but you seem to have a long history of getting things done, even against long odds. You're exactly the kind of person we want working in this administration."

"Thank you," Heat said.

"And I'm sorry if the delivery of the offer caught you a little bit by surprise. I told her I thought she should approach you privately first. But she said if she did it that way, you would just say no. She felt like doing it this way, so the whole world knew the incredible opportunity you'd been offered, and there'd be a better chance your friends and family would pressure you into saying yes."

"She's probably right about that," Heat said, adding a laugh.

"Lindsy Gardner is right about a lot of things. I know she's my boss, so I'm supposed to say this, but she really does have great instincts about people. We're not going to push you for an answer right now or anytime soon. I know this has just been sprung on you and it has to be a lot to take in. But is it something you can at least consider for a while?"

"Well, I have to say, I *am* flattered . . ." Heat began.

"Then stop right there. Stay flattered. That's a nice feeling," Null said. "Look, don't even try to make up your mind yet. Just think about it. Obviously, we wouldn't even need an answer until after the election. Gotta make sure we actually have a job to offer. Never know what those voters will do."

He offered a winning smile.

"No, but things are looking pretty good for you guys," Heat said. Overnight polls showed that, with Legs Kline out of the race, Gardner had picked up most of his voters, surging into the lead in a number of key battleground states. FiveThirtyEight was predicting a landslide.

"Well, we'll see. It's my job not to take anything for granted," he said. "But if I can give you my own sales pitch, it's that Lindsy is great to work for. I think in some ways she treats everything like she's still running a small-town library. She likes to really get to know the people who work for her on a personal level. I hope you'll at least consent to sitting down with her for a little chat?"

"Of course," Heat said.

"Terrific," Null said enthusiastically. "Her schedule is hopeless today. But we might be able to find some time for you tomorrow afternoon?"

"That would be fine. Just let me know," Heat said.

The two exchanged cell phone numbers—Heat's a 917 area code, Null's a 202—then went their separate ways. Heat had about a twenty-minute walk back to the Twentieth Precinct, which was preferable to what awaited her if she had decided to drive. The Secret Service had asked the NYPD to shut down half the streets in midtown Manhattan on account of Gardner's visit, and the other half were hopelessly jammed.

Heat was just under way and had already switched to thinking about the day that lay ahead—it consisted of more Legs Kline–related debriefings and a whole lot of backlogged paperwork, unfortunately—when her phone told her she had a text message.

Thinking it was going to be Null, Heat was expecting it to be a number from outside her contact list.

And it was. But it didn't come from Null.

It came from a 646 area code, which was overflow from New York's venerable 212.

It read: NIKKI. I AM YOUR NEW BEST FRIEND. OR PERHAPS YOUR NEW WORST ENEMY. IT'S REALLY GOING TO BE UP TO YOU. WILL YOU LISTEN TO ME?

It was signed, THE SERPENT.

Heat frowned. Was this some kind of prank? There were nine-year-olds in remedial schools who had more maturity than some of the guys back at the precinct, especially when they got in a group. This could have been their stupid idea of fun.

Or . . .

Well, at the very least, she could play along.

THAT DEPENDS, she texted back. WHAT IS IT YOU HAVE TO SAY?

Heat continued walking until she heard her phone chime again.

LEAVE YOUR MOTHER'S CASE ALONE. DO NOT TRY TO FIND HER. DO NOT TRY TO FIND THE BILLS. DO NOT INVESTIGATE IT IN ANY WAY. IT'S FOR YOUR OWN GOOD. YOU HAVE NO IDEA THE POWER YOU'RE DEALING WITH. TAKE THE JOB IN DC. FORGET YOUR MOTHER. TAKE THIS ADVICE OR SUFFER THE CONSEQUENCES.

Heat felt like someone had bounced a brick off her head. The idiots back at the precinct didn't know a thing about her mother. Only Rook and Storm did. And both of them knew better than to say anything.

WHAT CONSEQUENCES? Heat typed back.

By the time her walk had concluded, she still had not received an answer.

FOUR

STORM

The ruggedly handsome man turned off the television that had, until moments earlier, been showing footage of the Lindsy Gardner press event in New York City. The man was now standing in silence in a break room on the fifth floor of the Bureau of Prisons headquarters. He wore an exquisitely faked name tag that identified him as JACKSON, MICHAEL.

He smoothed his sideburns, also fake, apparently on loan from 1977. Then he pet his bushy mustache, which he had attached to his face with the aid of half a bottle of spirit gum, and which would have been familiar to aficionados of the pornographic films of the same era.

Derrick Storm had made this transformation somewhere above thirty thousand feet during his morning flight down to Washington, DC. Along the way, he had given himself a crash course on everything he would need to know to become Michael Jackson, an unfortunately monikered mid-level paper pusher at the Federal Bureau of Prisons.

He was determined not just to play the part, but to own it. His pleated khaki Dockers were just a little frayed at the cuffs, and the fly refused to stay closed, exposing the zipper. His short-sleeve button-down shirt was light blue and starched to attention. His tie looked like it was the lone survivor of a vicious food fight.

On his left wrist, he wore a plastic WWJD bracelet; on his left hand, a wedding ring. Studies had shown Americans considered married Christian men more trustworthy—studies that perhaps only proved that Americans had forgotten Jim Bakker.

So far, the disguise had worked beautifully. Storm had breezed his way past security in the lobby. No one had given him a first glance, much less a second one, as he rode the elevator to the top floor.

And now, having composed himself in the break room for a moment or two, he was ready. Someone—very likely someone in this building—had signed the order to transfer Bart Callan from supermax to the medium security facility from which he had ultimately escaped. And Storm, with the help of "Michael Jackson," was going to figure out who that signatory was.

Storm took one last deep breath. Then he turned out into the hallway, building up a good head of steam as he stalked past rows of half-height cubicles on his right, then turned into an office on the left that was three doors down from the corner.

"Well, *there* you are!" Storm half yelled in a nasal voice that was half an octave higher than his own.

A middle-aged black man with a shaved head looked up from his desktop computer, appropriately startled.

"I know the phone system here is cranky like a Yankee," Storm continued, "but the least you can do is pick up your extension when I call! You made me come all the way up from the third floor, you know!"

"Sorry. Can I . . . can I help you with something?" the man said.

"Yes, you can help me. I'm in the middle of a whoop-de-hoop

catastrophe here. So, yes, you can help me."

"I'm sorry, I don't think we've met, Mister—"

"Just read the tag!" Storm said petulantly, thrusting his chest in the man's direction.

"Mister . . . Michael Jackson? Is your name really *Michael Jackson?*"

"Yes. Yes it is. And, I know, you want to be starting something. And the girl is yours, not mine. And you want me to beat it. I've heard it all before. I can't help it that my parents never listened to contemporary popular music and decided to name me after my grandfather, okay? Are you really going to take me back to the sixth grade playground with your sophomoric banter? Because that's bullying. And may I remind you that under Directive Thirteen-Fifty-Seven-B, paragraph twelve, subset three, we have a very clearly stated no-bullying policy here at the Bureau of Prisons."

"Yeah, yeah, sorry," the man said. "Look, man, I didn't mean to step into a sensitive subject here. But . . . Well, shoot, have you ever thought of, I don't know, going by your middle name or something?"

"My first middle name is Tito."

"Oh. Damn."

"And my second middle name is Andrew. I'm afraid the seventh president of the United States kind of wrecked that one for me."

"Right."

Storm leaned in and whispered conspiratorially, "Though I'm glad they're taking him off the twenty. Aren't you?"

"Uh . . . I mean, yeah, I guess. Whatever."

"Also," Storm kept whispering, "I want you to know, I voted for Obama."

The man just arched an eyebrow.

"We should fist-bump, right? That's what you people do, isn't it?" Storm said, balling up his right hand and thrusting it toward the man.

The man, now caught somewhere between confused and horrified, knocked his fist against Storm's.

"And then we give each other 'the nod,'" Storm continued, bobbing his head and clarifying: "I watch *black-ish* on ABC, so I know."

The man was no longer caught in between. Now he was just horrified.

"Yeah, yeah," the man said. "Anyhow, you . . . you need something, Mister, uh . . . can I call you Mike?"

"Call me Michael, please. And, yes, I need something. I need to find an umbrella, and you're going to need one, too, because there's going to be a real poop storm if it gets out what's going on around this place! I'm talking congressional hearings, exposés in the *Washington Post*, tell-all books. Somewhere, someone is probably already deciding who's going to play your part in the movie."

"Relax, friend. Just relax. What's going on?"

"I'm not going to relax, that's what's going on!" Storm crowed. "I'm doing an audit of FCI-Cumberland and I'm missing a BP-T-oh-two-twelve for an inmate. Do you understand the consequences here? This is a disaster! I'm talking floods and locusts, hurricanes and typhoons, Justin Bieber on tour!"

The BP-T02-12, as Storm knew from his hasty research on the plane, was also known as the Place of Imprisonment form. And, within the Bureau of Prisons, every inmate was supposed to have one.

"Well," the man began, "I'm sure it just got misplaced. If you call down there and let them know there's been a little mix-up, I'm sure they'll—"

"No. No! This is *not* a quote-unquote 'little mix-up.' This is a complete and utter breakdown of the whole system. Heads are going to roll over this one, and you better be damn sure it's not going to be mine. I'm blowing the whistle. *Blowing the whistle,* you hear? That means there are laws that protect me. And I'm not going to stop blowing it. I'll blow my way all the way to the White House if I have to."

"Whoa, whoa. Just take it easy, Michael. This is fixable. Is it just one inmate we're talking about?"

"*Just one inmate?* I'm glad you can be so casual about this. But to me there's no such thing as 'just' one inmate in this system. Not with the kind of scum and villainy we've got locked up. You know who else is 'just one inmate' in the Bureau of Prisons? Ted Kaczynski."

The man cocked his head. Storm was now pointing at him.

"I'm getting to the bottom of this. I'm getting to the bottom of this if it's the last thing I do. Sometimes evil needs to be pulled up from the root. The BP-T-oh-two-twelve is really just a symptom. The real disease is the BP-C-eight-eight-eleven. I need to know who signed that, then we'll figure out what happened here."

The BP-C88-11 was also known as the Transfer Notice. It was a document that was required anytime an inmate changed prisons.

"Can't you just look that up yourself?" the man asked.

"Maybe up here on the well-to-do fifth floor you can just look it up," Storm said. "But down on the third floor, we don't have the access. Janet down in IT made sure of that."

"Janet . . ."

"Jackson," Storm said, then added: "My sister. She's nasty."

"All right, all right. Just cool down. I can look it up for you. Who's the inmate? Let's see if we can figure out what's going on here."

Storm rattled off Bart Callan's eight-digit federal inmate ID number, very pointedly not using his name—the name, Storm knew, would set off alarm bells.

"Well, let's see here," the man said, entering the number into his desktop computer as Storm recited it. "His transfer notice was signed by . . . Oh, here it is: Mason Wood."

"Mason Wood? As in Mason Wood, the associate director?"

"Yeah, his office is right over there in the corner if you want to—"

"I know where his office is," Storm said. "I'm just shocked! I'm shocked and appalled that someone like Associate Director Wood would make such a fundamental mistake like—"

"Now hang on a sec here," the man said, still looking at his screen. "The Place of Imprisonment form is right here."

The man tilted his screen so Storm could see it.

"Well, I'll be a . . ." Storm began. "How did I miss that?"

The man shrugged.

"Happens to everyone sometimes," he said.

Storm was now looking down at the carpet. "No. Not to me. I'm deeply, deeply embarrassed and I . . . I can't believe I had such awful thoughts about Associate Director Wood. Can you please, *please*, not mention this to him?"

"Yeah, man, no sweat."

"Thank you. You're a good man. *A good man*," Storm said reverently. "And I want you to know, I never thought for one second that OJ did it."

FIVE

HEAT

Unlike some of the New York Police Department's more stately structures, the Twentieth Precinct was not some architectural marvel or historic landmark. It was just a plain brick building hard up against 82nd Street, wholly lacking in decoration or ornamentation.

But to Captain Nikki Heat, it was a special place all the same. She had been assigned there shortly after graduating from the New York City Police Academy, after her mother's death had made her decide to change majors from theater to criminal justice and pursue a career in law enforcement.

Heat had since spent the majority of her waking hours in and around the Two-Oh, first as a beat cop, then as a sergeant, next as a detective, then as detective squad leader, and now as its first-ever female commander. Its walls had seen her laugh and cry, seen her break down the hardest con and yet also treat victims of crime with the softest touch. She had made a million mistakes there but also learned a million life lessons along the way.

It was, when you got right down to it, where she had grown up; it was her home as much as any she had ever had.

And so, as she pushed through the glass door shortly after eleven o'clock, having walked back from the press conference, she was entering comfortable turf. And she didn't have much of any reaction when the desk sergeant cheerfully called out, "Hey, Captain. I got something here for you. A bike messenger came by with it. He wanted to hand it to you personally, but I told him that wasn't happening. Anyway, here."

Then he handed her an envelope, and Heat felt her world lurch to a halt for a moment.

Her name was written on the outside, but that wasn't the shocking part. It was *how* her name was written that made everything come to a stop. It was the graceful curve of the N, the slant of the two Is, the hurried Ks, the loop in the H, the way the E and the A were like mere speed bumps on the way to the T.

Cynthia Heat's penmanship was always very distinctive.

"Thank . . . thank you," Heat said, accepting the envelope, hoping the man didn't notice that she had suddenly lost color.

Heat skipped the elevator, walking with a slight wobble toward the back stairwell, where she could have some privacy. She sat on the second step and stared at the envelope again, looking at that style of cursive she hadn't seen in seventeen years.

When she opened the envelope, whatever small doubts Nikki might have still harbored that her mother was the author of the missive inside instantly disappeared. Cynthia Heat had always written to her daughter in longhand. Nikki recognized not only her lettering, but also the spacing between lines; the cream-colored heavy stationery that Cynthia preferred; the way she heavily dotted a period; the way she capitalized the first letter of a sentence a little higher than any other capital letters.

If the fleeting glance in the bus shelter and the contents of the urn didn't confirm it, this did. Cynthia Heat was alive.

Nikki felt tears rolling down her cheeks already. She dabbed at them with her uniform sleeve, took a deep breath, then started reading:

My Dearest Nikki,

After seventeen years, I'm not sure how to even begin this letter. I know you must be angry with me. And I don't blame you. I'm angry with myself, too. More than you could possibly understand. I've missed so much of your life.

But the fact is I didn't miss everything. Your college graduation? I was there, three-quarters of the way back, by that magnificent elm tree. I saw you taking pictures afterwards with your friends, in that white dress with the blue trim. Your captain's promotion ceremony? I rented an NYPD uniform and dyed my hair brown for that one. It was one of the proudest days of my life. Your wedding? I'm sure you didn't realize the caterer had a new dishwasher. I loved the looks on everyone's faces when that lovely husband of yours announced you were going to Reykjavík for your honeymoon.

Beyond those occasions, you were never far from my heart, even when the rest of me was quite distant. In seventeen years, there hasn't been a day when I didn't think about you. I have had many homes during that time, some for years, some for no more than a few weeks. The first thing I unpacked in every single one of them was my framed pictures of you.

I can't believe, after all the times I've dropped in on your life—to check on you, to make sure you were okay, to see you with my own eyes—you spotted me in that bus shelter. It was clumsy of me. I guess I must be losing my touch in my old age.

But now that you know my secret, I have to beg something of you: Forget that I exist. Forget that I ever existed. Your life will be much happier and safer that way.

Long ago, I had to die so you could stay alive. Nothing has happened over the last seventeen years to change that. If certain people become aware I'm alive, you will be in grave danger. The threat is even greater now than it was back then. Maybe there will be some day when I will be able to come out of hiding. But that day is not now. And I'm very sorry to say it is not close.

In the meantime, please do not try to find me. I know that runs counter to the instincts you've developed as a detective, but I'm begging you: Leave this whole thing alone. I've already thrown away a big chunk of my life because I couldn't do that. Please don't throw away your life, too.

Love always,
Mom

Nikki sat hunched in the stairway and reread the letter three times. Her emotions took a cross-country journey as she did so, from anger to sadness, from joy to yearning.

The anger was that her mother had not only abandoned her in the first place, but that she now refused to come out of hiding for more than these brief cameo appearances. The sadness was that Cynthia felt she couldn't. The joy was knowing her mother had not, in fact, suffered an agonizing death. The yearning was to be with her again, whether it was to bake a pie with her, as they used to enjoy doing, or to share the simple pleasure of a mother-daughter coffee.

Eventually, however, Nikki arrived at frustration. And determination. The frustration was that Cynthia wouldn't just come forward and help Nikki help her. Reveal where the bills were. Say how she got them. Help unravel the mystery.

The determination was to do it even without her mother's assistance.

There were now two very loud voices that were telling Nikki Heat not to dig into her mother's past. First The Serpent—whoever that was. And now Cynthia herself.

They were having the opposite effect. It went to Nikki Heat's doggedness—which she had inherited from Cynthia—and from a basic fact of her psychological makeup. The more she was threatened, cajoled, or beseeched not to do something, the more it became the thing she most wanted to do.

Maybe that made her too stubborn for her own good.

But it was also a big part of what made her Nikki Heat.

Once she had taken enough deep breaths to compose herself, Heat stood. She tucked the letter in her jacket. She dried the tears off her face carefully, so she wouldn't smear the makeup the media relations people had insisted she slather on her face for the press conference.

Then she lifted her chin and completed her walk up to the detective's bull pen.

As she pushed through the door at the top of the landing, she told herself she was going to be all business that day. Nothing would distract her. Not her mother's letter. Not the very intriguing—and excessively public—offer from Lindsy Gardner.

First she'd dispatch with the lingering issues in the Legs Kline case. Then she'd power through the mound of paperwork that was being so fruitful and multiplicative on her desk.

Then, when Derrick Storm gave her the name of who sprang Bart Callan, she would throw herself into following the trail until it arrived on the Shanghai Seven's doorstep.

She was ready for anything.

Just not what actually awaited her as she rounded the corner.

Jameson Rook was wearing one of his best bespoke suits, an elegant gray pinstripe outfit from Gieves & Hawkes in London. He paired it with a lavender Christian Lacroix tie and an Hermès silk pocket square that had been a six-month anniversary present from Heat.

He was surrounded by dozens of roses in different hues, enough that the bull pen—whose aroma normally approximated what you'd get if you moved a coffee shop into a locker room—suddenly smelled like a florist's convention.

When he saw her, Rook leapt to his feet so forcefully the chair with the wonky wheel—the orphan chair that always seemed to be left over for him—wobbled into the desk next to it with a jarring bang.

During their last conversation, Heat had told him she needed to take a break from their marriage. She couldn't be with him as long as her mother was somewhere out there. She knew how obsessed she got with ordinary cases, much less when the subject was her mother. Beyond that, she could sense how dangerous the search was going to be. She couldn't involve Rook in any of that.

Her exact words were, "I have to get my head right so we can have a happily ever after."

She had since blocked his phone number so he couldn't send her texts or call her, and she had rigged her in-box to route his e-mails straight into the spam folder, so she wouldn't be tempted to read them as she went through the rest of her mail.

But there was nothing she could do to block the man himself. Rook wasn't going to give up on the woman he loved, the woman he had patiently wooed over the course of years until he had worn down her every objection. Rook had fought for her love before. And Heat could see he fully intended to do it again.

"Rook! What are you—"

"Wait," Rook cut her off. "Before you say anything, I need to show these roses how beautiful you are."

Looking scrumptious in his perfect suit, he started plucking bouquets off the desk.

"This," he said, starting with the red ones, "signifies my love for you, and the enduring passion we share for one another."

Then he handed her the yellow roses. "These are because, in addition to being lovers, we are also best friends who put our caring for one another at the center of our relationship every day."

Next he went orange. "This is for the admiration I have for you and how you approach everything in your life with full and total effort. And even when the thing you're approaching is trying to kick me to the curb, I *still* admire you."

Then it was on to purple. "I'm not actually sure what these mean. But doesn't it remind you of the purple marshmallow in Lucky Charms? I guess that accounts for the 'natural' in 'natural and artificial flavors.' "

He finished with white. "And this, of course, represents peace. So please understand I come in peace. And while I respect everything you said last night, I just want another chance to talk with you about this. When I married you, I signed up for 'in sickness and in health' but also 'in the event someone totally unexpected resurfaces after seventeen years.' We didn't say that last part out loud, but I swear it was in the legal disclaimers at the end."

Then he fished a white card out of his pocket. "But I'm not done," he said, as if this were an amazing TV offer that was just about to get better. "Because I've also booked us for the Island-Hopping Special with Captain Tyler's Airborne Escapades."

He handed her what she now saw was a gift card.

"The Island-Hopping Special?" Heat asked.

"That's right. Captain Tyler is my friend Gregory Tyler. He's a corporate law burnout who now takes his former clients and their superrich Wall Street buddies on adventures. He claims to be the only sea skydiving operation in the New York area, though I'm not sure anyone has ever checked him out on that. The Island-Hopping Special is one of his packages for couples. You and your loved one jump out of his specially modified seaplane— with a prepackaged picnic lunch that includes champagne, of course—and parachute gently down to the uninhabited island of your choosing. You have your picnic. You enjoy your afternoon. Then a few hours later, he comes back and picks you up. How cool is that?"

"Rook, I—"

"Wait, don't answer. I got a little excited and went off script. I'm not done yet."

He closed in and took her hands in his. "Look, I know you're going through some stuff right now. But I can help. That's what we're about. That's what marriage is about."

Heat glanced to her right, aware she had an audience. Detective squad coleaders Miguel Ochoa and Sean Raley—who went by the mash-up nickname Roach—were watching carefully. They probably thought this was just some kind of marital spat. She knew they would be cheering for Rook. And he didn't need any more encouragement.

All she wanted was for Rook to go away. She thought about making up some wild story about how Rook had cheated on her with a Russian bimbo named Svetlana. Roach would forcibly throw Rook out of the precinct once they heard something like that. If they believed it. She doubted anyone would.

So she cleared her throat and said, "Can you come into my office, please?"

As soon as the door was closed behind him, he went to kiss her. But Heat, afraid she wouldn't be able to resist him, fended him off with a stiff arm.

Rook looked appropriately wounded. "Nikki, seriously, what's this about? I don't understand why you're doing this."

"Neither do I," Heat admitted. "My head is a mess. I just . . . I can't focus on our marriage right now. I feel like all my energy needs to be on my mother."

"Okay. I get that. There are times in a marriage when the relationship takes a little bit of a backseat. And that's fine—as long as I get to be in the front seat with you while it happens."

"No. No, I can't involve you like that."

"Involve me like what? Nikki Heat, I am your lawfully wedded husband. It's too late to not involve me in your life. You're not making any sense."

"I know I'm not," Heat said. "It's deeper than anything I can explain."

"Can't you try?"

Heat took in a large breath. "When I was growing up, my mother was . . . She was the safe port from which I launched all my adventures. I could go out and explore with confidence, knowing I always had her to come back to, and she would always help me comprehend what I had discovered. When I thought she had been killed, I was suddenly just this grief-stricken teenager who couldn't understand anything anymore. That's why solving her murder consumed me the way it did. It was the only way the world was going to make sense again. I knew I wasn't going to have the luxury of thinking about my own happiness or being in a real relationship—or even taking a normal breath—until she got justice. Then, finally, I thought she did. Petar Matic was dead. Bart Callan was in jail. Carey Maggs was in jail. And that's when I was able to marry the most wonderful man alive.

"But now? It's like everything has been ripped apart again. I can't breathe normally anymore. I can't think about happiness or a relationship. On some level, I've gone back to being that grief-stricken teenager who doesn't know how to make sense of anything. And I know you want to help me find my center again. But the fact is, I have to make that journey alone. That's how I did it last time. And that's how I'm doing it again. I'm sorry."

She rose on her tiptoes to kiss him on the cheek. "Now, please. Just go."

Heat walked behind her desk, sat down, and pointed her nose down toward her paperwork. She kept it there even as she felt Rook's eyes boring into her.

It was only when he started to leave the room that she allowed herself a brief glance at him. He looked utterly lost.

She felt terrible about it. But it was how it had to be.

SIX

STORM

Derrick Storm's last act as Michael Jackson was to take two passes by the corner office of Mason Wood, the associate director of the Bureau of Prisons.

Wood was standing, talking on a headset, not paying any particular attention to the man walking quickly by his office.

In those two passes, Storm imprinted into his memory everything he needed to recognize Wood: the short-cropped white hair, the jowly face, the bags under the eyes, the belly that bulged against the constraints of the suit pants, the loafers with tassels.

This was the man who signed the order to transfer Bart Callan to a medium security prison from which he could more easily escape. And Storm could guess there was likely a large and fresh pile of counterfeit bills, courtesy of the Shanghai Seven, hidden somewhere in the Wood household because of it.

It was the kind of bribe perfect for a cautious, conservatively minded career civil servant. You couldn't use bricks of twenty-dollar bills—no matter how perfectly forged—to buy a Bentley or purchase a second home in the Caribbean. It would attract too much attention, inviting a scrutiny someone on Mason Wood's income wouldn't be able to withstand.

But you could use those twenties to go out to dinner whenever you wanted. Or to scalp tickets to whatever ball game or concert you felt like attending. Or to pay for gas and groceries so you could use your legitimate income to buy a *slightly* nicer car, the kind that wasn't too flashy or too noticeable.

Yes, Mason Wood probably thought he had done things just about right, setting himself up for a comfortable existence. And all it cost him was his signature.

If anyone asked, he probably had a story at the ready: It was just a mix-up; he meant to sign a different inmate's order; how was he supposed to know screwing up one digit in the inmate's ID number would have such disastrous consequences?

Maybe he'd get suspended for a little while. But he now had more than enough cushion, one near-flawless twenty-dollar bill at a time, to survive for as long as he needed.

Michael Jackson had it all figured out as he departed the Bureau of Prison's offices, spilled out onto 1st Street in Northwest Washington, DC, dumped the fake ID badge into one street-side trashcan, then ripped off the ridiculous porn-stache and fake sideburns and deposited them into another.

Now that he was Derrick Storm again, his first act was to text Nikki Heat and tell her he had found their man. Next he waltzed into a clothing store on D Street and grabbed some more Derrick Storm-like clothes. Not wanting to take too much time, he just grabbed whatever stuck out at him on his way back to the dressing room. Storm had one of those fortunate bodies that off-the-rack items fit perfectly.

He got his first text from Heat right around the time he was pulling a snug black T-shirt over his head.

GOT HIM. MASON K. WOOD. LIVES AT 182 CALHOUN LANE, BETHESDA, MD. CAREER BOP EMPLOYEE. UNDERGRADUATE AT JAMES MADISON UNIVERSITY. MASTERS FROM GEORGE MASON.

Storm continued dressing, ditching his khakis in favor of a

pair of jeans that, he knew from experience, would have women checking out his ass all afternoon. Such was his cross to bear.

MAKES $121,780 A YEAR AS ASSOCIATE DIRECTOR. LIEN ON HOUSE FROM MORTGAGE. TWO CAR PAYMENTS. THREE CREDIT CARDS, TWO WITH ZERO OUTSTANDING BALANCE. ONE MASTERCARD WITH DEBT TOTALING $14,050.

Credit card debt? That was strange. As he threaded a wide black belt through the loops on his jeans, Storm wondered: Why would a man with Wood's access to cash be racking up credit card debt? Unless it was in an effort to throw off someone doing exactly what Heat was doing. Anyone who suspected fraud would pull up Wood's financials, looking for signs of hidden wealth. Credit card debt would be a red herring taking an investigator in the opposite direction.

WIFE AMANDA WORKS IN MONTGOMERY COUNTY SCHOOLS, MAKES $72,010 AS A SCHOOL COUNSELOR.

Which, again, made the credit card debt strange. Why would a couple making close to two hundred large a year be so stupid as to let a credit card company charge them such usurious interest rates when, in theory, it would only take a small amount of fiscal discipline for a few months to get rid of it?

NO CRIMINAL RECORD. NO SPEEDING TICKETS. NO PARKING TICKETS. NO CIVIL COMPLAINTS. NO RUN-INS WITH THE LAW THAT I CAN FIND IN MD/VA/DC.

Which made sense. Someone who worked for the Bureau of Prisons would understand all too well the dire consequences of running afoul of the law.

Storm finished off his outfit with a pair of black Doc Martens. It wasn't fancy. But he looked—and, more importantly, felt—like himself again.

Except now he was curious. What was Mason Wood up to?

Had he not, in fact, taken a bribe from the Shanghai Seven? Was he just doing what he thought was a solid for Bart Callan, who he knew somehow from their shared time in law enforcement? But what would make a man in Wood's position want to do favors for felons?

Storm brought his mental picture of Wood back into his mind and studied the man for a moment or two. Was there anything about him Storm had missed?

Of course. The pants. They were too small. Wood had gained weight recently—stress eating?—and now his pants didn't fit. But he hadn't gone out and bought new suits that fit better, because he wasn't swimming in cash. He was, in fact, in debt to MasterCard.

Storm had, by that point, wandered back to the Bureau of Prisons building, an impressive chunk of limestone designed to impress upon passersby that the federal government took the construction, administration, and maintenance of its detention facilities quite seriously. Storm looked up at the fifth-floor corner office of Mason Wood, as if he might see something that would solve this mystery.

"What are you up to, Mason Wood?" Storm muttered to himself.

Lost in this thought—and busily staring skyward—he nearly missed what was happening at street level: a man with a jowly face and white hair was walking out of the building's main entrance. Wood was on the move. Storm quickly glanced at the time on his cell phone. 12:02. Lunchtime.

With Storm lagging fifteen or twenty yards back, Wood turned up 1st Street, then right on D Street, where he ducked into a parking garage. He was walking with purpose and without glancing back. There was no reason for him to think he had someone tailing him. Other than fellow professionals, most people Storm followed were delightfully oblivious this way.

That said, Wood's destination gave Storm a problem. People typically only went to parking garages for one reason: to retrieve their cars. Mason Wood was about to have four wheels under him, which would make him difficult to tail on foot.

Storm kept a car stored near Dulles Airport. He just hadn't anticipated needing it. He had taken a cab from the airport, because it was quicker than taking a detour by the garage.

He looked around, his head swiveling up and down the street until he found what he was looking for:

A rusting 1985 Ford Thunderbird, parked at a meter. Perfect.

Storm's first car had been a well-used 1987 Thunderbird that he'd bought in high school for five hundred dollars and lovingly fixed up. It carried him all through college, and by the time he surrendered it to a junkyard a year or two into his working life, it was more duct tape and bailing wire than car.

He knew that make and model better than any car made before or since. There was one important difference between the '87 model and the '85. By '87, the first onboard computers had started regulating many of the car's functions, including ignition. In '85, the Thunderbird still started in a way that would have been fundamentally familiar to Henry Ford himself.

Storm yanked the Thunderbird's door handle, hoping anyone who drove a junker like that wouldn't bother locking it.

The door held firm. A lesser man might have uttered an indelicate phrase or two. Storm just looked around at the rest of the street. To his mild dismay, there was no other vehicle that would do. It was the T-bird or nothing.

Then his eyes fell on the clothing store he had just patronized. Perfect. He ran in and grabbed the first hanger he saw, hollering a hasty, "Hi. Me again. I'll be right back with this. Thanks!"

He rationalized the temporary theft by telling himself he had probably overpaid for the T-shirt.

The hanger's hook was metal, but its body was plastic, and therefore a little chunkier than Storm might have preferred. But the rubber seal in such an old door had been loosened by time. Storm was able to work the hanger in until he found the latch he was looking for.

He pulled up and watched on the other side of the window as a slender metal knob, which had previously been flush against the top of the door, slid into its unlocked position. Then he yanked open the door. He was in.

With one quick jab, Storm bashed off the covering underneath the steering wheel and quickly found the two wires he was looking for. He ripped them out of their mooring, exposing their braided metal ends. The moment he touched them together, current surged through the solenoid, and soon Storm heard the delightful sound of a V-8 engine stuttering to life.

Back in this vehicle's heyday, a professional car thief could break into and hot-wire a car in less than sixty seconds. It had taken Storm about a minute and a half. But that was good enough. He had gotten himself seated behind the wheel by the time Wood, driving a blue Acura, emerged from the parking ramp.

Wood took a hasty look at the lack of oncoming traffic and pointed himself west on D Street. Storm did the same and continued following as Wood descended into the 395 tunnel that ran under the Capitol Mall.

"Where are you going, Mason Wood?" Storm asked as the Thunderbird rattled along a dozen car lengths back. "Aren't there enough lunch places in downtown DC for you? What are you hungry for?"

Wood eased into the left lanes, then followed signs for 295 south. He stayed on the freeway as it passed within sight of Nationals Park and neared the Washington Navy Yard. There had been massive redevelopment and a certain amount of gentrification in what had previously been a downtrodden part of the city. A number of upscale restaurants had sprung up. It made sense that a well-paid government worker might seek out one of them for a decent meal.

"What, you want Chinese fusion?" Storm asked. "Italian? Farm-to-table contemporary southern?"

But Wood didn't exit the freeway. Instead, he crossed the river into Anacostia. The gentrification, quite clearly, had not. This part of Southeast DC was still desperately poor, a pocket of multigenerational poverty and stubbornly high crime less than four miles from the Capitol of the most powerful nation on Earth.

This, of all places, was where Wood chose to exit. He passed the Anacostia Metro Station near Suitland Parkway, then worked his way into the neighborhood. He was making a series of turns, and it was all Storm could do to keep up. He didn't worry about Wood noticing he was being followed. That was another advantage to an '85 Thunderbird: perfect ghetto camouflage.

Storm was starting to wonder just how long a journey into the 'hood he was in for when the Acura's signal indicated it was turning into a small driveway. Storm kept driving past a former single-family house that had been converted into a business.

The neon sign attached to the ancient siding had several of its letters missing. Had it been nighttime, Storm would have thought Wood was entering an "ASS AG" establishment.

But in daylight, Storm could make out the letters just fine: MASSAGE.

Storm had finally figured out what Wood was hungry for. And it wasn't food.

Storm parked the Thunderbird just down the street and did some quick reckoning.

What was the right amount of time to wait to catch Wood in flagrante delicto? Five minutes felt like too few. He might not be *flagrante* yet. Fifteen felt like too long. The *delicto* might have already happened.

So Storm decided to wait ten minutes before making his move. In that time, he solved at least one of the mysteries of Mason Wood: the credit card debt. He had two cards—the two his wife knew about—fully paid off. It was the card his wife likely didn't know about, the one he used to fund his happy endings, that carried the balance.

Did the amount of money he was able to squirrel away each month for his escapades simply not equal his appetites? Did he have some plan in place to pay it off—some stock he could sell without his wife knowing it—that he simply hadn't executed yet? Or was he slowly working himself toward a financial and matrimonial disaster, one rub-a-dub-dub at a time?

Whatever the case, Storm was betting Mrs. Wood, dignified school counselor, would be very interested to know how her hubby was spending his lunch break.

With that in mind, Storm pulled out his phone and began documenting his walk toward the building. He took a picture of the sidewalk, strewn with litter and glistening with glass pebbles. He perfectly framed the "ASS AG" sign. He only wished he could play with his phone's f-stop so he could get the composition right. Automatic cameras were the worst.

He kept snapping as he barged through the door. The waiting

room was aged and tacky, with plastic chairs and a decorating style some ill-informed soul had once called "oriental." He was immediately greeted by a creased-faced woman of Southeast Asian origin. Vietnamese. Filipino. It was difficult to say.

"Hi!" she said, with a wide grin. "You need massage? We give nice massage to nice gentleman!"

Storm took her picture then kept walking, through a curtain into a dimly lit hallway lined with doors.

"Hello? You no go there! You no go!" the woman chirped after him, trying to grab his arm.

Storm shook his arm free and said in Mandarin, "I'm going. And you can't stop me."

He then repeated some approximation of that phrase in both Vietnamese and Malay. Not that he really spoke either of those languages as well as he spoke, say, Arabic or French. But he could fake it.

Finally, back to English, he said, "I'm going where I please. You can call the cops if you want. I'm sure they'd be happy to be invited in here for a tour. I'm sure your customers would like it even more."

He opened the first door, finding only a small room with an empty massage table. The second door revealed a man with a towel draped over his butt, moaning as a woman young enough to be his granddaughter kneaded the muscles in his back.

It was the third door where Storm found what he was looking for—or, rather, what he immediately wished he could unsee.

The Bureau of Prisons associate director was lying faceup on a table wearing only his socks. An Asian woman with well-toned forearms was pouring her considerable efforts on one particular portion of his midsection. She was wearing a robe, which she had opened, exposing her bare breasts.

As the door swung fully open and Storm clicked away, her rhythmic stroking ceased. She looked at Storm with more curiosity than hostility.

It was Wood, with his oak tree rapidly turning into an acorn, who moaned, "Oh, God. Not again."

Storm had switched to video for the ending—which most assuredly wasn't happy—as the woman took her hand away from Wood's now-shriveled manhood and closed her robe.

"Sorry for the interruption," Storm said. He stowed his phone, then dug two twenties out of his wallet and handed them to her. "Your work is done for today. Here's your tip. Thank you. You can close the door behind you."

Wood had swung around into a sitting position and was leaning toward a towel, which was clumped on a nearby counter. In one quick move, Storm swatted it on the floor. Wood looked at it helplessly, his defeat now total.

"Look, do you people really need more dirt on me?" he said miserably. "You've already got the photos from last time. Was this really necessary?"

"What are you talking about?" Storm said.

"I'm talking . . . Wait, what are you talking about?" Wood asked.

"I'm talking about your wife and how much she'd like to see the photos I've just shot."

"Yeah, yeah, I know," Wood said. "I thought we had already gone through this before."

"Who is 'we'?"

"You work for Jedediah Jones, right?"

Storm said nothing. *How could Wood possibly know that?*

"You do. I can see it on your face," Wood said. "So, yeah, *this*. The photos. The . . . blackmail, I guess you'd call it. Look,

I have a weakness, okay? I thought we already established that. No one's perfect. Do you guys really have to keep humiliating me like this? I'm just trying to blow off a little steam. This is all very aboveboard below-board entertainment. No one is being hurt here."

"I'm not here to debate the morality of prostitution with you, Mr. Wood."

"Ouch. Isn't 'prostitution' a little bit of a strong word? Mimi is a sensual massage artist. She's got a certificate and everything. She performs a valuable service for me."

"With her breasts hanging out."

"She works hard. It gets warm under that robe. That's her choice."

"Right. Of course."

"Look, is there something else your boss needs me to do for him?" Wood asked. "Because, if not, I really do need to be getting back to work."

"That depends. What did you do for him the first time?"

Wood had hopped down off the table, brushing close enough to Storm that he could smell the massage oil on the man's wrinkled, flaccid skin. Naked looked good on some people. Not on Mason Wood.

"If you don't know already, I'm certainly not telling you," Wood said.

"Yes, you are," Storm said, holding up the phone.

Wood looked at the phone and frowned as he pulled on his underwear. "This is ridiculous. The left hand doesn't even know what the right hand is doing. You're worse than the BoP. I thought you guys had your act together more than that."

Storm watched as Wood yanked up his pants while shaking his head.

"I'll give you a hint," Wood said. "It was about three weeks ago? And now it's all over the news? And the only reason it's not getting me fired is because I claimed the signature was forged? Which it was, because I made that woman do it."

"What woman? Clara Strike?"

"Is that her last name? Yeah. Clara. All I know is she's so gorgeous, she probably could have charmed me into doing whatever she wanted even without the blackmail."

Storm was ignoring the commentary. Clara Strike had been the woman who first recruited him into Jones's employ, rescuing him from life as a ham-and-egg private investigator when she became aware he had abilities far beyond that low station. She had since become the love—and torment—of Derrick Storm's life. Her brains, beauty, and dedication to Jedediah Jones's sometimes twisted priorities made her one of his most formidable assets. It also made the prospect of a long-term relationship with her all but impossible.

And yet, when they were together . . .

Storm shook the thought from his head. He had to focus on what Wood had just confessed.

"Wait, the order for Bart Callan's transfer. You signed it because *Jedediah Jones* blackmailed you?"

"Well, yeah," Wood said. "You think that was my idea? You should see Callan's psych evals. He's got an IQ of one-forty-five and the worst case of narcissistic personality disorder I've ever seen. Plus, he's trained in, like, ten different disciplines of martial arts. We had to put him in one of those supermax cells where the inmate is never touched by human hands, because he kept beating the crap out of the guards when he got pissed at them. That guy is a total piece of work. I can't believe you guys helped him escape. He's a—"

"Excuse me, Mr. Wood," Storm said. "I have a phone call to make."

Storm stumbled back out in the street, so momentarily stunned he just stood on the sidewalk, looking for all the world like a satisfied John who was just soaking in a bit of afternoon sunshine after some afternoon delight.

But on the inside, his mind was a jumble.

Jedediah Jones wanted Callan released—then, apparently, helped him escape.

But how could that be? Storm couldn't imagine what possible value Callan would have to Jones. Callan had skills, yes, but Jones had access to a lot of skilled operatives who *weren't* convicted serial killers. It made no sense that Jones would free a psycho whose only real usefulness was to the Shanghai Seven, unless . . .

Unless Jones was in bed with the Shanghai Seven.

It was the only possible explanation. But it made no sense. Hadn't Jones been the one who had not only ordered the raid on the Shanghai Seven but had asked that Storm come home with evidence Jones would use to get the criminal syndicate shut down?

Then again, the raid had clearly been compromised. Colonel Feng didn't have an entire squadron at the ready by accident. Had Jones both arranged the operation and then conspired to scuttle it? That would be classic Jones.

But then what, in the bigger picture, was Jones looking to exploit from a relationship with the Shanghai Seven? What could seven corrupt Chinese businessmen do for him? Who was the cat? Who was the mouse? It was beyond Storm's fathoming. The motivation for Jones's actions often defied conventional explanation.

Storm took halting steps back toward his car. Generally speaking, white people only went to Anacostia for one reason. And, sure enough, as he approached the Thunderbird, a young black kid who looked like he should have been in school was crossing the street, making a straight line toward Storm. He wore a long white T-shirt covering a waistband that likely had a pistol tucked in it.

"Hey, mister, you looking for something?" he asked.

Ordinarily, Storm would have disarmed the kid, twisted his elbow within a quarter inch of dislocation, made him confess where his stash was hidden, flushed the drugs down the toilet, then marched the kid back to school with certain threats about what would happen to him if he didn't stay and graduate.

It spoke to Storm's state of agitated distraction that he just brushed the kid away with a "No. Sorry."

Storm sat in the Thunderbird. He was dimly aware Wood had walked out of the massage parlor behind him, soon to be making the trip back to middle-class America in his Acura. Storm ignored him. Mason Wood was now a nonissue, a pathetic example of a man who was no longer a concern to anyone other than his unfortunate wife.

Before Storm fully knew what he planned on saying, he pulled out his phone and rang Clara Strike.

"Hey, babe. Long time," she answered easily, as if the last time they had seen each other hadn't been in the eastern Sahara, where she had abandoned him in a huff over their differing interpretations of a mission's objectives.

"Too long in some ways, and yet not long enough in others," Storm said. "Isn't that always how it is with us?"

"I guess that's fair. But don't tell me you're still pissed about Egypt. Egypt was . . . Well, I think it was pretty spectacular at first, if I do say so myself. And, yeah, it got a little messy in the middle. But then the good guys won, so all's well that ends well, right?"

"Because the ends always justify the means, Miss Machiavelli?"

"Cute," she said. "Look, is this just a poorly executed booty call? Or did you really just call me up to pick at old scabs?"

"No. Where are you right now?"

"The Cubby."

The Cubby was the nickname the operatives had given Jones's headquarters, a secret subterranean CIA lair whose precise location remained a mystery to Storm, even after all the years and all the contracts he had fulfilled for Jones.

"Can you talk?" Storm asked.

"It depends. About what?"

"What I mean is: Is Jones around? Can he hear you right now?"

"Probably. I always tell you, Jones is like a really skinny Santa Claus. He sees you when you're sleeping, he knows when you're awake. I've found it's best to live my life as if he can *always* hear me. It's safer that way."

"But is he in the room?"

"No. I'm in my office and now . . ." Strike paused, and Storm heard a soft thunk. "There, the door is closed. What's up?"

"I was just spending some quality time at the massage parlor with your friend, Mason Wood."

"Jeez, Storm, why didn't you just tell me you were that hard up? Even if you are still pissed at me about Egypt, I've got to be a better option than Mimi."

Storm ignored the jab. Strike knew Storm's intentions toward women were far too virtuous for him to ever contribute to an economy he felt demeaned them.

"Why did you blackmail Wood into signing an order to

transfer a cretin like Bart Callan to a medium security prison?" Storm asked.

"Uh . . . because Jones told me to and I was following orders?"

"That's always a good enough answer for you, isn't it?"

Strike sighed audibly. That was an old fight for them, one they had engaged in many times.

"Look, if you have a question for Jones, just come in and ask him. He'll deal with you straight."

"Yeah, straight from the bottom of the deck," Storm said.

"Don't be ridiculous. I keep telling you, Jones may not be a Boy Scout like you all the time, but he's ultimately on the right side. In a strange way, I've never met anyone more dedicated to his country. I'm sure he had a perfectly good reason for wanting Callan transferred."

"I'm just as sure he didn't."

"Yeah, yeah. Because Derrick Storm is the only white-hat cowboy out there. Sorry that the rest of us recognize the world has other colors in it."

Rather than come up with one last retort, Storm hung up. It was pointless. If the past was any guide, the more angelic Strike insisted Jones was being, the closer he was to the demons.

With his phone still out, Storm composed a quick text to Nikki Heat, explaining what he had learned.

SO BE CAREFUL, it finished. IT SEEMS MY PEOPLE ARE WORKING AGAINST US.

SEVEN

HEAT

Nikki Heat set her phone down on her desk. She had, for the last two hours or so, pretended that she could bury herself in paperwork, even as she picked at the details of Mason Wood's life.

She had yearned to do more than that, of course. She wanted to kick down the front door of his house and demand answers. She wanted to threaten to toss him into a nearby incinerator if he didn't cooperate.

But now it seemed Mason Wood was an investigational dead end, in addition to being a dead end as a human being.

And Heat could no longer shuffle through requisition and overtime requests. She picked up the phone again and reread Storm's text.

His people were working against them. Who *were* Storm's people, exactly? And what did that mean for Nikki's mother?

Certainly, it explained why Cynthia had stayed in the shadows for so long. To have made enemies with seven rich, crooked Chinese businessmen *and* a top secret division within the CIA was like winning some kind of perverse Powerball lottery where the reward was a big pile of malevolence.

But why would some counterfeit bills matter so much? Was the CIA involved in the counterfeiting somehow? Even thinking it was absurd, and yet . . . Well, anyone who knew the history of the CIA knew the agency was capable of just about anything.

Still, Heat did her best to banish those kinds of imponderable, high-level thoughts from her mind. If her years as a detective had taught her one thing, it was that an excessive focus on the big picture could be detrimental in certain cases. Sometimes you just needed to keep filling out one small corner of the frame until it helped the whole thing make sense.

Much of what she knew about the time period around her mother's death was old—and old news. But there was that one new piece of evidence.

Cynthia's conversation with Nicole Bernardin. Nikki had played it several more times the previous night, enough that she had some of its key revelations more or less memorized. She played it back in her mind.

I've dealt with those phony bills. I found a place to hide them. . . .

They definitely have fingerprints on them. I dusted them. They're faint, but they're there. . . .

Let me put it this way: I'd not only trust this spot with my life, I'd trust it with my best Scotch. . . .

Counterfeit bills with fingerprints on them, a key piece of evidence, hidden in a spot where—

Of course.

There was only one place where Cynthia Heat kept her best Scotch. And it wasn't in their apartment. It was a few blocks away, at her favorite hangout.

The Players Club was one of the most venerable and elegant social clubs in New York. Mark Twain had been a member. So had William Tecumseh Sherman. And Helen Hayes. And Cynthia Heat.

But for all its reputation and history, Cynthia had never treated it like some kind of exclusive, elitist enclave. And so Nikki never thought of it that way. If anything, it was like her mother's second living room, filled with interesting, affable, approachable people. Like a low-key dinner party with friends that was there five days a week, whenever you felt like a little company. Nikki had her first drink there, as a sixteen-and-a-half-year-old celebrating a successful piano recital. It was that kind of place.

If Cynthia was going to keep her best Scotch anywhere, it would be there. And the man who would be called on to safeguard it was George The Bartender, who had been working at The Players since Nikki first started being allowed to join her mother there as a little girl.

George's hair had been dark then. It was shock white now. His shift—which for all Nikki knew had been the same since Jack Lemmon had been a regular there—started at four o'clock and went until midnight.

Heat took a precinct pool car down to Gramercy Park. She locked her weapon in the trunk—no guns allowed inside, per club policy—then walked inside. It was a little after three o'clock. But, of course, George was already there, just as he often stayed after midnight when duty called.

"Ms. Heat. Lovely to see you," he greeted her as he wiped down the slab of lacquered mahogany in front him, even though it was already spotless. George's bow tie was just as crisply knotted as ever.

"Hi, George," she said, selecting a stool at the otherwise empty bar. "Good to see you, too."

Upon her demise—as falsely constructed as it now appeared to be—Cynthia Heat's membership had transferred to Nikki, who wished she had the time to use it more often. She and Rook used to make it a point to make a pilgrimage over there around the anniversary of Cynthia's death. Otherwise, Nikki's visits were few and far between.

"What can I get you?"

"How about a sidecar?"

"Of course," he said.

George disappeared into the back, to retrieve the necessary booze from her mother's liquor cabinet—or, well, technically, Nikki's. Every member at The Players Club had one. They were not alphabetized, and there was no discernible system as to how they were organized. Yet George knew where each was as surely as he knew where to find his own fingers.

The brass nameplate on Nikki's still read CYNTHIA HEAT. No one could bring themselves to change it.

Years before, Nikki had discovered a bottle of Durdles' Finest Pale Ale in there. It was one of the clues that had led her to Carey Maggs, who owned the Durdles brand, and then ultimately to Bart Callan.

George reappeared and, with a practiced hand, mixed Nikki's sidecar. Heat could spend every night for the rest of her life in her apartment practicing how to make one. It would never taste as good as George's.

She took her first sip. Perfect as ever.

"So George," she said.

"Yes, Ms. Heat?"

The bar was still empty. She was thankful it was so early. She didn't need anyone hearing what she was about to say. She took a deep breath and plunged in:

"Before my mother's . . . passing . . . did she ever give you something? Something to hide?"

Heat studied George intently. His face was blank. But as he

returned to wiping down the bar, which was no less immaculate than it had been before, she thought she saw a glimmer of a memory dancing in his eyes.

"No. Can't say anything like that ever happened," he said, without looking up.

"Can't say or won't say?"

George stopped wiping and raised his eyebrows. "I'm sure I don't know what you're talking about, Ms. Heat."

But he did know. Heat could see it in the way his skillful hands, which held a bottle so steadily, now had a slight shake to them.

Heat knew she was treading on sacred ground for a man in George's profession. A bad bartender kept your secrets only until you left the bar. A good one kept them until you died. A great one, like George, took them to his own grave.

"I think you do, George," Heat said softly.

George looked down, staring at his own reflection in the lacquer's high shine, almost like he was trying to look at himself in a mirror. The turmoil in his head was plain. *Ms. Heat is a trusted friend. . . . You've known her family since she was a girl. . . . She's asking about her own mother, who has been dead for many years now. . . . There's no harm in telling her now. But what kind of man are you if you betray a confidence?*

Heat knew why George had never pursued life as a professional poker player. He had tells all over the place. His breathing had grown rapid. His Adam's apple bobbed up and down. His suddenly sweaty palms were leaving little steam marks on the bar top.

She reached out and grabbed him by the wrist. He looked up, surprised. But at least he was now making eye contact. This was her chance.

"George, there's something I need to tell you. And I know I can trust you with this, because I see how careful you've been with my mother's privacy. But what's happening now is . . . Well, I hope you can see it supersedes whatever promises you made to her seventeen years ago. My mother is alive, George. It seems she faked her own death. I had no idea until I saw her on the street the other day. Then she sent me a letter this morning. She's alive and she's in trouble. Very, very serious trouble. And what she asked you to hide might be able to help me get her out of trouble. Please, George, I need your help."

Heat pulled the letter out of her jacket pocket. "This is her handwriting," she said, unfolding the letter. "I don't know if you recognize it like I do. But it's hers. No doubt. And the ink is fresh."

George took a glance at it and nodded.

"She's alive, George."

George pulled his arm away and turned his back. Heat was losing him to shock. Heat knew, from hard experience, this was a lot to process.

"Let's start with what I already know," she said, like the seasoned interrogator she was. "My mother gave you something to hide right before she died, didn't she?"

George was studying some spot on the counter behind the bar. But Heat saw him nod.

"Was it some money? Some bills?" Heat asked.

"It was an envelope," he said grimly.

"Could it have contained some twenty-dollar bills?"

"That sounds about right."

"When did she give it to you?"

"Three days before she . . ."

"Before you thought she died?"

George nodded again.

"And she told you to hide it where no one would find it. She told you not to even tell *her* where it was—that way no one could torture the location out of her or use some advanced truth serum on her or anything like that. Is that right?"

"Yes," he said.

"She even told you this directive had to survive her death. She told you no matter what happened, you had to keep that envelope hidden."

His head bobbed.

"But she also told you if she ever contacted you sometime in the future and asked for them, you were to give them to her. Unless she was under some kind of obvious duress—like next to a man who had a big bulge in his jacket pocket—you'd hand them over, am I right?"

"Yes," he said again. "She even made me put a codicil in my will. There's a letter in my safety-deposit box that will be mailed to the executor of my estate upon my death. Cynthia insisted on it."

Of course she would have. Cynthia Heat thought of everything.

"Okay, George. This right here? This is her contacting you. This is that future moment she was waiting for. Just hand that envelope over to me and you'll probably have Cynthia back here asking for a vodka martini by Friday. You'd like that, right?"

"Of course I would, but . . ." George began. Then he turned back to Nikki. The old man had tears in his eyes. "But if Mrs. Heat is alive, why isn't she contacting me herself, like she said she would?"

It was a question Nikki couldn't answer. Not to George's satisfaction.

"I'm sorry, Ms. Heat. I truly am," George said. "But I made

a promise to your mother long ago. And I aim to keep it now."

"Even if it means she'll never be able to come out of hiding?"

"I'm sorry," he said again. "Maybe she'll come to me soon. Maybe the time isn't quite right yet. Your mother was a brilliant, brilliant woman, Ms. Heat. Sorry—*is* a brilliant woman. I have to believe she knows what's best."

George's biorhythms seemed to have steadied. Heat could see he wasn't going to change his mind.

"But if you do find a way to write a letter back to her," George said, "tell her I'd very much like to see her again."

"So would I," Heat said. "So would I."

Heat wanted to leave and would have done so if she felt she could do it without hurting George's feelings.

Instead, she just sat there and sipped her sidecar, which suddenly didn't taste very good.

Having finished the drink, Heat made excuses about having places to go and police work to accomplish. George was gracious about letting her go with sincere wishes that she come back soon.

She stepped out onto Gramercy Park South, blinking in the afternoon sunshine, which suddenly seemed perversely bright. Across the way, Gramercy Park itself, that tiny sylvan sanctuary on the hard streets of Manhattan, hid in the gloom.

Heat didn't want to go back to the precinct. There was nothing there except paperwork that wouldn't get her one inch closer to her mother. And closer to her mother was the only place she felt like being.

Maybe she should call John Null and tell him she would be pleased to accept soon-to-be-President Gardner's invitation to head up Homeland Security. She could resign from the NYPD, effectively immediately, spending unused vacation time as her two weeks' notice. That would allow her to focus all her attention on her mother's case. Surely by the time the Gardner administration began their new jobs, Nikki would have brought things to a conclusion.

And if not, her new job title—director of Homeland Security—would be a heck of a club to wield against her mother's enemies.

Her phone bleeped to notify her of an incoming text message. Heat looked down at it with disinterest until she saw who it was from.

That 646 area code.

The Serpent.

YOU'RE NOT LISTENING TO ME, AND IT'S MAKING ME ANGRY. FOR THE LAST TIME: DO NOT INVESTIGATE YOUR MOTHER'S DISAPPEARANCE. IT WILL ONLY LEAD TO PAIN. DROP IT. NOW. OR DO I HAVE TO PROVE TO YOU HOW POWERFUL I AM? DO YOU NEED TO SEE A MANIFESTATION OF MY WRATH?

Heat read it twice, feeling the frown weighing on her forehead. It was hard to know what to do with this. Dismiss it as a prank? Take it seriously? Demand The Serpent show himself?

She knew one thing for sure: She wasn't going to listen to him. There was no way she was going to stop this investigation. Not for The Serpent. Not for anyone.

Heat jotted down the 646 number in a notepad, then called the number for the detective's bull pen.

"Yo," Ochoa answered. "What's up, Captain?"

"I need a quick favor. What's Roach up to right now?"

"We're sick and tired of filing reports, that's what. I think we're happy to do anything that doesn't involve more typing."

"Good. Can you run down this number for me?" Heat asked, then read off the 646 number. Ochoa read it back.

"That's it," Heat said. "Tell me anything you can about that number. Who owns it. Who it's been calling. If it's a cell, what towers has it been pinging off of. The usual."

"You got it, Cap. Is this something from Legs Kline or . . ."

"No," Heat said. "It's personal."

EIGHT

STORM

I f you steal someone's car, you return it with a full tank of gas. That's just common courtesy.

Derrick Storm would have also run the '85 Thunderbird through a car wash, just as an extra little thank-you, had he not been afraid there'd be nothing left of the vehicle by the time it came out on the other side.

The metered spot from which Storm had taken the T-bird was now occupied. But there was another spot available on D Street, two down from the original. So Storm parallel parked it, wondering what the owner would think about its magical teleportation and the sudden ability of the gas tank to fill itself.

Storm's last act was to tuck two twenties under the sun visor, deeming that an acceptable price for a short-term rental.

He then hailed a cab and asked it to take him to his private garage near Dulles, where he would have gone in the first place had he realized his stay in the DC area was going to be extended.

But, yes, Storm now realized he might be there for more than just a quick blackmail errand. Jedediah Jones was steeping himself in treachery, as usual, and until Storm could figure out why— why free Bart Callan? why do favors for the Shanghai Seven?—he wouldn't be able to rest.

He had an idea of a safe house where he could find sanctuary for the evening, where there was a man who might at least be able to help him brainstorm some ideas.

However, first things first: wheels that weren't stolen.

A man of Derrick Storm's wealth and connections could surely have afforded and procured any vehicle he chose. But none of the normal choices for a man in his profession felt quite right to him. A Lamborghini was too clichéd—and, plus, they were a pain to repair. A Maserati was too effete. An Aston Martin was too James Bond.

No, there was only one make of car that felt right to Storm, and that was a Ford. As far as he was concerned, there was no finer automaker in the world.

Commonplace? Certainly.

Boring? Only to some.

Unsexy? Don't you dare think it.

Storm just never felt better than when he was in a Detroit-made (or, okay, Kentucky, Alabama, or wherever it was Ford was assembling cars these days) product. It seemed only right for an American operative to have a great American car propelling him forward.

He owned a small fleet of Fords, strategically stashed in the cities he was most likely to frequent. In Washington, his choice was a Ford Taurus. It was the SHO model, which meant it was the best Ford's engineers—who were the best engineers in the world—could come up with, including a 365-horsepower twin-turbo engine that could shame anything Mercedes put on the road in the same class, a finely tuned suspension that Lexus would be proud to call its own, and a handling that compared favorably to any BMW you'd care to pick.

But the Taurus took all that automotive excellence and wrapped it in the ordinary everyday package that was a midsize family sedan. It was, much like Storm himself, a car that hid its full capacity.

By the time he felt the thrill of its engine vibrating in his heart, it was getting to be afternoon rush hour, a phrase that was something of a misnomer in the nation's capital—it was really like rush *four* hours. Storm experienced the schadenfreude that was traveling east on the Dulles Toll Road at ten to fifteen miles above the speed limit while the entire population of Virginia's Loudoun County sat inhaling its own exhaust fumes on the westbound side.

His destination was a place where he often went to find solace from life's thorniest problems. For some people that might have been a place of worship, a high-end day spa, or a trail high in the mountains.

For Storm, it was a dowdy split-level ranch tucked in an unremarkable subdivision in suburban northern Virginia. Decades ago, every other house on the block had been more or less just like it, with only small allowances for individual variation. Since that time, the entire area seemed to have been swallowed by the suburban propensity for bigger, better, and more. What had slowly been regurgitated back out, one addition and one teardown at a time, would have been unrecognizable to the neighborhood's original settlers.

Only this one split-level remained in its original unaltered state. Storm pulled up the driveway until his progress was blocked about halfway by a thick block of a man whose hair was completely white—except for his eyebrows, which had somehow stayed black. His face was full of character, some would even say wisdom, but his age-defying chin had not gone watery and run down his neck, like some men his age. It was a chin that was strong as ever.

The man didn't own anything mechanical that was less than

twenty-five years old. Even his car—a tank of a 1986 Buick—was older than a lot of the hipsters who were now starting to discover the neighborhood (but only ironically, of course).

Arrayed in front of the man were the pieces of a machine that was even older. It may have once been a lawn mower. It was currently looking improbable it would ever become one again.

"Don't give me that look," the man said as Storm approached. "If I had gone to the parts store they would have tried to sell me on a whole new spark plug."

"Yes. Heaven forbid if you had wasted an entire two dollars and forty-nine cents on that ridiculous suggestion."

"Well, come on," the man protested. "Anyone could see the contacts just needed to be cleaned a little."

"And then, for the sins of the spark plug, you decided to punish the rest of the lawn mower?"

"No. The carburetor was looking gummy. You don't want to store it for the winter dirty. It just gets that much harder to clean it come spring. And then I had noticed the throttle was getting sticky. And I've been wanting to sharpen the blade for a while now. Just a little routine maintenance. What do you want me to do, go to the goddamn Lame Depot and buy one of those crappy Yamaguchis, or whatever the hell they're called? They're nothing but plastic and tinfoil. I'd just have to buy a new one in five years. But a Craftsman like this? Now, this is solid. This is worth taking care of. How many times I gotta tell you, if you get a good machine and you take good care of it—"

"It'll last forever," Storm finished.

"Damn right it will," the man growled, wiping his brow on a grease rag.

"Hi, Dad," Derrick Storm said. "I'm glad to see nothing has changed around here."

"Hi, Son," Carl Storm replied. "I'm glad to see you're not wearing one of those two-thousand-dollar suits of yours."

"And why's that?"

"Because it means you can give your greasy old man a hug. C'mere, ya big lug."

The men embraced. Derrick, at six foot two, used to be two inches taller than his father. Now it was more like four. No one escapes gravity forever.

"Now, I realize that the moment I kick it, you're going to send this beautiful machine to the landfill," Carl said. "And then someone is going to buy this place, knock it down, and build some palace where they get a lawn service to take care of the three square feet of grass that's left. But, for now, why don't you help me put this thing back together so I can get the damn lawn mowed?"

Three hours later, after they had reassembled the Craftsman and then mowed, trimmed, and blown the grass clippings off the driveway and sidewalk, the Storm boys were sitting out back.

Carl's deck chairs were from the 1980s, making them new by his standards. They were made of forged aluminum spanned by a series of plastic strips, the kind that left their dented impressions on your hamstrings and backside after you sat in them for more than thirteen seconds.

Had the men been inside, it would have been Carl sitting on a Barcalounger and Derrick on a paisley sofa, also items that easily predated the first Bush presidency. And a blond woman with feathered hair would have been looking down on both of them from her picture on the mantel.

That so little ever changed about the house was, in a strange way, that blond woman's fault. Derrick's mother had died in a car accident when he was five, leaving both her boys alone and bereft. Derrick slowly got over it—sort of. Carl never even made it to sort of.

"She was a heck of a woman," was the most Carl usually ever said about his wife before he had to excuse himself from whatever company he was in.

The loss had brought Carl and Derrick together like nothing else could. A boy who grows up without a mother will become unusually close to his father—just like a boy without a dad will become steadfast in his love for his mother. It doesn't matter if that woman is a steady homemaker, an eccentric actress, or some combination of the two. He'll love her with ferocity.

The same was true with Derrick and Carl Storm. And one of the things that bonded them was a kind of unspoken covenant that they would keep things in the house just as she had left them. Because if Mom made it that way, who were they to change it? The Storm residence had become a kind of living time capsule as a result.

Carl's fidelity to The Way Things Were went even beyond home decoration. Most men who became widowers at such a young age would have eventually started dating again and probably remarried. He was not only ruggedly handsome in his own right, he was also devoted, dependable, loyal, and gainfully employed—all the things women lust after once they reach the age when they finally realize Prince Charming is really just a guy who remembers to buy tampons at the grocery store.

Yet, for all his desirability as a mate, Carl never seemed to look at other women, much less date them. He said it wasn't out of some strange sense of allegiance to a ghost who could not love him back in the corporeal sense. He swore it was just because his dead wife had spoiled him for all other women.

Derrick had asked him about it—just once—when he was

seventeen, when sex was pretty much all he thought about and when that surge of teenage hormones had filled him with a keen appreciation for how much a heterosexual man (of any age) would yearn for certain comforts only a woman could provide. Derrick had fumbled his way through the wording of a question that had come out something like: *Jeez, Dad, don't you miss, you know, getting to, uh, have someone to, you know, sorta be with?*

"You mean, do I wish I could get a little ink for my quill now and then?" Carl had asked with a laugh.

Then he dismissed his son with one sentence: "Once a man has been with a woman like your mother, it makes his standards a bit too high to go hopping in the sack with just anyone. Someday you'll understand."

And Derrick did, eventually coming to see that sex was meant to be more than just an aerobic activity between consenting adults. Still, he wasn't sure how much he bought his father's "just waiting for the right woman" line. It probably would have been more convincing if Carl ever took off his wedding ring.

The hand with the ring was now wrapped around a Pabst Blue Ribbon, Carl's beer of choice. Ordinarily, Derrick would rather have drunk the old motor oil they had drained out of the lawn mower. Except even he had to admit that under these circumstances—a good sweat on the brow, the stink of grass and gasoline on his hands, the sun starting to get low in the sky after a few hours of manual labor—a PBR hit the spot.

"So what's going on?" Carl asked. "There aren't airplanes dropping out of the sky, terrorists on the doorstep of the White House, or a biological threat that's about to wipe out half the East Coast. At least not that I know of. Don't tell me you're just popping in on your old man for a visit?"

"Not quite, Dad."

"Thank God. Because that would have been pretty damn boring."

Carl Storm was retired from the FBI. He still missed the action.

Derrick grinned. "Okay, so when you were at the Bureau, did you ever hear of a consortium of Chinese businessmen referred to as the Shanghai Seven?"

"Oh, sure. They were to the nineties what Cosa Nostra was to the fifties. They had their greasy fingers in all sorts of things. Anywhere you found a large Chinese population—New York, LA, wherever—you found offshoots of the Shanghai Seven. They had protection rackets, gambling operations, exotic animal smuggling, you name it. Chances were if you found a Chinese restaurant that couldn't be bothered to do a brisk takeout business, it was really a front for the Shanghai Seven. A lot of what was sloppily referred to by the locals as 'the Chinese mob' was actually Shanghai Seven. We could just never seem to get any traction against them to get their slippery asses in court."

"Why not?"

"I don't know," Carl said, taking a pull of his beer. "Part of it was they were good. And by good, I mean bad. They were willing to do whatever it took to keep their asses out of court. Witnesses changed their stories or disappeared. Coconspirators were either bribed or pressured into staying quiet. They ran a tight ship. I forget what the Chinese word for 'omertà' is, but the Shanghai Seven had it down pat.

"The other part of it was just that we were, for lack of a better word, a little lazy. You had to dig pretty hard to find the connection between the punks on the streets and the bastards behind it all. It's like those dandelions you were taking down with the Weedwacker just now. If you take the top off you can go to the special agent in charge, smile, and say, 'See? All cleaned up.' And from the curb, which is about as close as the SAC is going to get, it looks pretty good. But if you really want to get rid of them, you have to dig all the way down to the root. And the root can go pretty damn deep. In this case, when the root is all the way down in China, I think the Bureau kind of took the attitude that it was just unreachable."

"So they kept lopping the stem off the dandelion," Derrick began.

"And a new stem would grow back somewhere else," Carl finished.

"Still, I would have thought the Bureau would have eventually gotten tired of playing Whac-a-Mole. I mean, we do have an extradition treaty with China. Between that and RICO statutes, you could have gotten it done, right?"

"Well, yeah," Carl said. "But I think around the time we were really going to get serious about things, our government gave them a golden opportunity to go legit."

"What are you talking about?"

"There was a big trade deal that opened up a lot of their markets to our stuff and vice versa. Suddenly, the Shanghai Seven could make money legally, so they left the illegal stuff behind."

"When was this? I'm not sure I've ever heard of it."

"Most Americans haven't. It was the late nineties. It was one of those deals that sort of slid under most folks' radar at the time, but it turned out to be a huge game changer in US-China relations. You want to know why we now have a three-hundred-sixty-whatever-billion-dollar trade deficit with China? That deal was a big part of it."

Derrick was curious enough that he slid out his phone and fired up a powerful leading technology, a proprietary investigative algorithm that he had learned was one of his best assets when he was under pressure to learn world secrets. It was called Google.

"Huh, I'll be damned," he said.

There on his screen was a long-forgotten press release about the United States agreeing to support China's entry into the World Trade Organization in exchange for China lowering tariffs and opening its market to US goods. It was dated November 15, 1999.

Derrick could feel his brain crackle. November 1999. Just like the taped recording of Cynthia Heat and Nicole Bernardin. Did one have anything to do with the other?

"So try out a hypothetical with me," Derrick said. "Say you're the Shanghai Seven. This trade bill has just been passed, and you're seeing dollar signs, because McDonald's is about to move into half the neighborhoods in China—and someone is going to have to build all those McDonald's. And on the other side of the globe, you know there are a bunch of American corporations who are eying the world's largest labor force, knowing it'll be willing to work for cheap. And if you're the Shanghai Seven, you're figuring you can get a piece of that, too."

"Right, exactly. It would have been a time of boundless possibility."

"Except, of course, you've got this little problem—and this brings me to the case I'm working on now," Derrick said. "Because you've been into all this dirty stuff that might make the American corporations take their business elsewhere. Like, for example, you have this counterfeiting operation, and suddenly there's this American intelligence agent who's onto it and is now trying to gather more evidence. And the agent may have tripped across some funny money that has one of the Shanghai Seven's fingerprints on it."

Carl Storm chortled.

"What's so funny?" Derrick asked.

"I can already tell you, that American intelligence agent is in a world of trouble. The Shanghai Seven went into a mode for a while right when it was shifting operations where it had a bunch of loose ends to tie up. That agent would have been one of those loose ends. The Shanghai Seven would have done whatever it could to put that guy in the ground."

"That gal, actually."

Carl cocked one of his dark eyebrows. "Really?"

"Really. And somehow she survived. She faked her own death and has been in hiding for seventeen years."

"She sounds like a heck of a woman," Carl said, draining what was left of his PBR.

Derrick studied his father for a moment. It wasn't often Derrick heard the old man compliment a woman who wasn't his late wife—with the same phrase, no less. But Derrick decided not to make an issue of it.

"Okay, so then here's another question," Derrick said. "I was just in Shanghai last week. I blew up a counterfeiting operation that was allegedly connected to the Shanghai Seven. What would make them want to go back into that kind of business?"

"Didn't the Chinese stock market drop something like half its value not long ago? If I know the Shanghai Seven, they were probably up to their necks in it, and leveraged to the hilt on top of it. Now that they've lost their shirts, they're falling back on old bad habits. Counterfeiting is an art as much as anything. Once you have people skilled in it, it's probably hard to resist using their talents when you suddenly find yourself short on dough."

"Yeah, that makes sense," Derrick said.

"I'm assuming this is something that weasel Jedediah Jones has you tied up in?"

Carl knew all about Jones's duplicity. Half the reason Derrick talked through his cases with his father was because the old man had such solid instincts. The other half was as a kind of backup plan: If Derrick ever disappeared, Carl would know where to start looking for him when Jones couldn't be bothered.

"Yeah, and it's worse than usual," Derrick said. Then he told his father about Jones ordering the transfer of Bart Callan and how it tied back to Cynthia Heat and the counterfeit bills.

"You say 'worse than usual,' but that sounds like his typical MO, if you ask me," Carl said when Derrick was through. "That sonofabitch would double-cross his own grandmother."

Carl crushed his beer can in his powerful hands. "Anyhow, you need another? That first one always goes fast when you're thirsty."

"Sure does," Derrick said, handing over his empty can.

Derrick sat on the back deck, enjoying the familiar peace of his boyhood neighborhood on a fine fall afternoon. He heard another lawn mower going a few doors away. Overhead in the cloudless blue sky, an airplane on its way to Dulles left a contrail that glowed pinkish in the setting sun. He breathed deeply. The air smelled fresh and clean.

Carl emerged from the sliding glass doors with two more PBRs. Then his face grew hard.

"Get down!" he yelled.

Before Derrick could react, Carl grabbed his son by the shirt and easily tossed his two hundred and thirty solid pounds to the floor of the deck.

As Derrick bounced on the wood, a volley of bullets exploded into the side of the house with a hail of splinters.

NINE

HEAT

They didn't teach you to think like that at the New York City Police Academy—for a very good reason—yet Nikki Heat couldn't banish the irrational voice in her head:

If only The Serpent would try to take a shot at me. That way I could have it out with him rather than have him delivering all these vague threats.

But as she sat on a bench in Gramercy Park there was no one firing weaponry—just a bunch of pigeons pecking apart a bagel that had been left behind for them.

Nikki wished she could be one of the pigeons. Right then, The Serpent—and a slew of other factors—had her feeling more like the bagel.

She was itching for something to do, rather than something to think about—which was all her mother's mysterious reappearance seemed to leave her with. When her phone rang, she was relieved just to be able to answer it.

"Heat."

"Yo," Miguel Ochoa said. "We managed to run down that phone number."

"That was fast."

"You complaining?"

"Certainly not. What do you got?"

"No, it seems to be more about what *you* got," Ochoa said. "It was a burner phone, bought in cash at a drugstore right around the corner from the precinct this morning by a guy who wore a sling."

"A sling?" Heat asked, not sure if she had heard him right.

"Yeah, like his arm was broken or something. And he was wearing a blue hat. There were two people working up front at the time, and that was all they could remember about the guy between the two of them. Next time I rob a store, remind me to wear a hat and a sling, because people can't seem to see beyond them."

"But Rales got surveillance footage, right?"

"Negative. The recorder broke a long time ago. There was a street camera and we were able to find a man with a blue hat and a sling entering the store and then leaving a short time later. The problem is, he entered from the south, with his back to the camera. And then he exited heading north, again with his back to the camera. We never saw his face."

"Perfect. What else?"

"We contacted the service provider and leaned on them to give us call data. I thought they were going to make us get a warrant but we convinced them to play nice."

"That's a break."

"It is and it's not. The phone hasn't made any calls, just texts."

Heat already had a sinking feeling before the next words came out of Ochoa's mouth: "And the only number it has texted is yours. What's going on, Captain?"

"Nothing," Heat said quickly. One of the pigeons ripped off a particularly large chunk of bagel as the word escaped her mouth.

"This guy bothering you or something?"

"No, it's . . ." Heat wasn't sure how to complete the thought. Ochoa didn't need to know that she was being anonymously warned away from investigating her non-dead mother's disappearance.

She came up with "Don't worry about it."

"You know we're always saying we're like a family at the Two-Oh. If you were my sister—"

"But I'm not," she snapped. "I'm your boss."

Ochoa was silent.

"Sorry, I'm just . . . I think I'm coming down with something. Are you guys doing okay up there? I think I might just call it a day."

"Yeah, yeah, of course, Cap. You need anything, you know we're just a call away."

"Thanks, Miguel."

She hung up, then stood from where she'd been seated at her park bench. The pigeons were mostly done with their dinner. Heat decided it was time to get home so she could make her own. She retrieved her gun from the trunk of her unmarked car and set herself on a slow meander toward her mother's apartment, a short distance away.

Her apartment. It was still strange to think of it that way again.

Then she reached her block and stopped to gawk at the building. Two strands of yellow police tape stretched across the front door. Standing in front of that was a uniformed officer.

And parked in front of him, just down the steps and beyond the sidewalk, was a truck from the coroner's office.

For the first time all day, Heat was glad she had been forced to wear her captain's uniform to the press conference. It spared her having to identify herself to the young officer who had been stationed in front of the building.

He saluted nervously as she approached and said, "Evening, Captain."

"At ease," Heat said. "I live here. What's going on?"

"There was a crime committed inside, sir," the officer said.

Thank you, Officer Obvious. "Gee, someone should put some crime tape up," she said.

Heat began to walk past him into the building, but the officer slid to the side to block her path.

"I've been told to keep residents out for the time being, sir," he said. "It's pretty gross in there. You might not want to go in."

Heat fixed him with a look. The man—boy, really—never would have said that if a male captain had shown up.

"Officer, do you see these bars on my collar?"

He nodded. She put down her bags so she could close the distance between them.

"They signify many things," she said. "But one of the things they indicate is that I can handle 'gross.' I can also handle yucky, icky, and pukey. Am I making myself clear?"

"Yes, sir," he said, moving out of the way.

Then Heat walked inside.

It was not just gross. It was like a set designer for a chain saw movie had gone overboard. There was blood on the walls, blood on the ceiling, blood on the floor, blood on the vase that held the silk flowers, blood on the silk flowers, blood on the table that held the vase, and blood on the mirror behind the vase.

And that was just what registered with Heat in her first glance. She was aware the typical adult male contained approximately one and a half gallons of blood. She had just never seen such a high percentage of it splattered on the walls of her lobby.

A team of CSU techs were hovering over a body that was lying behind the front desk. Heat walked over.

She immediately recognized the bowling-pin-like shape of Bob Aaronson, but little else about him.

He had been brutally butchered. His scalp was partially separated from his skull and peeled back, revealing the whiteness of bone. His eyeballs were missing, as if they had been pecked out by hungry vultures. His jaw hung, obviously dislocated, at a grotesque angle. His fingers ended in meaty stumps where the nails had once been. His throat and wrists had been slashed.

For good measure, he had also been disemboweled.

Death, whenever it had come, had been a blessing. The amount of pain he had suffered before then had to be unreal.

Heat paused, as she always did, to honor the victim of a crime. It was the ritual she always performed so she never forgot what police work was ultimately about.

In truth, Bob Aaronson had been a terrible doorman. It wasn't just Derrick Storm who slipped past him. So did delivery people, neighborhood bums, heroin addicts, religious zealots, charitable solicitors, political pollsters, and pretty much every other undesirable visitor imaginable. The only people he managed to reliably stop were Girl Scouts selling cookies. He was that bad.

Aaronson probably should have been fired for incompetence at least ten times, except that no one on the building's co-op board could be bothered to do it. Plus, he always sucked up to them.

Still, this was a terrible way to go, even for someone as worthless at his job as Aaronson.

Heat turned so she didn't have to look at the carnage any longer.

On the other side of the lobby, talking to one of Heat's sheet-white-faced neighbors, was a pair of plainclothes detectives who Heat recognized as being from the Thirteenth Precinct.

One of them walked over when he saw her.

"Captain Heat," he said, not bothering to hide his surprise. "Did . . . did someone called you about this already?"

"This is my building. You guys got any leads on what happened here?"

"You mean other than someone going to town on the doorman with a fillet knife?" the detective asked.

"I figured that out already. You got a time of death?"

"We talked to one resident who entered the building at around 4:35 and found Mr. Aaronson alive and well. The resident who found him called 911 at 4:52. So we've got a pretty tight window, yeah."

"Any idea who?"

"We were hoping you might be able to tell us that," he said.

Heat tilted her head to the side. Then the detective pointed to the wall behind the desk, where there was something written in blood. Heat hadn't noticed it at first, what with all the other blood sprayed everywhere. Even now it was hard to make out, because of the smearing, running, and clotting of the blood that the writer had used as his ink.

Except once she focused on it, there was no doubt what had been spelled out:

NIKKI HEAT.

Heat drew in her breath sharply, despite herself. She had been threatened and intimidated before, though not, perhaps, in such sanguinolent fashion.

She rocked back on her heels and had to fight the urge to steady herself on the desk. She didn't want to smudge any of the blood spatters or leave her prints in a way that might contaminate the scene.

"You got a friend you want to tell us about?" the detective asked. "Maybe someone handy with a knife?"

All she could think about was The Serpent. Was this his idea of taking a shot at her?

What was it he had said in his last text? Something about proving how powerful he was and manifesting his wrath? There was certainly a lot of wrath involved in what had happened to Bob Aaronson.

Yet she already knew she wasn't going to tell this detective about The Serpent. Maybe she would have to tell Roach about him, but . . .

In the meantime, the detective was staring at her hard, waiting for her answer.

"I don't know," Heat said. "I don't recognize this as being anyone's work in particular."

"You think maybe this could be related to Legs Kline somehow? Maybe one of his people trying to avenge his ex-boss's death, trying to rattle your cage?"

"I don't know if any of his people were that loyal, but . . . I guess I wouldn't rule anything out."

The detective had his pad out, but he hadn't written anything on it. Truly, Heat hadn't given him anything useful.

"We certainly haven't," he said. "If you don't mind, we're going to go through your old cases, see if anyone special just made parole or something like that."

"Good plan," Heat said. "I'm happy to assist, of course."

"Thank you, sir," he said, handing her a business card. "And, certainly, if you have any ideas about who might have done this—"

"You'll be my first phone call."

That seemed to satisfy him, so Heat made noises about wanting to head upstairs. More than anything, she wanted the Crime Scene Unit to complete its job so someone could begin cleaning up. She didn't want her neighbors walking past and seeing her name painted in blood. They were already leery enough about her, given past history.

She punched the button for the elevator and rode up by herself. As she entered her apartment, the first thing she saw was that the small end table in the vestibule had been tipped over, and the vase that normally sat on the table was lying on the ground in two large pieces and several more small ones.

Someone had been in her apartment, someone who still might have been inside.

Heat froze for a moment. The prudent thing—the thing she would have done, had it been any other apartment but her own—would have been to go back downstairs and request backup before she entered.

She drew her 9mm instead. That would have to serve as her prudence and her backup.

TEN

STORM

Derrick Storm had sprawled flat on the surface of the deck, making himself as small a target as possible.

Carl Storm had fallen on top of him. For as much as Derrick wished he wouldn't, Carl Storm was using his body as a shield to protect his son.

Derrick always knew his dad would take a bullet for him. And vice versa. He just hoped to never have the occasion to confirm it.

They had their faces down—Derrick on the deck, Carl on Derrick's back—to protect themselves from the shards of wood raining down on them.

The gunfire was automatic, making it impossible for them to keep track of the rounds expended. It just kept coming in a sustained burst. There is nothing quite like being pinned down by a heavy blanket of machine-gun fire to make a person feel overmatched.

The only thing keeping them alive was the deck's elevation and the gentle downward sloping of the backyard beyond it. Had it been the opposite, subjecting them to fire from above, they would have been shredded. Ask any military commander, anywhere, throughout history, from the Huns to Hannibal: There's a reason why the high ground is considered an advantage.

Finally, the gunfire ceased.

"Reload," the Storm boys said at almost precisely the same moment.

They didn't need to communicate what that meant they needed to do. Carl sprung off Derrick's back and scrambled toward the sliding door. Derrick low-crawled after him into the family room.

But not before he risked a brief glance at where the gunfire had been coming from. That was what allowed him to see the shooter plainly.

He was Caucasian, with a buzz cut flat enough on top to land a remote control airplane on and ears that stuck up from the sides of his shaved head. He had a slightly psychotic look about him, like he had spent his childhood wearing too much camouflage, pretending to play soldier, and his summers torturing frogs with leftover Fourth of July fireworks.

Whether or not he actually spent time in the armed forces, he was now clearly some kind of mercenary.

But who sent him? And how had he tracked Storm to his father's house?

There was no time to even think about it. Once inside the family room, still in a crouch, Derrick looked at the Barcalounger and the paisley couch. They were the familiar furnishings of his boyhood, and he couldn't believe he was now wondering how he might use them to keep himself alive as the gunfire resumed.

But no matter how ugly a couch was, it couldn't stop a bullet. The attacker was now pumping rounds into the side of the house, aiming for the room the Storm boys had disappeared into. Chunks of plaster flew as the bullets pierced the wall.

"Come on! In here!" Carl yelled, staying low as he entered the kitchen, where at least there were cabinets to provide extra cover.

They sat together on the linoleum floor as bullets shattered the windows in the next room.

"We can't stay in here," Carl said. "He'll move into the kitchen next and we'll get shredded. You want to make a break for the front door?"

"No," Derrick said. "That's exactly what they want us to do. I'll bet you anything the guy in the back's job is simply to flush us out toward the front, where the rest of the team is waiting to finish us off."

"Good point. So what's your plan?"

Ordinarily, Derrick Storm's plan when someone was shooting at him would have been to shoot back. Storm's favorite gun was a Smith & Wesson Model 629 that he called Dirty Harry. Like the revolver Clint Eastwood had once used when asking someone to go ahead and make his day, it used .44 Magnum cartridges.

Unfortunately, Dirty Harry was currently stored in the trunk of his Ford Taurus, which was currently parked in the driveway, which was currently among the least safe places in America.

But just as Storm was about to draw a breath to answer his father's question, he was interrupted by the cacophonous sound of the front door being broken down.

"Go, go, go," someone was saying.

"Cellar," Carl whispered fiercely.

It was a terrible direction to head in. And also the only one with a chance of keeping them alive.

As silently as possible, they slid toward the door to the basement, which was off the kitchen. Carl went in first. Derrick was just behind, locking the door as he went, for what little good that would do.

The Storm basement was unfinished, with a bare concrete floor and a series of naked lightbulbs hanging from the two-by-ten rafters. Small head-height windows, each of them no more than twelve inches from top to bottom—too small to crawl out of—let in some ambient light. There was a storm door with steps leading up to it. But, of course, that only emptied into the backyard, where that machine gunner would have been all too happy to rip them in half.

For better or worse—probably the latter—they were now trapped down there.

Derrick looked up at the rafters, as if he could see the men who trod on the floors above. He was counting the assailants who were systematically working their way through the first floor of the house.

"I think there are four of them," he whispered. "Plus the guy out back."

His father nodded.

"Please tell me you have a gun down here," Derrick said.

Carl was immediately agitated. "Me? Christ, I thought *you'd* have a weapon on you. That's the only reason I said we should come down here." He bristled. "I'm just an old retired fart. You're the damn superspy."

"Where's yours?"

"Upstairs. In the gun safe. Like usual."

"Did you really have to be that responsible?"

"Look, between the kids who live in this neighborhood and the OxyContin addicts who don't, you've got to—"

"Okay, fine, fine," Derrick said, feeling his frustration mount. "Do you have any weapons on you?"

"Just my knife."

Ever since Derrick could remember, his father had carried a folding knife with a three-inch blade. It was handy to have around on Christmas Day, when there was suddenly a package in need of opening, or for when he was doing chores around the house. It was substantially less useful as instrumentality for a homicide—particularly when up against firearms.

"Dad, that thing is like a half step up from a butter knife. I'm not making toast here," Derrick said, then swore. "How did these guys even know where I was? I wasn't followed here. I made sure of it."

"Well, you've got your phone on you, right?"

"Yeah."

"Let me see it," Carl said.

As soon as Derrick pulled out the sleek silver device that came courtesy of a top secret government lab—and therefore had capabilities far beyond your typical iPhone—Carl struck it out of his hand. It didn't break when it hit the floor, so Carl brought his boot down on it heavily and repeatedly until it was a shattered mess.

"You know damn well that snake Jones knows where you are every second when you have that thing on you," Carl said. "You said he's working for the Shanghai Seven. I'm sure he gave them your exact GPS coordinates. They were just waiting for you to stay in the same place long enough so they could assemble a team and make a move."

Derrick nodded. He knew his father was very likely correct.

"So what do we have down here we can use to get rid of those guys?" Derrick asked. "We've got about three minutes, five tops, before they figure out we're not upstairs bleeding to death."

The Storm boys let their gazes sweep across the basement. There was a long workbench that took up most of the far wall. Tools hung neatly on a pegboard above it. Wrenches. Hammers. Screwdrivers. A laser level—the one modern gadget Carl Storm had allowed into his home, and only because even he grudgingly agreed it was better than The Old Way. Each utensil had its own spot that had been so unaltered over time it created a silhouette on the wood in its exact shape.

"Clear downstairs," Derrick heard one of the thugs shout. "Let's go up."

"I'll cover downstairs," another replied.

The Storms were running out of time.

Underneath the workbench were a Shop-Vac, a bread maker that someone had given Carl long ago (and he had never even bothered to take out of the box), some milk crates filled with wires and other assorted junk, two flats of bottled water, a kiddie pool Derrick had reveled in as a child . . .

Great, Derrick thought hopelessly. *We can fill up the pool with bottled water and then drown them one by one.*

"Clear," Derrick heard. Then, maybe five seconds later, again: "Clear."

Derrick moved his eyes away from the workbench. There was a water heater. *Could that be turned into a weapon? Not without a blowtorch and at least four hours to work on it.* An old furnace. *Ditto.* A washer and dryer. *Not bad for defensive purposes, but hopeless on offense.*

And then, parked near the dryer, Derrick spied an air compressor large enough to come up to his knee.

Carl had bought it eons ago in defiance of the local gas station when it decided to start charging four quarters for use of its air hose. Carl, who was a fanatic about maintaining proper tire pressure, had been irate: *Who charges for air? What kind of damn world is that?*

Then he went out and bought a top-of-the-line commercial air compressor. Derrick had done the math and figured out that even if his dad filled his tires every two weeks, it would take seventy-seven years for the thing to pay for itself. Carl didn't care. It was the principle of the thing.

Derrick had never been so grateful to have a stubborn donkey for a dad.

"Please tell me you have a nail gun that goes with that air compressor," he said.

"I always found a hammer worked just fine. What would I need a nail gun for?"

"For when five mercenaries have you cornered in a basement with no hope of escape."

"I hear you. But . . . Oh," he said, having just figured out what his son wanted to do. Then he looked at it with a special glint in his eye, and a small grin appeared on his face.

"Son, we don't *need* a nail gun. I've got a bunch of different size nozzles and all kinds of nails over there. If we rig it right, this thing could *be* a nail gun."

Derrick didn't wait for more. He walked quickly to the air compressor and grabbed it. Carl had already gone to the workbench and began scooping up boxes of nails in his thick hands.

They met by the stairs that led up to the kitchen. The box Carl settled on was filled with two-inch common nails. They were 11.5 gauge, with just the right weight to turn into a deadly projectile.

Carl fitted a hose to the compressor's tank, then tried the first of several nozzle options. Derrick watched his father work, feeling like he was nine years old again and they had reached the part of some project that Daddy had to do for him.

"There," Carl said finally. "Perfect fit."

He held the hose aloft. It had roughly three-quarters of the nail sticking out of it, with the pointed end leading the way and the flat end anchored inside the nozzle. "Should be just tight enough that it'll build a lot of pressure behind it and then, whammo, it flies out with deadly force."

"You sure it's going to work?"

"No," Carl said. "In the Bureau we used to call something like this TITS."

"TITS?"

"A Totally Insane Try at Something."

"Perfect," Derrick said. "How are we going to aim it? That thing doesn't exactly come with a scope."

They both looked around the basement for a moment. Then Derrick found himself settling on the one item down there that wasn't old enough to rent a car.

"The laser level," he said. "We can clamp it right on top of the nozzle."

"And then just aim a bit high?"

"Exactly."

"You think the nail is going to fly straight?" Carl asked.

Boring on rifle barrels was invented for that very reason—to give a bullet the rotation it needed to slice through the air on a line. Without that rotation, a projectile turned into a knuckleball, dancing and weaving as it reacted chaotically with the air around it. It was why muskets were so inaccurate that Revolutionary or Civil War–era soldiers could line up fifty feet apart, unleash volleys on each other, and still miss.

"Probably not," Derrick admitted. "But we're firing from such a short distance, it's only going to go off by so much."

"I wish we could test it."

Derrick was shaking his head. "As soon as we start this thing," he said, gesturing toward the air compressor, "those guys are going to know we're down here. We'll have company."

"Right," Carl said. "So this either works, or . . ."

"Or," Derrick finished for him, "we're dead."

The compressor's engine came to life on the first pull and was soon rumbling loud and strong, making enough of a racket that Derrick could no longer hear the footfalls of the men above them.

All he could do was wait for the first assailant to descend on him and hope like hell his TITS worked.

Derrick was crouched to the side of the stairs. He had hastily removed the cover of the water heater and was using it as a shield. It was a good, thick piece of aluminum, old and heavy. Whether it would actually stop a bullet depended on the kind of rounds the thugs were using and the kind of weapons firing those rounds, two factors Derrick couldn't predict.

Only his arm and hand, which held the nozzle, were exposed if one of the thugs decided to lay down a blanket of cover fire before coming down the steps. Derrick's job was to aim this crude weapon he and his father had created and to release the air pressure that had built up in the tank when he was ready to fire— the air compressor gun equivalent of a trigger pull.

Carl was next to him, slightly farther away from the stairs, and thus more out of the line of fire. His job was to be ready to reload the nozzle with another nail as quickly as possible after Derrick fired.

They didn't have long to wait.

The door to the basement burst open with a crack loud enough to be heard over the racket of the compressor. But the door had been broken down by someone who immediately retreated, so there was no one filling the doorframe.

Then one of the thugs took a quick peek around the corner

before quickly pulling back. What he would have seen in that glimpse was surely curious: an arm, with its elbow braced on one of the steps, holding a hose that had something—it's unlikely he would have recognized it as a nail in that fleeting look—sticking out its end.

Whatever it was the thug thought he was seeing had not, apparently, scared him much. He soon whirled around the edge of the doorframe and assumed a shooting position, a long-barrel rifle nestled against his shoulder.

It gave Derrick a nice target. By his best guess, he had to aim the laser level two inches higher than where he wanted the nail to end up.

If the nail flew straight.

Or at all.

The real issue was what would happen to the air pressure when Derrick released it from the tank and it slammed into the head of the nail. All those pounds per square inch would need somewhere to go. If air could leak around the sides of the nail, it would—and the nail would either stay in place or lamely dribble out.

If, on the other hand, the nail was in there too tight, the nozzle itself might explode, probably taking a chunk of Derrick's hand with it.

Everything had to be just right.

And there was only one way to find out if it was. As soon as the laser's red line touched the start of the man's hairline, Derrick released the pressure in the tank.

The air flowed through the hose with a tremendous burst and a loud whooshing sound until it hit up against the head of the nail, nestled firmly in the nozzle.

The pressure built in some fraction of a second that was far too small for a human to register in any meaningful way. But it would all come down to what happened in those nanoseconds. Would the nail give first or the nozzle? Or would nothing happen at all?

Derrick was just holding on as firmly as he could, which was a good thing, because the kickback soon thrust his arm backward, as if he had lost an arm wrestling contest with an invisible giant.

But not before the nail burst from the hose at supersonic speed and buried itself in the attacker's forehead.

The man was thrown back into the kitchen by the force of the blow. Derrick could only see his feet. But from the way those feet seemed to have gone instantly still, he could tell the nail had done its job.

He let out a ragged hoot as he brought the nozzle back down to his father, who stuffed another nail in the end, sort of like muzzle-loading a shotgun. Then Derrick brought his arm back up into firing position.

There had been a burst of excited swearing from the kitchen, and it was coming from at least three different voices. It melded in such a way that Derrick couldn't make out what they were saying.

But they were pissed. And maybe—hopefully—a little scared.

The next man who dared ease around the corner did so with greater caution. The first thing Derrick saw was the muzzle of what appeared to be either an AR-15 or an AK-47. Derrick flattened his arm against the step just as the gun fired a short burst of rounds that plowed harmlessly into the basement's concrete wall. Chunks of the wall scattered on the basement floor.

The man repeated this procedure twice more, continuing to fire blindly each time, accomplishing little more than heaping greater injury on Carl Storm's basement.

Derrick just waited. He didn't have the luxury of spraying

multiple shots all over in the wild hope of hitting something. He only had one shot at a time.

Finally, the thug—perhaps thinking his fire had sent the Storm boys hiding farther in the basement—cautiously edged around the corner.

Derrick held off until the man's left eye was showing. Then he calmly brought his arm back up, aimed the laser level the same two inches high he had calculated before, and released the pressure.

The nail buried itself in the man's eye. It didn't kill him. But his howls of pain—loud, wracked, and agonized—were barely human. Then, suddenly, they ended with a single gunshot.

One of his comrades had decided to put him out of his misery.

In the meantime, Carl had already reloaded the nozzle. Derrick's breathing remained steady and he deliberately did not allow himself to start calculating the odds. There were still three assailants upstairs trying to figure out how to kill him and his father. Their weaponry—with all due respect to what Derrick and Carl had rigged up—was far superior. They were now reassessing their options.

There was hushed conversation happening above them. Derrick did not dare take his eyes off the door.

The next attack didn't come from that direction. A spasm of automatic weapon fire rained down on them from above. One of the thugs was trying to get lucky, shooting at them through the floor, attempting to find an angle of fire that would strike one of the Storm boys.

Really, all it was accomplishing was harassing them. Between the linoleum, the subfloor, and the two-by-tens that supported it, very few of the bullets were getting through. And even those were striking harmlessly into the basement floor.

Then the firing stopped. The chattering of the air compressor felt quiet in comparison, and Derrick was able to make out the noise of what sounded like three men fleeing the house.

And something else.

A police siren.

No, make that several of them.

"Are you buddy-buddy with the Fairfax County Sheriff's Office by any chance?" Derrick shouted at his father.

"No. Does local law enforcement ever really like the FBI that much?"

"Fair point. I think we're about to get a visit from them. Do you want to explain to them why there are two dead men in our kitchen?"

"Not really."

"Me neither."

"Let's get out of here."

"Okay, but there's one thing I need to do first," Derrick said. "Let me see your phone."

"What phone? The one in the kitchen?"

"No, Dad. The cell phone I bought you for Christmas two years ago."

"Oh. I handed that thing back in. I couldn't hear for crap on it. I never got any calls anyway."

"Dad, I keep telling you, you have to *turn it on* before it can receive calls."

"There's a perfectly functional landline up in the kitchen. I promise you won't have to worry about bad reception."

"I'm not making a call. I need a camera, and you just smashed mine," Derrick said, pointing to the shiny pieces of high technology in pieces on the floor. "I want to take pictures of the two guys we just killed."

Carl Storm recoiled in horror. "What are you, collecting souvenirs or something?"

"I'll explain later. Do you have a camera or not?"

"Well, I mean, yeah, I got the old Polaroid. Still has film in it. Will that do?"

"Are you *ever* going to join us in this millennium?" Derrick said.

"Not unless I really have to," Carl said.

The sirens were getting louder. They were running out of time.

"Fine," Derrick said. "Get me the Polaroid."

ELEVEN

HEAT

With her 9mm at shoulder height, Heat trained her eyes toward the interior of the apartment, where any threat might be coming from.

There were no lights on. The setting sun was now low enough behind the buildings to the west that the apartment was cast into a pre-twilight gloom.

She took one step forward, waiting for The Serpent—or whoever it was who sliced apart Bob Aaronson—to make his move.

Another step. She felt hyperalert, a surge of chemicals jangling in her bloodstream that came from knowing it was entirely possibly someone was about to die, her body having the innate sense to make sure it wasn't her. She was ready to shoot at anything that moved.

Heat widened her eyes, trying to will her pupils into allowing more light in. Any intruder who had been lying in wait for some time would have the advantage of full dilation.

With her next step, Heat could now see partially into her living room. Another end table had been toppled. The lamp the table had held was on its side on the floor. The arm of the couch had been ripped. Chunks of stuffing were lying on the floor next to it. So were some feathers that looked like they had once belonged inside a pillow.

Heat was trying to stay connected to her every sense, to things as delicate as the tiny hairs on her cheeks, which might give her a moment's warning that a stirring of air molecules had occurred, signifying an attack was imminent.

Except everything in the apartment seemed still. She was the only one moving. At least for the moment.

Heat took one more step, bringing her more fully into the living room, at which point she became aware of just how total the destruction was. From her current vantage point, it appeared every inch of the apartment had been violated in one way or another.

She was trying to stay vigilant, mindful the intruder might still be in there. But there were certain physiological responses, all involuntary, that were making it difficult. Her pulse had quickened. She had broken into a sweat. Her hands were shaking.

Having your home thoroughly ransacked will trigger those kinds of responses.

It's just stuff, Heat tried to tell herself. *It's either replaceable or it's not. Focus on what's coming at you around the next corner. Stay vigilant and—*

Then Heat saw the window to the fire escape was still open. The Serpent—and this just felt like the work of The Serpent, who had threatened mayhem and destruction and seemed to be carrying through with it—had apparently already made his exit.

On the chance that it was a decoy, Heat performed a sweep of the remaining rooms, closets, and bathrooms, with the 9mm still up and her finger on the trigger. But that pass only confirmed what she knew the moment she saw that open window: She was alone in the apartment, after all.

She returned to the living room, holstered her gun, and allowed herself to more thoroughly assess the damage.

It was something beyond substantial. It seemed there was

no piece of furniture that hadn't been attacked, no pillow left unripped, no table that remained upright, no chair that hadn't been overturned. Heat's shoes crunched on glass from broken picture frames no matter where she tried to walk. Knickknacks and mementos of varying levels of sentimental importance— many of them either owned by, gifted to, or gifted from her mother—were haphazardly strewn about the room.

Heat blocked out every thought about where those trinkets and talismans had originated from and the stories behind them. That would only distract her from what mattered at the moment, which was figuring out if anything was missing.

So far, the only thing that she noticed for sure was the tape player Storm had given her. She had left it on the coffee table, which was still there, albeit on its side. But there was no sign of the tape player next to it, or under the torn-up couch, or anywhere else, for that matter. The intruder appeared to have made off with it.

But that meant he didn't just get the device itself. The player still had the cassette inside it. Heat had been listening to it just that morning.

Heat continued her tour of the wreckage. Back in the bedroom, which had her home office shoved in one corner, the filing cabinet seemed to have been a target that received The Serpent's particular attention. Files had been opened and emptied onto the floor, then tossed aside. Sealed envelopes had been jaggedly torn open. It was everything from credit card statements to old insurance policies to product handbooks to health records to who-knows-what, all littering the floor in a pile several inches thick and several feet wide, in a haphazard pattern surrounding the now-empty filing cabinet.

The intruder had obviously been looking for something in there.

The bills, right? It had to be the bills. If The Serpent was working for the Shanghai Seven—and it made sense that he was—and the bills were of utmost importance to them, then it logically followed that recovering the bills had been the real objective there.

Killing Bob Aaronson had just been a kind of shot across Heat's bow, a demonstration of The Serpent's ferocity and the Shanghai Seven's brutality. And he had died for essentially no reason. Nikki's mother never would have hid the bills in her own apartment. That's why she entrusted them with George The Bartender, who wouldn't have hid them in Cynthia's place, either.

But The Serpent obviously didn't know that. Because The Serpent hadn't listened to the cassette tape yet.

Except . . . the Shanghai Seven clearly knew about the recording—that's who Storm had stolen it from in the first place. So was it possible The Serpent didn't really work for the Shanghai Seven? Or had the Shanghai Seven simply not told The Serpent about the recording?

Or was this not really the work of The Serpent? Was this some other actor?

So many question marks. So few periods.

Heat continued farther into the bedroom. What few clothes she still kept in the apartment had been strewn about. The drawers had been yanked out of the dresser bureau and turned upside down. The mattress was torn open and leaning against the side of the wall. The box spring had lines where a knife had slashed through it. The books on her nightstand—including a riveting thriller by Brad Parks, one of her new favorite authors—had been toppled.

She moved on to the bathroom. The medicine cabinet was open and barren, half its contents lying at the bottom of the bathtub, the other half in the sink. The contents of the vanity had been pulled out and strewn on the floor. The lid on the back of the toilet had been lifted off and was now only half in place.

Back through the disarray of the bedroom, she went next to the kitchen, which had not been spared. Pots and pans had been pulled out of cabinets and left where they had been thrown. The utensils had been treated the same. Things that had once been tidy and cool in the refrigerator were now messy and warm on the tile below.

As with most of the rest of the apartment, nothing was missing. It had all just been violently pushed, pulled, and torn askew. Every surface, be it vertical or horizontal, had been explored in some manner.

That included the liquor cabinet above the fridge. Bottles had been tossed out. Some had shattered, making the kitchen smell like a bar fight. But it didn't seem to have been the subject of any greater—or lesser—attention than anything else, which was another sign that made Heat think this burglar had been unaware of Cynthia's long-ago words. *I'd not only trust this spot with my life, I'd trust it with my best Scotch.*

Heat checked the last bathroom—a little half bath off the living room that had been largely unscathed, mostly because it had so little in it—then returned to the living room.

She stood there, hands on her hips, taking stock of the catastrophe. She could feel her heart tearing. It wasn't just that it would take weeks to clean it. It wasn't just the money it would cost, regardless of whatever insurance would or wouldn't cover. It wasn't just that some of what had been broken was irreplaceable.

It was that while this was her place, it was also—in a more essential way—her mother's place. And that made it feel like some part of her mother had been attacked and now could never be put back together—again.

Heat walked over to the front door and shut it. What good that would do, she couldn't even guess. Maybe she wanted to restore some shred of a sense of security.

She knew there were two detectives downstairs who would want to know that the murder of Bob Aaronson had only been a prelude to another crime, and that the pillaging of the apartment had been the killer's real purpose.

But Heat couldn't bring herself to alert them. She didn't want those detectives working this. She wanted her own people on it. And there was one person in particular she needed: the man known in the Twentieth Precinct as the King of All Surveillance Media.

She pulled out her phone and punched one of the speed-dial settings. Two rings later she heard:

"Raley."

"Hey, Rales. Is the king feeling lordship over his kingdom today?"

"The king is, indeed, sitting on his throne."

"Lovely image. Anyhow, I need a favor. You up for doing one?"

"Go."

She told him about the apartment and about what had happened to Bob Aaronson sometime between 4:35 and 4:52 that afternoon.

"I'm sure the Thirteenth Precinct is going to have someone going through the neighborhood, looking for surveillance footage," Heat finished. "But that someone won't be the king. Do you think you could take a run at it?"

"I can," he said. "What are the rules of engagement?"

"For the One-Three, the Fourth Amendment is fully in force. For you?"

She could practically feel Raley leaning forward, then said, "Don't worry your head about it. You get what you can get by any means necessary."

"Any means?"

"Whoever did this is never going to let himself wind up in a courtroom," she said. "So, yes, have at it."

"Absolutely, Captain. Consider it done."

Heat ended the call, then once again surveyed the disaster scene that was her apartment. Where did she even begin?

She bent down and picked up one of the shattered picture frames. It was a picture she knew well, having walked by it thousands of times over the years. But it had been some time since she had actually studied it. Through the pieces of jagged glass, she saw two people.

One was practically a stranger. It was a much-younger version of herself, on her high school graduation day. She was wearing the ridiculous mortarboard hat foisted on graduates the world over, and a purple—had her class color really been purple?—polyester gown. Her face was rounder, still with residual pockets of baby fat clinging to it. She looked both happy and optimistic, in the way that perhaps only a naive eighteen-year-old who thinks she's about to take over the world can be.

The other person was Cynthia Heat. She was wearing a classic A-line dress with a sash across the waistline that accented her still-trim figure, a dress that was much like the woman who wore it: simple but elegant, a latter-day Jackie O, a modern-day Princess Kate. Her mother would have been, what, about two years shy of fifty at that point? Back when that photo was snapped, Nikki probably thought of her mother as being just, well, old. It struck thirty-six-year-old Nikki that she now was closer in age to the woman in the photo than to the girl.

Yet whereas she had been able to track her own aging in such minute detail—watching each day as her features sharpened, as she lost her wide-eyed innocence, as fine lines appeared around her mouth—she had no idea what the years had done to her mother. In Nikki's imagination, Cynthia Heat was still frozen in time.

But she had been out there, somewhere, maturing and changing, day by day, year by year, just like everyone else. And if Nikki felt anything as she looked at that picture, it was mostly a sense of sadness that she had been deprived of all those days and all those years.

There was nothing she could do to get them back. The best she could do was make sure that she didn't allow any more of them to slip away.

TWELVE

STORM

There are those who might have denigrated Carl Storm's 1986 Buick Electra.

Its design was boxy—nothing but straight lines, almost as if it had been drawn by a fourth grader who was just learning to use a ruler as a straightedge. Its hood hinged at the front, so that it opened away from the passenger compartment, a feature so universally scorned that Buick discarded it, along with the entire Electra line, just a few years later. It was so impossible to get parts for it anymore, it had actually driven Carl Storm to the Internet, because eBay was one of the only places where you could find, say, a fuse box or a headlight or a bearing that actually fit.

Beyond that, Carl's vehicle had its own unique peccadilloes. The column shifter had gotten so finicky, you needed to bang it down with your palm and just hope it ended up on drive. The fan sometimes blew hot air straight from the engine no matter how low you turned the AC setting, and then magically fixed itself the next time you drove it. The windows rolled down slowly, or sometimes not at all, depending on what kind of mood the motors powering them were in. Parts of its undercarriage creaked no matter how often Carl lubed them, making even a drive through a parking lot a somewhat noisy experience.

RICHARD CASTLE

But when it came to slipping past wary law enforcement, it turned out a 1986 Buick Electra driven by a man in his late sixties was a pretty good bet.

As the Fairfax County Sheriff's Office descended upon the Storm residence, where there had been multiple reports of gunshots flooding the switchboard, the deputies did not pay the slightest attention to the boxy old car being driven by the cranky old man heading in the opposite direction, out of the neighborhood.

They had left Derrick's Ford behind at Carl's insistence. He was sure it had a tracking device on it, as well as listening devices. Derrick agreed, removing Dirty Harry from it on his way out, not worrying about the police connecting him to the car. It was registered to a shell company they would never be able to trace.

"Now, you want to explain to me why you took those pictures of those dead guys?" Carl asked. "Because otherwise I'm starting to worry my son is a fetish-driven serial killer who saves souvenirs of his victims."

"Cripes, Dad, I took their photos, not their ears."

"Still."

"Well, okay. I snapped those pictures so I can figure out who's after us."

"Well, it's that snake Jones, isn't it?"

"Maybe. Maybe not. I'd rather know for sure than guess, wouldn't you?"

"Okay. I hear you. But what can you do with a couple of Polaroids?"

"I can use Jones's technology again him," Derrick said.

"Uh, you want to explain that?"

"Jones is, at his core, a hoarder of information. He understands that in today's world, that's the ultimate currency.

He's developed an intelligence database over the years that is second to none. People have literally died just so Jones can have a few more megabytes of data. Every foreign operative. Every mercenary. Every freelancer. If anyone has pulled a job anywhere in the world, there's a pretty good chance he's in the system. Those guys who were after us were clearly pros. They'll be in there. Sometimes I think everyone alive is in there."

Carl grimaced. "Couldn't the guy just collect stamps or something?"

"Collecting humans is more fun," Derrick said, then pointed to an on-ramp. "Hop on the Beltway, then get us on 395 North."

"Got it."

"Anyway, as I was saying, Jones has everything the rest of the CIA has, plus some stuff he doesn't share with anyone else outside of his unit. In addition, he employs a cadre of tech savants—I call them 'the nerds'—who sign nondisclosure agreements that basically ensure Jones can kill the next six generations of their families if they let anything leak. So it's buttoned up pretty tight. But if we can get into his database, I can take those Polaroids and get an ID faster than you can say 'facial recognition software.'"

"Yeah, yeah, fancy pants, I got you," Carl said. "I get that Jones has all the beeps, whistles, and bells. But how are we going to get access to his information? You don't even know where the Cubby is. And even if you did, I'm sure it's impenetrable."

"It is. We're not going there. We're heading to Kevin Bryan's apartment in Crystal City."

"Bryan. He's that Irish fella who works for Jones, right?"

"That's him."

They had merged onto the Capital Beltway. Carl Storm was doing a steady fifty-five, which earned him a long and growing number of cars stacked up behind him, waiting for opportunities to pass. One lane over, cars were ripping past him doing seventy-five. Farther over, in the true passing lane, a pair of dueling Hyundais were tempting Mach one.

Derrick ignored them, along with the temptation to ask his father to speed up. Carl Storm was former FBI. He railed all the time about state troopers tacitly allowing a certain level of speeding. His argument was that if you made the de facto speed limit different from the posted one, you essentially made the law seem arbitrary or somehow negotiable, which ultimately weakened the entire legal system.

When Carl went on that rant, Derrick just nodded and waited until his dad wasn't in the car to take one of his Fords up to ninety. In theory, he agreed with his father. In practice, Derrick Storm had places to go.

Shortly after they merged onto 395, Carl broke the silence. "Are you sure you can trust Bryan? Don't get me wrong, he's always struck me as a good guy. But if he works for Jones, he's part of the wolf pack, isn't he?"

Derrick didn't know how to explain that within the Cubby, there were varying levels of loyalty to Jones's tactics and methodologies. At one end—never asking why, just following blindly—was Clara Strike. Storm was the opposite pole. Agent Kevin Bryan and his partner, Agent Javier Rodriguez, were somewhere in the middle. They carried out their orders unless they realized there was a good reason not to.

And every time Derrick had provided that reason, they had come around to his way of thinking. They had gone behind Jones's back often enough that Derrick knew they'd do it again.

"We can trust him," Derrick said. "Besides, we don't really have a choice. At this point, it's pretty much trust Agent Bryan or stay in the dark."

"Got it. So, what, we go over there, explain ourselves, and hope he helps us out?"

"It's not quite that simple," Derrick explained.

"Nothing is with that human reptile."

"Yep. I think if he had his way, his agents would just sleep in the Cubby like he often does. He grudgingly recognizes they want to have their own lives. He just doesn't like it. He considers it a point of weakness. He knows agents are far more vulnerable in their own homes, where they'll relax and take their guard down, than they are out in the field. So he has the nerds monitor all of the agents' places of residence."

"Then we can't get in after all?"

"No, we can. The nerds can't cover everything all the time. Even Jones has limits. He relies on the fact that bad guys will *think* there aren't security precautions at an agent's home, and will therefore be more reckless. Depending on the agent's living setup, the countermeasures in place vary. In Bryan's case, he lives in one of the high-rises in Crystal City. Jones has the security cameras in the lobby patched into the Cubby. And he has the door to Bryan's unit wired to alert the nerds in the case of unauthorized entry. But that's it. So I've got an idea of how I can get in."

"How? It sounds like you'd be detected."

"Not the way I'm planning on getting in. Get off here."

Derrick was pointing to the Duke Street exit on 395.

"I thought you said we were going to Crystal City," Carl said.

"We have some stops to make."

"What for?"

"Supplies. Westbound please."

"Where are we stopping?"

"I'm not sure I should tell you," Derrick said. "This is top secret. Above top secret. It's like double-secret probation."

"Would you stop bullshitting a bullshitter?"

"You're not going to like it."

"Tell me."

"Fine. You see that big orange sign up ahead?"

Derrick pointed to the large sign, which had an even larger boxy store behind it, with a massive fake facade.

"No," Carl said. "Not there."

"Yes, Dad. Turn in there."

"Anywhere but there."

"I'm sorry. We have no choice."

"Can't we go get shot at again? That was more fun."

"Dad, just make the turn."

Carl appeared to still be fighting the instruction. Then he gave up, eased over into the left-turn lane, and put on his turn signal.

As he pulled into the parking lot, Carl just sighed and muttered, "The goddamn Lame Depot."

They purchased the most expensive glass cutter they could find— which, at the Home Depot, meant they had just been separated from $6.98.

A Hart twenty-one-ounce milled-face steel framing hammer—whose weight Derrick liked the moment he picked it up—was their big-ticket item, at $25.97.

Next, and perhaps mostly importantly, there was a window squeegee ($3.79) and a bottle of Windex ($3.17).

And then there was the impulse buy: a vintage twill hat with the Home Depot logo that Carl Storm absolutely insisted on acquiring, as a memento of his first—and, he hoped, last—trip to the hardware mega-store. That was another $11.36.

Altogether, with 5 percent Virginia sales tax—because, hey,

state legislators have to eat, too—it came to $53.83.

Next it was on to REI, the outdoor store, where things got a little more expensive. In short order, Derrick racked up a $716.88 tab while Carl rolled his eyes.

Then it was on to Crystal City, which quite literally towers over its more famous neighbor to the north. When members of the US Congress, in their infinite ego, decided that nothing in the nation's capital should be taller than the building where they spent their work time, they passed the Height of Buildings Act of 1910. As has often been the case when Congress decides to meddle in something, they screwed up: by regulating the height of buildings based on the width of the street outside them, rather than setting an absolute limit, they enabled the local Catholic diocese to outdo them in the 1950s, when it built the Basilica of the National Shrine of the Immaculate Conception. In addition, by limiting the height of buildings within the district, they doomed it to the lack of affordable housing and outward sprawling development pressure that continues to plague the region today.

Nevertheless, those onerous and byzantine height restrictions did not cross the Potomac River to the west. And so when Crystal City began booming in lockstep with the size of the federal government in the 1970s and '80s, it did so upward, not outward.

Which was why the building where Kevin Bryan lived was, at 312 feet, actually taller than the US Capitol. And that was where Derrick asked his father to stay parked on the street outside.

"All right. I should be about an hour or so," Derrick said. "Would you mind getting us some sandwiches? I'm starving."

Carl grunted.

"Fine. Just stay here then. I'll be back."

His father grunted again. Ignoring him, Derrick grabbed his

gear out of the trunk, donned a vest lined with useful pockets, slipped the two Polaroid pictures inside the vest, and began making his way out. But not to the building where Bryan lived; instead he made his way to an identical one that was just across a narrow street.

Carl pressed the down direction on the Buick's passenger side window power button. For a moment, there was only an agonized grinding noise. Then, slowly, the window began to lower.

"Hey, where are you going?" Carl said. "I thought your boyfriend lives in that one."

"He does," Derrick said. "That's why I'm going over here."

Carl frowned. "There's got to be a quicker way."

"No," Derrick said. "There's not. Not without getting caught. Just sit tight."

He disappeared into the lobby of the neighboring building. Laden with his recent purchases, which he had stowed in a mesh bag he bought from REI, he walked up to the security guard.

The man was young and smartly dressed, with short brown hair and earnest blue eyes. Storm sized him up for an eager-to-please type, a guy who would have been at home in the mountains of New Hampshire, running a summer camp for kids.

His name tag identified him as Devin Clifford.

"Can I help you?" Clifford asked.

"You sure can, Mr. Clifford," Storm said, as if he was one of those campers, putting a big smile behind it. "Do you have a newspaper by any chance?"

"A newspaper?" Clifford asked. "Today's? Or . . ."

"Today's, yesterday's, last week's, doesn't matter," Storm said, taking the Windex and squeegee out of the mesh bag and waving them in the air. "I'm with the Streak-Free Window Company. I'm here to clean some exterior windows on the twenty-second floor. But I forgot to bring newspaper with me. And you know what that means."

Clifford looked confused.

"Streaks," Storm said, as if he would rather be subjected to the bubonic plague and repeated viewings of the entire Real Housewives franchise.

"You have to understand, my company has the Ultimate No-Streak Guarantee™," Storm continued, somehow managing to pronounce it in a way that communicated the trademark. "If we leave streaks, we not only have to refund a hundred and twenty percent of the customer's fee, but we have to—"

Storm stopped, apparently too traumatized to continue.

"What?" Clifford asked.

Storm leaned in and whispered: "We have to do it again, in the nude. Get it? Like we're streaking? I had to do it once. My third job, I left streaks. And believe me, after that, I said never again. First of all, I got my, *y'know*, caught in a carabiner."

Clifford reflexively crossed his legs behind the desk. Storm's voice had returned to normal volume.

"Then once you get up there, it's even more humiliation. Do you know what it's like to have your junk suspended two-hundred-something feet in the air, just flopping around in the breeze for everyone to see? It's like . . . it's like . . . Well, it'd be like if you were forced to do this job in the nude."

Unsure if Clifford looked suitably horrified, Storm finished it off with: "And *your mother* lives in the building."

Clifford immediately reached below the desk and brought up that day's edition of the *Washington Post*. "Here," he said. "Take it."

"Great," Storm said. "Do you need a bypass key for roof access or anything?"

"Yeah, let me take care of that for you," Clifford said, walking over to the elevator and pressing the button. Storm whistled innocently while they waited for a car. When it arrived, Clifford eagerly plunged his round bypass key into the panel, then punched the button for the roof.

"No streaks, okay?" Clifford said.

"No streaks," Storm promised.

Storm was soon riding in solitude up to the roof. When he walked out, he was twenty-four stories above street level. He went over to the edge and peered down to see his father's Buick, in all its straight-lined glory, still parked in the same spot.

So much for sandwiches. Storm ignored the gnawing in his stomach and got to work. The sun was down but the lights of the city gave him enough illumination to see what he was doing as he began unpacking his bag.

Once he had everything laid out, he grabbed the C.A.M.P. USA Wing 2 traveling pulley he had bought from REI and threaded an entire seventy-meter length of 9.5-millimeter Mammut Infinity dry rope through the wheel. Then he secured one end of the rope to the skyscraper's railing, tugging on it with as much strength as he could muster to make sure it held.

Next he tied the other end of the dry rope to the handle of the hammer. An expert with knots of all kind—nautical, climbing, ranching, and otherwise—Storm used a slipped buntline hitch, which he greatly preferred over the standard buntline hitch, because the slipped version wouldn't jam on him.

Having just created a do-it-yourselfer's grappling hook, he was now ready for the tricky part: hurling it over to the other building and getting it to catch on that railing.

Storm was not entirely unfamiliar with ropework. Briefly confused by the notion he was meant to be a cowboy, Storm had worked a summer at a cattle ranch in his early twenties. He had gotten a great tan and some new muscles. He had also learned just how average he was going to be at his job if he decided to make a living as a rancher.

But if there was one appreciable difference between the cows he lassoed back then and the building he was now trying to rope, it was that at least the building wasn't moving.

He peered at his target, which was about sixty feet away. Getting the hammer's tines hooked onto the railing wasn't good enough. He didn't trust the grip of two short slices of stainless steel. His goal was to get the rope itself wrapped around the railing—with the hammer anchoring the rope.

The throw would have to be perfect. He began swinging the rope over his head, letting that twenty-one-ounce hammer out slowly, building more and more centrifugal force with every foot of rope he let slip through his hand.

When he felt he had both the momentum and aim perfect, he let go of the rope and watched the hammer sail through the night air.

He knew almost immediately he had too much behind it. The hammer went high over the railing, then landed with a barely audible thud on the roof. Storm hoped it might snare on the railing post when he dragged it back. But, no, it passed in the middle.

Try number two went short, hitting against the side of the building. The third try hit the railing, but too squarely: The hammer bounced off.

Number four was long again. Number five was short.

It was on his sixth try that Storm got it just right. He watched with satisfaction as the hammer twirled around the railing, like an Olympic gymnast doing giant swings on the parallel bars.

He gave his end of the rope a series of hard tugs from several different angles, until he was sure the improvised grapple was going to hold. Then he tied off his end, as tight as he could get it to go, to eliminate slack. The last thing he wanted was to get stranded in the middle of a droopy rope and end up having to climb hand over hand the rest of the way.

After slipping his legs through the Arc'teryx AR-395a climbing harness he had just acquired, he hooked himself to the pulley. Then he attached a second safety rope. If the hook on the other end didn't hold, he'd become a human pendulum, smacking into the side of the building with tremendous force. Many climbers had been killed that way in the mountains. But he'd have a better chance of surviving that than he would the three-hundred-plus-foot plunge he'd be facing without the safety rope.

He grabbed the pulley with both hands and slid it back and forth across an arm's-length arc. Then he gathered the mesh bag, which contained the remainder of his gear.

Storm was an experienced mountaineer, a man who had climbed the north face of the Eiger in under four hours, a man with multiple 20K summits on his resume. But there was still that moment of truth when you were facing a chasm—whether it was across a crevasse or across two buildings—when you simply had to decide to trust your ropes.

Some climbers reported relishing the thrill. In Storm's experience, those were the climbers most likely to end up leaving the mountain in a body bag.

He double- and triple-checked his knots, carabiners, and harness. Once he was satisfied, he got himself perched on the edge of the building and readied himself for a ride on what was essentially an untested high-stakes zip line.

Then, with legs made powerful from six-hundred-pound

squats, and with his eyes focused only on the other side, he launched himself.

Storm felt the wind in his hair and the updrafts from the city streets as the asphalt released the last of its heat from the day.

If anyone had happened to look up from the sidewalk at that moment, he might not have been able to make out the rope in the darkness. What he would have seen was the unlikely sight of a man who appeared to be levitating from one building to the next, like some kind of Jedi trick.

The entire trip, which took an hour to shop and prepare for, was over in seconds. Storm was just about out of momentum when he made it to the other side, giving him a soft landing.

He clambered up over the railing, happy to have something solid under his feet again. He left the ropes in place, in case he needed to exit the same way, then unhooked himself from the pulley.

It was time for part two of his journey, which was simpler from a technical standpoint, if no less dangerous. He extracted a Black Diamond ATC-XP belay device from his bag, gave it a little kiss, then got to work. Before long, he had tied both a main line and a safety line to separate parts of the railing and gotten his harness attached. Then he rappelled down to Kevin Bryan's living room window.

The apartment was dark, as Storm suspected it would be. He took out the one purchase he had yet to make use of—the seven-dollar glass cutter—and, doing his best to ignore that he was dangling many stories up, began carving a hole for himself.

It took about ten minutes of determined effort, scoring and then re-scoring the same lines, but he eventually removed a section of glass large enough that he was able to clamber through the opening and into the apartment.

Kevin Bryan was not there.

But Carl Storm was.

He wore his Home Depot hat and a self-satisfied grin.

Derrick stammered, "How . . . How did you—"

"I did it old school. I pulled this down low over my eyes when I walked through the lobby," Carl said, giving the hat a tug. "So you don't have to worry about the cameras."

"And the front door?" Derrick asked.

"I had my lock tools in the back of the Buick," Carl said. "Took me about a minute and a half. There was a magnetic sensor, but I used a wire and some chewing gum to keep the circuit in place."

"Nice job, MacGyver."

"I told you there was a quicker way. You waste too much time with this action-adventure hero crap."

THIRTEEN

HEAT

Nikki Heat didn't stay long in her apartment. Her nascent attempt at a cleanup job quickly sputtered due to some combination of being too overwhelming and too emotional to consider tackling that evening. It was difficult to even breathe in there.

She changed out of her captain's uniform and into fresh clothes, then stuffed a few outfits into a duffel bag. It was enough to last a few days, no more. At some point, she'd have to sneak into Rook's place in Chelsea when he wasn't around and resupply herself.

Then she got out, feeling ridiculous for locking the door behind her when it was clear The Serpent could get in anytime he wanted.

The only place she wanted to be even less than her apartment was the lobby of the building, which was still covered in the bloody remains of Bob Aaronson—and her name, that scarlet message from Aaronson's killer.

The detective she had spoken to before nodded at her as she passed. She made noises about coming back later. If he noted that the duffel bag slung over her shoulder seemed inconsistent with that declaration, he didn't say anything.

Unsure where else to go, she decided to head toward the

only home she had left. She went back to the unmarked car she had parked near The Players Club, then pointed it toward the Twentieth Precinct.

Once in the detective bull pen, she was greeted by the familiar and comforting sight of Sean Raley, who was hunched over an extra-large monitor, doing his magic. He didn't so much as look up when Heat entered, which was always a good sign. It meant he was locked in on something.

After depositing her bag in her office, Heat cruised up behind his shoulder and began hovering there. He appeared to be in some kind of chat room. Heat hadn't even realized people used those anymore. It was like being transported to some pre-Facebook remnant of the early Internet.

Raley finally noticed her presence after sending a particularly long missive.

"Just about there," he said, as if wherever "there" was should have been obvious to all. "With luck, I'll give you a shout in ten minutes."

Ten turned out to be more like thirty. Heat distracted herself with the nonsense on her desk until Raley's face appeared at her door.

"Okay," he said. "I got it. You want to come have a look?"

Heat followed the King of All Surveillance Media back to his throne room.

"Just so we're clear, you said 'any means necessary,' and I took you at your word," Raley said. "With how I had to acquire it, what I'm about to show you won't come close to standing up in court. It also might have you feeling like you need hand sanitizer."

"I understand."

"Good. The One-Three has already done a good job going up and down the street, doing the usual canvass. The problem is, our perp did them one better. There were three cameras with various angles on the street outside your place. One was shot out by a BB gun. One was spray-painted. Another was hacked so thoroughly the owner couldn't even log into his own computer. This guy was very thorough, and very determined."

"So we're dead in the water?"

"Not at all. I was just forced to resort to desperate measures."

"How desperate?"

"Are you familiar with the Gotham Voyeurs?" Raley asked.

"Uhh . . . no."

"Keep it that way. Trust me, you'll feel better when you're getting dressed in the morning."

"I don't follow."

"The Gotham Voyeurs are a network of high-tech Peeping Toms. Normal pornography just doesn't do it for them. They get off on knowing they're watching someone who wasn't aware they were being watched. You know what I mean?"

"Uhh . . ." Heat said again.

"Oh, trust me, it gets worse. The Gotham Voyeurs aren't just ordinary run-of-the-mill perverts who are happy to spy on their neighbors and keep it to themselves. They interface with each other on message boards and in chat rooms and brag about who can get the best footage. They're constantly trying to outdo each other. They compete on who can upload the best, most graphic, most unusual stuff. The freakier the better. They also do what they call challenges."

"Challenges?"

"It's not enough for some of these guys to get random strangers. They go after specific targets. So, say one of the GVs—that's what they call themselves—really wants to see his coworker go at it with her boyfriend. He puts out the call to other GVs: 'Sally Smith lives on the fourth floor of a co-op on

Eighty-Sixth Street, with a south-facing window. Who can get her?' And then another GVer will say, 'You're in luck. I'm at Eighty-Sixth Street, seventh floor, with a north-facing window. I'll get you Sally.' They assign points based on the difficulty of the assignment and the quality of what's returned, keep leaderboards and everything. It's really quite involved."

"It's depraved. Has vice ever tried to shut these guys down?"

"Nope. What they're doing is not actually illegal. You can film anything you want from the window of your apartment, or from anywhere you have legally accessed, or from a public street for that matter. That's the narrow moral and legal ledge the GVers stand on. If people don't have the good sense to shut their blinds, they're really making themselves fair game. And some of these guys are so good, they might still be able to find a way to—"

"Okay, stop. Just stop. I get it. There are degenerates everywhere in this world. I'm changing in my closet from now on. Please say you've told me all this for a reason."

"I have," Raley said. "Except now we get to the good-news-slash-bad-news part of this presentation. The bad news is, one of the more active GVers lives across the street from your building."

"I think I'm going to be sick."

"The good news is he had a very powerful, very expensive camera trained on your building all day."

"That's the good news?"

"You'll start thinking so when you see the footage he got. He was doing what they call 'fishing,' or sometimes 'trolling.' The camera is wide-angle but also high resolution. So you set it on an entire building, like a fisher setting a net, then you go back later and see if you caught anything. If you did, you isolate it, then enlarge it. It comes across like a lower-quality camera that was zoomed in on the right place."

"Okay. So one of these jerks was fishing on my building today?"

"Yeah, that's about the size of it."

"And you got him to send you his material . . . how, exactly?" Heat asked, with some mixture of amazement and disgust.

"Remember how you said 'any means necessary'?"

"Yeah."

"Let's just leave it at that."

"Okay," Heat said. "I think I need that hand sanitizer now."

"Yeah, I need whole-body sanitizer," he said. "Anyway, here goes."

Raley's screen, which had been black, was now in living color, showing the street outside Heat's apartment.

"I asked the guy to give me the entire stretch of footage between four-thirty and five, just so I had a little bit of a buffer on either side," Raley said. "At 4:36 you see a lady going in."

"That's the resident who told the detective Aaronson was alive."

"Sure is. And at 4:51, you see another woman entering."

"That's the resident who called 911."

"Right. But at 4:42, a man enters. Unless the killer was already hiding in the building, this would have to be our guy. He'll be coming shortly. We never do see him leave. I'm assuming he found some other means of exit."

Yeah, my fire escape, Heat thought.

She studied the screen. The footage was being shot from above—roughly the level of a fourth-floor apartment, perhaps a quarter of a block east of her mother's place. It was an angle that didn't afford any viewpoint into the lobby itself, which was fine with Heat. She didn't need to watch her doorman get slaughtered. Seeing him afterward was bad enough.

The foot traffic on the street looked like any other day in

Gramercy Park, a Manhattan neighborhood that was well-to-do, but not *too* well-to-do. That meant unlike, say, Central Park West, the people who owned the apartments, co-ops, and condos actually lived there.

They were ordinary people, and they were strolling along, coming and going, blissfully unaware they were being filmed or that something so very violent was going to happen nearby.

Heat actually recognized some of the folks—mainly the ones who came from the west, due to the camera angle. To newcomers, Manhattan seems like an endless succession of strangers. But to those who have lived there long enough, the island becomes a series of small towns stitched together into a city of eight million. You start to see the same people all the time.

And so Heat was, in some ways, unsurprised when she saw a familiar face coming from the direction of the setting sun. The man had done his best to obscure his features with a black baseball cap and dark glasses.

But Heat knew him immediately. She knew his walk, which was athletic and precise. It propelled him through space like the leading edge of blade, full of dangerous purpose.

He was wearing a black long-sleeve shirt, black jeans, and, most ominously, black gloves. He had a black satchel slung casually over one shoulder. It was just the right size for a hunting knife and some lock tools, with some room left over to carry out whatever he felt like taking from Heat's apartment.

It had been a few years since Heat had seen him. He had never been anything close to fat, but he had clearly slimmed down. Yet he was not only leaner. He was also harder.

Time in prison will do that to a man.

And it had clearly done it to Bart Callan.

⁂

Raley waited until Heat finished watching the segment he had selected. It was, on its own, not terribly instructive. All it showed was a man in dark clothing walking into an apartment building.

It was only when you understood what came next that it became chilling.

"That's Bart Callan, isn't it?" Raley asked.

"Yeah," Heat said.

"Should I tell the Thirteenth? They could never use this video in court—because there's just no way I could explain on the record how I got it—but knowing it was Callan would let them narrow their investigation on him. I'm sure they'd be able to get other evidence once they knew who to look at."

"Might as well," she said. "You should also put in a call to our friends at the US Marshals Service. They've had their fugitive apprehension team turning the state of Maryland inside out looking for him. They'd probably like to know he's been seen here."

For what little good it would do them. There were basically two kinds of fugitives: those with means, smarts, and friends in high places, and those without.

The latter, which was most of them, were relatively easy to catch. They were inevitably found in some local flophouse, at their former girlfriend's place, or thumbing a ride on the interstate. The former—and Callan was not only in that class, he was basically the valedictorian—were far more difficult. They had a tendency to become one with the wind.

Especially given what Storm had relayed to her about Callan being aided and abetted by Jedediah Jones and the Shanghai Seven. Between Callan's skill set, Jones's endless intelligence resources, and the depth of the Shanghai Seven's pockets, Callan could remain at large indefinitely.

Until he decided to strike again.

Which he could do at basically any time.

"You okay, Captain?" Raley said. "You look a little spooked."

"Yeah, I am," she admitted. There was no point trying to deny it.

"Do you think . . . I mean, I don't mean to get you even more spooked, but do you think Callan is coming after you?"

"Callan is too much of a coward for that," Heat said. "He couldn't take me out four years ago, and he won't be able to do it now."

Raley looked unconvinced. "Okay, Captain. But . . . I mean, you know we've got your back, right? Any time. Any place. You get a bad feeling about something, you call us, right? No hesitation. No second thoughts."

"Right," Heat said. "Anyway, I've got some stuff to do here. But great work, Rales. Really, really great work. You've outdone yourself. You've earned a shower."

"Yeah, but if it's all the same to you, I'm going to take it with my swim trunks on."

She offered him a weary smile. He gave her a loose salute that only momentarily hid the concern on his face.

Heat returned to her office, closing the door and dialing the blinds to the closed position. She sat in her desk chair, whose pneumatic piston sighed at the same time she did.

She peered out the dark window and ordered her thoughts. She had been convinced The Serpent, who made threats about evincing his power, had killed Bob Aaronson. She now had clear and convincing evidence Bart Callan had been the man behind the knife.

Did that mean Callan was The Serpent?

It certainly made sense. The Shanghai Seven had Callan

sprung from prison because he was more qualified than anyone to suss out where Cynthia Heat would have hid her counterfeit bills. Callan had ransacked Cynthia's former apartment as part of that effort.

But he also probably had been tasked with keeping Nikki Heat off the case—all the better to prevent her from finding the bills or other damning evidence against the Shanghai Seven. And so Callan had come up with a pseudonym behind which he could attempt to harass and intimidate her.

And this particular pseudonym was laden with meaning. The Serpent was a harkening to the code name Cynthia Heat had once given Callan: The Dragon. Callan was practically taunting her with it, trying to add to the psychological warfare.

And it wasn't going to work. Heat was more determined than ever about that now. And she wanted The Serpent, aka Callan, to know it.

She pulled out her phone, brought up The Serpent's last text, then hit REPLY and started typing.

HEY, CALLAN, NICE WORK AT MY MOTHER'S APARTMENT. KILLING AN UNARMED DOORMAN. YOU'RE BRAVE. BUT YOU'RE ALSO STUPID. WE GOT YOU ON CAMERA, GENIUS.

She hit SEND, feeling some mild satisfaction about being on the offensive for once. She could imagine the smug look on Callan's face disappearing as he read the text and realized he wasn't as smart as he thought he was.

Two minutes later, her phone notified her of an incoming message.

THIS IS NOT BART CALLAN. AND I HAD NOTHING TO DO WITH YOUR MOTHER'S APARTMENT. YOU'VE GOT ME ALL WRONG. AND YOU'RE NOT LISTENING. I AM OUT OF PATIENCE. NO MORE WARNINGS. THIS IS NOW WAR. YOU EITHER CEASE ALL ACTIVITIES REGARDING YOUR MOTHER OR YOU DIE.

Heat was shaking her head as she angrily tapped out her reply, bristling at the man's arrogance.

HOW DUMB DO YOU THINK I AM, CALLAN? I'M NOT SCARED OF YOU. I WASN'T WHEN I PUT YOU IN JAIL FOUR YEARS AGO AND I WON'T BE WHEN I PUT YOU BACK THERE THIS TIME.

She fired off the message with a testy jab of her finger, then considered the piles of paperwork in front of her. It was now after eight o'clock. There was just no way she could summon the willpower to concentrate on it.

There was also the small logistical issue that she had no place to sleep. Her thoroughly violated apartment was clearly not an option. She couldn't face the mess and heartache. She also—if she was being perfectly honest with herself—didn't feel safe there.

At the same time, she couldn't crawl back to Rook's place. Not only would it be putting him in the crosshairs, but it would send mixed messages.

And so, with another sigh, Heat booked a room for one night at The Lucerne, a hotel three blocks south of the precinct. She splurged for a deluxe room with a king bed, but sadly clicked "one" on the slider that asked her to signify the number of total guests. Then she gathered her duffel bag, turned off her desk lamp, and walked out of her office.

The bull pen was empty. Raley was now gone. Ochoa had preceded his exit by several hours. They were still tired from the Legs Kline case.

The detectives on night duty were out responding to calls. She took the stairs to the first floor and bid good night to the desk sergeant, then walked out into the night.

The front door of the Twentieth Precinct opened onto a sidewalk alongside 82nd Street with little fanfare. The sidewalk itself was narrow, no more than about six feet wide, which was why Heat had to juke to the side when a party of well-dressed thirtysomething restaurant-goers—semi-oblivious and fully drunk—practically ran her over.

And that, in turn, was why Heat's head wasn't quite where it should have been when three bullets crashed into the glass door behind her.

FOURTEEN

STORM

They didn't bother turning on the lights. Nor did they speak. Though decades apart in age, and schooled in different tactics by very different parts of the government, the men were united by something universal about waiting for someone who hadn't let you into their place, didn't know you were there—and might not appreciate you being there. Announcing one's presence under those conditions offered no tactical advantage.

And so the Storm boys sat in darkened silence. Carl was lying on a couch that faced the man-sized hole in the living room window. Derrick was watching the front door while seated on a stool that fronted the island between the living room and kitchen. They were waiting for the rasping of a key, the sliding of a lock, the turning of a door handle.

It was 8:32 when they finally heard those sounds. And soon the smallish form of Agent Kevin Bryan, backlit by the overhead lights in the hallway, was filling the doorway. He closed the door, set his keys in a bowl, and hung up his jacket. His actions were nonchalant, unhurried, seemingly unaware of his visitors.

Then he whirled and, in one remarkably quick movement, withdrew his Sig Sauer and trained it on Derrick Storm.

"Whoa! Take it easy," Derrick said quickly, sticking his hands in the air.

"Jesus, Mary, and Joseph, Storm!" Bryan said. "What the hell is wrong with you? I was just about to pull the trigger. What are you doing here?"

Bryan flicked a switch, and light flooded from the pendant lights that dangled from the ceiling. His small living area was fashionably and minimally decorated: The couch Carl was lying on had a matching love seat with a coffee table in front of it and a tasteful area rug underneath, all of which sat atop well-polished hardwood floors. On the other side of the island, the wood gave way to the tile of the kitchen. The granite countertops shone softly.

Carl sat up as Bryan entered the room.

"Oh. Hello, Mr. Storm," he said. "I didn't see you there."

"Fer Chrissakes, son, how many times do I have to tell you to call me Carl?"

"Sorry, sir."

"That's no better."

"Sorry, uh, Carl," Bryan said. But he still hadn't shaken all of his rage at the intrusion. "So, seriously, Storm. What are you doing here? I mean, I could have killed you if I—"

And then his gaze fell on the window.

"That's it. I'm going to kill you," he said.

"Sorry," Storm said.

"No, no. Sorry doesn't cut it. 'Sorry' is for when you accidentally spill a drink on the rug. 'Sorry' is fine when you break the handle on the toilet. You don't carve a hole in someone's living room window and just say, 'Sorry.' What did you do? You have some kind of problem with using the door?"

"I thought this place needed a little fresh air. You know these buildings can get very unhealthy when not properly ventilated."

"Stop screwing around," Bryan said, staring at the window furiously.

"Stop looking so pissed," Derrick said. "I'll pay for the new window. You know that."

Bryan's mouth hadn't moved.

"And tickets to a Nationals game," Derrick added. "First base side. Down low. You'll be practically right next to Bryce Harper."

"I don't care if Bryce Harper is sitting in my damn lap whispering sweet nothings in my ear. That's not going to fix my window."

"Come on. I'll talk to him about hitting a foul pop-up your way," Derrick said.

"Is there any other damage I should know about? You didn't take down a wall or something, did you?"

"No. I was going to wait until we left to do that. Unless you'd rather we used the door."

"Don't tell me you made your dad come through the window, too."

"I did it the old-fashioned way," Carl said, holding up his bag of lock-pick tools.

"But didn't you set off the . . . Oh, never mind," Bryan said, shaking his head. "Look, what do you want? Because I can tell you, all I want is for you to get the hell out of here right now."

"We had a little dinner party this evening. Five friends of ours. They came with automatic weapons, even though we told them they didn't have to bring anything," Derrick said, removing the Polaroid pictures from the climbing vest and holding them out for Bryan. "Can you run these guys through Jones's rogue gallery and give us a rundown on them?"

The Irishman accepted them, then recoiled as soon as he parsed what they depicted.

"Good lord, Storm. Your friends aren't in very good health," he said.

"We'll tell them to take it up with their family physician."

"Their family mortician might be better," Bryan said. "But, look, that doesn't excuse what you did to my window. Why didn't you just e-mail these to me?"

"I'm a little bit technologically challenged at the moment. And this is . . . not something I want to get on your boss's radar."

"Are you two girls fighting again?" Bryan said. "Let me guess: You went to the prom in the same dress and now you're fighting over who looks prettier."

"Something like that."

"Seriously, what's going on?" Bryan asked.

"At the moment, I'd say we have conflicting motivations," Derrick said.

"With you two? That's every moment."

"You have a point."

"So, let me get this straight: You break into my apartment, vandalizing it in the process," Bryan said. "And now I'm not only supposed to overlook that and help you, I'm supposed to help you even though this is another one of those times when doing so will greatly increase the chances that Jones decides to order an air strike on my head and then hide what's left of my corpse in a cave in Afghanistan, where it will be feasted on by scorpions until it is nothing more than a scattered skeleton."

"The birds and vermin will pick you clean before the scorpions," Derrick pointed out. "And the cave might technically be in Pakistan. Jones gets that special thrill in violating their sovereignty without their knowledge. He does it whenever he needs a pick-me-up."

"Fantastic. Either way, I don't care. I know you're going to pout and go on about how Jones is up to something underhanded that only Derrick Storm can prevent from turning into a full-blown diabolical plot, and how the very future of freedom, justice, and democracy is at stake."

"Freedom, justice, democracy, and my pale white ass," Derrick said.

"I still don't care. And, in case I haven't made it clear, you can forget it. I'm not helping you," Bryan said. "I'd rather take my chances with the pouting than with the cave. I hate scorpions. And birds. And vermin."

"You're going to force me to make this ugly, aren't you," Derrick said.

"It wouldn't matter even if you did. Even if I wanted to help you, I couldn't. I don't have access to the database from here."

"Except you do," Derrick said. "You have a work-around that gets you in."

"No, I don't," Bryan said.

"You do too. You told me about it in Antigua."

Bryan's eyes narrowed. "I did not. You're making that up. When was I—"

"Buff," Derrick said.

"What?"

"Buff. That's when I learned that 'buff' is actually another way of saying yellow. This was Antigua, after the Whitaker Holdings job. We were celebrating. Maybe a little too much. You ended up dancing a jig for the Alpha Gams from the University of Alabama. They made you an honorary sister and even dressed you up like one. And their colors are red, buff, and green. As I think about it, I'm pretty sure I still have the photos saved in the cloud . . ."

Bryan crossed his arms. His lips were pursed. "Oh, this gets better. So first you vandalize my apartment and now you threaten me with blackmail. You're a real charmer, you know that, Storm?"

"It's because I'm so ruggedly handsome."

"You know what? I don't care. You go ahead and do whatever you want with those photos. Publish them in the *Washington Post* for all I care. Heck, that would probably make me un-fireable. Transgender is totally in right now. I bet the women's bathroom in the Cubby is a lot nicer than the men's anyway. And, in any event, that work-around doesn't work anymore. Jones found out about it and shut it down."

"Oh, come on, you know you can."

"I can't. And I won't. That's final."

"All right. I didn't want to bring this up, but—"

Suddenly, Carl Storm rose from the couch and, with a growl in his throat, brought a halt to the bickering: "All right, knock it off and sit down. Both of you."

Agent Bryan and the younger Storm exchanged curious glances.

"Sit. Now," Carl reiterated.

The two men complied.

"Look," Carl said, once they were settled. "When I was your age, I used to enjoy this crap, too. The chest-thumping. The macho bullshit. The posturing. The horse-trading. And it's all fine for you, because you're young and you have the energy. But I'm an old man. I'm tired. My prostate is the size of a watermelon, so I have to pee every twelve seconds; I'm cranky because I haven't had dinner; and I've had more bullets fired in my direction today than is really good for a man. So I'm going to cut to the chase a little bit here.

"Right now, you're young. You're powerful. You're at the peak of your lives, and so the government needs you. And you think it's always going to be that way. But eventually the government is going to move on, like it always does. It'll be relying on younger men who are themselves in the prime of their lives. Jones will be dead, and you two will be kicked to the curb like yesterday's garbage, and you know the only thing you'll have then?"

Bryan and Storm exchanged glances, like schoolboys who had missed a reading assignment and were now being stumped by the teacher.

"Each other," Carl finished. "That's it: your former colleagues, the guys who were in the trenches with you, the ones who saved the world at your side, the ones who will remember what you could do back when you were young and will still appreciate that you did it even though you can't do it anymore. And you probably don't believe me now, but that's going to mean more to you than you can possibly know. You'll even come to recognize you love each other. You won't say it, because who does that? And you'll probably still give each other a hard time. But deep down, you'll come to understand those bonds you have with your former colleagues are some of the most meaningful relationships in your lives, and you'll come to realize you were blessed enough in this crappy world to be given two families: the one you were born with and the one you found on the job. So you!"

Carl was pointing at his son. "You're not going to threaten him or find some way to get leverage on him or any of that other macho crap guys do. You're going to tell him how much you value him, how much you appreciate his skills, and how much you really need him right now, because you're in a world of trouble if he doesn't help you."

Derrick looked down at the hardwood floor and began mumbling, "So, Kevin, I—"

"To his face!" Carl ordered.

Derrick lifted his gaze. "I, uh . . . Look, you really are one of the best in the world at hacking into computer networks and cracking the seemingly uncrackable. And Dad is right. I'm kind of screwed if you don't help me."

Bryan was grinning, perhaps a bit uncomfortably, but Carl pointed at him next.

"And you! Wipe that silly smile off your face. You're going to tell him it's your pleasure to help him, because you know he'd do the same for you. Because you know if Jones ever did turn on you, he's the one guy who would go to the ends of the earth to save your sorry ass, because that's what brothers do for each other."

Bryan eyed Derrick. "Yeah, what he said. And I guess I could add that you're one of the best in the world, too."

"Good," Carl said. "Now shake hands, you two."

Derrick stuck out his hand first. Bryan accepted it with a firm grasp.

"So this is naturally something I wouldn't share with Jones," Bryan said. "But I might just have a work-around I've been wanting to try out."

"Because you're the man," Derrick said.

"No," Bryan said, pointing at Carl. "*He's* the man. You're just lucky to have him as a dad."

Bryan had set up his laptop on the kitchen island.

Derrick was plating grilled cheese sandwiches and bacon, because that was all he could scrounge out of Bryan's typical bachelor's refrigerator.

And Carl was peeing. For the second time.

"Okay, I think I'm in," Bryan said.

"Attaboy," Derrick said. "I knew you could do it."

"Just make sure you give me a beautiful eulogy after Jones

has me killed," Bryan said. "I don't want there to be a dry eye in the house."

"I'll get choked up myself midway through, just to encourage any of the holdouts."

Carl had rejoined them in the kitchen. "Two buttons but no handle," he was grumbling. "It's a goddamn toilet, not the space shuttle."

"Hand me those pictures," Bryan said. When Derrick complied, Bryan fed the first through a small scanner he had hooked up.

"Shouldn't take long now," he said.

A small bar on his screen filled, then it was replaced by a window featuring a man's mug shot.

"Okay, meet Alexi Hawley," Bryan said. "Age thirty-three. American by birth. His mother is German, so he has dual citizenship and the passport to go with it. Grew up in Minnesota, where he was your basic juvenile delinquent: shoplifting and, oh, look at this, vandalism. He's a man after your own heart, Storm."

Derrick smiled.

"By the time he was eighteen it looks like he had acquired a real taste for crystal meth," Bryan continued. "By twenty-one, he had run through his second and third chances with law enforcement. He had some serious time hanging over his head and had just gotten picked up again, but he was in luck, because the army was involved in two wars and it was starting to run out of bodies. He enlisted as an alternative to incarceration."

"And people say patriotism is dead," Carl commented.

"After basic training he shipped out, but it seems— unsurprisingly—he had a bit of a problem with authority. His platoon in Afghanistan had standing orders not to engage the enemy unless the enemy shot first. Apparently he wasn't real keen to sit around and wait for Tommy Taliban to get an itchy trigger finger, so he'd either find ways to provoke them or just ignore orders and start firing. He wound up with a bad conduct discharge after he shot up a village that was suspected of harboring Taliban fighters."

"In other words, the guys in his platoon loved him, but everyone in the command structure couldn't wait to get rid of him, because he kept making them have to fill out reports," Derrick said.

"Yeah, that's not in the file. All I can tell you is that he went right back to the Middle East, doing private security for anyone who would give him a bulletproof vest and a big gun. Then he started moving farther east and freelancing and . . . let's see, looks like he popped up with the Tamil Tigers. Lovely. He spent six months in a jail in Laos on suspicion of treason. Bet that was fun. And then he ended up in China, where he—"

"Started working for the Shanghai Seven," Carl filled in.

"Yeah, how did you know?"

Carl wagged his bushy eyebrows in his son's direction. "Just a hunch," he said.

"All right. Well, that's where the file on Alexi Hawley ends. As for this other one . . . Is that a carpentry nail in his forehead?"

"That's actually referred to as a common nail," Carl said.

"I don't want to know," Bryan said as he fed the photo through his scanner and waited for a result to pop up. When it did, Bryan studied it for a minute or so.

"Okay, here we go," he said. "Terence Paul Winter. A real Boy Scout, this guy. And I mean that literally. He was an Eagle Scout with Troop Eighty-Seven out of Davenport, Iowa. Member of the Future Farmers of America. Never in trouble with the law. Went to Iowa State. Double-majored in business and Asian studies with an emphasis on Chinese. Got his MBA in international business at Stanford then started consulting in the logistics industry."

"How would a guy like *that* wind up associating with a scumbag tweaker like Alexi Hawley?"

"I'm getting to that. After he did his time as a consultant, he caught on with OOCL, Oriental Overseas Container Line. They're one of the real big boys in global shipping, as I'm sure you know. And then . . ."

Bryan started chuckling. "Oh. Oh, Storm. You have *really* outdone yourself this time."

"What?" Derrick said.

"Well, it seems OOCL assigned Winter to Shanghai. That's one of China's major ports, so his career was obviously doing pretty well. And he started getting to know the movers and shakers there."

"Including, let me guess, the Shanghai Seven," Carl said.

"Yeah, but not how you think. Imagine this, if you will. He's this young executive; a big, good-looking kid from Iowa who spoke the language. He's going to all the right parties. He's got a good job. And it looks like he caught the eye of one of the Shanghai Seven's daughters. A whirlwind romance ensued, followed by a high-profile wedding that was reported to cost three million dollars. Congratulations, Storm, you just killed one of the Shanghai Seven's son-in-laws."

Derrick rolled his eyes while Carl clapped him on the back. "I always encouraged you to aim high, son. Nicely done."

"It looks like the Shanghai Seven assigned the son-in-law to help run their American operations. So he was over here, along with the daughter. My guess is Big Daddy called him up and said, 'Hey, we've got this problem in America right now. I'm going to send some mercenaries over. Have them help you take care of it.' Or maybe Hawley was the only one with Shanghai Seven connections and the others were more recent hires. Tough to say when I can't run the other three through the system."

"Yeah, they didn't stick around long enough for us to take nicely lit portraits," Derrick said.

"It doesn't really matter at this point anyway," Carl said. "We've got the Shanghai Seven on our ass. And now it's personal. That's the takeaway."

Bryan was nodding. "For what it's worth, we were hearing a lot of chatter today that the Shanghai Seven were assembling some kind of operation. They're apparently looking for something. But we didn't know what—or who is doing all the looking. One of our assets just said they were prepared to pump a quote-unquote 'small army' over here until they found it."

"An operative. You know who?"

"Negative. I got that from Jones."

"That's because . . ." Derrick began, then completed the thought in his mind: *Jones is the operative, and he's getting his scoop straight from the Shanghai Seven. He's leaking out a little bit of information so it seems like he's on the right side. Really, he's working both. Classic Jones.*

"Because what?" Bryan asked.

Derrick studied his friend. It wasn't that he didn't trust Bryan. It was that he wasn't sure it was good for Bryan's health, short- or long-term, to know too much. Sometimes, especially when you were one of Jedediah Jones's agents, ignorance really was bliss. People who knew too much tended to become targets.

"Just forget about it," Derrick said.

"No, no. Look, you need to come in. The Shanghai Seven was already bringing the pain on you, and that was *before* you went and killed part of the family. I don't even want to think about what they're going to do now. Just come into the Cubby. Jones will protect you."

Yeah, right. Jones will hand me over with my head resting on a platter and an apple in my mouth, Derrick thought.

"I really appreciate your help," Derrick said. "Dad's right. All we really have in this big bad world is each other. You know I'll always have your back. You might . . . You might not see me for a while."

"What are you talking about? I swear, I don't think Jones is up to anything. Or at least not anything more than usual. You can trust him."

"Let's go, Dad," Derrick said.

"Jeez, guys," Bryan whined. "Don't you at least want the grilled cheese?"

"Sorry we can't stick around," Derrick said, knowing that each minute they spent at Bryan's apartment increased the risk that Jones might have a way of finding them there. "Don't worry. We'll take the elevator this time."

And then, Storm thought, *we run.*

FIFTEEN

HEAT

Nikki Heat hit the concrete and rolled, then crawled behind a parked car, an older Mercedes station wagon long enough and wide enough to provide effective cover. She hoped.

The drunk restaurant-goers, in all their fancy clothing, were scattered. Some were screaming. Others were ducking. One had started running up the street in the direction of Columbus Avenue. Heat couldn't tell if any of them had been hit.

She leaned into the door panel of the Mercedes, feeling its cold steel against her side like a warm blanket. She had pulled out her 9mm and now just needed to know where to aim it.

Daring to raise her head just a little, she scanned the buildings on the other side of the street. She was looking for movement on the roof, an open window, a curtain being blown by the breeze, anything to indicate where the shooter was.

All was still.

But not for long. Two cops, clutching large, bulletproof shields against their torsos, had emerged from the pockmarked front door of the Twentieth Precinct. If they were armed, they were not pulling their weapons. Their entire focus was on protecting the civilians.

There were eight of them altogether—seven, if you didn't

count the guy who was still running up the block until he disappeared around the corner, seemingly determined to start his own version of the New York City Marathon. Working steadily, the cops grabbed each one of the remaining seven, hauling them to safety behind the shields.

Heat kept her gaze across the street, moving her eyes constantly in the hopes she would see something that stood out. Occasionally, she stole glances at the door. Given enough time, the Crime Scene Unit could perform a ballistics analysis and determine the approximate position and angle the bullets had been shot from. Heat was trying to do a quick-and-dirty version of that calculation on her own.

But each time her glance went back to one of the buildings on the other side of 82nd Street, she didn't see anything out of the ordinary.

A few times, she thrust her head above the station wagon, then immediately brought it back down, playing peekaboo with a would-be sniper. She varied where she did it, popping up from behind the trunk one time, then the hood the next, then the middle of the vehicle. She was trying to see if she could draw any more fire.

None came. Other than the sobs and panicked shouting of the restaurant-goers—and the soft, insistent professional coaching of the cops who were rescuing them—there were no unusual sounds.

Eventually, one of the shield-toting cops came for her.

"Sir," he said. "Please come with me."

"No," Heat said stubbornly. "I want to draw this bastard out."

"Sir, I don't think that's advisable. Please come with me."

She looked at the cop's babyish face. He was one of her recent hires, a greenhorn no more than three months out of the academy.

This kid still doesn't even need to shave more than twice a week, and he's acting smarter than I am, Heat thought.

"Right," Heat said. "Sorry. Good call, officer. I lost my head for a second."

"Actually, sir, I'm here to see that you don't," he said. "Now, we're going to stand, on three. Then we're going to walk to the door."

With the kid holding the shield in a place where it offered both of them protection, they made it to the safety of the precinct.

The desk sergeant, who had coordinated the response, appeared in front of Heat.

"What was that about?" he asked.

"I have no idea," Heat said, even though she did. "Maybe someone has been hit up for a PBA fund-raiser once too often."

Then her phone indicated she had a text message.

"Excuse me," she said.

She quickly checked the screen. The message was from The Serpent.

NEXT TIME, it said. I WON'T MISS.

There would have to be a report filled out. And the aforementioned ballistics analysis needed to be performed. And the slugs, which were badly deformed from their encounter with the bulletproof glass, would have to be put through the system.

Heat knew it wouldn't come to anything. Ultimately, which rooftop Callan used—or what caliber of gun he selected—wasn't going to help find him. And so she didn't feel the need to stick around for the confirmation of the inevitable nothing. She was tired. And demoralized. And scared. And lonely.

She put all the official matters in the hands of the Crime Scene Unit and the night detective shift, then began a three-block walk to The Lucerne. She expected her shoes would feel heavy, what with all she had been through during yet another long day in a series of very long days.

Instead, a spurt of nervous energy put a spring in her step. She realized she was taking countermeasures against a shooter, ducking behind barriers when they presented themselves, varying the speed of her walk from fast to faster.

This is ridiculous, she told herself. *There's no way Callan knows I've chosen a hotel three blocks south, versus going to Rook's place, versus a hotel four blocks west.*

Still, she was frightened. Might as well admit it to herself. She thought about Bart Callan. The first time she had met him, he was an agent with the Department of Homeland Security—ironically, the agency Heat just might soon be the head of. She had thought, for a long time, he was one of the good guys. It had taken her a while to unravel his mendacity.

She thought back to the day, four years earlier, when she had finally put it together. They had scheduled what Callan thought was a friendly sparring session. They met in Heat's gym, the bare-bones, this-ain't-your-two-hundred-dollar-a-month-hook-up-haven health club. She knew Callan was a traitor and a criminal by that point. She was just trying to lure him into admitting it.

When Callan had arrived, he was wearing a ripped T-shirt that showed off his guns. Heat had taken one look at him and read him for an overconfident pretty boy she'd be able to take down easily. Any martial artist can tell you that while biceps may look nice, they are not a terribly useful muscle. Core strength beats bulging biceps any day.

Except their first several rounds had actually gone to Callan, who caught Heat by surprise, putting her back with ease. She eventually got the better of him, dislocating his shoulder before she arrested him.

But that was only because she had managed to distract him. One-on-one, when his attention was fully on her, Callan had proven himself to be a worthy adversary. It's not overconfidence when you really are good.

And Callan was good. Very good. She didn't want to repeat the mistake of not giving him the respect he deserved.

Even now, when he should have been running scared—he was the fugitive, after all—he had her completely off-balance, making it a nervous walk to The Lucerne. She was relieved when she finally arrived without an extra hole or two in her body.

The lobby was small—as tends to be the case at any Manhattan hotel where you're not spending $350 a night—and she tried not to feel an extra stab of remorse when she had to answer "one" to the desk clerk's question: "How many key cards would you like?"

She took the elevator up to the deluxe room, which still had the typically tiny dimensions of a Manhattan hotel room. It was just a bed, a desk, a television, and a minibar, with narrow channels left open around the furniture for navigation.

It should have been a sanctuary. Except as soon as she closed the door behind her, all the things she had been semi-successfully keeping in their own compartments suddenly ran together. Her ransacked apartment. The taunting of Bart Callan/The Serpent. Being shot at. Her mother, alive but still not with her. Her husband, estranged from her because that was what was best for him.

It was, wasn't it?

Heat's resolve began to crumble, almost like someone knocking into a brick wall with a five-ton wrecking ball, sending shattered pieces of masonry and mortar to the ground below. She imagined herself crawling back to Rook and snuggling up next to that gorgeous hunk of a husband.

There were a lot of reasons they had survived so much as a couple. Some were, relatively speaking, superficial: he could make her insides feel gooey with one winsome smile; he could make her laugh, even when she didn't want to; he was the first person she wanted to share news with, whether it was good or bad.

But more important than all that was the way he accepted her, no matter what condition she happened to be in when she crawled, limped, or ran toward him. In sickness or in health. Sane or crazy.

When she needed him to listen, he did that. When she needed to be embraced, he did that, too—and sometimes so, so much more, if that happened to be where things led.

She knew this was another time when Rook would take her exactly as she was.

A memory from their early dating life came to her. It was their one-month anniversary. She was still a sergeant who was subject to the whims of whatever case came up next in the rotation. Rook had secured a seven o'clock reservation at Joie de Vivre, a place so exclusive even celebrity two-time Pulitzer Prize–winners had a hard time getting a table. She had happily accepted, even though they were so new in their relationship—and she still had so many walls built up around her feelings—she had to pretend she wasn't abundantly impressed by his pull.

Before heading to work that day, she had packed a smoking-hot dress, one that plunged and clung and flowed in all the right ways. She matched it with a pair of knockout heels. She planned to change and then run out the door, hoping none of her fellow detectives would see her in it—because, after that, they'd never be able to think of Sergeant Heat as one of the guys again.

Mostly, she was excited for the date. Who wouldn't be?

But then it rained. And she wound up trooping through the projects, looking for a perp suspected of B&E. But even when she found him, hiding amidst rat droppings in the cellar of his cousin's apartment, it wasn't clear whether they had enough evidence to hold him, because a confidential informant was playing hard-to-get with the prosecutor's office.

When the snitch finally gave it up, it was raining even harder, hopelessly delaying the last bus from Rikers, which should have been there hours earlier. And the only other detective working was a lieutenant, and the squad leader at that, so she couldn't just lay it off on him while she ran out the door in a scorching dress and six-inch heels. On top of that, her hair looked like it belonged on a troll pencil topper.

Even worse, she had lost track of time. It was 8:12 P.M. by the time she called Rook, saying she was dreadfully sorry, but she couldn't make it.

"It's fine," he said calmly. "We'll just reschedule."

But she could only imagine what he was feeling inside. For one hour and twelve minutes, Jameson Rook had sat in that swank restaurant by himself, across from a table setting that made it abundantly clear he expected company, getting surreptitiously eyeballed by a high-society crowd that was whispering behind its hands about how the two-time Pulitzer Prize–winner was being stood up.

He had every reason to be furious with her. She was furious with herself.

And yet, as she walked out of the precinct forty-five minutes later, thinking she'd go home to ramen noodles and an answering machine message from her new boyfriend saying he was thinking about seeing other people, there was Rook. He was wearing his best suit, though he was so soaked from the waist down—a twenty-five-block walk through a driving rainstorm will do that, no matter how good your umbrella is—that the pants appeared to be twelve shades darker than the jacket.

He was carrying two Styrofoam containers, marking the first time that Joie de Vivre had ever agreed to do takeout. He had stopped off at a drugstore to buy the only two candles they had left. One claimed to be kiwi scented. The other supposedly smelled of maple syrup.

"I was thinking we could reschedule for right now," he said. "Do you think the bull pen has a table for two?"

"But Rook, I ruined our romantic evening," Heat said.

"Nonsense," Rook said as the water continued dripping from his pants into his shoes. "Every time I'm with you, it's the most romantic thing that's ever happened to me."

That was Rook then. And she knew—even though they had never discussed that evening again in all the years since—it was still Rook now. If he held grudges at all, he got over them in the blink of an eye. He loved her. Unconditionally.

And she loved him. Unconditionally. So why was she pushing him away? Why couldn't she do both: be a wife *and* a daughter?

She threw her bag down on the bed, then emptied her pockets. She grimaced when she pulled out the gift card for Captain Tyler's Airborne Escapades. The Island-Hopping Special. It was such a classic Rook move. He was always finding ways to keep things fresh.

And she was always finding ways to screw things up. With that thought, she went for the minibar, which was well stocked with small bottles. Each one contained a full shot. But they felt so small and inconsequential she had tossed back three of them before the alcohol from the first one even had time to seep into her bloodstream.

She drank because of her mother. She drank because of Rook. She drank because of all she had lost and all she seemed to be losing.

SIXTEEN

STORM

Back in the ancient boxy Buick, the Storm boys pointed south, away from the lights of Crystal City and Washington, DC, toward the promise of anonymity.

Derrick drove. If there did happen to be anyone to outrun or evade, it made sense they might want to be able to exceed fifty-seven miles an hour. The Buick was, as Derrick soon proved, capable of more.

But there didn't seem to be any tail, or anyone who cared that sometimes a Buick was going ninety in the far left lane, and then sometimes it was lagging back at fifty in the far right.

They were clean. For now.

"So what's our plan?" Carl asked.

"To run. To hide. Then to regroup," Derrick answered.

"I have to tell you, in my line of work, I was always the hunter, not the hunted."

"Unfortunately, I've had experience with both. Welcome to the lower reaches of the food chain. Sometimes it helps just to accept it as fact."

"I don't accept—"

"Dad, seriously. We've got a major criminal syndicate after us, and they're being tipped off by a top secret division of the CIA. We're a little bit outgunned at the moment."

They were passing near the Potomac Mills mall. In the glow cast by the massive overhead lights, Derrick could see his father's jaw working.

"Okay, so if I accept your premise that we're in duck-and-cover mode, what are the rules of engagement?" Carl asked.

"For tonight? We don't engage at all. We find a place where we can hunker down. But we have to do it in a way that keeps us completely off the grid. Jones will be looking for us, and he has eyes everywhere. You've already destroyed my phone, so that's a good start. But we also have to avoid using credit cards, ATM machines, anything that would leave electronic bread crumbs for Jones to follow. How much cash do you have on you?"

Carl took his wallet out of his back pocket and eyed its contents. "Eighty-four dollars," he said. "How about you?"

"You don't want to ask."

"Oh, fer Chrissakes . . ."

"Sorry, Dad. I stopped using cash a while ago. I'm in and out of so many countries it doesn't even make sense to try to keep up. Even small villages in Mongolia take plastic now."

Carl grumbled about that development, recasting an argument first made by recalcitrant ancient Mesopotamians who were resisting the move to the shekel as a unit of currency, replacing the use of livestock.

"Look, Dad, I know things are a little bleak right now, but . . ."

There was a pause. Then it became pregnant. Then it had babies.

"But what?" Carl finally asked.

"Actually, I'm not sure," Derrick said. "I was going for the big pep talk and I realized I didn't actually have any material for it."

"Oh, great. That's really confidence-inspiring. I'm moved.

Churchill. Patton. None of them could have said it better."

"Well, okay, okay, no need to get snarky, here. We just have to think about this rationally. Jones is the ultimate pragmatist. There's no way he and the Shanghai Seven are cooperating based on some alignment of long-term goals. They're temporary bedmates, based on a mutual exchange of needed goods or services. But maybe we can change that arrangement somehow. We know what Jones is giving the Shanghai Seven: information about our whereabouts. The question is, what is the Shanghai Seven giving him in return?"

"Money?" Carl asked.

"Unlikely. Jones already has all the money he needs. Besides, money isn't Jones's god. Power is. They must be giving him some kind of advantage over someone, some kind of perceived influence, I don't know."

"All right. How are we going to figure out what it is?"

"Not a clue."

"Wonderful. Again, if this spy thing doesn't work out for you, you have a great future as a motivational speaker."

"If you want someone to sing 'Tomorrow' from *Annie*, you're in the wrong car," Derrick spat. Then he adopted a more conciliatory tone. "Look, let's just try to get a hot meal and a good night's sleep."

They were at the exit that led to Quantico, the Marine base. Derrick put on his turn signal and was soon cruising down a row of fast-food restaurants and low-end chain motels. When he got to one that wasn't a chain, he pulled in.

The man at the front desk informed them he had one room left for fifty-four dollars a night, plus tax. The man absolutely insisted he needed a photo ID and to swipe a credit card for incidentals, until Derrick kicked in an extra twenty. Then that insistence faded.

One falsified registration form later, Mort S. Dricker Jr. and his father, Mort Sr., were officially registered at the Oorah Hotel.

With lodging taken care of, they went across the street to a convenience store. Their remaining $7.30 covered two cans of Hormel hot chili, which had an added nostalgia bonus, having been a staple of Derrick's childhood—it was one of the few things his father knew how to cook. The store clerk kicked in two plastic forks and two paper plates, free of charge.

Then they made their way to room 216, which was on the ground floor, around the corner from the front desk. Carl parked the Buick just outside, backing it into the space as if they had a trunk full of bags to unpack.

In reality, they didn't even have a toothbrush between them, much less the toothpaste to put on it. Much less the money to afford such luxuries.

Derrick tried not to think about that as he inserted the key card in the flimsy door. It led to a dimly lit interior, with heavy curtains that appeared to date to a time when the Marines who checked in were worried about what they were going to face when they shipped off to Korea.

The air smelled stale. There were stains of dubious origin on the walls, cigarette burns on the threadbare carpet—even though the room was labeled nonsmoking—and a certain overly lived-in feeling about the beds. Neither of the Storms wanted to think about the frantic sexual energy that had been expended during too-short twenty-four-hour leaves in this space.

Immediately facing them as they entered the room was an ancient dorm-sized refrigerator with a big boxy microwave— possibly the newest item in the room, sheets included—set on top. Up against the wall, the dresser held an item that was sure to be a curiosity to any of the young recruits who used the room: a non-flat-screen television.

In the corner by the window, there was a small round table with a noticeable slant to it, and two wooden chairs. In the other corner, there was a shelf at head height, underneath which was a rod with four bare metal hangers on it. On the floor, beneath the hangers, the maid had left a small plastic caddy with generic cleaning supplies.

That was probably the best news of all. It suggested someone had actually once cleaned the place.

"Home sweet home," Derrick said, closing the door behind them.

"You spies really lead a glamorous life."

"James Bond never had it so good."

"They must have skipped those scenes in the movies," Carl said.

Derrick pulled the cans of chili out of the plastic bag and began waving them vigorously back and forth.

"What are you doing?" Carl asked.

"I like my Hormel hot chili shaken, not stirred."

Derrick doubled-up the paper plates, the better to prevent leaking, then dumped the contents of both cans on top. He gave that delightful culinary creation a few minutes of nuking in the microwave, then pulled it out, using a bath towel as a hot pad.

"Bon appétit," he said, placing it in the middle of the round table.

"So this is a hot meal and a good night's sleep?" Carl said.

"It could be worse," Derrick said.

"How?"

"If the chili didn't have pop-tops. At this point, I don't think we could afford a can opener."

Derrick was already digging in with his plastic fork. Carl soon followed. In truth, it tasted pretty good. Everything does when you're starving—and when you're reasonably certain it might be your last meal for some time.

With no conversation, they attacked the pile of chili until it had diminished to about a quarter of its original size. Then their gustation was interrupted by a knock at the door.

"Pizza delivery for you, Mr. Dricker," a man said. It was the man from the front desk. Except his voice was suddenly an octave higher than it had been.

The Storms exchanged a glance. They hadn't ordered pizza.

They didn't need to say this to each other. Nor did they need to look outside to know the front desk man was nervously holding an empty pizza box while someone else held a gun to his head.

Derrick was already on his feet, already studying the room, what possibilities it offered, and how they might escape from this trap.

Except there was no escape. The room didn't have any side doors, nor did it have a back window. The front door was the only way out.

Having made that determination, he began cataloguing the contents of the room, looking for anything he might be able to use to his advantage.

The knock came again. "Mr. Dricker," the man said. "Pizza for you."

"I think you have the wrong room," Derrick said, to stall for time.

"It comes free with a one-night stay, sir. Compliments of the Oorah."

Carl Storm was standing now, too. He formed his fingers into the shape of a gun, then pointed the imaginary barrel at the door and pantomimed a shooting motion, complete with kickback.

Derrick shook his head. There was no point in wasting an innocent hotel clerk. Especially when all it would do was alert the thugs on the other side that they did not have the element of surprise on their hands, and so they might as well enter with guns blazing.

Besides, he already had a plan.

"Okay, terrific," Derrick said to the man. "I'm just getting out of the shower. Give me a second to get some clothes on."

Derrick shooed his father out the way. "Pull the mattresses up on the far side of the room and get behind one of them," Derrick whispered.

Then he began putting his plan into place. He grabbed the microwave and quickly transferred it over to the round table in front of the window, which was to the left of the door as he faced out. He pointed the back of the microwave toward the interior of the room. Then he tilted over the refrigerator, ripped out the Freon tube, and stuffed it inside the microwave.

Freon, by itself, is an inert gas. That's one of the reasons it's used as a refrigerant. However, even an inert gas, when put under enough pressure—and then heated to the point where it bursts—can turn into a weapon.

But Derrick wasn't done. He added the two empty cans of chili, two of the four hangers, which he bent to make fit, and all of the cleaning supplies he could stuff inside.

He set the microwave for ten minutes then ran to the back of the room, where his father was already crouched behind one mattress. The other mattress was for Derrick. He hid behind it, stuffed his fingers in his ears, and closed his eyes.

In truth, he had no idea what he had just created. Perhaps it was a powerful improvised explosive device. Perhaps it was just a mess that would spark and fizzle until it shorted the microwave.

It wouldn't take long to find out.

The metal inside caught fire within a few seconds. A few seconds after that, the plastic of the cleaning supply bottles began melting. From there, it was hard to say what exactly occurred. Was it the cleaning supplies igniting, causing the Freon tube to burst? Or was it the detonation of the Freon tube that addled the chemicals?

Whatever the case, the resulting explosion was more terrific than anything Derrick could have hoped for. And the outer covering of the microwave gave the blast a shape, propelling most of that energy outward.

The window shattered, sending a hail of glass and shrapnel toward the parking lot. Derrick's hope was that anyone in its vicinity would have been knocked flat—or at least stunned.

Which was what gave the Storm boys their only chance.

"Go, go," Derrick whispered fiercely, pulling out Dirty Harry as he went for the door. Carl was right behind him, moving at a speed that was distinctly preretirement.

Derrick didn't bother looking to his left, trusting on the explosion to clear out that side. As soon as he crossed the threshold, Derrick turned to his right, ready to put Dirty Harry to deadly use.

The first thing he saw was the hotel clerk. The poor man was lying on the concrete walkway, moaning. He had brought his arms up to his face, one side of which was a mess of raw meat.

Beyond him was the man who, Derrick guessed, had been holding the clerk at gunpoint. He had taken the explosion face-on and had been thrown on his back. He wasn't moving.

There were two other men who appeared to have been loitering a little farther back. They were also shielding their faces with their arms, like they were expecting another blast.

One was crouched into a small ball. Derrick deemed that

man to be effectively ineffective for at least as long as it would take the Storms to reach the safety of the Buick.

But the other man, while still flinching, seemed to be coming out of his shell-shocked stupor a little faster. He was already raising the rifle that had been at his side and was perhaps a second or two away from being able to start firing.

Derrick would have moved on from his field of fire by that point. But his dad would be square in the crosshairs.

Still moving, not daring to stop and aim, Derrick pulled Dirty Harry's trigger twice in rapid succession. The first bullet hit just south of the man's collarbone and spun him. The next buried in his side.

It was unclear whether either shot was fatal. It would depend on which way the bullets tumbled inside the body and how skilled the trauma surgeons were. But the wounds were, at the very least, incapacitating for the time being.

Derrick was in the Buick's driver's seat by the time the man fell. That the vehicle was pointed outward—with Carl having backed the car into its spot—was looking like genius forethought. As Derrick twisted the ignition key, Carl piled into the seat next to him.

"Hit the gas," Carl said. "And duck."

Derrick followed both instructions, steering half blind into the parking lot, aiming for what he judged to be the open space at the exit. Gunshots sounded out. The man who had been crouching and shielding himself had obviously found his gumption and was now up and firing.

And not inaccurately. One bullet slammed into the vicinity of the trunk. Another buried itself in one of the taillights, putting it out of commission. Then the back window of the Buick shattered when a third bullet found it.

But by then, Storm was already back out on the main drag, putting distance between them and the gunman with every pump of the roaring engine's pistons. There were two more shots, both misses, and then the guy stopped bothering.

Derrick merged onto Interstate 95, pointed northbound, if only because that was the first entrance ramp that presented itself. He accelerated but didn't bother going any more than the speed of the other traffic.

They were out of danger.

For the moment.

But how long until it caught up to them again?

Derrick tried to sort out what he had seen. There were three attackers, not counting the poor front desk guy. Those had been the three survivors from the assault on Carl's place in Fairfax before. They hadn't had time to recruit reinforcements.

Yet. But that was clearly coming.

And if they didn't find a better hiding spot, there were only going to be so many daring escapes they could muster before the odds caught up to them.

"Okay, so how *the hell* did they find us?" Carl asked. "We used cash. We don't have phones on us. We were in the very definition of a no-tell motel with a clerk we had bought off. What happened?"

"My guess? Satellites," Derrick said.

"What about them?"

"Let's start with the assumption Jones knew we were at Bryan's place."

"But you went in through the roof, and my Lame Depot hat was a foolproof disguise. How would he know?"

"Because Jones knows everything. One way or another, he just does. He didn't want to tip off the Shanghai Seven when we were at Bryan's place, because he didn't want to endanger one of his agents. But as soon as we were on the move, he had eyes in the sky. That's why we didn't have a tail coming out of Bryan's place. Jones knew it was a lot easier to have one of the nerds track us in real time from high up in the geosynchronous orbit. He waited until we had bunked in for the night, then told his Shanghai Seven friends where to find us."

"Well, if that's the case, then aren't we screwed? There's nowhere we can hide."

"Oh, Jones can't see everything. He doesn't have regular access to geothermal satellites. Only the military has that, and I'm willing to bet Jones doesn't want to burn through a favor with the Pentagon just to help out the Shanghai Seven."

"So where do we hide?"

"In the trees," Derrick said, already slowing for the next exit.

It was labeled with signs for Prince William Forest Park.

"First things first, though. We have to let Nikki Heat know what's going on down here. She's as much a threat to the Shanghai Seven as we are. She has to know Jones might be using his resources against her."

"Great. But how are we going to tell her? We can't even use a phone."

"We can't use *my* phone," Derrick said. "That doesn't mean we can't use *a* phone."

Having turned off the highway, Derrick was soon pulling into an Exxon with an accompanying convenience store, one of the large modern ones that had a little bit of everything. Before long, he had convinced a fellow customer that a lightly used Arc'teryx AR-395a climbing harness would go for at least a hundred bucks on eBay, and that made it worth at least forty bucks in the parking lot of an Exxon.

And forty bucks was enough to buy a refurbished burner phone and a card with enough minutes to suit his purpose. Before long, he had banged out a text to Heat's cell phone number.

Then Derrick Storm and his father disappeared into the deep recesses of the Prince William Forest Park.

SEVENTEEN

HEAT

At the speed of light, the text had traveled to a cell tower, then to a server, which then located Nikki Heat's phone as being near another cell tower, which then sent out the message. The whole transaction, from transmission to receipt, took less than a second.

The processing of it, by a woman who was already four bottles into the minibar—and contemplating a fifth—was quite a bit slower. The words blurred on the screen in front of Nikki Heat's eyes before coming into focus.

NIKKI: IT'S DERRICK ON A BURNER PHONE, it read. I AM COMPLETELY COMPROMISED. WE ARE ON THE RUN. MY PEOPLE ARE INFORMING THE S7 OF MY EVERY MOVE. THEY MIGHT BE DOING THE SAME TO YOU. WATCH YOUR BACK.

At that moment, Heat's back was firmly planted in the only chair in that tiny Manhattan hotel room. The shades were drawn. No one knew where she was. No one was going to be bothering her.

She let out a long exhale, telling herself she was as safe as could be.

And then, just as the last oxygen molecules exited her lungs, there was a knock at the door that made her anxiety spike.

"Room service," said a voice.

She hadn't ordered room service.

It was like Storm's text had not been a warning, but rather a prophecy. Had Storm's "people" found her that quickly? Was the Shanghai Seven on the other side of the door?

Or was this Callan again? Since he seemed to be acting as Shanghai Seven muscle, was he now doing this errand for them as well?

Heat pulled out her 9mm and tried to begin a correspondence with a more sober part of her brain. She cursed herself for diving into the minibar with such ferocity. Just when she needed her wits about her, just when she needed everything to be totally sharp, she felt like she was moving through peanut butter.

On her way to the door, she stumbled against the bed, which seemed to have grown by several feet since she had last walked around it. She fell into the wall, barely able to maintain enough agility to brace herself with her free hand.

The knock came again.

"Room service."

Yeah, right. Couldn't you people at least come up with something more creative? Say it was free pizza or something?

She was breathing more heavily than a short walk across the room ought to have required. She reached the door and paused, trying to gather herself. Was there any way she could wrest some advantage from this situation?

Peering through the peephole, she saw what appeared to be a hotel waiter, dressed in a black vest and matching bow tie, with a long-sleeve white shirt underneath. With one hand, he was holding aloft a large platter with three covered plates on it. The other hand was tucked behind his back, in the manner that a courteous waiter might.

Or a guy hiding a Glock.

Heat thought about shooting first and asking questions later, either by cracking the door open or just firing straight through it. That Glock, or whatever he was packing, wouldn't matter if she could put him down before he could get a shot off.

Except, even in her inebriated state, she still remembered her training, which was buried in a place deep enough the booze couldn't touch it. Lethal force was only justified when an assailant posed a threat of serious physical harm. She had not yet seen a weapon and did not have definitive proof he was there to kill her.

She thought of Michael Brown. She thought of Eric Garner. She thought of all the cops who, when faced with that split-second judgment, had chosen poorly, ruining so many lives in the process. Nikki Heat didn't want to find herself trending on Twitter for all the wrong reasons.

At the same time, she couldn't let this goon get the drop on her. She took in a deep breath, let it go, then counted in her head.

When she reached three, she threw open the door, planted her left leg firmly, then aimed her right foot at the underside of the guy's chin. Heat was trained in Brazilian jujitsu. She had delivered this kind of kick at imagined or simulated targets several times a week for years. Drunk or not, muscle memory took over.

Her shoe connected with a solid, meaty sound. Had the blow been slightly to one side or another, it probably would have dislocated the man's jaw. Being that it was straight on, all that force transferred into a jarring, concussive blow to his brain. Both the waiter and the tray he had been holding jerked backward, separated from each other as sure as the man was now separated from consciousness.

Nikki already had her gun up and had it steadied on the man's midsection all the same. If there was a next move, she didn't want it to catch her off guard. She was ready for the gun to come out, for this encounter to turn deadly. Then she would have the justification to bury this punk.

But wait. Why were there potatoes au gratin flying in the air? And why was she watching a rib eye bouncing against the far wall? And were those snow peas, lightly sautéed in a balsamic soy sauce and garnished with almond slivers?

"Well, so much for you being a meat and potatoes girl," she heard a very familiar voice say.

She turned and faced her next opponent.

It was Jameson Rook, dressed in a tuxedo accented with a rose boutonniere.

"Next time," he continued, "you can just tell me you prefer the fish."

It took a while for the waiter to return to consciousness and then be mollified by a sincere apology, an ice pack, and the largest tip in room service history.

But after that was taken care of—and the au gratin slime was washed off the walls and carpet—Heat and Rook had retreated back into her room.

"It appears I have interrupted a looming tragedy," Rook said, surveying the quartet of small bottles on the desk. "Surely you realize there are quicker and less painful ways to go than death by minibar?"

Heat, who was feeling sufficiently more sober—thanks to the adrenaline chaser she got when the waiter knocked on the door—swept the bottles off the top of the desk and into the trash.

"How did you find me?" she asked.

"I'm afraid I can't tell you without revealing closely guarded, top secret, proprietary information, and neither subpoena nor threat of imprisonment will force me to do so. I daresay, not even the future director of the Department of

Homeland Security could get me to confess."

Heat fixed him with one of her classic "I'm done playing now" looks. It had distinct "I'm going to kick your ass now" overtones.

"You have the Find My iPhone app installed," Rook said hastily. "Remember? When we lost it in the couch cushions after that time we . . . well, you know."

She nodded. She remembered, of course. It just seemed like another century, when she had been a different person.

He closed in, grabbed her hands, and looked deep into her eyes: "My plan was that we would talk over dinner. But now that you seemed to have dispatched with that, we *could* skip right to dessert, if you like."

Heat was still in such a confused mental state, she offered no response. Rook, whose focus was suddenly quite singular, thought for sure that meant he had sealed the deal.

But as he narrowed the gap between them to plant the kiss that would be the first act of mind-blowing makeup sex, Heat turned away. Rook's lips ended up colliding with her ear. And not the soft, sensuous, fleshy lobe underneath. The hard cartilaginous top part.

"Oh," he said, after his mouth bounced off the side of her head. "Ouch."

Still, Rook was not deterred. He had lured Heat out of bad moods with his playful man-child charm many times. And, with his typical confidence, he seemed sure he could do it again.

"Sorry. It's the lights, isn't it? Too much light," he said, walking over toward the switch. "Rookie mistake. But do you mind if I leave on the one in the bathroom? You know I like to be able to watch you—"

"Rook. Stop," she managed.

This was no mere mood. And after so many years of being in

love with her, Rook didn't need a secret decoder ring to be able to read it.

"Hey," he said, recrossing the room, trying to take her hands. She wouldn't let him. She was looking away.

"Hey," he tried again. "It's me. Come on. What's going on?"

"Rook, just go," she said.

"No. Sorry, Captain Heat. I'll do anything you want. Except that. I've been thinking about it all day, and I shouldn't have left your office this morning. You're not getting rid of me that easily tonight."

"It's too dangerous for you to stay."

"I don't care."

"I do."

"And I appreciate that. But, look, do you know what's more important to me in this world than you?"

She looked at him expectantly. He waited. It was, for Rook—a man not long on patience—a considerable wait.

"Nothing," he said finally. "Nothing is more important. I would have thought you knew that by now, but maybe I need to say it again. Look, living without you, it's not even living. So if the choice is safety or you, I'll take you every time. I decided that a long, long time ago. I haven't regretted it for one second since then, and even if staying with you meant this was my last night alive, I still wouldn't regret it."

His eyes were wide and his gaze was so penetrating, she felt like he could see her soul. It was so intense, she had to look away.

"Do you know when I knew that?" he said. She wasn't answering, so he continued: "Well, probably the first second I ever saw you. But that makes me seem shallow, so I'll give you another time. I don't know if you remember it, but we had just started dating. We had a special night out for our one-month anniversary and—"

"Joie de Vivre," she said.

"Yes. We had a reservation—"

"For seven o'clock."

"Right. And I was sitting at the bar, waiting for you. Seven. Seven-oh-five. Seven-fifteen. The maître d' kept wanting to give away the table, but I told him the most incredible woman in the world was going to be coming through the door any moment. Eventually he said he had to either seat me or let it go, so I sat there, by myself, for an hour. I could see everyone in the restaurant looking at me while trying to pretend they weren't looking at me. There was even an item in the gossip column of the *Ledger* the next day about Jameson Rook being stood up.

"And there was a point where I can remember thinking, 'Why am I not mad right now? I should be mad. Look at me, I'm Jameson Rook. I've made all those ridiculous Most Eligible Bachelor lists. There are thousands of women who would love to be at this table right now. I should call one of them and have a great time. Why am I waiting for this chick?' And that's when I realized I was going to do whatever it took to be with you. Then. And always."

"Even walking twenty-six blocks in the rain with a takeout bag and two stinky candles?" Heat said. She was facing him now.

"I can never smell the unforgettable combination of kiwi and maple syrup without becoming instantly aroused," he said in a low growl.

And there. That did it. Much to her astonishment, Heat actually smiled.

"There's my Nikki," he said softly. "I knew she was in there."

The smile got just a little wider. The way Rook was looking at her—with total love—she just couldn't help it.

"So, really, what's going on?" he asked. "I'm not going away, so you might as well tell me and then let me help."

She recounted all that had happened over the last day, ever since she had left him alone in his Tribeca loft. When she finished, she expected him to come up with one of his usual wacky theories—about how the Shanghai Seven were really aliens there to provoke a war among humans by creating a massive trade imbalance, or something similarly absurd. Instead, the first sentence out of his mouth was remarkably cogent:

"George is the key," he said. "He knows where those bills are. And he wants to tell you. I know he wants to tell you. I'll bet you anything he had a crush on your mother, so he wants to see her again, too. He just needs a little more . . . inducement."

"What kind of 'inducement' did you have in mind?"

"I was just going to talk to him."

"I already tried that. What makes you think you'll have any more success?"

"Well, I wasn't going to mention this, lest I seem immodest, but he *is* a fan."

Of course George was a fan of Jameson Rook. George and the rest of the literate world.

"I'm willing to bet he'll come around," Rook said. "In fact, he might even come around if we don't talk to him. George is the kind of guy who needs some time to absorb things. But once he does, he'll see turning over those bills is the best thing for everyone."

"Do you want to go over there now? I don't think his shift ends until midnight."

"No, no. It's only been a few hours since you talked to him. Give it a little more time. It'll be more effective tomorrow."

Heat knew Rook's insights into these sorts of things were often uncannily accurate. "Okay," she said. "If you think so."

"I do. Now promise me you won't get impatient and run off in the middle of the night."

"I would never do that."

"Yes, you would."

She thought about it for a moment. "That's true. But in this case I'm not going to. Because I have a big problem."

"Oh?"

She was again smiling coquettishly. "Yes. It's just you and me, alone in this small hotel room with this large bed," she said. "Whatever will we do to fill the time?"

"Well," Rook said. "Since I am in such mortal danger, and since this might well be my last night alive . . ."

Rook's hands found her ass. Heat felt a flush coming to her face. "Yes?"

He went to kiss her ear. And this time, he managed to get the soft, fleshy part gently between his teeth. "You wouldn't deny a dying man his last request, would you?"

She would not.

Nor did he deny hers.

Multiple times.

EIGHTEEN

STORM

At sixteen thousand acres, the Prince William Forest Park was the largest protected natural area in the Washington, DC metropolitan area.

From high in the air, which would have been Jones's vantage point of it, it was the first significant chunk of solid greenery as you headed south from the nation's capital.

Except not now. Now it was just gray. A cool fog had rolled in, blanketing the Potomac River valley in a fine mist. Between that and the trees, Derrick Storm was sure he had confounded Jones's satellites. Even geothermal couldn't penetrate that kind of soup.

Derrick could imagine the rueful, dour countenances the nerds wore as they told Jones they had lost their quarry; he could see Jones, always unflappable, tugging at his collar, which was about as demonstrative as he ever got. He could practically hear them admitting defeat.

That thought warmed Derrick. Little else about their surroundings did. The broken back window of the Buick allowed the damp, chilly night air to pour in. They had turned off the engine to save what little gas they had left. The $9.57 Derrick now had in his pocket wouldn't get them very far once they needed more.

Having gone as deep into the forest as they could, they had

finally pulled off the main road. They were sitting in the middle of a narrow dirt service road used by the park rangers and perhaps the occasional hiker who was looking for a shortcut back to asphalt. They didn't know where the road led, or how it ended—or if it ended at all. But it was, they deemed, a safe spot to ride out the night—or at least as safe as they could get under the circumstances.

Carl Storm had moved to the backseat, where he was lying uncomfortably on his side. Much like Carl himself, the cushioning under the Buick's cloth seats had grown stiff with age.

His son was in the passenger seat, which he had reclined as far as it would go. He crossed his arms inside his T-shirt, which made him a little warmer. But only by so much.

Neither bothered complaining. And even though they had their eyes shut, neither was sleeping, either. Their ears were tuned to the sounds of the forest, which was—save for the occasional hooting of an owl bragging to his girlfriend that he had caught dinner—silent.

It was for this reason they were able to hear the hum of an engine in the distance. Derrick was the first to sit up and turn toward the sound. His movement made Carl do the same.

The vehicle was still a ways off. But it sounded like it was getting closer.

"Okay, I am *sure* I didn't order pizza this time," Carl said. "You?"

"Definitely not," Derrick said, already shifting to the front seat.

He started the Buick, wishing it were quieter, hoping the fog and the sound of the other engine would dampen their noise. He kept the lights off as he began rolling forward over the rugged road.

"Okay, how did they find us this time?" Carl asked, now turning and looking out the glassless back window.

"They didn't," Derrick said. "It's not them. It can't be. There's no way they could get eyes on us in this pea soup."

"Just like there was no way they could find us at the no-tell motel," Carl said.

"It could be a park ranger."

"Out for a little jaunt in the middle of the night?"

"Well, then it's kids looking for a place to do whatever it is kids like to do in the forest after dark."

"I've got an idea," Carl said. "Let's play a game where we pretend it's them until we know otherwise."

"Good game. What are the rules?"

"Rule one: Get us the hell out of here. I'll come up with the rest of the rules after that."

"Good rule," Derrick said. "Let me see if I can play along."

Derrick squinted into the fog and darkness as he brought the Buick up to perhaps twenty-five miles per hour, which was as fast as he dared go. There was almost no ambient light. He was relying on his eyes being well adjusted to the gloom. Now and then, he'd feel one side of the Buick or the other scraping against underbrush. That was his sign to tug the steering wheel in the opposite direction, to keep them from going off the road. The ruts helped, too.

The Buick's ancient suspension groaned as it lurched over bumps and through potholes. The other vehicle's engine was definitely coming closer. Derrick guessed it was going perhaps forty or forty-five. It sounded more like a truck. Not diesel—it didn't have that diesel rumble to it—but definitely eight-cylinder.

He pressed down on the accelerator a little more, easing them up to thirty, not daring to go too much faster with the lights off. All it would take was one sudden bend in the road and they'd plow into a pine tree. Then they'd be in even more trouble.

The road continued sloping upward. It wasn't a mountain—there weren't any of those in that part of Virginia—but more like a small hill.

Then they reached the top. Derrick had the sense they had entered a clearing roughly the length and width of a football field. There were no longer trees looming overhead. Just mist.

They passed an area with picnic benches and a fire pit just off to their left.

"You gonna turn the lights on so we can see where we're going?" Carl asked.

"No. Shhh," said Derrick, who had been using a kind of echolocation to find his way, counting on the sound waves bouncing back him to tell him if he was about to hit something.

"Look, these guys are getting closer. Are you really going to let them get on top of us? Why don't you just turn the lights on and floor it?"

"Because I don't even know where this road goes. I think we might have reached the end. Now shhh and let me concen—"

Then he slammed on the brakes. A log cabin, complete with notched corner joints and rough-hewn windows, had jumped out at them from the darkness. The Buick stopped inches short of one of the logs, which was even more solid than that steel 1985 bumper.

Derrick put the car in reverse and eased away from the cabin, just so he could drive around to the other side of it. Then he shut off the Buick's engine.

"Okay," Derrick said. "This is where we make our stand."

"In a log cabin," Carl said. "Definitely old school. I like it."

The Storm boys quickly scrambled out. The back door to the cabin had a padlock across it, but it was really only a deterrent to the most law-abiding of trespassers. The lock was attached to a flimsy metal hasp. Gripping Dirty Harry firmly, Derrick had it loosened after just two ferocious downward chops. Then, using the gun like a crowbar, he pried it off.

They entered the cabin, which had a plastic folding table inside the main living area, a small kitchen off to the left, and a loft up top. Derrick scrambled up the ladder to the loft, and using Dirty Harry like a hammer, he bashed one pane of glass away from the window so he'd have a clean shot should he decide to take one.

He had just cleared away the last glass shards when the headlights from their pursuers burst into the clearing, cutting through the fog. The lights were higher than a standard sedan. It was an SUV, and not one issued by the National Park Service. It was dark. The windows were tinted.

A black SUV. The vehicle of choice of discerning bad guys everywhere.

Now that the clearing was better illuminated, Derrick could see that it was, in fact, the end of the road. The driver could clearly see that, too, because the SUV was coming to a halt, roughly two hundred feet short of the cabin, near the fire pit.

Carl had joined Derrick up in the loft.

"All right, so what do we got here?" he asked his son in a hushed voice. He was breathing a bit more heavily from the climb up the ladder than Derrick was.

"Not hikers, that's for sure," Derrick whispered back.

"Yeah, but are they hostile?"

"I don't know."

The SUV was just sitting there, idling. The driver had shifted into park. Derrick could make out the dim blue glow of an electronic device—a laptop? an iPad? something of that nature—being used inside.

In that low light, and from that distance in the fog, Derrick couldn't say whether he was seeing one of the Shanghai Seven's men or a group of kids who liked geocaching at night. He hadn't exactly had time to imprint the faces of any of the men who had been chasing him before he shot at them.

The blue glow vanished just as the backup lights of the SUV flickered briefly, the driver putting the car back in drive. Then, ominously, the SUV began making a slow counterclockwise circle around the edge of the clearing, maintaining a distance of several hundred feet from the cabin.

"Yeah, I'm thinking they're hostile," Carl said.

"And pretty soon they're going to know we're in here," Derrick said. "They'll see the Buick parked behind the house."

Derrick followed the progress of the SUV as it rolled around the outskirts of the clearing.

"You gonna use that shiny gun of yours, or is it just there for show?" Carl asked.

"Harry only has six rounds, and I've already used two of them. I'm waiting until I actually have something to shoot at."

The men in the SUV were not going to be quite as sparing with their ammunition. When they reached roughly six o'clock in their circumnavigation of the clearing, the passenger side window lowered. The barrel of a rifle emerged, and suddenly the rapid muzzle flashes of an automatic weapon were filling the night.

Both Storms hid behind the thick wooden walls of the cabin. But it soon became clear the shooter's target wasn't human. It was vehicular. Carl Storm's 1985 Buick was under assault like nothing it had ever been designed to sustain, and it was quickly debilitated. Its tires were shredded. The windows were reduced to pebbles of glass on the ground. The doors on the driver's side, which were exposed to the fire, soon became riddled with bullet holes.

Derrick thought about aiming a potshot in the direction of the window. But he knew it would likely be a waste of precious ammo. The .44 Magnum Stealth Hunter is a terrific short-range weapon. At that distance, and without a scope, he'd just be guessing.

Besides, he didn't want to give away their position. Not until he needed to. He was fairly certain he'd be facing two assailants—the only two left alive from the original five after the first two encounters. He wanted to be able to take one out before the other knew where the Storms were hiding.

The thug emptied an entire thirty-round magazine into the car, stopped to reload, then did it again, filling the air with a fiery racket and battering the Buick to where it was unsalvageable. Carl's face was stricken the entire time. A car that had been faithful to him for the last thirty-two years of his life had been decimated in about thirty-two seconds.

Finally, there was silence.

"Bastards," Carl whispered. "I was just about to flip the odometer for the fifth time. I was going to celebrate with new floor mats."

"This is war now," Derrick said.

The SUV got back under way until it completed its journey around the clearing, then came to a stop roughly in the same spot it had the last time, with its front grill toward the cabin.

Then there came a shout.

"Derrick Storm," a man's voice said.

Derrick didn't reply.

"Storm, we know you're in there. We just want the CD."

Carl looked at his son curiously.

"I confiscated a CD from a Shanghai Seven counterfeiting operation last week," Derrick whispered.

"What's on it?" Carl asked.

"Not sure. I couldn't crack the encryption."

"Must be something important if they've sent five guys after you to get it."

"Must be."

From outside, the voice continued: "Come on, Storm. We've got all the ammo we need. And we've got some other surprises for you, too. You won't stand a chance in that cabin. We'll kill you for it if we have to. Or you can just turn it over. What's it going to be, Storm? Is that CD worth dying for?"

Thugs who wanted to negotiate. The world really was becoming more civilized. What was this "other surprise," anyway?

But forget it. Derrick wasn't giving up the CD, especially now that he knew how valuable it was. Just let the thugs try to come after him. He had the advantage of the high ground in the cabin's loft. And the logs would protect them from machine-gun fire. They were untouchable in there.

"Storm, I know you can hear me," the man said. "What's it going to be? You want to turn over the CD or die trying to keep it?"

Replying would only give the thugs an idea of where to aim their guns, so Derrick stayed quiet.

Then he heard the back hatch of the SUV open. He couldn't really see what was happening until a bright flash emanated from behind the SUV. It traced a high arc toward them, and Derrick looked at it with a kind of detached interest until it finally occurred to him: *An RPG. These goons actually have an RPG.*

Carl had just reached the same conclusion, because he shouted "grenade" just as it bounced off the roof and landed beside the cabin.

The Storms huddled down as the explosion went off. The percussion rocked the cabin. So that was the "other surprise" they had promised. The only thing that kept it from doing serious damage was that it was easier for the blast's energy to head into the open air next to the cabin than to tear into the cabin itself.

If they managed to get a grenade through a window . . .

"We got more where that came from, Storm!" the voice, now exultant, hollered. "We'll keep lobbing them at you until you're bleeding out your eyes. Is that how you want to go, Storm? All because you wouldn't hand over a CD?"

For all their bluster, Derrick understood why the thugs wanted him to surrender the CD without a fight. They were down to two men, one of whom was cringing through a face full of shrapnel. They were tired and demoralized. Sifting through the rubble of a cabin, hoping to find a CD that may have been damaged in the melee . . . It wasn't their idea of a nice nightcap.

At the same time, Derrick began reconsidering his own options, which had been substantially altered by his enemy's additional firepower. Running was pointless. Even if the Storms did manage to get away from this particular predicament, it was pretty clear Jones had found a way to track them anywhere they went. It was like he had the whole planet bugged.

But the alternative—staying put—was suicide. If they stayed in the cabin, it would be reduced to toothpicks, one grenade at a time, leaving them ever more concussed and shell-shocked until the cabin fell on top of them. But if they left the cabin and took the battle out in the open, it exposed them to savage machine-gun fire.

It was a bit like choosing between being drowned or being hanged. One death was slow. The other was quick. They both ended in the same place.

"Okay, okay," Storm shouted. "You win. How do you want to do the exchange?"

"There are some picnic tables just to our left," the voice replied.

"We're going to back down the driveway until we're just out of range. You can come out and place the CD on one of the tables. In five minutes, we'll come back and get it. Do we have a deal?"

"Absolutely," Derrick hollered.

Carl looked at him, stunned. "You realize you just signed our death certificates. They're going to start lobbing grenades in here the moment they have the CD. You're really going to just hand it over?"

Derrick grinned. "Absolutely not."

The SUV was soon backing out of the clearing. Derrick set a timer in his head: five minutes. He had five minutes to figure something out.

He only had one gun. Taking down one man with superior weaponry was hard enough. Taking down both—and doing it so quickly the second man couldn't launch a deadly counterattack—was nearly impossible.

But that's exactly what Derrick Storm had made a living out of doing for a long time now.

Five minutes later, the CD, safely ensconced in its clear jewel case, had been set atop the picnic table. Its shiny multihued surface was barely able to find any light to reflect until the mist-filtered headlights of the SUV bounced back into the clearing.

The vehicle crept slowly up the path until it reached the fire pit, then came to a stop.

The passenger side window rolled down.

"Derrick Storm," the passenger yelled. "Have you done as we asked?"

The words sped out to the trees that formed a wall around the edge of the clearing, then bounced back at the man. Derrick didn't reply.

"Derrick Storm," the passenger yelled again.

But again, all the man heard was the faint echo of his own voice.

The passenger swore. "If that sonofabitch tried to run, I swear I'm going to tear off his balls and stuff them down his throat."

He unleashed one more "DERRICK . . . STORM!"

"Stop yelling," the driver said. "The CD is on the table. I can see it from here. I'm just going to grab it and then let's get the hell out of here."

"You sure you don't want to pump a few grenades at them? I bet that sonofabitch is in that cabin right now, lining you up, waiting to put one in your ear as soon as you pop out."

"Yeah, you're probably right," the driver said, subconsciously bringing his hand to his throbbing face. At least his wounds had stopped oozing. "Give him hell. You can tell the bosses we did it for Terence Paul Winter."

The passenger went to the back of the SUV through the seats—less exposure that way. He grabbed the RPG, which still had five grenades loaded in it.

Then he popped the hatchback and scrambled out, using the SUV as a shield from any small arms fire that might come from the cabin, exactly as he had done before. He tilted the RPG at roughly a sixty-degree angle, then pulled the trigger.

A bright line flashed through the night. The grenade landed just short of the cabin, then rolled under the front porch. Three seconds later, the explosion took off the entire front part of the house.

"Ha! Take that, Storm!" the passenger yelled.

He fired off three more grenades in quick succession, tilting his angle a little closer to fifty so that the grenades all landed inside the gaping hole in the cabin created by the first grenade.

By the time the last of the grenades detonated, there was very little left beyond a pile of splintered logs, which were now on fire. Adding to the conflagration, the Buick had also been set ablaze. The last explosion was when the flames reached its fuel tank. No one—not even Derrick Storm—could still be alive inside.

"All right," the passenger said as he climbed back into the front seat. "We don't have to worry about that asshole anymore. Let's get the CD and get out of here."

"You got it," the driver said.

Moving confidently now that the threat had been eliminated, the driver opened the door, swung his legs out, and took six purposeful strides toward the nearby picnic bench, where the CD beckoned him. His right hand held the pistol grip of an AR-15, the weapon that had so thoroughly obliterated the Buick.

His left hand was perhaps a foot away from grabbing the CD when two things happened in rapid succession.

First, from about twenty-five feet away, Carl Storm popped up from the small hollow where he had been hiding in a prone position. He quickly brought Dirty Harry up to shoulder height and pumped two rounds through the open passenger side window of the SUV. The passenger's skull exploded, sending a glob of red against the tan leather seats and a finer red spray for many feet beyond that. The driver's head whipped back toward the SUV. He was bringing up his AR-15, his trigger finger mere moments away from putting down a blanket of fire that would cut Carl in half.

And then the second thing happened. Derrick Storm, his face and hands blackened by charcoal from the fire pit—perfectly camouflaging him against the night—emerged from the other side of the picnic bench like a wraith from the shadows. The driver, whose attention had been refocused toward the gunfire, never saw him coming until Derrick was on top of him, crushing him to the ground with his full weight, plunging the entirety of the three-inch blade into the man's ribs.

The AR-15 flew from the man's hand. He landed on his belly, his face mashed into the ground by Derrick's weight. The gun landed in the grass a few feet from the man's grasp. He began trying to crawl after it, but he could barely move with two hundred thirty pounds of Storm on top of him.

Correction: two hundred thirty pounds of *angry* Storm.

Derrick withdrew the knife then drove it into the man's side, burying it up to the hilt. Then he did it again. And again. The man bellowed, but Derrick was not about to show mercy.

It was Carl, instead, who did that. The elder Storm had run toward the fight and, once he had kicked the AR-15 farther away, took careful aim at the driver's head and pulled the trigger.

The driver's body immediately went slack. Derrick, who had been interrupted mid-stab, paused with the knife at the top of its path. Then he brought it slowly down.

"Thanks," Derrick said. "I didn't know how many swipes it was going to take with this butter knife."

"Yeah, well, it doesn't matter now," Carl said, nodding toward the driver's lifeless form. "He's toast anyway."

They carried the bodies toward the cabin, which by then was burning hot, and tossed them on top, turning it into an impromptu funeral pyre.

There might have been a few pieces of charred bone left by the time the thing burned out. Or there might not. Either way, it wouldn't be enough to identify the remains.

Then, as best they could, they wiped down the interior of the SUV. Derrick didn't kid himself into thinking this would escape the notice of a well-trained Crime Scene Unit with an ultraviolet light. It just had to be good enough to fool a highway patrol officer during a traffic stop.

Upon closer inspection, the SUV—which was now the Storms' only transportation—turned out to be a Ford Expedition, much to Derrick's delight.

Derrick drove. Carl counted the money they had taken out of the dead men's wallets. It totaled $389. Enough for a few tanks of gas and a few meals that just might beat microwave-heated chili on a paper plate.

They also now had a cache of weapons at their disposal and a trunk full of ammo. And even if that felt like a BB gun and some pellets compared to the arsenal Jones and the Shanghai Seven could put together, it was still something.

"So this was really all about that CD you swiped?" Carl said as they rolled out of the forest.

"Yeah, I guess so. My guess is it's some kind of records or files that definitively tie the Shanghai Seven to the counterfeiting operation. Maybe there's even dirt against Jones on there. Maybe that's why he's been helping them."

"Instead of the smoking gun, the smoking compact disc?" Carl asked.

"Something like that."

"Speaking of Jones, you know all we've done is bought ourselves a little bit of time, right? Jones is going to keep finding us until we figure out how he's doing it. And I have to think now that we've killed off five of the Shanghai Seven's guys, they'll send ten at us next time. Then twenty. I'm sure they're paying top dollar and don't particularly care about burning through their inventory of mercenaries."

"I know," Derrick said, his tone empty.

"That's why I keep telling you we need to take the fight to them. We can't keep running and hoping we keep getting lucky. We have to go on the offensive."

"Against a conglomeration that size? I wouldn't know where to start. Besides, they're on the other side of the world right now."

"No, no. I'm not talking about taking on the Shanghai Seven. They have way too many tentacles. I'm talking about Jones."

"Jones?"

"Yeah," Carl said. "He's the one who keeps selling us out."

"Well, I know. Which is all the more reason we can't approach him with the expectation he'll engage us in a polite chat."

"I'm not talking about a polite chat. I'm talking sticking a gun in his face and demanding he tell us what the hell is going on. There's got to be some reason why he's helping the Shanghai Seven, and there's got to be some way to convince him to stop."

"Even if I agree with you, how are we going to do it? I don't even know where the Cubby is. I mean, it's somewhere underground at Langley, but where? I wouldn't know where to start. I've been blindfolded every time I've been taken there, and the CIA wouldn't exactly take kindly to someone trying to comb over their property in a search grid pattern."

Carl's glance went toward the clock on the dashboard. "It's 1:52 A.M. I'm sure Jones is at home, asleep."

"And, what, you want to raid his house? Forget it. You know how many foreign agents, terrorists, and domestic ne'er-do-wells have tried and failed over the years? Every inch of the house is wired to a security system that—"

"You think I can't beat a home security system?"

"I know you can. But my point is that you'll never even get that far. Jones lives on ten acres with the house square in the middle, set up on this hill like a little fortress. There's a huge open yard surrounding it on all sides—I'm talking zero natural cover, unless you can hide behind a blade of Bermuda grass. Jones has the nerds monitoring cameras that are conventional during the day and then automatically switch to thermal at night."

"The cameras are mounted on the house, right?"

"Yes. But don't go thinking you'll disable two cameras and be done with the job. There are thirty-six of them: eighteen primary and eighteen duplicate backups. Each camera is assigned to a twenty-degree arc, even though it captures much more than that, so there's overlap on top of overlap in the coverage. If a primary camera goes down, the backup comes online immediately. If more than one camera malfunctions, the Cubby is immediately notified.

"And don't go thinking you'll just catch them napping. They've written programs so if anything much larger than a sparrow moves in any one of those camera's fields of vision, alarms start going off. If Jones is home, he's notified immediately. He and his wife go into a panic room while the nerds launch a drone hidden on the property that goes from dormant to airborne in about ten seconds. If there's anything left of the trespasser once the drone is done, a team of agents arrives about five minutes later to finish him off."

"So you're saying you doubt me?"

"Aww, come on, Dad. You're the one who just gave that beautiful speech about how we need to cut out the chest-thumping macho bullshit. Don't make this about some kind of test of fealty."

"He lives in Potomac Falls, right?"

"Yeah, but—"

"Drive north, son. Your old man still has some tricks up his sleeve."

NINETEEN

HEAT

Nikki Heat was having one of those dreams that was so intense, so vivid, it felt absolutely real.

She was in high school again. It was piano recital time. Cynthia Heat always rented out a small performance space for her students to be able to put on a show for their parents, relatives, and friends. Everyone dressed up like they were going to the opera or ballet—dark suits for the dads, pearls and high heels for the moms—and made like it was a big deal.

Because, for the students, it was.

Nikki's dream started with her backstage, just behind a curtain. There were other students around her, nervously buzzing about, though they were on the fringes, indistinct. Nikki couldn't see their faces.

Her attention was focused on the stage. The girl who preceded her in the program was finishing up her piece. Nikki could feel her nerves rising. Her sweaty palms grasped her sheet music. There was no more anxious time for a performer than when she was just about to walk onstage.

The girl struck her final chord. The audience clapped enthusiastically. The girl stood and bowed. Then from the corner of the stage, in a spot Nikki couldn't quite see, there came the voice of her mother, who always served as the emcee for the evening.

"Again, that was Elizabeth Flanders playing Rachmaninov's Prelude in G Minor. That is such a spirited piece, and I think we can all agree Beth brought wonderful energy to it. Thank you, Beth," Cynthia said.

The audience applauded again. Beth Flanders bowed one last time, then walked offstage.

Cynthia waited until she was gone, then said, "And now, please welcome our next performer, Nikki Heat."

Polite clapping followed. Nikki knew that was her cue. Everyone in the auditorium knew that was her cue.

There was just one problem: She couldn't get her legs to move.

"Nikki Heat," Cynthia said again.

The applause was a little more reserved this time. Nikki was trying desperately to lift her right foot, straining with all her might. But she couldn't get the thing even one inch off the ground.

"Nikki, it's time. Come out now, please," Cynthia called.

The crowd was murmuring now. It knew something wasn't right. Nikki was trying to move her left leg. It was every bit as unresponsive as the right one had been. She wanted to walk out on that stage. She wanted it more than anything. Her muscles just wouldn't cooperate.

"Nikki, are you there?" Cynthia asked.

Desperate, Nikki tried calling to her mother. It came out as a whimper. Her voice was weak. So weak.

"Nikki Heat . . . Nikki Heat . . . Come find me, Nikki Heat."

There were tears streaming down Nikki's face now. *I'm coming, Mom. I'm coming*, she wanted to scream. But the paralysis that had started in her legs was now total. Nothing in her body worked anymore. She was frozen in place. Her mother was just on the other side of the curtain—so very, very close— but Nikki couldn't get to her.

Then a phone started ringing. Loudly, insistently. And so close to her ear it actually felt . . .

Real. Because it *was* real. Someone was actually calling her. Heat forced her eyes open, relieved the dream was over, then untangled herself from the meaty left arm of Jameson Rook, which had been draped over her naked body.

She answered just before it went to voice mail with: "Heat."

"Nikki, it's George."

George The Bartender. Why was he—

"I'm sorry to call so late. And I'm sorry if I woke you up."

"Not at all," Nikki lied. "I was just getting some paperwork done."

"Oh, good. Good. I just . . . I got off my shift about an hour ago, and I've just been at home, thinking about what we talked about earlier today. Or, I guess I should say, yesterday."

Heat's eyes focused on the nightstand clock, which read 2:05 A.M. Rook was nude, too. He was on his right side, not stirring. She began easing herself off the bed.

"Right, right," she said, keeping her voice low so she wouldn't disturb him.

"Anyway, it's been tearing me up and . . . would you mind coming over so we can talk about it a little more? I know it's late, but I just feel like we should discuss things some more. Would that be okay?"

"Sure," Heat said quickly. So much for the promise she wouldn't run off in the middle of the night. She was in the bathroom now, with the door closed so she wouldn't disturb Rook's slumber.

"I've just been thinking about it, about your mother's wishes, and I think . . . Well, I'm hoping I can convince you about what she really wanted. I think she had very specific wishes about where she wanted those bills to end up."

"Absolutely, George. I think you're absolutely right."

"Good. We'll talk about it when you get here. And, again, I'm sorry to call so late. But I just can't get it out of my mind and I think . . . Well, I think maybe a change of heart might be in order."

"I agree. I'm already on my way," Heat said, even though that would have put her in opposition to several New York City indecent exposure statutes—while giving at least a few citizens a cheap thrill. "I know you live close to my mother's place, but what's your address, George?"

George rattled off a number on East 18th Street, adding, "Apartment 5F. You want some coffee? I'm just about to put some on. You just never know when you're going to have unexpected company, if you know what I mean."

"That'd be great, George. Thanks," said Heat, already sensing her night's slumber was done.

She was expecting him to say something else—"good-bye" or "see you soon"—but George seemed to have already hung up. Heat ended the call and exited the bathroom so she could begin scrambling into her clothes. As she dressed, she looked at Rook, still sacked out, his chiseled chest rising and falling in a steady rhythm.

He had been right about George having second and third thoughts—"a change of heart," George had called it. Of course Rook was right. A journalist spends his career observing people and drawing conclusions about them, and Rook was better at it than most.

A warmth spread to her lower extremities as she thought about the intimacy they had shared that evening. He was better than most at some other things, too.

As she left The Lucerne, Heat ordered up a Lyft to take her

down to Chelsea. Traffic at that time of night was flowing easily, and with the lights well timed, the car was able to roll through chunks of ten or twenty blocks at a time before coming to a halt.

As midtown Manhattan passed by her, Heat's excitement mounted. George would take her to the bills. She would take them to the crime lab personally and demand the technicians scan them and put them through the system immediately. They'd give her a little bit of a hard time, but ultimately a captain got what she wanted.

And then? Well then, after seventeen years, she'd start getting some answers. If the prints weren't in the city of New York's database—and she doubted they would be—she'd send them on to the FBI, then to the CIA. Surely no one would deny the perhaps-future director of Homeland Security a favor.

She was feeling wired as the car came to a halt in front of the address George had provided. She might not need his coffee, after all. The possibility of all that lay ahead was a natural stimulant.

George's apartment was a fifth-floor walk-up in a smaller building that had no doorman and was almost certainly rent-controlled, judging from how little about the building had been updated.

Heat pressed the button for 5F and was buzzed up. She practically flew up the stairs and was soon at George's door, knocking softly so she didn't wake the neighbor in 5R.

George came to the door still dressed in the same clothes he had been in earlier. He opened the door without speaking, allowing Heat to enter his small, tidy living room. He looked odd, almost like he had been crying.

Then he closed the door behind her.

"Good work, George," another man's voice said. "Now let's raise those hands nice and high, Captain Heat."

Heat slowly did as the man said. It had been four years since she'd last heard that voice, but she didn't need to turn around to know who it belonged to.

Bart Callan had found her.

George had his hands pressed together in a supplicant pose, like he was already begging for Heat's forgiveness.

"I'm sorry, Nikki," George said pathetically. "He made me."

"Shut up, old man," Callan said. "Go back over in the corner and don't move."

George retreated meekly into the far corner as Callan advanced toward Heat from behind.

"Now, Nikki, you are going to stand absolutely still. You are going to keep your hands nice and high, and you are not going to move a single muscle. Do you understand me?"

"Screw you, Callan."

"I would like that very much, believe me. When we sparred that time, feeling that body of yours underneath me . . . I would like nothing more. I thought about that a lot in prison, you know—thought about what I'd like to do to you.

"But I'm afraid that's not why I'm here. Now, not a move."

She felt the cold muzzle of a gun against the base of her skull, pointed upward such that any bullet would obliterate her medulla oblongata—the part of the brain responsible for respiration, circulation, and a host of other functions a body couldn't do without for very long.

Then she felt Callan's hand working its way up her torso. It started at her stomach, then went to her rib cage, then paused for a grope of her breast. Her skin crawled. She would have rather been felt up by a reptile.

"Nice," he said, giving her a squeeze. Then he moved to her

shoulder holster, which he expertly unsnapped before removing her 9mm.

With any other assailant, Heat would have picked a moment to whirl and deliver an elbow to the Adam's apple, followed quickly by a back kick to the groin.

But not with Callan. He was too good. And too careful. And his gun was dug too far into the back of her head.

Callan stepped back quickly, getting himself out of range of Heat's fists and feet. Then he walked over to one of the living room's two windows, which was already open. He tossed the gun out, letting it fall five stories to the sidewalk, unconcerned about who might find it or whether it would strike someone on the head.

Heat heard it clang off the concrete, feeling a special sense of helplessness as she thought about some kid—or some criminal—scooping it up.

Quickly, though, that gun became less of a concern than the one Callan now had trained on her face.

"Surprised to see me? Thought you had gotten rid of Bart Callan for good, didn't you? Well, let me tell you something you obviously didn't learn four years ago: I win in the end. I always win in the end."

"You're going to fry this time, Callan. You're an escaped inmate who committed murder while on the lam. That's a capital offense. The federal government will be happy to give you the needle for that."

"If I were you, I'd be a little more worried about your own death than mine," Callan said. "Now, you're going to tell me where your mother hid those bills."

Heat was fairly certain her confusion showed on her face. "*I'm* going to tell you? What are you talking about? I have no—"

"I know you were a theater major, Nikki, so I'll give you a

B-plus for that performance. But it's not fooling me. I heard your mother on that recording you had in your apartment. I heard all the stuff about how she hid the bills in the same place as her best liquor. I know that didn't mean her apartment, because I turned that inside out pretty good—yes, that was me. Then I went and had a talk with your buddy George here."

Callan jerked his head toward George. "And your bartender told me everything. He told me that Cynthia knew her phone was tapped and that it was just a misdirection to fool the people listening and how you had the bills all along. In case you're wondering, it took about twelve seconds before he gave you up. I didn't even have to touch one of those silver hairs of his."

Heat's eyes flashed toward George, who mouthed "I'm sorry" one more time. She could plainly see his desperation for her to do something, anything.

She could now guess how it had gone. Callan had gotten the jump on the old man, who then started lying just to stall for time. Maybe he also thought Heat, as a cop, would come with backup, or that she would be smart enough to sniff out the trap. When she thought back to his last words, she realized he had even tried to warn her:

You just never know when you're going to have unexpected company, if you know what I mean.

But, of course, Heat had been so excited about the possibility of finally getting the bills in her possession, she had ignored that sign.

And now it seemed to have been a deadly mistake.

"So now," Callan continued, "you're going to tell me where those bills are. And you're going to tell me right now, because if you don't, I'll gut your friend George like a fish."

"If you touch him, you'll never get those bills," Heat said.

"That's a promise. Leave him out of it. This is between you and me, Callan."

"So you admit you know where the bills are?"

Heat acted like she couldn't decide whether to confess, like she was struggling with the weight of the thing. In reality, she was trying to think of some way out.

If she could keep Callan talking, she could then lead him to some other place, some place where she could find some advantage against him. But where would that place be? It wasn't like she'd be able to convince Callan she had left the bills at the precinct and have him march in there with her. Could she tell him what he was looking for was at The Players Club? George had keys. She could take Callan there. Perhaps his focus would drop for a moment along the way, giving her the opportunity to pounce.

Finally, because he was expecting an answer, she said: "Yes, I do."

"Good. Where?"

"No. Not yet. First, George here is going to walk out of the apartment."

"And run straight to the cops? Not a chance."

"He's an innocent. He has nothing to do with this."

"You are not in a position to bargain here, Captain Heat," Callan said, brandishing the gun at her, as if she needed the reminder.

"Oh, but I am. I'm the only person alive who knows where those bills are," Heat bluffed. "And if you kill me, you'll never recover them. But the executor of my estate has very specific instructions about what to do with them in the event of my untimely passing."

Callan clenched his jaw.

"I should have gotten those bills off your mother when she first told me she had them," he said.

"What are you talking about?"

Callan actually smiled, then said: "Oh, I guess you wouldn't know about that. That was why I first had the pleasure of interacting with your mother—because of those counterfeit bills. I was part of a task force with the Secret Service that was looking into foreign counterfeiting, and she came to me. After she told me about where she had gotten them from, it was clear she had to die. That's when I ordered Petar Matic to kill her."

"I thought it was because she had gotten onto your smallpox plot with Carey Maggs."

"Well, yes. That, too. I had a couple irons in the fire back then, and your mother was trying to tug at all of them. She was circling around a bunch of stuff she could never quite grab. The smallpox plot was actually pretty far from being hatched at that point—Maggs needed a lot of time to get his operation up and running. The bills were actually the much more immediate issue on my mind when I dispatched Petar."

Except Matic had never made it there—and obviously hadn't admitted his failure to Callan. Tyler Wynn, who knew about Cynthia's death sentence, had helped her fake her own death first. Not that Callan knew it.

"So you were working for the Shanghai Seven even back then?"

Callan got a funny look on his face. "Who I'm working for is none of your business. Now, I'm getting very tired of this conversation. You've got five seconds to tell me where the bills are before I shoot the old man, and then another five seconds before I shoot you."

TWENTY

STORM

"This is *never* going to work," Derrick Storm said.

He was wearing two pairs of long johns and a pair of boots and standing next to his father on a winding country road just down from Jedediah Jones's house. They were in Potomac Falls, amidst some of the most expensive real estate in the DC area, an enclave of the superrich and ultra-connected. It was still dark.

"Of course it's going to work," Carl said. "Haven't I taught you anything about technology? If human beings are clever enough to design it, they're usually clever enough to defeat it."

"*This* is never going to work," Derrick repeated.

His eyes were fixed on his father's creation, which was the end result of an hour or so of odd errand running. It began with a pre-dawn raid of a sod farm, which went off mostly smoothly—sod farms not being known for their excessive concern with theft. The only hitch was that the sod didn't have any price tags on it. The Storms could only hope the one hundred dollars they left behind covered what they took.

It continued at a twenty-four-hour Walmart, where a tired checkout woman didn't blink at the strange combination of purchases: two king-size blankets, four bags of tent pegs, two pairs of insulated boots, four pairs of long johns that were going to be far too snug on the men purchasing them, sweatpants and sweatshirts that were going to be too large, a package of razor blades, and Saran Wrap.

Lots and lots of Saran Wrap.

Finally, they stopped at a 7-Eleven not far from Jones's house, where the Storms had emptied the freezer of ice bags.

"Thermal cameras rely on the fact that human beings emit body heat in the infrared spectrum," Carl lectured. "But if there's no body heat, there's nothing for the camera to see. Now hurry up. We haven't got all night here. Dawn will be here before you know it."

Derrick was still shaking his head as he looked at what Carl had insisted they make. They had attached thick layers of sod to the king-sized blankets with the metal tent pegs, which had been bent to keep them in place after they were inserted. The result, a blanket of grass, looked ridiculous and weighed about two hundred pounds, so they weren't exactly going to be flying across Jones's front yard.

Then there was what Carl insisted they do to themselves.

"This is never going to *work*," Derrick said.

"You keep emphasizing a different word in that sentence like it's somehow going to change my mind. Your pessimism is disturbing. I thought I raised an optimist."

"You did. You just didn't raise a crazy person."

"They said Van Gogh was crazy."

"Because he was," Derrick said. "The man chopped off his own ear and then later killed himself."

"But he left behind art that is still being studied and marveled at."

Derrick pointed to the grass blankets: "Yeah, Dad, these? No one is confusing these with *Sunflowers* or *Irises*."

"Shut up and start wrapping," Carl said.

This was the other part of Carl's plan. After putting on their long johns to give them insulation, they were going to pack as much of their bodies in ice as they could stand. Then they were going to put clothes around the ice. Between that and the boots, very little of their body heat would be able to escape. Any that did would be absorbed by the blanket, and then ultimately by the grass, which would naturally maintain the same temperature as the surrounding atmosphere.

And that, in turn, would make them invisible to the infrared cameras.

Or at least that was the hope.

"This is nuts," Derrick said as he flattened the first ice bag against his father's chest.

"This is genius."

"Yeah. Of the Van Gogh variety."

Once Derrick had Carl wrapped, Carl returned the favor—if, in fact, having bags of ice strapped to one's body could be characterized as such. They finished by putting the final layer of supersized clothing on over top, providing even more insulation.

Then they grabbed their grass blankets and began the walk toward Jones's property.

"So run through this for me one more time," Derrick said. "We're going to sneak across the grass in this ridiculous getup until we reach the base of the house."

"Right. The cameras are on the house, and they're fixed, not moving. Once we're snuggled up next to the foundation, they'll no longer be able to see us. We slice off the ice bags—you did remember to grab your razor blade, right?"

"Yeah. It's in my pocket."

"Good. So as I was saying, cut away the ice bags, shed the grass, pop the latch on a window, and climb in the house."

"Being careful to take countermeasures against whatever security system is in place."

"If it's a window, it's going to be one of three things: pressure sensitive, magnetic, or motion detecting," Carl said. "There are ways of defeating all three."

"Then we escort ourselves to Jones's bedroom, stick a gun in his face, and make him start talking."

"Exactly."

"And I suppose you're going to tell me this is old school?"

"No. I believe this is TITS."

Derrick shook his head one last time. *"This is never going to work."*

The perimeter of Jones's property was ringed with shrubs and trees meant to make it look like any other in the neighborhood.

They were, in fact, strategically placed to ensure that no vehicle larger than a scooter would be able to thread through them. Nature was sometimes as effective as anything humankind could design in that respect. Plus, it was prettier.

The driveway was also fortified in ways hidden from the casual observer. The tasteful brick pillars and the black wrought iron gate were reinforced by steel rods that were anchored in a huge block of underground concrete. The asphalt was embedded with spikes that deployed if the system detected an unauthorized entry attempt.

An M1A2 Abrams tank probably would be able to get over and through it. Anything short of that would be thwarted.

There was nothing, however, to prevent a person on foot from entering the property. The CIA's security people were relying on the cameras to intercept that kind of security breach.

And so the Storm boys were simply able to stroll onto Jones's property, carrying their grass blankets on their backs. Contrary to popular belief, thermal cameras can't see through thick tree or leaf coverage. The vegetation, which adopts the same temperature as the ambient air, acts as a screen.

The easy part of the journey ended once they reached the edge of the forest. From there, it was several hundred yards of upward-sloping lawn all the way to Jones's house, which was surrounded by flower beds filled with tasteful but insubstantial landscaping: some low shrubs, some perennials that had begun to wilt as the fall days grew short, some mums that had been planted to give the place a little late-season color.

In between them and the flower beds, there was nothing—not even a clump of daffodils—to give them cover.

Derrick had been here before, not as an infiltrator but as a guest. He and Jones had been celebrating the disruption of the sale of enriched Plutonium 239 to an international arms dealer who could have then sold it to the North Koreans, the Iranians, or half a dozen other undesirable buyers. Jones had given Derrick a tour of the property, followed by a meal of roasted pheasant. Then they had retired to the back porch for cigars and brandy. It was during the second brandy that Derrick spied one of the cameras and Jones, flush-faced and uncharacteristically loose-tongued, began bragging.

Now Derrick was looking at the property again, albeit with a very different objective. His chief concern was navigational. Even if Carl's ridiculous ice-and-grass suit worked, how would they see to find the house if they were covered in sod? Carl had insisted they could lie down, then lift up the grass for a moment when they needed to make sure they were still on the right course.

Derrick immediately saw a better solution.

"The mow lines," he said, pointing at the striped pattern that the landscapers had left behind. "We can follow them straight to the house."

"Good plan," Carl said. "Let's suit up."

Derrick gave a resigned sigh, then pulled the grass blanket over his head, supporting the edges of it with his hands so the seams between the square chunks wouldn't show.

As soon as he took his first steps out of the forest, he expected to hear the whir of a drone, the shout of an alarm, something that would indicate what a terrific failure Carl's plan was. To anyone watching during the day, it would have been a most curious sight: two walls of grass that suddenly started walking out from beneath the trees.

But, of course, there was no one watching at night. Just a camera that, if Carl's theory was correct, couldn't see a thing.

Derrick's first steps were halting. It was an odd sensation. His body, which was packed in ice, was so numb he could barely feel it. And yet his face was already perspiring from the effort it took to walk from the car, through the forest, and now up the yard, all while carrying the heavy blanket.

For Derrick, who kept himself in prime shape by eschewing conventional weights and health club contraptions in favor of real-world workouts—flipping huge tires, carrying rocks, hauling weighted sleds up hills—this was a manageable, even familiar type of exercise. But he worried about his father. While still solidly built, Carl Storm wasn't quite the horse he had once been.

Derrick could hear the old man grunting and straining from underneath his grass cloak. Carl's breathing was growing more labored with each step.

Finally, after about two hundred yards, he stopped.

"Sorry," he said softly. "I need a blow."

"Yeah, me too," Derrick said, to make his dad feel better about taking his time. It wouldn't help anything to have Carl suffer a heart attack on Jedediah Jones's lawn. Derrick hunkered down and tried to think about not emitting heat.

After a minute or two, during which time Carl's breathing went from a strained wheeze to a more manageable heavy pant, he said, "Okay, let's get going."

Derrick's legs started churning again. He could see only the grass at his feet, and remained cognizant of staying in the same mow line. He corrected his course as soon as he was about to walk into grass that had been mowed in a different direction.

The water, which began as a trickle down his legs and arms, was really pouring off him now. It was some combination of melted ice and sweat, and it had both soaked his clothes and pooled in his boots.

A hundred yards or so later, Carl again huffed, "Rest." They settled down for about three minutes this time. Carl was clearly giving it everything he had. It took longer for his breathing to get down to an acceptable level again. Derrick felt uneasy the whole time, but he knew his father was doing his best.

"All right," Carl whispered.

They were moving again. The slope of the lawn had leveled off some, which told Storm they were getting closer to the house. How close, he couldn't say—and he didn't dare lift up the blanket for a look. Despite the ice, he felt like he was creating a lot of heat, which would escape if given the chance. He didn't know what that would look like on the screen that was piped into the Cubby—like a cloud of red, floating up?—or to the program that monitored the cameras, constantly searching for anything large and mobile.

This time, they only made it about fifty yards before Carl let out a ragged, "Break."

The break itself last even longer. Five minutes? Seven? Trapped underneath a grass blanket, feeling incredibly exposed, still convinced this couldn't possibly work, it felt like five or seven hours. Derrick was trying not to get impatient with his father. But, at the same time, there was a reason men in their seventies were no longer considered fit for duty. And this was it.

Derrick was shedding so much water, the grass actually squeaked a little as he stood back up.

"Come on, Dad. We've got to move. I think we're almost there. One last good push and I think we'll make it."

"Okay. I'll give it everything I got," Carl said.

The yard was almost flat now. Any moment, Derrick expected to see the grass give way to some dirt, then to the mums that had been planted at the flower bed's edge.

Ten steps. Twenty. Derrick was trying to keep at his father's ever-slowing pace, so they were really baby steps. Carl was really struggling, but they were almost there. Derrick was sure of it.

"Just a little farther," he whispered, as much for his own morale as anything.

He was daring to feel confident. For as hot and wet as he was, for as much as his boots sloshed, for as ridiculous as the whole thing was, the grass shield had stayed cool. Carl's plan had actually worked.

Or at least that's what Derrick thought.

Then all hell broke loose.

From the perspective of the computer tasked with monitoring the infrared cameras, the questionable data was not the moving walls of grass, because the cameras truly couldn't see them.

It was that the walls of grass were occasionally leaving behind slicks of warm water that grew in size as they went up the hill. There were two puddles about two hundred yards up the hill; two more a hundred yards later; then, and this is what tripped the alarm, two fifty yards after that.

It was the last pair that caused the computer to alert one of the nerds, who studied those blotches of warmth with great interest. To the nerd, it almost looked like a slug was leaving behind a trail of ooze. Except she couldn't see the slug—just the ooze.

The nerd ordered the drone, which had its own infrared camera, up into the sky. Unlike the fixed cameras mounted on the house, the drone could move around and study this unusual pattern from a variety of angles. The nerd still wasn't sure what she was seeing, only that it was happening in front of her boss's house, and that therefore she'd rather apologize for a false negative than face unemployment (or worse) for an unreported positive.

Once she determined the blobs were moving, she made the call, dispatching a team of agents with human eyes that could not see infrared, but most surely could see the two walls of walking grass advancing on Jones's house.

The Storms, who were underneath their blankets—which blocked heat from getting out but also sound from coming in—were unaware of this. They couldn't hear the drone when it took flight. They also hadn't heard the agents who had quietly moved into position around them.

No, all they could hear was when a very stern voice finally shouted: "CIA security! Freeze!"

The Storm boys hadn't discussed what they would do if they were detected. Maybe it was because no conversation was really necessary. As father and son, Carl and Derrick Storm had 50 percent of their genetic material in common: long chains of identical nucleotides twisted into a double helix of adenine, thymine, cytosine, and guanine; the language of life.

And the word *surrender* wasn't written in any of it.

As Derrick flashed out his razor blade and began furiously slashing at the Saran Wrap, he knew his father was doing the same. The wrapping had been a slow, laborious process. The unwrapping was accomplished with a few quick wrist flicks.

Then Derrick threw the blanket off his head. The lawn was still mostly dark, though it was now split by flashlight beams that made it difficult for him to know how many agents there were or where they were standing—other than that they seemed to have positioned themselves between him and the house.

He started running, semi-blinded by the light, in the opposite direction, toward the dark of the forest. It was, perhaps, a long shot he'd make it. But it was the only option. He couldn't start a gun battle against trained agents who were, on a different day, on the same team he was.

Out of the corner of his eye, he saw his father had also cast off his ice bags and grass blanket and was making a similar mad dash to safety.

They had three hundred fifty yards to cover. Under optimal conditions, Derrick could run that distance in forty seconds. Weighed down by three layers of sodden clothing and running in boots, he knew he would be substantially slower. But he had to try.

His numbed thigh muscles flexed. His boots dug into the ground. His arms began to churn. Ten strides and he could reach top speed.

Instead, he made it all of four steps before he heard a loud rush of air, then felt something sharp plunge into his back, just to the left of his spinal cord.

His next two steps were unaffected. Then his legs started feeling heavy. Then his arms stopped obeying his commands. The world started to get spinny.

The last coherent thought to pass through Derrick Storm's brain was one of the worst a person can have: that he had let his father down.

Then everything went black.

TWENTY-ONE

HEAT

Bart Callan had shifted his aim from Nikki Heat to George The Bartender, who was cowering in the far corner of the apartment, his hands over his face—as if that could protect him from what was about to come out of Callan's gun.

"Five," Callan said.

He was standing approximately ten feet from Heat. His back was slightly turned away from her. Did it give her an angle from which to approach him?

"Four," he said.

No. He was too far away for her to even consider some kind of move. Ten feet was three steps before he'd be in range of a kick. And there was no way she could take three steps, then plant, then deliver a strike in the time it would take Callan to respond. Her feet may have been powerful, but Callan's gun truly had more kick.

"Three," he said.

She had to think of something. Somewhere to take him. Something to say that would stall him. Anything that would give her more time.

"Two," he said.

"Okay, okay, take it easy, Bart," Heat said. "You win, okay?

We'll take you to where the bills are, *won't we, George*?"

"Yes, yes, of course, Ms. Heat."

"I thought you'd see it my way," Callan said. "Now where are they?"

"They . . . they are," Heat began and looked imploringly at George.

But George wasn't saying anything. He was just glancing from her, to Callan, back to her. After all that time—even with his own life so clearly threatened—George wasn't going to go back on the promise he had made to Cynthia Heat. Nikki didn't know whether to be incensed or deeply touched. It was a gesture of loyalty that surely would have secured George's place in the Bartender Hall of Fame. The only downside was that it appeared he was going to be enshrined posthumously.

"They're at my apartment," Heat blurted, just to have something to say.

"Yeah? Where?" Callan demanded.

"They're . . . they're in my bureau, in my bedroom."

He walked several steps closer to George.

"No, they're not. I turned that bureau inside out. I removed every single drawer and checked them all over to make sure there were no hidden compartments, no false bottoms or fronts, nothing taped to the side somewhere."

"You missed one," Heat said. "It was my underwear drawer, okay? You were probably just too distracted to—"

"I didn't miss anything. Those bills weren't there. This is bullshit, and I'm done playing around. The old man gets it," Callan said, raising the gun just a little higher. "Five, four, three, two—"

Callan was just beginning to form his lips into an oval to make the W sound that began the word *one* when the door to the apartment burst open.

A man with Asian features burst into the room. Heat bent slightly at the knees and brought up her hands, reflexively assuming a fighting stance. Callan was turning toward the man, whipping his gun in that direction.

Neither Heat nor Callan was fast enough. With his pistol already in a firing position, the Asian man pulled the trigger twice. Heat was so close she could feel the air being expelled from the gun and the powder lacing her skin, but neither bullet was aimed at her.

Callan's head snapped backward, his neck going at an angle it was not designed to assume. Then he dropped, bouncing off the far wall on his way down, landing in a crumpled, bloodied heap. On the wall behind him, there was a thick red splotch of plasma, bits of skull, and brain matter.

Bart Callan—former FBI, former Homeland Security, the man whose designs on Cynthia Heat's life had forced her into hiding for seventeen years, the man who would have allowed thousands of New Yorkers to die of smallpox in the name of profit—was no more.

As soon as the echo of gunfire ceased, it was replaced by George's scream. The bartender had pressed himself as far into the corner as possible, as if he was trying to get even farther away from the dead man.

Heat had stayed in her defensive crouch but was now frozen with uncertainty, not knowing if the shooter was a friend, a foe, or just some kind of freelance guardian angel. The gunman brushed past her on his way across the room, where he was already inspecting his handiwork.

Two more Asian men came in immediately behind him with their guns raised. But the first man said something to them—in

Mandarin? that was Mandarin Chinese, yes?—that made them immediately relax.

Then a fourth Asian man came in. But whereas the first three had walked with stern purpose, this one seemed to be on more of a leisurely stroll.

He was dressed in polyester pants with a ten-thousand-year crease ironed into them. His sandals were inexpensive and plastic. His short-sleeve button-down shirt, also made of a cheap synthetic material—imitation polyester, if such a thing existed—was red with a few yellow stripes.

A Chinese communist on holiday.

In his fingers he held a cigarette, which he languidly brought to his mouth. The lit end glowed. Then the air was filled with a peculiar odor. Scent memory being the strong force it is, Heat was immediately transported to her junior year at Northeastern, where she was sitting on the rooftop of an apartment with a theater friend who was smoking . . .

Clove cigarettes. The man was smoking cloves. *Storm had been talking about a man who smoked cloves.*

Colonel Feng. Could this be Colonel Feng, the Shanghai Seven's bought-and-paid-for policeman? But what was he doing here, thousands of miles from his beat?

Heat was now officially perplexed. Wasn't Callan working for the Shanghai Seven? Why would Feng kill one of his own men?

Had Callan gone rogue or . . .

Or was he never working for the Shanghai Seven in the first place? Heat flashed back to the look on Callan's face moments earlier, when she had said something about his long-standing employment with the Shanghai Seven. It had seemed to be genuine confusion, like she had reached a conclusion that was not only unfounded, it was so out of the realm of possibility he had never even considered it until that moment.

Heat had done enough interrogations in her life to know Callan had been off-balance for that split second, almost like if she had asked a perp who thought he was about to be collared for a murder if he had committed a rape.

Then he'd recovered in time to snap back with, *Who I'm working for is none of your business.*

It wasn't exactly a denial of Shanghai Seven ties. Yet there was something about it—coupled with the look—that told Heat there was something else going on.

But if Callan wasn't with the Shanghai Seven, whose bidding was he doing? Why had he ransacked Heat's apartment? Why was he looking for the bills? Why was he harassing her as The Serpent? Who had sprung him from prison in the first place?

Heat looked at the bloody hole where the back of Callan's head had been and realized she might never know. The secret may have died at the same time Callan hit the floor.

Meanwhile, Colonel Feng—it was indeed Colonel Feng—had walked toward Callan's inert form and toed it briefly, even though it was abundantly clear Callan was beyond feeling that or anything else. Then, showing no hesitation or outward distaste over his task, he began patting Callan down and searching his pockets. He skipped what was left of the head—there was clearly no place to hide anything up there anymore—but otherwise gave the body a thorough inspection.

Then he turned to Heat.

"Where is the CD?" he said in English.

CD? Heat thought. *Isn't the Shanghai Seven after the counterfeit bills, like Callan?*

"What CD?" Heat asked, legitimately confused. "I don't know what you're talking about."

Feng sighed, like he was already impatient with the interview. "Captain Heat, I'm talking about the CD that was stolen from a warehouse in Shanghai and is"—he seemed to catch himself before he said too much—"evidence in an ongoing investigation I am conducting."

Heat now remembered the compact disc Storm had mentioned in her apartment. He had talked about how it was so effectively encrypted that he hadn't been able to figure out what was on it.

"Evidence? Really?" Heat said. "So this is official police business?"

"Yes, of course," Feng said, a pinched smile on his thin lips.

"In that case, you won't mind if I call NYPD headquarters at One Police Plaza so I can confirm that you've registered with them, as all visiting law enforcement—especially foreign law enforcement—is required to do."

Heat pulled out her phone. Feng barked an order in Mandarin. The man who ended Callan's life advanced quickly across the room and knocked Heat's phone out of her hand.

"He thinks it's rude to make a phone call in the middle of a conversation," Feng said. "And I'm afraid he's going to insist on your continued politeness until we're done here. You see, manners are very important in Chinese culture."

Feng sneered. His underling's pistol was casually aimed at Heat's midsection.

Heat kept her gaze steady. "You won't get away with this, *Colonel Feng.*"

Her use of his name seemed to startle Feng for a brief moment. But he recovered quickly.

"I am not interested in your threats. I am interested in the CD. It was taken by a man named Derrick Storm, an American intelligence operative who failed to register himself with my country, making both his theft and his mere presence there illegal."

"You'll have to take that up with the State Department. I'm just a captain with the New York Police Department. I have nothing to do with foreign intelligence."

He smiled. "I'm sure. Just as I am merely a colonel in the People's Armed Police."

"I'm telling the truth."

"Then why was Derrick Storm in your apartment for several hours on Thursday evening?"

Heat tried not to show any reaction. How did Feng know where Storm was? Certainly, Derrick Storm would have been careful enough to make sure he wasn't followed. For a man in Storm's line of work, that was second nature.

"Yes, we know about that, Captain Heat," Feng continued. "I think you'll find we know a lot of things. Which is why, if you have nothing to hide, and if you really are a regular police captain, as you claim, you will answer my question truthfully. Why was Derrick Storm in your apartment two nights ago?"

"There have been a lot of people in my apartment lately. Most of them didn't knock before entering. Callan was one of them. Up until a few minutes ago, I thought he was working for you."

Feng looked down at Callan, but did not comment.

"Captain Heat, your evasiveness is boring me. Derrick Storm gave you the CD and Bart Callan, who we have been following for quite some time, was about to take it from you. But obviously he didn't quite get around to it. So it is still in your possession. This is the last time I will make this request politely. Hand it over so we can end this unpleasantness and be on our way."

"I don't have any CD," Heat said.

"Very well. If that's how we have to do things."

Feng gave another instruction in Mandarin to the

pistol-packing man nearest Heat. He advanced on Heat with the gun raised.

"My associate is going to search you," Feng said. "I suggest you—"

But Heat was having none of it. She had already been groped more than enough for one day. Brazilian jujitsu is useful for any number of things. Disarming an attacker is one of them.

Her hand flashed and the man no longer possessed his gun. Then she stomped her foot on the side of his knee, expertly tearing his medial collateral ligament. The man collapsed, howling in pain. Heat assumed a defensive position, daring the next guy to try anything.

Feng was just considering what to do about this when they heard a commotion five floors down. The front door to the building had opened and several pairs of heavy feet were tromping up the stairs quickly. There were times—like when there had been reports of shots fired—when the NYPD liked to make a noisy entrance.

Heat was looking toward the staircase through the still-open apartment door as a quartet of New York's Finest completed their ascent.

"NYPD," one of them said.

"Gun!" another shouted.

"Hands up," the first said. "Let's see those hands everyone. Hands."

All four officers had their weapons out. Feng considered them without consternation, as if the dead fugitive on the floor was of no particular concern.

"This isn't over," Feng hissed at Heat.

Heat had never seen a man who seemed as calm about having just participated in a conspiracy to commit murder as Colonel

Feng. He issued an order in Mandarin to his men, who immediately holstered their weapons. Then he strolled breezily toward the armed cops.

"Good morning, gentlemen," he said genially. "I'd like you to meet Captain Heat. She's one of yours. Or at least she claims to be."

"Sir. I need to see your hands up *now*," the officer replied.

"Yes, yes," Feng said, taking a long drag on his cigarette before holding up his hands in a desultory manner. "Now why don't you get some handcuffs on me? I would be delighted to pay a brief visit to your precinct."

Feng held his arms out. His men followed suit. As they were led out of the room, none of them took a glance back at Callan, nor did they seem especially concerned about having just killed a man.

Heat watched them go. She knew she would get a chance to question Feng later in an NYPD interrogation room, which meant it would be on her terms, not his. She didn't think she'd get anything out of him about the Shanghai Seven or what was on the CD that mattered so much. But it was possible he'd be willing to give up information about Bart Callan, like who he was working for.

In the meantime, Heat had to play a different role—not the interviewer, but the interviewee. She gave the patrolman a short narrative on what had occurred. She knew it was a story she was going to have to repeat at least a few more times. It was going to be a long night.

Once the officer put in the call to his desk sergeant that a homicide had occurred, Heat herded George out of his apartment so the cops could get in and crawl around—and so he wouldn't have to be further traumatized by having to spend any more time with Callan's remains.

"You going to be okay?" she asked.

"Yeah, I . . . I think so. Thanks to that Chinese gentleman. Who was he, anyway?"

"It's a long story."

"Will you tell it to me? I'm starting to think it's something I might need to know."

Heat nodded. "Okay. But first I'm afraid you have to be a witness to a homicide. Stay here until the detectives get here and tell them everything that happened."

"You got it, Ms. Heat."

"Now, if you'll excuse me, I have a few things to attend to outside."

She walked down the five flights of stairs and went back out into the street. Her first task was to locate her gun before someone else did. She walked over toward the window it had flown out of, discovered a small hole in the pavement that lined up with that window, then found the gun a few feet away.

After pulling out the magazine, she dry-fired it at the ground a few times. It seemed no worse for wear after its five-story fall. It made the same well-oiled snapping sound it usually did. She reloaded it, then returned it to the empty spot in her shoulder holster, immediately feeling the relief of having its weight back in its proper place.

Then she pulled out her phone and dialed the number for Storm's new burner phone.

It rang several times before going to a voice mail box that hadn't yet been set up. She tried the number again, getting the same result.

She didn't think Storm was sleeping. From the tone of his last text, it didn't seem like he would be doing that anytime soon. So where was he? What was he doing?

Heat dialed one more time, then settled for a text. She first wrote about Callan, who had long ago put the hit on Cynthia Heat because she was in possession of counterfeit bills, and who now seemed to have been working for someone else—Heat didn't know who—before the Shanghai Seven cut him down.

HAVE ASCERTAINED S7 IS AFTER THE CD, she finished. BARELY ESCAPED AN EFFORT TO FIND IT BY YOUR FRIEND, COL. FENG. I WILL HAVE A CHANCE TO INTERROGATE FENG LATER. FOR NOW, CAN YOU CRACK THE ENCRYPTION SO WE CAN SEE WHAT IS SO IMPORTANT ON THERE? CALL WHEN YOU CAN. PLEASE CONFIRM RECEIPT OF THIS MESSAGE.

She hit SEND, wondering why Storm wasn't answering, pondering where he might be when it found him.

TWENTY-TWO

STORM

Derrick Storm had performed extraordinary feats of strength in his life.

He had once, to aid a Filipino farmer, stepped in for a faltering ox and hitched himself to a plow, removing it from the field where it had become stuck. In Mozambique, he had once saved a life by lifting a small car off a little girl's legs before she bled to death. On the occasions when he did meander into a weight room, he could bench-press over three hundred pounds and squat over six hundred.

That's what made it all the more strange when, as he slowly regained consciousness, he found he lacked the ability to lift his eyelids.

They seemed to be attached to his eyeballs with mortar and concrete. And no amount of effort could pry the two surfaces apart.

That wasn't all. As Storm began slowly performing a systems check, he found he had a slight ache in his back. That he could explain. A projectile of some sort—fired from a tranquilizer gun, perhaps?—had hit him there as he ran away.

But why was his butt so sore? There was a definite throbbing coming from the gluteus maximus on his left side.

Storm's hand—he could move his hand!—began exploring his lower half. He was wearing pants, which was always a good sign when one was coming out of a blackout; however, they weren't the same pants he had been wearing before the blackout. That was a bad sign.

Why had someone changed his pants?

He remembered he had been wearing a somewhat unwieldy outfit: two pairs of long johns and a bulky pair of sweatpants. Which meant someone had peeled off not one but three layers from his slumbering body. He wasn't sure he wanted to know the circumstances.

His hand kept going, pressing here and there until—

Ouch! Yes, there was definitely a tender spot on the side of his butt. It was throbbing lightly. Had he been shot there, or . . .

He moved his left leg and felt the tug of a few stitches. It was like someone had performed surgery to remove a bullet. But it must have been a small bullet, maybe one that had only barely penetrated, because it felt like there were only a few stitches.

Storm's success with being able to move both his leg and his hand made him determined to try again with his eyelids. And, yes, this time he was able to break through the layer of masonry that held them down.

He blinked a few times, restoring a thin layer of moisture to his eyeballs, which slowly came into focus. He was lying on a black leather couch. The couch was in an office. The office was in the Cubby. And the Cubby was deep underground at CIA headquarters in Langley, Virginia.

Storm recognized the carpet, the lighting, the general hum of the place. He was not restrained in any way, so he was not being held prisoner in the strictest sense of that word. Except it was impossible to leave the Cubby unescorted. So, in that way, he was a captive.

There was still the possibility he was going to be handed

over to the Shanghai Seven like some kind of offering. It just hadn't happened yet. Perhaps Jones wanted to debrief him first. Perhaps Jones would propose a deal.

"Hey, look who's awake!" a woman's voice said.

Storm looked up and saw her coming around a desk toward the couch. She had wavy brown hair that fell just right, alluring brown eyes, and the kind of symmetrical face that typically ended up on a movie screen.

Clara Strike was that kind of gorgeous. Breathtaking, really. And for a moment, Storm's heart forgot all the times it had been shattered because of her. It thumped in his chest much the same way it had the first time he had ever seen her.

She was wearing a conservative dark pantsuit, pairing it with heels that were definitely not standard CIA issue and a blouse that had just enough buttons undone to put certain thoughts in Storm's head.

Storm was reminded of a theory in physics known as quantum entanglement. First posed as a theoretical possibility many decades ago, quantum entanglement posits that once two particles have been brought together, they are never again truly separate. If you tickle one particle by altering its spin, its partner feels the change instantaneously, no matter how far away it has traveled—even if it's across the galaxy.

It's one of those wildly counterintuitive aspects of quantum physics that makes no sense to those doomed to the limited realm of the human senses. Einstein himself denounced the theory, which he derided as "spooky actions at a distance," as a logical impossibility.

And yet a team of researchers at Delft University of Technology in the Netherlands recently concocted an experiment, using electrons trapped inside diamonds, which seemed to prove quantum entanglement was, in fact, real.

Storm could have saved them the trouble and expense. His interactions with Clara Strike long ago confirmed quantum entanglement. For as much as he wanted to separate from her, for as far apart as they sometimes were, he could never seem to pull it off. She could always change his spin.

Still, while the heart beats on its own, it needs to be protected from itself by the head. This was Clara Strike, he reminded himself. He needed to be cautious.

"How are you feeling?" she asked. She sat down next to where he was lying and placed a warm hand on his hip.

Storm sat up. "Like a million bucks, all green and wrinkled."

"Do I want to know what you were doing on Jones's lawn, dressed up like a football field?"

"No."

"Well, just to warn you, one of those agents out there had his phone on camera mode. I'm told the footage of you throwing that grass rug off your head, making a break for it, and then getting put down like a rampaging elephant is absolutely priceless comedy. Apparently the only thing that's stopping it from becoming a viral YouTube sensation are all those strongly worded nondisclosure agreements we sign. But I wouldn't be surprised if it's playing on a loop at the office Christmas party."

"Great. I'm sure it'll go well with the virgin eggnog. Where's my dad?"

"He's still out, as far as I know. We put him in the medical wing in the main part of Langley rather than bring him down here. We felt it would be best if he had a doctor keeping an eye on him. He's not quite the young stud that his son is and we were worried about the combination of overexertion and the tranquilizer those agents used."

She had moved her hand from his hip to his chest. Storm sat up rather than allow himself to continue to be fondled.

"Take it easy, big guy," Strike said playfully. "You've been through a lot, too."

"Yeah. Speaking of which, why does my ass hurt?"

She gave him an arch smile. "While you were out, we turned you over to the aliens for an anal probe."

"Seriously."

"Then I don't know. You were up in medical before they brought you down here. That's all I know."

"Wonderful. Surgery without my consent, performed while I was unconscious by the always trustworthy medical staff of the Central Intelligence Agency. I'm sure I have nothing to worry about."

"You look fine to me. If you want to turn the tables on the CIA, I'll let you play doctor with me later when I get off work. We'll go to my place and turn the lights low. You can probe whatever you like."

"I'm not joking," Storm said with a testy frown. "What the hell did they do to me up there?"

"Take it easy, take it easy. I'm sure it was nothing. Look, if you want to know, ask Jones."

"Yeah," Storm huffed, "because I'm sure I'll get the truth out of him."

Strike rolled her eyes. "Would you stop being paranoid? Jones isn't—"

Her desk phone rang. Strike rose to answer it, grabbing it upside down.

"Oh, hello, sir."

Storm could tell from Strike's tone that it was Jones, who seemed to be endowed with the Voldemort-like sense that someone had dared speak his name.

"Yes, sir, he's awake. I'll send him right down."

Strike replaced the phone. "Looks like you'll get the chance to ask Jones all the questions you want. He needs to see you."

Storm stood. Strike placed her hand on his hip again.

"Let me know if you're free later," she said.

He nodded, even if he was quite sure he wouldn't be.

Jedediah Jones's office was, like so much else about the man, spare and functional.

He had maintained a personal relationship with every president since the first Bush, and yet there was not a single grip-and-grin photograph to suggest it. He had won nearly every award that the US government gave out, but they were all stored in a box somewhere. There was no ego wall behind him, no personal photos on the desk, nothing beyond what was needed to do the job.

Jones was in his sixties but, with daily five-mile jogs and only occasional indulgences in his diet, he had not allowed so much as an extra ounce of fat to creep onto his waistline. He was slightly below average in height, well above average in presence. He had brush-cut gray hair and steely blue eyes that were already glaring as Storm walked into the room.

"Sit," Jones said in a voice that sounded like it came from the bottom of a gravel pit.

Storm complied.

"You want to tell me what you were doing on my lawn this morning?" Jones asked.

"I've been thinking it would be perfect for a croquet course. Dad and I were just planning where we wanted to put the wickets."

"Stop screwing around," Jones growled. "Why were you trying to break into my house?"

Storm said nothing. He had long ago learned that the less real content he released around Jones the better.

"I can't imagine you wanted to steal something," Jones pressed. "I've paid you far too well over the years for you to have any material needs. I can't even speculate you have gambling debts to cover, because I know you always win. And, besides, I've seen all your IQ testing. You're more than smart enough to recognize there are easier targets than my living room."

Storm's lips stayed pressed together.

"Were you looking for some technology? I know you love your so-called toys. I keep all the good stuff in here, of course. Besides, all you need to do is ask. You know that."

Storm crossed his arms.

Jones continued: "I realize you are only in my employ on a contract basis. But I'd like to remind you that right now you are under contract to deliver me evidence against the Shanghai Seven, and you have not done so yet. Therefore, at the very least, you owe me an answer. What do I have to do? Threaten to press charges for trespassing? Don't make me play bad cop, here. Come on, Storm. We're on the same team."

Storm couldn't help himself. "Are we?" he said icily.

"Of course we are," Jones said.

"Then why are you playing footsie with the Shanghai Seven?"

"What are you talking about?"

"You know exactly what I'm talking about," Storm said. "You've been selling me out to them faster than you can take a breath. What did they offer you? A direct line to the top reaches of the Chinese Communist Party? Cuddle time with Chairman Mao's remains? Ping-Pong lessons?"

"Stop it. I'm not helping them, and I resent any implication to the contrary. For God's sake, Storm. I'm trying to get them put out of business. In fact, I'm paying you handsomely to help me do so. Did you forget that raid I sent you on last week?"

"That raid was compromised from the start."

"Not because of anything on this end," Jones said. "Use that big brain of yours, Storm. I'm not denying the Shanghai Seven seems to have been tipped off about that operation. But do you really think the tip came from this office? Why would I have bothered going through all the legwork and expense of organizing that raid in the first place if all I was going to do was scuttle it?"

"As a misdirection? Because you get off on stuff like that? Who knows? It's not actually the raid that bothered me. I expected that. It's that a team of mercenaries hired by the Shanghai Seven has been following me from my father's house to a shady motel in Quantico to the depths of the Prince William Forest Park. Do you really want to sit there and tell me they were able to do that all by themselves, with no help from you?"

Jones slid open his top desk drawer, removed a large manila envelope, and opened it. From inside, he removed a Ziploc bag containing a small black chip.

"This is quite a little marvel," he said, tossing it across the desk at Storm. "We heard the Chinese were working on something like this, though our intelligence indicated they hadn't gotten out of the lab yet. I guess we were wrong. It's real next-generation stuff. They're calling it TPT."

"TPT?"

"Total planet tracking. It's a cutting-edge combination of GPS and USBL, which means they can track you anywhere, anytime, whether you're on top of Mount Everest or twenty thousand leagues under the sea."

"Good for them. What's your point?"

"Our surgical team pulled it out of your ass this morning," Jones said. "We caught it during a routine bug sweep before we brought you down here. You were a walking transponder, transmitting on multiple frequencies. It's a wonder you couldn't hear *American Bandstand* pouring out of your backside."

Storm's brow furrowed as his hand went to the stitches on his posterior, which he began absentmindedly rubbing. *A tracking device?* How had anyone managed to implant a tracking device on him without . . .

And then he remembered the dart that had buried into the side of his buttock the week earlier, during the raid on the counterfeiting operation. He had immediately pulled it out, worried it was laced with poison.

But it hadn't been delivering toxins. It had inserted that tiny black chip into him.

He thought back to when that SUV had first come into the clearing by the cabin. One of the mercenaries had an electronic device open. Storm had been able to see the blue glow from his perch on the second floor. That must have been what they were using to monitor where the tracking device was.

"All right," Storm said. "Fair enough. Let's say I believe you about that. It still doesn't explain why you blackmailed that pathetic Mason Wood into ordering Bart Callan's transfer."

Jones got a curious look on his face, almost like he was discussing Hegel and someone brought up Kierkegaard. "Bart Callan? What does he have to do with any of this?"

"Don't play around. You know perfectly well the Shanghai Seven helped him escape from that flimsy jail you sent him to and now he's working for them."

Jones allowed his left eyebrow to rise a nanometer before

settling it gently back down. "I think you might be mistaken. Did Strike tell you about Mason Wood?"

"No. I found that out for myself."

"Well, I can assure you Bart Callan has nothing to do with the Shanghai Seven. They have enough murderous psychopaths lined up, waiting to work for them. They don't need the complication of hiring one who is a wanted federal fugitive."

"Then why did you have Wood order Callan's transfer?"

A rare smile appeared on Jones's face, then passed away just as quickly. "That was a favor for a friend," he said.

When Jones called someone a "friend" it was always tinged with meanings not normally attached to that word. To Jones, friends were fungible assets.

"Who?" Storm asked.

"Just a friend. A good friend. Soon to be an even better friend, hopefully, but that is truly not your concern. I assure you it's unrelated to the troubles you now seem to have with the Shanghai Seven," Jones said. "But hopefully, now that the TPT device has been removed, those troubles will be lessened. If you'd like, I can assign some agents to accompany you and provide additional security."

Storm knew the agents' other job, in addition to providing security, would be to report back to Jones everything they heard and saw. Storm would rather drink bleach.

"No thanks," he said.

Jones pushed away from his desk and stood. "Well, not that it isn't pleasant to see you again, but if you're done accusing me of treason, I have work to do. And I believe you do, as well. The next time you'd like to visit my house, please just call first. You know my wife has a soft spot for you. I daresay she has a bit of a crush on you. I'm sure she'd love to cook for you anytime you'd like to stop by. In the meantime, if you can promise you'll now go about fulfilling the terms of your contract—and if you can promise you'll stop being a threat to national security by trying to breach my security system—I'll have you and your father escorted out."

"Thanks," Storm said. "You know how much I appreciate your hospitality."

"Yes, indeed. Let's just get you your things, shall we?" Jones said. His hand was back in the manila envelope. He pulled out the burner phone.

"This is nice, by the way," Jones said. "Very nice. Very next gen. Are you going to start using a pager next? Maybe cups and strings?"

Storm snatched it from the desk.

"What happened to the phone I gave you?" Jones asked.

"It broke."

"Well, have the quartermaster get you a new one on the way out. There's no reason to have you bumbling around in the technological darkness that was the first decade of this millennium."

Jones then extracted the CD that had nearly cost Storm his life. "I suppose I should also return this to you. We've heard chatter the Shanghai Seven is after something in your possession. Might this be it?"

The disc glinted in the artificial light of Jones's office. Storm was careful not to grab at it, lest he seem overeager.

"It could be," he said. "That's a rare studio recording of the Doobie Brothers' greatest hits. It stands to reason the Shanghai Seven would have a special affinity for 'China Grove.'"

"Ah," Jones said, clearly not believing anything Storm was saying. "Perhaps that explains why the data on it was encrypted."

"Well, we can't let an iconic American treasure like the

Doobie Brothers fall so easily into foreign hands. Their fans would be 'takin' it to the streets' in protest."

"Well, I have to say the encryption was very thorough. Very exotic. Our techs gave it their best shot, but they couldn't crack it. I never would have thought the Doobie Brothers were so clever."

"You can underestimate the Doobie Brothers if you like," Storm said. "But that's only 'what a fool believes.'"

TWENTY-THREE

HEAT

The detectives who arrived on the scene made her tell the story, then go over it again.

Then they did the same to George The Bartender.

Then the US Marshals Service arrived—having been alerted that their prisoner had been found—and the process started all over. Heat was patient, cooperative. She understood everyone had a job to do, and it was important they did it well.

She also knew they were right then interrogating Colonel Feng. Heat wished she had the chance to talk to him first. But she knew a murder investigation took priority. She would have to wait.

By the time Nikki and George were told they could go, it was after five o'clock in the morning. And Heat, who was suffering a mild minibar hangover, was badly in need of some grease.

They found an all-night diner filled with that quintessential Manhattan combination of people on their way to work and people on their way back from a night out. This was no kind of establishment for a grande skim latte with two pumps of sugar-free vanilla. It was a place for eggs, pancakes, bacon, and coffee. Lots of coffee.

Heat asked for a western omelet, a side of bacon, and to keep the coffee refills coming.

George, who had yet to recover his appetite, ordered orange juice. When it came, he barely sipped it.

The old man had been through so much . . . too much for one night, for sure. Heat's plan was to let him process what had happened, then approach him later—maybe that evening, after he had slept—to discuss what, to her, now seemed obvious and inevitable: George had to turn over the bills.

But she could let it wait for a little while. There was a time to be a cop and force an investigation forward. There was also a time to realize human beings can only be pushed so far. The young Nikki Heat hadn't always understood that distinction. The older Nikki Heat had learned it well.

"I'm sorry I involved you in this," he said meekly, taking another sip of his drink. "When that guy came in and started asking for those bills, I . . . I panicked. All I could think of was how you had been asking about them, so I blurted out your name."

"I understand," Heat said, feeling some much-needed caffeine seeping into her bloodstream. "It's okay, really."

"Your mother didn't think anyone would ever figure out she had asked me to hide them, but she made me come up with a contingency plan just in case. She was always thinking, your mother. Sorry: *is* always thinking. I'm still having a hard time remembering she's alive."

"Me too," Heat said.

George pulled himself a little closer and leaned in from the other side of the table. "I was supposed to hide another envelope. That was the backup. If anyone ever came at me, I'd lead them to the phony set of bills. The problem was, I forgot where I hid them."

Heat just nodded.

"It's been seventeen years," he said, still pleading for her forgiveness even though she had already given it. "It's a wonder I remember where the originals are."

"Yeah," Heat said softly.

George's head bowed. "I guess now you're going to tell me I should give them to you."

She wasn't, of course—because of that instinct not to push things. But since George was the one bringing it up . . .

"Here's the problem, George. Bart Callan—that's the man who was killed—was working for someone who wants those bills. That someone is going to probably hire another man to get them now. And if Callan had told his employer that he suspected you had them—"

"They'll just come after me again," George said morosely. He was no longer even touching his orange juice.

"Then there's the problem of that Chinese man, Colonel Feng. He works for a group called the Shanghai Seven. Even though he was asking about a CD, the Shanghai Seven is eventually going to try to retrieve those bills, too. And they might put two and two together and realize that if whoever Callan worked for was concerned about the bills, they should be concerned about the bills, too."

"And then I'll have even more folks after me," George said.

"Yeah, that's about the size of it."

"And you really think . . . you really think you'll be able to make things safe for Cynthia to come out of hiding if you get those bills? You really think you'll be able to unravel whatever it was that made her need to hide in the first place?"

"I don't want to mislead you, because it might be a dead end," Heat said. "Having the bills wasn't enough for my mother to be able to make a case against anyone. It might not be enough for me, either. But it also might be. The fact is I won't know until

I at least have the chance to try. And, yes, I think it's my mom's best chance."

George seemed to be taking it all in as he brought the orange juice back to his lips.

"Okay," he said. "Then I'll show you. But only because it's the best thing for Cynthia. Not because I'm trying to save my own neck. I hope I have the chance to tell her that in person."

"Me too, George. Me too."

The omelet and bacon arrived, but Heat was already throwing money on the table and shoving away from it.

"All right," she said. "Let's go."

"Aren't you going to eat?" George asked.

"I'm not hungry."

Not for an omelet, anyway.

Manhattan was coming alive as George led the way out of the diner. Newsstands were opening, their clerks unpacking the bundles of papers that had been laid there a short time before. Garbage truck drivers were hurrying to make it through their morning routes before traffic picked up. Bodega owners were rolling up the steel shields that protected their stores at night.

It was one of the things Nikki Heat loved about her city: that sense of purpose that powered so many of its citizens so relentlessly forward into the promise of a new day.

And, despite having slept no more than three hours the previous night, she felt the same hope and energy. She was letting George lead the way, not asking where they were going, lest it spook him. She was going to let him do this in his own way, even if she was dying for him to walk just a little faster.

Still, it didn't take long for her to figure out where they were going, especially once George made the turn on East 19th Street and she realized he was heading for the alley behind The Players Club. George must not have had a key to the front door. Just the back.

He paused when he got to the door.

"Your gun," he said.

"What about it?"

"I'm sorry, Ms. Heat. You know the policy."

She did—no firearms at The Players Club—she just didn't think it would be enforced at that time of the morning, when the club was empty.

But she wasn't going to argue with George. Not when she was so close to the bills. She couldn't believe she was going to be separated from her service weapon for the second time in four hours—and this time voluntarily, at that. She just quickly scouted around for a hiding spot.

The Dumpster. No one would disturb the gun if she hid it there. She asked George to get her a towel from the kitchen. When he returned with it, she wrapped her 9mm and hid it out of sight of anyone in the alley, save for the rats.

Then, finally, George escorted her inside. He had to turn on lights as he went, going through the tiny warren of hallways that only the staff ever really used. Heat felt like she was getting a behind-the-scenes tour at Walt Disney World, seeing all the unfamiliar parts of an otherwise familiar place.

George stopped briefly in the cramped quarters shared by the maintenance staff and rummaged around in a toolbox for a moment, pulling out a straightedge razor and a long flathead screwdriver that would have made for a decent weapon if wielded properly. Then he led her to the polished mahogany bar that was his realm.

"Here?" she asked. "All this time, you kept it here?"

"Not quite," he said. "You'll see. Come on."

He had an enigmatic glint in his eye as he bent low to grab

something—Heat couldn't see what—from behind the bar. When he came back up, a piece of his white hair had come loose, giving him a kind of mad professor look.

Then, without a second glance at Heat, he went back to where the members' liquor lockers were. The room was dark. It didn't seem possible George could see anything.

"Aren't you going to turn on a light?" Heat asked.

"The bulb blew out last night and we haven't been able to replace it yet," he said. "It's apparently some kind of specialty item. Doesn't matter to me. I've always said I could navigate this place blindfolded. This is my chance to prove it."

He had walked to one of the cabinets, seemingly at random. Heat fumbled with her phone until she found the flashlight feature. She switched it on just as George whirled to face her. He gestured at her with the screwdriver, gripping the plastic end and flashing the metal end dangerously close to her face.

"You can't tell anyone about this," he said.

"Of course not."

"I really shouldn't be doing this."

"You're doing the best thing for everyone involved," Heat assured him.

He fixed her with one long, strange glance. Then he inserted a key into a locker whose brass plate had CLEMENS etched on it.

"Clemens?" Heat said. "As in *Samuel Langhorne* Clemens?"

"Well, it's certainly not Roger Clemens."

"All these years, you've been hiding the bills in Mark Twain's old liquor locker?"

"No one is supposed to touch this," George said. "It's the first rule all the new bartenders are taught: 'Don't mess with Mr. Clemens's cabinet.' It seemed like the safest place."

George turned back to the cabinet. He took the straightedge

out of his pocket, then plunged his hand in. Heat could hear him scraping away at wood.

"It took a few tries to get the cherry stain on this to match the surroundings exactly," he said. "But then it was pretty simple. This is just a piece of lauan that I glued into place."

"So you created a false back to the cabinet?" Heat asked.

"Defacing Mark Twain's old stashing place in the process. It helped that the envelope was so thin. Made it easier than if I had to hide something with a lot of heft to it."

He took a few more swipes with the straightedge. "There," he said. "That ought to do it."

Now it was time for the screwdriver. Before long, Heat heard the sound of dry, old wood separating from another piece of even drier, older wood.

"If anyone on the board knew I was doing this, they'd have me crucified," George said.

He removed a shard of wood from the back. After one more percussive crack, he brought out an envelope. He clutched it for a few extra seconds, giving the moment a small amount of added drama.

"Here," he said finally, handing it to Heat.

She brought it out to the bar area, which the morning sun was just starting to illuminate. It gave her enough light to see it was a number ten envelope made of the thick linen stationery paper Cynthia Heat preferred.

For as tempted as she was to rip the envelope open, Nikki knew she needed to exercise caution.

"George, do you have any plastic gloves?"

"Hang on," he said, going behind the bar. He came up with a pair of black rubber gloves. "Will these do?"

"Thank you," Heat said, delicately placing the envelope on the shiny, meticulously clean bar top as she put on the gloves.

"Now that straightedge, please," she said, feeling almost like a surgeon asking for a scalpel.

George handed her the razor, which she used to slice a line at the top of the envelope, taking great care not to let the blade touch anything inside.

She peered into the opening she had created. There were five twenty-dollar bills, straight and crisp and perfect. Heat pulled out the first one and studied it, smiling immediately.

There was a fine layer of powder clinging to it, and it made Nikki instantly feel the kind of intrinsic connection to her mother that had so often been absent over the last seventeen years. The combined writing muscle of every Hallmark card writer in existence could scarcely have concocted a better greeting from the mother in question to this particular daughter.

Cynthia Heat had already dusted it for prints. And there were several that stood out quite vividly. Not exactly a full set, but certainly more than enough to make an identification.

Forgetting what time it was, even forgetting *where* she was, Nikki Heat had already hauled out her phone.

She pulled up a number and pressed the call button.

As she listened to the ring tone, she studied the thumbprint on the first bill. It was smack in the middle of Andrew Jackson's face, with all its arches, whorls, and loops standing out very clearly. Heat could have gotten a better image with an old-fashioned ink pad and print papers down at the precinct. But this was almost as good.

After four rings, she heard a groggy voice answer: "Hello?"

"DeJesus. It's Heat."

Benigno DeJesus was the best crime scene tech Heat had—which didn't necessarily mean he was thrilled to be serving in that role at six in the morning.

DeJesus sputtered an inventive series of curses in Spanish—a kind of pirouette of profanity—then finished with: *"Dios mío, ¿sabes qué hora es?"*

"Sorry, sorry. I know it's early. It's kind of a personal emergency."

"It had better be," DeJesus grumbled.

"I need you to run some prints just as fast as you can. How soon can you get to the precinct?"

"I'll be there as soon as I can. Can I get my pants on first?"

"Only if you have to."

He concocted another elegy made of expletives, then hung up.

TWENTY-FOUR

STORM

D errick Storm left the Cubby the way he always did: wearing a hood that obscured his vision, riding in an elevator that lurched and zoomed like it was taking them through the bowels of Willy Wonka's Chocolate Factory.

When he was allowed to take off the hood, he was back out in the main lobby of CIA headquarters. Parked outside was the Ford Expedition he had rightfully stolen, fresh from the impound lot where it had spent the early morning.

Storm quickly checked out the back. The RPG launcher, the machine guns, the copious supply of ammunition, all of it appeared to be untouched. The CIA apparently interpreted the Second Amendment at its theoretical maximum.

As he waited for his father to reappear, Storm checked his burner phone and saw the message from Heat about cracking the encryption on the CD. He stiffened when he read Colonel Feng's name. There was something about the man—his oiliness, his cool, a dispassion that seemed to go beyond anything natural—that Storm found unnerving.

Furthermore, it signaled just how seriously the Shanghai Seven was taking this matter that they felt it necessary to send their top fixer all the way across the world just to retrieve a compact disc.

He texted back that he would get right on it.

What he didn't add was that he wasn't sure how he'd go about it. He had just left a room filled with the most talented cryptologists he knew of. And they had surely tried—and, if Jones was to be believed, failed—to access the CD while Storm was unconscious.

There was no taking the CD back down to the Cubby. Jones may not have been giving Storm's location to the Shanghai Seven, but that didn't fully restore Storm's faith in the man. It seemed every bit as possible he'd take whatever evidence Storm was able to drum up against the Shanghai Seven and use it for a purpose other than its original lawful intention. The only way Storm could keep Jones from misbehaving was to see this thing through to the end.

Storm was so lost in thought he only looked up when he realized someone was pulling open the passenger side door.

"Fancy meeting you here," Carl Storm said. "Let's get out of here. This place makes my skin crawl."

"You got it," Derrick said. "I was thinking I'd take you to a hotel. You know it's not safe for you at home while the Shanghai Seven is still out and about looking for us. Don't worry, I'll find you a better place than the Oorah. You can stay there until it's safe."

"What, and make me miss all the fun?"

"Dad, this isn't going to be f—"

"I'm aware," Carl said. "I was just making a little joke. Sheesh. Loosen up."

"That's the thing, Dad. None of this is a joke right now. You know what my last thought was when that tranquilizer dart hit me? It was that I had let you down."

"What are you—"

"Let me finish. I let you down because I never should have let you get involved in this in the first place, and I should have done a better job protecting you once you got in it. It's ridiculous that I've put you in harm's way. If anything happened to you because of one of my stupid jobs, I would never forgive myself."

Carl absorbed this for a beat. But Derrick could tell from the way his black eyebrows were waggling that he wasn't agreeing with a word of it.

"Well, that's very nice of you, to be looking after your enfeebled old fart of a father," he said. "But now, because I'm your father, I have the full liberty to tell you that is one hundred percent pure, unadulterated horseshit."

"Dad, come on—"

"No, no. I let you finish. Now you're going to let me finish. You know what *my* last thought was when those bastards shot me? It was that if this was how I had to go, there was no better way: with my son at my side, fighting until the last breath. As a matter of fact, if I could sign up for that right now, I would. So you might as well realize I'm in this thing to the bitter end, no matter how it ends. And don't give me this 'I let you down' crap. You could *never* let me down, Derrick. I'm too damn proud of everything you've accomplished and of the man that you've become for that to even be possible."

He patted his son on the knee, making Derrick feel like he was twelve again. It was, for a moment, a terrific feeling to have.

Then the moment ended. Carl cleared his throat and said, "Anyhow, before I issue the fatherly command that you shut up and drive, tell me: Why did you look like you were trying to pass a kidney stone when I first got in the car?"

Derrick told him about Heat's text and about how the CD seemed to be at the forefront of the Shanghai Seven's efforts both in DC and in New York.

"Sounds like we need to find out what's on that thing," Carl said.

"Of course. But how? None of the nerds could do it."

"Are you sure?"

"Yeah, I'm sure. That's what Jones—"

He was about to finish the sentence with the word *said*, but never got there.

Carl was already shaking his head. "How many times do I have to tell you, you can't trust that snake? If he told you he didn't crack it, that means the odds are better than fifty percent that he did."

Derrick just stared straight ahead through the windshield. He couldn't disagree with his father.

"Okay, so here's what we're going to do. If Jones's guys—"

"Jones's people. Some of those guys are gals, Dad."

"Right. As I was saying: If Jones's people cracked it, I bet that means your buddy Kevin Bryan could do it, too."

"You think he'll help us?"

"Sure. I'm 'the man,' remember?" Carl said, then smiled and patted his son's knee one more time. "Okay, *now* you can shut up and drive."

Morning traffic was just starting to thicken as they made the short trip to Kevin Bryan's apartment building. Derrick went through the front door this time. If one of the nerds alerted Jones about his visit, so be it.

They were on the same team, after all.

A quick elevator ride later, they were on Bryan's floor. He came to the door freshly showered, dressed in boxers and a T-shirt. He wedged it open only an inch, keeping the chain in place as he glared at Derrick.

"Just so we're clear, I'm only answering because I'm afraid

you'll cut another hole in my apartment if I don't," he said.

"That was definitely a possibility, except I don't like to duplicate the same means of entry twice, and I thought using explosives would get a little messy."

"What do you want, Storm?"

"Your help. Same as last time. Do you need another lecture from Dad or can we skip the touchy-feely stuff this time?"

"Is your dad even here?"

"Over here, Kevin," Carl said from the other side of the door.

Bryan mulled this over for a moment, then said, "Forget it. No offense, Mr. Storm, but even the Irish have limits on how much guilt they can be made to feel. We have a staff meeting this morning, and you know Jones with his Vince Lombardi routine: 'If you're not five minutes early, you're five minutes late.' I'm not—"

He was interrupted by his phone ringing. With the chain still on the door, Bryan snuck the phone out of his pocket, looked at the screen, then answered it immediately.

"Yes, sir," he said.

Voldemort. Again.

"Yes, sir," Bryan repeated.

He listened a little more.

"Are you sure, sir?"

Another pause.

"Yes, sir. I'll get right on it."

Bryan returned his phone to his pants. "Okay. How did you pull that off?"

"Pull what off?" Derrick said.

"That was Jones. He said I'm supposed to help you with whatever it is you want me to do, and he said it's okay if I don't tell him what it is. It seems whatever you've done, you've earned my services as a valet."

The Storms exchanged astonished looks. Then Derrick rolled with it. "Great," he said. "Can you shine my shoes?"

"Don't push it," Bryan said, sliding the chain off the door. "Come on in."

Without further delay, Derrick explained the nature of what they needed. Bryan immediately forgot about whatever hurt feelings he was still harboring about the intrusion and listened well. The challenge clearly intrigued him.

Before long, Carl had fallen into a deep sleep on the couch, and the other men had retreated into Bryan's home office. Bryan slid the disc into his desktop computer, which connected him to the massive computer power of one of the CIA's mainframes. He was soon lost in a digital world whose contours were only vaguely familiar to Storm.

Storm's job was to fetch coffee and pretend to know what Bryan was talking about as he attempted various assaults on the disc's security measures.

As one after another failed, Bryan's agitation began increasing. So did his rate of coffee consumption. And yet, in his increasing mania to solve the puzzle, he didn't seem to notice or care as he broke into a caffeine-induced sweat, or when his legs started bouncing up and down like small pale jackhammers.

After an hour of this, Bryan suddenly looked up from the screen.

"Holy crap!" he exclaimed.

"Did you get it?"

"No. I *really* need to go to the bathroom," Bryan yelped, then disappeared into his bedroom.

When he returned, he looked bewildered.

"What is it?" Storm asked.

"I don't know . . . I just . . . You usually get a pretty good sense of how things are going after a couple of hours, and I'm just not getting anywhere. If cracking this thing was like trying to write a novel, I'd still be on the first sentence."

Storm nodded. A novelist he once knew had explained that coming up with that first sentence was like a teenage boy trying to lose his virginity: a long exercise in mounting frustration followed by a payoff that, afterward, seemed altogether too brief.

"So what do we do?" Storm asked.

Carl, who had recently awoken from his slumber, wandered into the room and was listening in.

"I don't know," Bryan said. "Find a dinosaur to help you bust through this thing?"

"What do you mean?"

"This is late nineties encryption. In the computer world, that's so long ago, it's not just Stone Age—it's like the cavemen haven't even evolved yet. They're still monkeys trying to figure out how to stand upright. But, in its own way, that makes it a special kind of genius, because it's so old and so many generations removed from current protocols, I don't have a clue how to go at it. I can tell the nerds didn't, either. This thing is locked up tight."

"So you're saying the encryption is old school?" Carl asked.

"Ancient school," Bryan confirmed.

"In that case, I think it's time we excuse ourselves," Carl said, then turned to Derrick. "I've got another trick up my sleeve."

Derrick stiffened. "This isn't going to end up with me wearing someone's lawn on my head, is it?"

"No, no. I know a guy who might be able to help. We should go visit him."

"Where does he live?"

"New York. Queens."

"That's going to be a bit of a hike," Derrick said. "Can you call him first? Make sure he's not on vacation or something?"

Carl looked down at his shoes. "We, uh, we can't."

"What do you mean, 'we can't'?"

"He doesn't exactly have a phone."

"He can crack this unbreakable encryption but he doesn't have a phone?"

"He's very serious about his privacy."

"And who, exactly, does he worry is going to invade his privacy?"

Carl just shook his head. "Everyone."

TWENTY-FIVE

HEAT

Nikki Heat slid her key card into the door of her room at The Lucerne.

It felt far longer than four hours since she had departed there. But after dropping off the bills for Benigno DeJesus to begin working on, she'd begun to feel every minute of the sleep she had lost.

She tiptoed in to find Jameson Rook in the exact same spot where she had left him. He was still naked, still lying on his right side, still in a deep sleep. About all that had changed was that there was now a small stream of drool running down his chin onto the pillow.

Rook always did look cute when he was sleeping. And he looked something better than cute naked. It suddenly struck Heat that a naked hunk was a terrible thing to waste.

Stealthily, she took off her clothes and slid into bed next to him, draping his left arm back over herself.

The jostling brought Rook's upper half awake. Then her lack of clothing began to do the same for his lower half.

As he moaned his approval, Heat gently took hold of him. His body responded instantly to her touch. Rook's manhood had certainly gotten a good workout the previous night, yet he was ready for more. The man's stamina knew no end.

He brought his lips to her nape, and she gasped in delight as he took a small nip of her neck. Realizing she was already wet, she guided him between her legs and enjoyed him thoroughly.

When they were through, he said, "That was fantastic."

"Thanks. You too."

"And now you're going to tell me where you've been."

"I've . . . I've been here all night."

"Then how come you've got coffee breath?" Rook said.

Busted. Sometimes, sleeping with a trained journalist really sucked.

"Where did you go?" Rook asked.

Knowing there was no fooling him—at least not this time—Heat relayed her adventures with George The Bartender and Captain Feng. Then she told him about George finally turning over the bills, which she had, in turn, entrusted to DeJesus.

"So what are you going to do when DeJesus gets a hit?" he asked when she was through.

"I don't know. Start asking someone a lot of difficult questions, I guess."

Rook nodded. Then a switch flipped inside him and he got a sly grin on his face. "And what are you going to do in the meantime?"

He began closing in, and she was already relishing the feel of him inside her again when—with terrible timing—her phone bleeped with an incoming text.

"Ignore it," he said throatily.

But she was already rolling away from him. "I can't. It's probably DeJesus."

He let out a different kind of moan this time.

"Sorry," Heat said. "But I won't be able to enjoy this until—"

"Okay. Get on with it."

Heat rolled out of bed and fetched her phone from her pants.

She sat on the edge of the bed as her eyes focused on the screen.

It wasn't a text from DeJesus.

It was from a 646 number she had already begun to recognize altogether too well.

The Serpent.

But how was that possible? Bart Callan was dead. She had watched him die. And there was no possibility of it having been faked. She had seen the back of his head blown away and the brain matter decorating the wall behind it. No one, no matter how good an actor, could have assumed the odd angle at which his neck had come to rest.

So was The Serpent really someone else? He had to be. She thought back to what convinced her it had been Callan in the first place. It was because he'd scrawled her name in blood on the wall behind the lobby desk after killing Bob Aaronson, which had seemed like The Serpent delivering on the threat he had promised, and because of the tie back to his code name, The Dragon.

But that could have been nothing more than coincidence. And it stood to reason Callan had plenty of reasons to write Nikki's name on that wall. After all, she had put him in jail for four years.

"What's going on?" Rook asked, crawling over next to her.

"It's another text from The Serpent."

Rook took a moment to absorb this. "But I thought . . ." he began, then stopped himself, having seemingly reached the same conclusion—or lack thereof—as Heat. "Okay, so if The Serpent isn't Callan, who is he?"

"I don't know," Heat said.

She swiped at her phone to read the text.

LAST WARNING, it said.

There was a video attached. Heat hit the play button and waited for what felt like an eternity for it to load. Then the screen went from blank to full color, and Heat nearly dropped her phone.

It was her mother. Alive. Tied to a chair at the wrists and ankles. With a newspaper propped against her lap.

"Oh my God," Rook said. Nikki was beyond words.

Cynthia Heat was just sitting there, looking straight ahead, showing no emotion. Whether she knew the camera had been turned on and was recording her was unclear.

It gave Nikki a moment to really study her mother in a way she hadn't been able to during that half-second glimpse in the bus shelter, when her mother had been made up as a street person. Cynthia Heat was now dressed exactly as Nikki remembered her: a simple pair of slacks, a blouse with an elegant pattern and subtle splashes of color, expensive but tasteful jewelry, a belt and shoes that brought the outfit perfectly together.

The camera zoomed in. The screen on Nikki's phone was small, but it still managed to pick up the new details this closer view brought. There were more lines around Cynthia's eyes than Nikki remembered. New wrinkles had cropped up on her forehead as well. Her face was narrower, more drawn. Her lips had thinned and her eyes had sunk, victims of that inexorable loss of collagen that time inflicts. Her hair was grayer, duller, more fragile.

And yet: Her cheekbones were still a marvel, as high and proud as ever. Her eyes continued to radiate an intense awareness, like she was right then figuring out the weaknesses of her captors and factoring her odds of overcoming them. She was holding her chin up, strong, defiant, and prideful. She still had her dignity.

More than that, there was life to her. Seventeen years had not taken the fight out of Cynthia Heat.

Which was good. Because it was pretty clear she was going

to need that and more to get her through whatever this was.

What scared Nikki more than anything was that her mother wasn't blindfolded. Whoever had detained her wasn't worried about her seeing their faces or being able to identify where she was being held. It suggested they didn't plan on leaving her alive long enough to do either.

Nikki pulled the sheet up over her naked body in some kind of futile attempt to feel less vulnerable. Rook had placed a protective hand on her back. Neither gesture provided much comfort.

The camera panned down to show the paper in her lap was the *New York Ledger*. Heat couldn't quite make out the date, but the front page featured a photo of Lindsy Gardner's visit to the city from the previous day. In the upper right corner, there was a teaser: HOMELAND HEAT? CELEB COP OFFERED DC JOB. It was that morning's edition, which Nikki had watched hit the newsstands only two hours earlier. This was new footage.

Once the shot of the newspaper had been established, the camera worked its way back up, then zoomed back out to show all of Cynthia, sitting in a room that was so nondescript it could have been across town or across the planet.

"Good morning, Cynthia," a deep disguised voice said from behind the camera.

Cynthia looked just to the right of the camera, where it seemed the operator was standing.

"Go to hell, you gutless coward," she spat.

The voice laughed like he found this amusing. "Yes, yes. Cynthia Heat, always talking a big game, always so brave."

"Take these restraints off me and we'll see whether it's talk or not."

The voice laughed again. "That might be fun. But that's not why we've taken you. We want you to say hello to someone."

"Is it the queen? Don't bother. I said hello to her last week."

"No, Cynthia," the voice said. "We want you to say hello to your daughter."

Cynthia had already inhaled to make another snappy retort when the last word seemed to hit her like a shock wave. Her strength seemed almost immediately sapped.

"My . . . my daughter?" she said.

"That's right. I'm sending this video to Nikki as soon as it's done. It will be on her cell phone a few minutes from now."

Tears immediately welled in Cynthia's eyes, even as she tried to remain defiant.

"Leave her out of this," Cynthia said fiercely. "She has nothing to do with this."

"It's too late. She keeps trying to insert herself. She keeps pressing the issue. She won't heed any of my messages. I've tried warning her. I've tried shooting at her. She still doesn't listen. But maybe she'll listen to her mother. Tell her. Tell her to stop looking for you. Tell her to stop investigating the circumstances of your disappearance. Tell her to leave the Shanghai Seven alone."

A solitary tear fell down the side of Cynthia's face, leaving a salty track behind. She seemed to be having a difficult time controlling her breathing.

"I . . . I tried telling her that," she said quietly. "She won't listen to me, either. I wrote her a letter. I told her to stop looking for me. But she won't stop. She just won't stop."

"Then tell her again," the voice urged. "Tell her now!"

Cynthia Heat was staring straight into the camera, which had zoomed back in. Nikki felt that stare in some deep part of her gut. This was her mother, talking to her, for real.

"Nikki, sweetheart. I know . . . I know what a terrible mother I've been. But you have to believe that I've only done what I've done to protect you. So now please, *please*, let me keep protecting you. Forget about me. Go on with your life. Enjoy your husband. Have children. Take that new job in Washington. Do whatever it is that makes you happy. That's all . . . That's all I've ever wanted for you. Please."

At that moment, a red dot appeared on her forehead. "That's enough," the voice said. And Cynthia Heat, who could obviously see the weapon whose laser scope was now trained on her, closed her mouth.

"Nikki Heat," the voice said. "You've heard your mother. Now listen to her. Listen to her or the next video you receive will be me pulling the trigger.

"To signify you intend to comply, you will leave the country. Now. Two tickets have been purchased for you and your husband on Alitalia. They are waiting for you at the Kennedy Airport ticket counter. The tickets will take you to Rome, then to Amalfi, where you will stay for three weeks, contacting no one. When you return, you will go about your life as usual. The flight leaves at two o'clock this afternoon. You will be on that flight, or your mother will die. We will be watching."

Cynthia Heat gave the camera another searing look. "Please, Nikki. Please, please. Just go on with your life. You've lived without me for seventeen years. Please, please just go on doing it . . ."

And that was how the video ended: with Nikki Heat's mother begging her daughter to forget she ever existed.

It was the worst kind of bargain, the kind even the devil wouldn't have offered.

If you don't stop working a case that might bring about the safe return of your mother, she'll be killed.

But if you do stop working the case, she'll never be part of your life—so it'll be like she died anyway.

Two choices. Both bad. And time was running out before she had to decide between them.

Heat slumped at the end of the bed with the unseen weight of her mother's life pressing on her shoulders.

"Is it too dumb to ask if you're all right?" Rook asked.

Heat hugged the sheet tighter around herself.

"No," she said. "But to answer the question: No, I'm not."

"I understand," he said. "Do you have any thoughts about what you want to do?"

"I'm not having any thoughts yet. All I seem to be able to do right now is feel. And don't ask what I feel, because all I know is that it's too terrible to have a word associated with it."

Rook didn't immediately reply. He slid out of bed, put on some pants, then faced her.

"I'd like to watch the video again," he said.

"I'm not sure I can."

"I understand. Why don't you go take a shower? It's a short video. Forward it to me so I can watch it a few times while you're getting cleaned up. Then I'll put on some coffee for us and we'll figure out what we should do."

"I wish you wouldn't say 'we.' It's bad enough my mother is in danger. I don't want you to—"

"Too late. I'm already in this. Now forward me that video."

Heat was so enervated she complied with Rook's request and then walked into the bathroom. She turned on the water as hot as she could stand and then stood under it, hoping it could wash away some of her misery.

But there wasn't enough water in all the oceans to do that, nor enough heat in the sun. Heat felt lost and wretched and despondent. But more than that, she felt the extraordinary impotence of her situation.

It was a feeling she seldom experienced. From the day she entered the Police Academy, the one message that had been impressed upon Cadet Heat was that she could do something about the evil of the world. She could track down burglars. She could punish violent offenders. She could bring killers to justice.

As a cop, it wasn't just a suggestion she could do something about bad guys. It was her sworn duty.

And yet now, faced with the worst kind of bad guys, she was being told she couldn't do anything. It was an order that took her worldview and put it on spin cycle. Nikki Heat wasn't very good at being helpless.

She finally shut off the shower, not because it had made her feel any better, but because she felt she had given Rook enough time to watch that horrible video a few more times and come to whatever conclusion he needed to reach about it.

After drying herself and wrapping the towel under her arms, she returned to the room. Rook had donned a bathrobe with The Lucerne's logo. He was looking at the video intently, though he had turned the sound off so she wouldn't have to hear her mother's pleading or that awful disguised voice. It spoke to his level of concentration that he didn't even look up as she slipped out of the towel and into the change of clothes—a navy blue power pantsuit—Rook had thoughtfully brought from home for her.

Finally, he put down the phone and announced, "Okay, I think I've got a handle on this. I've watched the video six times. Four with sound, two without."

"And?" Heat asked.

"I think The Serpent is basically the Incredible Hulk."

When she saw he was actually serious, Heat brought her hand to her forehead, which she expected to begin throbbing at any moment. She was accustomed to Rook's wild theories and nonsensical suppositions. She had even grudgingly come to recognize they were sometimes right. But this was absurd, even for Rook.

"Rook, I'm not sure I can handle a trip to Crazytown right now."

"This isn't a trip to Crazytown. I'm not even getting you on the highway that leads to Crazytown. Just hear me out. The first communiqué was The Serpent saying he could be a friend or an enemy, and that it was up to you. Am I right?"

"Right."

"So, right off the bat, that's a very Incredible Hulk play. At this point, he's still Dr. Bruce Banner. He's calm. He's rational. He's trying to use logic with you. Yes, there's an implied threat—because he might turn into the Hulk—but everything is still very safe."

"Okay," Heat said, unable to believe she was actually playing along with this.

"Next we get the more overt threat: Do it my way, or else suffer. That's obviously a minor escalation. But there's still this hesitance there. Dr. Banner is fighting the transformation with everything he has. Even someone who is not as passionate about Marvel Comics as I am—"

"That's pretty much everyone over the age of twelve, Rook."

"Point taken. But as I was saying, you have to recognize this is classic Hulk behavior. It's basically him saying, 'Don't make me angry. You won't like it when I'm angry.' In his heart, Dr. Banner doesn't *want* to turn into the Hulk. He tears up a nice outfit every time he does. But he knows if things keep going a certain way, he probably won't be able to control it anymore. Still, there's that sense of regret. Do you follow?"

"I guess."

"Good. Because your next contact with The Serpent was even more Hulk-like. Bear in mind, your next contact was *not* the Bob Aaronson murder. We know for a fact that was Callan. And Callan can't be The Serpent, because dead men send no video texts. Your next contact was those potshots he took at you. Shots that missed."

"He only missed because I was dodging out of the way of some drunk people coming back from a restaurant."

"No, I'd argue he missed on purpose. If he was really trying to kill you, he might have gotten unlucky, on account of the drunks. But he would have hit some drunks instead. Instead, he was aiming high, which is very Hulkian."

"Because . . . ?"

"Because the Hulk goes out of his way not to hurt people. No matter how complete his rage is, no matter how green his skin turns, he never hurts innocent people."

"This is ridiculous."

"No, this is so dead-on, I'm thinking the psychology literature is seriously lacking for not having identified this sooner. They could call it Incredible Hulk Syndrome. IHS. Lou Ferrigno could be the celebrity spokesman for the disease. Anyhow, where was I?"

"Turning green."

"Right. And that leads to our final contact from The Serpent. This video. Again, no one was actually hurt. Think about it: If The Serpent really meant business, wouldn't he beat your mother up a little first? Wouldn't he cut off a body part or bruise her face or inflict some real pain? It would make the video a hundred percent more scary and therefore a thousand percent more effective. It would tell you, beyond a doubt, that The Serpent was a vicious guy ready to do vicious things. But he doesn't do that. Because, on the inside, he's still Dr. Bruce Banner, a mild-mannered, very decent human being."

"Can you please put this in non-superhero terms for me?" Heat asked.

"Yes. This is a bluff. The Serpent is all hiss, no bite."

"I don't know, Rook. My mom doesn't scare easily, and she looked pretty scared."

"Actually, I'm not so sure that's true. The video is really the ultimate confirmation that I'm right here."

"How so?"

"I think it may have been scripted."

"Scripted? But if it was scripted, that means my mother is . . . cooperating with her captor?"

Rook had started pacing back and forth on the small patch of hotel carpet in front of the bed. "Well, I'm not ready to go quite that far. But I do think their end goals are aligned. In a way, we knew that already. Before she was captured, she had written you that letter. So when the kidnapper is telling her to call you off the case, he's really only reinforcing something she wants anyway."

"But that doesn't mean the video was scripted."

"I'm not sure you'll believe that after you have the chance to look at it more carefully, particularly when the sound is off," Rook replied, slipping into his professorial lecture mode. "With the sound on, it's too easy to get distracted by the creepiness of that voice, by the words being spoken. But when you mute it, all you have to look at is body language. That's when you can really see what I'm talking about. Here, let me show you."

He fiddled with her phone for a moment and got the video cued up to the part where Nikki's name had just been mentioned, where Cynthia Heat welled up with tears. He hit PLAY and handed the still-muted phone to Nikki, then stood behind her so he could watch along.

To Nikki, it was just the same bad movie all over again, but silent this time. She didn't know what Rook was possibly seeing on this small screen. Except she could practically feel his excitement rise just before Cynthia began talking.

"There," he said, pointing. "Right there. See how she leans forward a little bit right before she speaks? It's like she knows it's going to be her turn to talk. Her body has this expectation it's about to deliver a line. How would she know that unless it had been decided ahead of time?"

Nikki kept watching as Cynthia was now sitting still. Rook got excited again, just as Cynthia's lips began moving.

"There it is again," he said. "Don't you see it?"

And, actually, she did. What's more, she knew, from her theater training, that it was a trait that sometimes had to be drummed out of amateur actors who anticipated a fellow player's lines ahead of time instead of reacting to them after they were delivered.

"Yeah, I do," Heat said. "You're right. It's like she's been tipped off."

Rook, still the professor, was clearly pleased with his student. "So there's that. There's also the plane ticket. I mean, really, what kind of bad guy offers you a free trip to the Amalfi Coast? Don't get me wrong, I like his style. And I know a *great* restaurant in Amalfi if you want to take him up on his offer. But it's not exactly consistent with someone who really plans to put a bullet in your mother's head. A true evildoer wouldn't bother offering a carrot like that. All he'd worry about is the stick."

The absurdity of the Hulk analogy aside, Heat realized she actually agreed with Rook.

"Okay, so let's say this is a bluff," she said. "How does that affect us moving forward?"

"It doesn't," Rook said. "The Serpent is going to keep making his threats. Just ignore him and continue with your investigation."

"In other words, we call the bluff and pray it really is an empty threat."

"Exactly."

Heat took in a deep breath and held it. She had relied on Rook's hunches many times in the past. Some panned out. Some didn't.

The difference, this time, was the stakes of being wrong. This wasn't a murder investigation, where going along with Rook would possibly take her down the wrong path for a little while before she got herself back on the right one.

This was her mother's life.

And yet she knew Rook was right. There had been something off about The Serpent from the start. Heat still didn't have an inkling who he was or what his real motivations were. But she ultimately didn't believe he would kill her mother.

Heat let out the breath. "I hope you're right about this," she said.

Rook looked appropriately grim-faced. "So do I."

TWENTY-SIX

STORM

I t was with some regret that Derrick Storm left the Ford Expedition—and its attendant munitions—in short-term parking at Reagan National Airport.

He briefly thought about trying to smuggle the RPG launcher and a few grenades through security, reasonably certain the Transportation Security Administration would miss it if he was clever enough to redirect their attention toward something that would really set off alarm bells—like a 3.6-ounce bottle of shampoo.

But, ultimately, he had friends in the New York area who could outfit him with weapons if the need arose. Besides, he didn't want to waste the shampoo.

Thus unencumbered, Derrick and Carl Storm managed to grab two seats on the 8 A.M. Delta Shuttle. Fifty-nine minutes later, it touched down at LaGuardia. Another twenty minutes after that, they were in a rental car, headed east on the Grand Central Parkway. Derrick was following GPS instructions for the Dartmouth Street address in Queens his father had furnished him.

"Okay, so who is this guy again?" Derrick asked.

"Albert Gorithem," Carl said. "You can call him Al."

"Paul Simon would surely approve."

"I'm pretty sure Al doesn't know Paul Simon exists. He's not exactly hip to the latest fads."

"Dad, Paul Simon hasn't been the latest fad for thirty years."

Carl Storm just grunted.

"Are you sure he's going to want to see us?" Derrick asked. "You guys parted on good terms?"

"Yeah. The best. We were like this."

Carl crossed his middle finger over his forefinger.

"And he'll be able to tackle this CD," Derrick said, trying to signal his confidence by making it a statement, not a question.

"If anyone can, it would be Al. Back in the day, he was the best there was."

"So what happened to him?"

"Same thing that happened to all of us," Carl said. "We got old, obsolete. Then some snot-nosed kid came along and convinced people he could do the job better. Plus Al had some, ah, eccentricities that got the best of him."

"The no-phone thing?"

"That among other things, yes."

"We're not going to find him running around his house in a tinfoil hat, are we?"

Carl paused for what Derrick felt was a little too long before answering. "I don't think so, but . . ."

"Oh, perfect."

"Look, this guy is a virtuoso when it comes to cracking encryption, okay? But sometimes if you want to enjoy the art, you need to suffer the artist."

Derrick was cutting through the heart of the western tip of Long Island with five lanes of barely controlled chaos. Derrick first drove eighty, then forty, then back to eighty. As he did so, he weaved in and out of lanes, cut off other cars, roared through gaps in traffic that appeared inadequate for any wheeled vehicle larger than a tricycle, then left huge yawning gaps ahead of him.

To Derrick, this was prudent countersurveillance. To most New Yorkers, it was just driving.

As he passed Citi Field, home to New York's forever second-best professional baseball team, he became aware that one car—a blue midsize sedan with a Mazda logo on its grille—seemed to be shadowing his movements, speeding up when he sped up, lagging back when he laid off the gas. It was staying a few cars back, never in the same lane, trying to be subtle about it. But Derrick's sensitive nose had sniffed out a potential tail.

The exit for Al Gorithem's house was coming up quickly. If the blue Mazda sedan was a tail, he didn't want to lead his pursuers any closer to where he was going. At the same time, there was no better way to confirm that he was being followed than by taking the series of turns that the GPS was telling him came next.

"We might have company," Derrick said.

"What do you mean?"

"There's a blue sedan that seems to really like us."

"Since when?"

"Since the airport."

Carl chewed on this for a moment. "You think it's possible your Shanghai Seven buddies found a way to put another tracking device in you?"

"No. The CIA bug check would have tripped on it. And it's not like Jones would have told them to leave it in. He doesn't want anyone, not even someone he's working with, knowing about the Cubby. The better possibility is that the Shanghai Seven hacked into Delta's computer system. I've seen the nerds do it. They worm their way in and download passenger manifests all the time."

"So, in that scenario, they could have known what time we

were landing and been able to get a few people in place to follow us coming out of LaGuardia."

"And then, once they see where we're going, that gives them time to assemble a larger team to take us down," Derrick finished.

"Then I say lose the guy on surface streets. It shouldn't be hard to do. You know what Queens is like. Whoever laid out the streets there either had a sense of humor or a bad case of vertigo."

"Okay, then here goes nothing," Derrick said.

He took the exit for Al's place, staying along the Grand Central Parkway's frontage road for a short time. The blue sedan did the same.

He took a right on 69th Road. So did the Mazda. But so did a lot of other traffic. It was the first main road after the exit.

"Still on us?" Carl asked.

"Still on us," Derrick confirmed.

"Okay, pull into that drugstore," Carl said. "Let's get a look at this guy."

Derrick complied. The sedan cruised past. It wasn't a guy. It was a woman, wearing a hijab that covered her hair and neck.

"You think the Shanghai Seven has taken to hiring Muslim women to do their dirty work?" Derrick asked.

"Doubt it."

"Okay, then let's call that a false alarm," Derrick said.

They pulled back out onto 69th Road. The blue Mazda did not reappear. Derrick thought for a while a Toyota 4Runner might have been lurking behind them. Then it fell off and maybe—maybe—a Chrysler 300 had taken up the shadow.

Then Derrick dismissed it all as paranoia. A three-car follow required training, timing, and discipline. It was difficult to pull off without a high-degree of coordination. Even seasoned CIA agents had been known to botch it. They were clear.

After a series of turns, they were soon cruising down Dartmouth Street, which was as tree-lined and pleasant as any street named after that great institution of higher learning ought to have been. Derrick found a spot midway up the block and parallel parked.

On the left side was a row of tidy, well-kept brick houses that had all been built around the same time—likely after World War II, with the generosity of the GI Bill—and had remained more or less identical.

Except for one. Its soffits were decorated by a trio of medieval-looking gargoyles. Its roof had coils of razor wire around the edges. A variety of NO TRESPASSING signs festooned the lawn, which had been xeriscaped to eliminate the need for mowing. There were bars on the doors and windows. The shades were all drawn.

"What makes me think we've found the place?" Derrick said.

"I see all that private-eye training hasn't completely left you," Carl said. "Now just hang back and let me take the lead. This might get weird."

Carl headed up the short concrete walk, climbed a brief set of steps, then rang the doorbell.

Nothing happened. There was no chime, no buzz. Carl pressed the button again, harder this time. But no sound could be heard.

It stood to reason a man who wanted to be left alone would disable his doorbell. So Carl opened the screen door and rapped his knuckles on the narrow opening between the bars that overlaid the door.

Then he knocked again. And again.

"Maybe the guy isn't home," Derrick suggested from the sidewalk.

"No. He's home."

"How do you know?"

"Because Al is a bit of a shut-in."

"*A bit* of a shut-in?"

"Okay, so last I heard he hadn't left his house since 1998."

"Oh, Dad . . ." Derrick said.

Carl knocked again. And again. "Al!" he yelled. "Al, it's me. Carl Storm. From the Bureau."

More knocking. Nothing.

"I'm just going to keep knocking until you answer," Carl called out.

To make his point, he pounded on the door ten times in rapid succession.

Finally, from inside, there came a tense, high-pitched "Go away."

Derrick Storm, meet Albert Gorithem.

"Al, I need your help with something," Carl said. "Come on, open up."

"You're with them. I know you're with them. Piss off."

"Who's them?" Carl asked.

"You know perfectly well. Now go away. You're not fooling me into opening the door for you."

Derrick looked at his father with a half grin on his face. "Dad, I know you said you were like this." He overlapped his middle and pointer fingers. "But to me, that sounds more like this." He rotated his hand until only his middle finger was protruding from it.

Carl ignored him. "Al, come on, buddy. This is really important. I need an old encryption cracked. You're the only one who can help us."

For a brief moment, one of the living room shades parted

before immediately being returned to its place.

"It's got the CIA stumped," Carl continued, then made the important strategic switch from pleading to challenging. "I guess maybe it would stump you, too."

Derrick could practically feel Gorithem stirring uncomfortably from the other side of the door.

"There's a man who always tries to break into my house around this time," Gorithem said. "He's incredibly persistent. He comes every day except Sunday. How do I know you're not working for him?"

"Al, that guy who tries to break into your house every day? That's the mailman."

"That's just his cover. I'm not fooled."

"Well, look, I'm not him, okay?" Carl said. "Look at me. I know I've gotten old, but I'm Carl Storm. Just look at me."

The shade briefly parted again. "How do I know you're not just someone who looks like Carl?"

"Oh, fer Chrissakes."

"June 1996. Minnesota. What case were you working on?"

"Kiddie porn," Carl said. "You had figured out some of those sickos were swapping images by embedding them in what seemed like innocent chunks of research data. They were trading them back and forth using file transfer protocol. I went to Duluth to bust the guy. He was living in his parents' attic and doing it all on a server he had made himself. Uh . . . Willis was his name. Vernon Willis."

For a short while, nothing came from inside. Then: "That case got a lot of publicity. You could have read news accounts about that."

"Al, stop being—"

"Seattle. 1986. What case did you close?"

Carl's dark eyebrows furrowed. He put his hands on his hips. He looked up to the sky.

Finally, he said, "Trick question. I didn't have a case in Seattle in 1986."

"Liar! Fraud! Imposter!" Gorithem yelled. "I knew it! The real Carl Storm would have never forgotten the Bessinger kidnapping!"

"Oh, for the love of . . . The Bessinger kidnapping was in eighty-seven, you moron! Klaus Bessinger. His father was the principal violinist in the Seattle Symphony Orchestra and he had been loaned a Stradivarius that was valued at something like half a million bucks. The kidnappers wanted to swap the violin for the kid. We lured the kidnappers in with a violin we borrowed from a local Suzuki teacher named Jennifer Kovarovic. The decoy worked and the kidnapper we caught flipped on his coconspirators after I showed him footage of death by electrocution and promised him that's what he'd get if he didn't cooperate."

Gorithem considered this for a moment. "How do I know you didn't just study some of Carl Storm's bigger cases so you'd have answers in case I asked you about them?"

"Oh, Al. Would you cut it out and—"

"My retirement party. What kind of cake did they serve?"

"Another trick question. You didn't have a retirement party. You stopped leaving your house years before that. We had to mail you the cake. The rumor was you left it on your front porch because you were sure the SAC who sent it had poisoned it."

"That cake *was* poisoned. One of the neighborhood dogs eventually got to it and I swear I never saw that dog again."

Suddenly the front door to the house opened. Standing in the entryway was a thin man of about seventy. His skin was so pale it was practically translucent. His hair was matted on one side—from his pillow, perhaps—and wildly protuberant on the other. He wore black socks and no shoes, plaid shorts, and a blue checked shirt that was open to reveal scraggly chest hair.

"Now hurry!" he said. "That quote-unquote 'mailman' could be here any minute."

Carl walked quickly inside. Derrick made to follow him, but Gorithem stuck out a skinny arm, blocking his path.

"Wait. Who's this?"

"This is my son, Derrick."

Gorithem looked up at Derrick. "The day you were born, what brand of cigar did your father pass out at the office?"

"How should I know?" Derrick said.

"Cohibas," Carl said. "Now knock it off, Al. We've got work to do."

The interior of Albert Gorithem's home turned out to be just as strange as the man himself. The entire downstairs had been turned into one large workroom.

Its flooring was hard tile. It smelled of cleaning supplies. The walls were lined with dry-erase boards covered in multivariable equations, all of them written in painfully small handwriting and spiked with Greek letters Derrick only knew from college fraternity parties.

In the middle of the room there was a large array of computers of varying sizes and ages, all networked into each other through a jungle of cords that protruded out their backs. If Gorithem knew about the invention of wireless communications, it didn't show.

There was only one chair: the one in front of the computers. There was no other indication creature comfort had been more than a glancing consideration.

Security, on the other hand, had been lavished with attention. Hanging from the ceiling was a series of television screens that showed a variety of views of the stone front lawn, the small alleys on either side of the house, and the tiny space behind it. No one was sneaking up on Al Gorithem.

"Bet you didn't see any of those cameras on the way in," Gorithem said, clearly proud of himself.

"No," Derrick replied.

"The gargoyles. They're hidden *in* the gargoyles. Which means they're protected by stone. It would take a jackhammer to knock those things out of commission."

"What are you working on, Al?" Carl asked.

"That's classified," he said. "As a matter of fact, I'd ask that you not look at the boards. There are some mathematicians at Berkeley who would give anything to have a gander at them. I don't want you to tip them off to what I'm on the brink of."

"Yeah, not a real danger of that," Derrick assured him.

"I'd invite you to take a seat, but . . ." Gorithem looked around the room, which was devoid of furniture save for the one chair.

"That's okay," Carl said. "We might as well just get down to business."

"I thought you were retired," Gorithem said.

"I am." Carl jerked his thumb at Derrick. "He's not."

"And why should I help him?"

"Because I'm asking you to, and I'm the only reason they didn't fire you before you got your twenty in," Carl said. "Remember San Antonio?"

"Oh. Right," Gorithem said.

"And Branson."

"Yes, yes. Okay, so what's this encryption you can't crack?"

Carl nodded and Derrick extracted the CD from his jacket, where it had been safely nestled against his body. He handed it to Gorithem, who sat down without a word and inserted the disc into the drive of one of his computers.

He struck a few keys, then frowned as two of the screens in front of him filled with a baffling series of numbers, letters, and symbols.

To the Storm boys, it was unreadable. Derrick would have had an easier time unscrambling an egg. Carl would have had an easier time laying one.

But Gorithem's eyes were poring over the screen like it was as easy and pleasurable to read as a classic Stephen Cannell novel.

"Yes, yes," he said. "I haven't seen this in *a while*. You were right when you said it was old. *No one* uses this anymore. Oh, this is a gem."

"So can you crack it?" Derrick asked.

"Can I crack it?" Gorithem said, offended. "Would you listen to this kid, Carl? Can I crack it. What are you trying to say? That I'm just some Whit Diffie wannabe?"

Derrick and Carl exchanged blank looks.

"Please pretend you know he's the father of public-key cryptography, or I'll lose respect for you," Gorithem said.

"Uh, right."

"Anyhow, what we're dealing with here is a combination of MD5 and AES. It's 128-bit, so you're going to have a tough time brute-forcing this puppy. And it employs elements of the Rijndael block cipher. Before WAP2 came along I really thought it had a chance to go places, but it never really caught on with anything more than enthusiasts like me. It's known as the Bridget Two Cipher, or just the B2 for short."

"The Bridget Two?" Derrick asked. "So it was developed by a woman named Bridget?"

"No, no. It was developed by a guy who named it after the

only girl who ever slept with him, in the hopes she'd do it again."

"Did it work?"

"Of course not," Gorithem snorted. "Anyhow, this might take some time. So let me get to it."

TWENTY-SEVEN

HEAT

The call must have come in while Heat was in the shower or while Rook was performing his video analysis.

But as soon as Heat was aware she had missed the call— and that the caller had left a message, and that the caller was John Null, Lindsy Gardner's campaign manager—she eagerly checked her voice mail.

"Nikki Heat, John Null here," she heard. "Lindsy is really excited to meet with you. We've got a major rally in Phoenix tonight but she might be able to fit you into her schedule before she leaves. Or, better yet, you could join us for the trip. Whatever works. Call me."

Heat had been moments away from leaving The Lucerne and heading to the precinct. Without a word, she handed the phone to Rook, who was still wearing his bathrobe.

They had yet to discuss the offer or its implications. As if she didn't already have enough on her mind.

Rook listened to the message, then handed Heat her phone.

"So what do you think?" she asked.

"I think he likes you. By the way, is he bigger than me?"

"Stop it. I mean about the job."

Rook rubbed his chin for a moment. "I think if the future president of the United States offers you a position, you'd be a fool not to consider it pretty seriously."

"Yeah, but . . . I mean, I have too much paperwork *now*. Can you imagine what it would be like with that job?"

"You'd also be better resourced. You could delegate the stuff you didn't like."

"It'd be pretty high profile. I'm not sure I'd like that."

"I don't know if you've noticed, but you seem to get a lot of attention in this job, too," Rook pointed out. "Admittedly, I'm partly to blame—"

"Mostly to blame."

"Mostly to blame. But, my point is, that would follow you wherever you went."

Heat looked out the small window, down at 79th Street. "And what would you think about living in DC?"

Rook pantomimed typing. "I can do this from anywhere. It's one of the perks of my job. I'm sure *First Press* wouldn't mind if my stories got more of a Washington bent."

"So you think I should take it?"

"I think that's not my decision. It's yours. Do what you think is best. I'll support you either way. You know that."

"Do you think my mother would move to DC with us? I mean, you know, assuming this ends well."

"That's a nice thought," Rook said, then kissed her on the forehead. "And now, because I've already given up my hopes for another prework quickie, I'm going to hop in the shower."

Heat grabbed him before he could make it there and kissed him more deeply.

"There's more where that came from. But later. Now go," she said, swatting him on the ass.

She left the hotel with a bounce in her stride. She would check in with DeJesus to see if he had a hit on the fingerprints. Then she would see if she could arrange for some one-on-one time with Feng, who was hopefully tired from an evening of being grilled by all levels of law enforcement.

Despite the dearth of sleep, Heat felt so much more energy than she had when she'd made the same walk the previous night—or even when she'd first watched the video of her mother.

Rook was right. She was becoming increasingly sure of it. The Serpent wouldn't really harm her mother. The real threat was the owner of those fingerprints. Or it was whoever had hired Callan. Either way, she was close to learning the identity of those people and bringing them to justice.

As she picked up her pace, Heat recognized the beginnings of one of the more tricky emotions a detective has to deal with: hope.

In some ways, it's the most necessary of feelings. It propels a detective forward, gives her confidence. She has to *believe* she can solve a case or else she never will.

And yet it also comes with a certain amount of danger. Hope raises a person up.

Which only makes the fall that much more painful.

"What do you mean Feng is no longer in custody?" Heat snarled into her phone.

It had been her first act when she'd settled behind her desk: a quick call down to the Thirteenth Precinct to see when she could schedule some time with Feng; or, better yet, to have Feng brought up to the Two-Oh, where she could work him over in the friendly confines of Interrogation One.

Instead, she learned she was too late.

"He and his brute squad killed a man last night," she continued. "They did it right in front of my eyes. You don't just kill someone and then waltz out of police custody with a breezy,

'Oops, it won't happen again.' They're foreign nationals, for God's sake. They shouldn't even have guns. An incident like that should take days to untangle, not hours."

"I'm sorry, sir," the dayside detective told her. "I have no information for you. The order came down before I got here this morning."

"Came down from where?"

"As I understand it, it was straight from the commissioner's office."

"Oh, that's just perfect." Heat slammed down the phone.

She waited half a second, then picked it up again and dialed Zach Hamner. The senior administrative aide to the NYPD's deputy commissioner for legal matters answered with an officious "Hamner."

"What the hell, Hammer?" Heat began.

"Well, good morning, Captain Heat," he said, with false amiability.

"Shove it. Why did the commissioner spring Colonel Feng?"

Hamner rolled with the question like he had spent all morning expecting it. "Why is that any of your business?"

"Don't even try to get cute with me. You know damn well it's my business."

"Because you were a witness? Or because Bart Callan made you look ridiculously foolish by turning you into a damsel in distress, in need of rescue, by separating you from your service weapon? Honestly, Captain, you ought to be thanking me for sweeping this matter under the rug and assuring this does not receive any more of the department's attention. Or the media's."

"So this was your doing?"

"Call it a group decision that was made by a group whose membership may or may not have been larger than one," Hamner said. "And not that you deserve any explanation whatsoever, but since the commissioner is already dreaming of all the Homeland Security dollars you're going to shunt his way: Yes, we let Feng go, and we did it for at least three good reasons.

"One, he was here on a diplomatic visa and claimed immunity. Two, he reasonably believed the lives of two people—a police officer and a civilian—were in grave danger. And part of the corroboration to support that claim came from your mouth, Captain. Three, the man he killed was an armed escaped convict who was clearly a danger to the public. Do I really need to keep going here?"

Heat was gripping the phone so tight her forearm was starting to throb.

"Oh, I've actually just thought of a few more," Hamner said, clearly enjoying himself. "Four, our friends at the US Marshals Service were practically ready to pin a ribbon on Feng's chest, because he spared them the continued embarrassment of not being able to track down a high-profile fugitive. And, five, Feng made a phone call to the Chinese Embassy, which started making its own phone calls to some pretty important people in the middle of the night. There was no chance our government was going to risk an incident with the world's only other superpower over something like this. Hell, the Chinese are creating whole islands in the South China Sea and then populating them with missiles in blatant violation of international law and more treaties than I can name, and all we do about that is issue warnings and occasionally have a battleship sail into view. You think Uncle Sam is going to jam up a few Chinese diplomats for essentially doing us a favor? Dream on.

"Now," he finished, "any more questions?"

"No. I think we're done."

"Good. By the way, you looked great on TV yesterday, Captain Heat. Really represented the—"

Heat hung up. She fired off a quick text to Storm: FENG IS IN THE WIND. BE ON THE LOOKOUT. HOW'S IT GOING WITH THE ENCRYPTION?

Moments later, Storm texted back: WE'RE MAKING PROGRESS. ANOTHER HOUR? MAYBE TWO? THANKS FOR HEADS-UP ABOUT FENG.

Heat stood. There was nothing more she could do about Feng. Maybe once Storm got the encryption cracked—and they understood why the Shanghai Seven was so hot to recover the CD—Feng would cease to be of importance.

Or he'd be joining his employers in a jail cell. Extradition from China was not impossible. Better yet, if she managed to track him down while he was still in the country, no extradition would be necessary.

With that end still loose for the time being, Heat stood and made the walk downstairs to Benigno DeJesus's domain.

She found him stirring some coffee, staring down thoughtfully at the brown liquid as if it held all of life's answers. Heat only wished it were so easy. She tapped on his door, even though it was open.

"Oh, hey, Captain," he said. "I was just about to call you about those fingerprints."

"With good news or bad?" she asked.

"The latter, I'm afraid. I ran them through our system and of course struck out. Then I went to NGI."

DeJesus didn't have to bother explaining that the FBI's Criminal Justice Information Services Division had developed what it called the Next Generation Identification system to house all of its biometric data. NGI's crown jewel was Advanced Fingerprint Identification Technology, which now claimed a matching accuracy of beyond 99.6 percent and included more than a hundred million unique entries. In addition, DeJesus could access the Repository for Individuals of Special Concern, which included convicted sex offenders, suspected terrorists, and a host of other unsavory characters.

"And you struck out there, too?" Heat asked.

"Not exactly," DeJesus said. "There's a hit on the print. But it's classified."

Of course it was. That's likely why Cynthia Heat hadn't been able to do anything with the prints seventeen years ago. She had hit the same wall her daughter was hitting now.

"How classified?" Heat asked.

"You need something called T-A1 clearance."

"What's that?"

"I had never seen it before, so I had to call down to the FBI in Washington to ask. It turns out T-A1 is the highest level of classification. Apparently, it was created during the Nixon administration—go figure—and it's not used very often anymore. The fibby I talked to had never actually seen it, either. But it means only the president, the vice president, the Joint Chiefs of Staff, or members of the president's cabinet can access it."

As soon as he said the word "cabinet," Heat brought her hand to her mouth.

She wasn't a cabinet member. Yet. But as head of Homeland Security, she would be. It would mean having to wait a few months before she could act . . . But what was a few more months compared to seventeen years? Could her mother hold out that long? Could she even hop on that flight to Amalfi and make The Serpent think she was standing down, when really she was just lying low for a little while?

"What?" DeJesus asked, reacting to her obvious shock.

"Nothing," Heat said. "I just . . . I have to make a phone call. Good work, DeJesus."

"Sure, Captain. Would you like me to put the bills in evidence, or . . ."

"No, why don't you just give them to me?"

He handed Heat the envelope, and soon she was charging back up the steps toward her office.

Director of Homeland Security. Could Nikki Heat, onetime beat cop, really ascend to one of the highest law enforcement positions in America?

When she reached her office, she pulled the door shut and tried to collect her wits. She took some slow breaths to steady herself.

Almost without thinking, she sat at her desk, opened the top drawer, and was about to place the envelope inside. Then she considered the advisability of that move. George had stashed the bills for years in the most secure place he could find, a hidden compartment no one knew about in a place people were forbidden to go. Sticking the bills in a desk drawer—even in a secure police precinct—was hardly showing the same level of concern.

Not knowing what else to do with it, Heat slipped the envelope into the jacket pocket of her pantsuit. That would have to do for now, until she found a better place. A safe-deposit box seemed like a good call.

She took a few more deep breaths and thought about the set of circumstances that had led her to this spot. The entire narrative—from her mother's murder all those years ago, to Legs Kline's more recent shenanigans, to Storm's raid on the Shanghai Seven, to her learning about those bills and their importance, to Lindsy Gardner's job offer—played out in her head.

Nikki Heat didn't believe in fate, or kismet, or destiny.

She believed there were always explanations for seemingly inexplicable things—even if she couldn't necessarily find them right away. Mysticism, the occult, voodoo, those were areas she left to Rook, who always seized on the supernatural with special zest. In her experience, if the killer had mysteriously vanished without a trace, it wasn't because he was a ghost. It was because no one realized he was still hiding in the closet.

Yet even Heat felt this strange gravitational pull toward what she was about to do next, like all the stars in the universe had arranged themselves to tug her in this direction.

She drew out her cell phone and was soon ringing a certain 202 area code.

"John Null," she heard.

"John, it's Nikki Heat."

"Captain Heat, do you believe in ESP?" he asked.

Heat, now thoroughly spooked, said, "Uh, n-no, why?"

"Because I was *just* about to call you again," he said. "Lindsy had a cancellation in her schedule for lunch and I wanted to see if we could fit you in. Could you be over here at noon?"

"Sure. Where are you?"

"Campaign headquarters. We're in The Marlowe."

The Marlowe was in the Financial District.

"Yeah, I think I can still make it in time," Heat said.

"Terrific. We'll see you shortly."

Heat ended the call, then hurried out of her office, making noises to Roach about how she had a lunch date—without saying who it was with—and how she'd be back in a few hours. She rattled off a quick text to Storm about the classified fingerprint results. She typed an even briefer text to Rook about where she was heading, spending most of her 160 characters on reminding him he couldn't tell any of his reporter buddies about it.

Then she took the subway downtown. The Marlowe was one of the sparkling gems of lower Manhattan, a ninety-two-story testament to the success of the American experiment.

Certain members of the liberal press had given candidate Gardner a hard time about her choice for campaign headquarters. The Marlowe was home to some of the more vital cogs in the nation's financial machinery—the kinds of banks, venture capitalist firms, and hedge funds that made capitalism such a ruthless creature.

They were the very beasts Gardner was trying to tame in her efforts to diffuse the intense concentration of wealth among a very select few. Yet Gardner argued if she was ever going to reform the zoo, she needed help from the animals. Hence her selection of The Marlowe.

As Heat walked toward the building, it was three minutes before noon. She was pleased to see there were no members of the press camped outside. She pushed through the brass revolving doors, then confronted a security desk, which had been told to document all visitors to Gardner campaign headquarters and then send them on to the eightieth floor. Nikki flashed her NYPD tin, then made the ride up.

When she got off the elevator, John Null was waiting for her in the vestibule. He was wearing a different tailored suit than the day before, but if anything it draped across his long body even more nicely.

"Thanks so much for coming, Captain," he said, giving her a sincere smile and a sloppy salute. "Lindsy is ready for you. If you can just submit yourself to these gentlemen for a moment, we can be on our way. Sorry, not even decorated NYPD captains get to bypass the Secret Service."

He nodded toward a trio of men in dark suits who were

clustered near a metal detector. Each of the men was certainly armed, though their weapons were not visible. They wore earpieces connected to tightly coiled wires that disappeared down their backs. With a minimum of fuss, the Secret Service collected her phone, explaining they had to keep it because it could be used to set off explosives, and her gun, a threat that was a little more obvious.

Heat couldn't believe she was giving up her service weapon for a third time in one day. It didn't make her feel any less naked than she had the previous two.

But there was no time to dwell on it. She and Null passed through the metal detector. Then Null escorted Heat through a thick set of double doors. They were immediately confronted by a divider behind which a receptionist could have sat if there had been one. Half the floor space was off to the right, the other half to the left.

Null went left into a vast open area that had been furnished with a maze of desks, all of them jammed up against one another in haphazard clumps of varying sizes. Some of the desk pods were empty, while others were filled with cadres of idealistic-looking young adults whose wide-eyed zeal reminded Heat of cult videos she had seen.

"We occupy three floors of the building," Null narrated. "We have phone banks upstairs and direct mail downstairs. This is in the middle. A few of the folks we're seeing are staff people, but most are volunteers. Lindsy gets them from all over. They're split into two groups: the true believers, who want to be part of something bigger than themselves, and the opportunists, who want a job in her administration when this is over."

He laughed at his own joke as he continued through the room. None of the volunteers seemed to recognize Heat or acknowledged her presence.

"We sometimes call this the hive," he said as they continued their journey toward the back. "We talk about the buzz they create. We talk about the honey they make. We're just one big happy colony here, and we refer to Lindsy as the queen bee. Speaking of which . . ."

They had arrived at a corner office suite whose door was closed. Null opened it, stuck his head inside, then proceeded through an empty area with a desk holding a computer and a multi-split screen that showed various camera angles of the two main rooms. From there, the people toiling diligently in the hive really did look like worker bees.

At the next door, he tapped lightly but did not wait for a reply before wedging it open.

"She's here," was all he said.

Then he turned toward Heat. "Okay," he said. "Lindsy is ready for you."

TWENTY-EIGHT

STORM

I t didn't seem possible Al Gorithem could appear any crazier than he had upon their initial meeting, what with his shut-in pallor, his bedhead hair, and his security camera gargoyles.

And yet, somehow, as he got closer to cracking the encryption on the compact disc, he grew even more manic.

He began bouncing in his chair in an arrhythmic fashion, bobbing to the left and right like he was either trying to dodge punches thrown by a heavyweight fighter or he was riding out an 8.0-magnitude earthquake. Now and then he reached into his open button-down shirt to scratch at his white chest hair or pet the small doughy paunch of flab that puffed out just above his waistline.

His eyes stayed glued to one of the several monitors on which he had programs working—except for when they made sojourns to the security camera footage, which they did frequently, even though the closest there came to an intruder was a wandering neighborhood squirrel.

But that was downright ordinary behavior compared to when he began talking at the screen.

Sometimes he would plead: "That's right, little baby girl, come to Papa! Come here!"

Other times he would chastise: "Bridget, you nasty whore, don't do that to me!"

Still other times he would taunt: "You think you can play that game, but I gotcha. You can't play hide-and-seek with me. I'm the black mamba of hide-and-seek."

And on. And on. Derrick and Carl would exchange glances when his monologue got especially strange ("You think I'm going to stop and whistle in the churchyard, but I'm walking on past!") or especially clichéd ("You're the trash, but I'm the trash compactor, honey!") or when he started repeating a name for no apparent reason ("Edilberto, Edilberto, Edilberto").

The only interruption was the visit from the mailman, which Gorithem saw coming on the cameras. He scrambled up to what he called his "panic room" on the second floor before Carl Storm was able to coax him back down to work.

An hour passed. Then two. Noon was coming, but it was clear Gorithem was unaware of the passage of time, or the need for food, or anything other than the variety of screens facing him.

They knew he was getting close when his self-talk grew increasingly exultant ("Yes, yes, yes!"). And then, finally, at five minutes after twelve, he announced, "Okay, I've got it."

Derrick, who had been sitting on the floor by the window, and Carl, who had been pacing back and forth because his butt was numb from the floor, rushed to the bank of computers.

"You know, I have to tell you, there's a good reason why WAP2 beat out B2. Bridget really does have some flaws," Gorithem said. "If you'll indulge me for a few moments, I'd like to guide you through the process by which I exploited them."

"No," Derrick and Carl said in perfect unison.

"Okay, okay. Sheesh," Gorithem said, lifting up his arm to act as a shield. "Then what do you want?"

"That depends. What's on there?"

"Just one file with a WAV extension—an audio file. It's dated October 27, 1999."

Derrick thought about the timeline he had been establishing in his head for 1999. October twenty-seventh was three weeks before the announcement of the trade deal that made it profitable for the Shanghai Seven to go legitimate. And it was four weeks before Cynthia Heat made her exit. Whatever this was could have been a precipitating incident.

"Terrific, if you can just e-mail it to me, we'll be on our way," Derrick said.

"E-mail it, what . . . using the Internet?" Gorithem asked, suddenly even more ashen-faced than usual.

"Well, yeah, what else do you—"

"Are you mad?" he crowed. "This network I've created is like a pristine forest where every grass and tree has only been nurtured by the purest springwater. It has never been tended by any hand except my own. The Internet is . . . I mean, it's a cesspool. It's digital filth. It's like if you took that forest, sprayed it with toxic waste, then had all of humanity defecate on it every day for—"

"Okay, okay, take it easy," Derrick said, holding up his hands traffic-cop style. "Why don't you just play it for us and we'll worry about the rest later."

"You got it," Gorithem said, then pressed PLAY.

It began with a foreign-sounding dial tone, not the familiar 350/440 hertz of a "Ma Bell" landline. Then there was a long series of buttons being pushed. Like a country code, followed by an area code, followed by an exchange, followed by a number.

Then:

"Hello?" A woman's voice. American.

"Hello." A man's voice. Chinese.

Both voices could be heard clearly.

"Is your line secure?" she asked.

"Yes. It was swept earlier today," he said.

A pause. Then the man again. "Is it done?"

"Well, that depends."

"Oh? On what?"

"What it's worth to you," she said.

"But you're sure you have the votes?"

"I've got the votes. Locked up the last one last night. The senior senator from Colorado said he'd swap his vote on WTO for my vote on an incredibly porky hydro-dam project."

"Pause it," Derrick said, then looked at his father. "By WTO, I assume she means the bill that allowed China to enter into the World Trade Organization?"

"That'd be my guess," Carl said.

Derrick nodded at Gorithem to continue the recording.

"So that's fifty-one votes?" the man asked. "We won't need the vice president?"

"That's right. Fifty-one signed, sealed, and soon-to-be delivered."

"And what are you proposing as your fee?"

"Fifty million dollars," she said coolly. "A million for each vote. You get mine for free."

"That's outrageous. Some of those people would vote for WTO anyway."

"Fifty million," she said again. "Fifty million, or that senator from Colorado is going to have a change of heart. So will senators from Kentucky, Washington, Indiana, and at least three other states. I'm not playing around here."

"But we've never . . . we've never had to pay anything close to that."

"Because you've never stood to benefit so much. There's about to be a line of American companies eager to throw money at you. If you're smart about it, you and your Shanghai buddies will recover your investment within the first three months. I'm giving you a bargain."

There was a pause on the other end. Then the man said, "Very well. Fifty million."

"You can wire it to my account in the Caymans."

"No wire. Cash."

"Cash? Are you kidding?"

"Our businesses in America are cash businesses. It's cash or it's nothing."

"Fine. Cash."

"It will take us a little time to get it together. We'll deliver it to you in ten days."

"I can be patient. But you won't get your vote until I get my money."

"I understand," the man said.

"You'd better," the woman said.

And then the call ended.

For a moment, all three men in that strange Queens house— one sitting, two standing—just stared at the screen.

They understood full well they had just heard the negotiation of a fifty-million-dollar bribe. The Chinese man was clearly a member of the Shanghai Seven. They could figure out which one later.

It was the identity of the woman that had them a little stunned. There was no question about her voice. It was strong and authoritative, yet somehow still quiet. Even a man who hadn't left his house since 1998 recognized who it belonged to:

White House front-runner Lindsy Gardner.

***

Carl Storm was the first to break the silence.

"I'd bet you anything she got that fifty million, and that it was all counterfeit," he said. "They made the best fakes in the world back then."

"Just as they do now," Derrick said. "So she gets the fifty million and doesn't realize it's fake. She knows she can't really do anything with it right away. Maybe someday she's going to find a way to tuck some in an offshore account. But even then she wouldn't be able to use it. The financial disclosures required of a US senator would make it very difficult to bring the money back onshore. She can't really touch it until she's out of office. Long-term, it's her retirement money. Short-term, it's her walking-around money. It's the luxury of not having to worry about what you spend on the day-to-day. She uses it for gas, groceries, clothes, the small stuff. It's all purchases under ten thousand dollars, all cash so no one can—"

Then Derrick snapped his fingers. *"Of course,"* he said. "Cynthia Heat used to teach piano lessons to Lindsy Gardner's kids. The senator even talked about it during the press conference the other day. I bet she paid Cynthia with the bad bills. Cynthia recognized they were fakes and started making inquiries. After all, why would a US senator be passing around funny money? There's no way Cynthia could have just let that go."

"This Cynthia Heat really sounds like a heck of a woman," Carl said. And not for the first time.

"She is. The problem is, according to one of the texts I got from Nikki earlier today, Cynthia showed the bills to Bart Callan, who was part of some kind of foreign-counterfeiting task force—"

Derrick snapped his fingers again. "Of course. Nikki texted me about this, too. Callan told her that Cynthia came to him with the fake bills when he was on that task force. Callan realized he had just been handed a golden opportunity to blackmail a US senator. But only if he could silence Cynthia Heat. At that point, Gardner and Callan became partners of sorts, and they both needed Cynthia Heat dead: Gardner needed it so her secret stayed safe; Callan needed it so he could maintain leverage on Gardner and so Gardner remained valuable to him. That's why Callan put the hit on Cynthia, and also why she needed to appear to stay dead. As long as Lindsy Gardner was alive and in public life, Cynthia was a huge threat. Meanwhile, Cynthia was caught between a rock and a hard place. She knew Lindsy Gardner was wrapped up in something fishy. But she couldn't definitively prove Gardner had been passing around phony bills, because the fingerprint results were always classified at a level that was well above her pay grade."

"So you think Callan has been working for Gardner all this time?" Carl asked.

"Yeah," Derrick said. "And I can prove it."

He pulled out the shiny new phone the quartermaster had given him and dialed Jedediah Jones's direct line.

"What is it, Storm?" Jones growled.

"You still want the Shanghai Seven put away?"

"I believe I've made that clear."

"Good. I'll be able to deliver the evidence you want to the field office in New York within the hour. But I need one thing first."

"And what's that?"

"The truth about something," Derrick said. "You said you ordered Callan's transfer to a medium security facility as a favor to a friend, someone who was about to be an even better friend, yes?"

"That's right."

"That friend was Senator Lindsy Gardner, wasn't it."

There was dead silence on the other end of the line.

Derrick pressed ahead: "Right now, you're weighing whether you should burn her, because she's about to be president. And it's good to have the president feeling like she owes you some favors. But I'm telling you her candidacy is maybe two hours away from being dead. Because after I go to the field office, I'm going to the *New York Ledger*. I've got a recording of her asking the Shanghai Seven to pay her fifty million dollars to deliver a vote on a trade bill."

"You're sure the recording is authentic?"

"And good quality. All you'll have to do is listen to it. There's no question it's her. You know no one can do a Lindsy Gardner voice except Lindsy Gardner."

Jones just chuckled. "Well, well. It seems I've been played by a librarian."

"So it *was* Gardner."

"She called me up not long ago, said Bart's mother was a friend, said the mother was worried about poor little Bart having a rough time in prison," Jones said. "Lindsy said she knew the request for a transfer couldn't come from her. Not during an election. If it got out, she'd be crucified. So she asked me to do it."

"And you were all too happy to comply," Storm said.

"She was trailing in the polls to Legs Kline at that point. But even if she didn't get elected, she was still going to have a lot of pull in the Senate."

Jones chuckled again, a rarity for a man whose laugh was usually a monthly occurrence.

"What?" Derrick asked.

"It seems I was played by a librarian twice," Jones said. "It was during that same conversation she gave me the tip about the

Shanghai Seven counterfeiting operation that you raided. She told me not to ask how she knew about it but that she had it on good authority it was occurring and that I should take care of it quietly, off the books, because she didn't want to run the risk of upsetting US-China relations. That's why I called you. And you delivered. Just like you always do."

Derrick got a glint in his eye. "I'll be in touch," was all he said. Then he ended the call.

It was all making sense. Gardner had been waiting seventeen years for the Shanghai Seven to return to illegal activities so she could get them put out of business. It was her revenge for the Shanghai Seven bribing her with fake bills all those years ago.

As for Callan? He had been monitoring Gardner's presidential campaign from prison, waiting for the perfect moment to deliver the threat: Get me out of here, or I'll tell everything I know. Gardner realized if she wanted to be president, she had to help him. And then as soon as he was out, Callan started chasing the counterfeit bills with Lindsy Gardner's fingerprints on them. Because then he'd own the president of the United States.

Then there was the Shanghai Seven, which had been sitting on that recording of Gardner accepting the bribe for seventeen years—also waiting for the perfect moment to spring it on her. It was even possible, if not likely, that the Shanghai Seven had made contact with her and made her aware of the existence of the tape. That's what made Gardner decide it was time to make her move against them. And she used her friend Jedediah Jones to do the dirty work.

But now it was all about to unravel on her. Derrick Storm had the compact disc with the recording. Nikki Heat had the bills with Gardner's fingerprints, which would be unclassified just as soon as the attorney general—who was, after all, a cabinet member—decided the recording demanded a full investigation. Maybe Cynthia Heat could even testify when she came out of hiding.

Derrick's attention went toward Gorithem's computer. He didn't like that this recording, this vital piece of evidence, existed only as a series of zeros and ones on a flimsy piece of plastic. At the very least, he wanted the zeros and ones of that WAV file duplicated so there was backup.

He turned to Gorithem. "Now that you've broken the encryption, we can treat that file like any other file, yes?"

"That's right."

"Great. Then would you mind making a copy of that recording and putting it on your machine just so that CD isn't the only copy of it?"

Gorithem looked like someone had just asked permission for a US Post Office to be located in his living room. "And pollute my network? Not. A. Chance. That file could have all kinds of—"

"Okay, okay. Take it easy."

"Do you want to listen to it again?" Gorithem asked.

"No. We've heard enough."

Gorithem ejected the CD and handed it to Derrick, who placed it gingerly back in its jewel case.

Derrick then looked at his father. "Okay," he said. "We have to go."

As Carl and Al Gorithem said their good-byes, Derrick placed a phone call to Nikki Heat.

There was no answer. So he sent a text:

CD IS A RECORDING OF LINDSY GARDNER ACCEPTING A $50M BRIBE FROM S7. YES: LINDSY GARDNER. THOSE BILLS YOU HAVE IN YOUR POSSESSION CONTAIN HER FINGERPRINTS. YOUR MOTHER KNEW IT BUT COULDN'T PROVE IT BECAUSE OF THE CLASSIFIED

RESTRICTION. IN NEW YORK NOW. WILL EXPLAIN EVERYTHING SOON. CALL ME IMMEDIATELY. 911.

After thanking Gorithem, the Storm boys walked back outside, blinking in sunlight that seemed incredibly bright after their time in the shut-in's cave.

Automatically Derrick's training kicked in and he scanned his environment for threats. There were none. A bird chirped. One or two blocks away, someone was operating a leaf blower. Farther away, heard but not seen, a 727 was making its final descent into LaGuardia.

It was an ordinary day in an ordinary New York neighborhood. And yet . . .

There was something off. Derrick sensed it. Were there eyes on them? Was an ambush about to be sprung? Or was he just being paranoid again?

He waited, soaking in all the input he could, down to the molecules of air drifting into his nose. If anyone could smell trouble, it would be Derrick Storm. His head swiveled from side to side. His ears pricked up just slightly.

But really there was nothing. He had been wrong about being followed coming out of the airport. He was wrong now.

He took two steps down the short concrete pathway toward the rental car. Nothing happened. They were fine. That bird wasn't any more of a danger to them than that 727 was.

Three more steps. Still nothing. Situation completely normal. They would get in the car, drive into Manhattan . . . No, better yet, they would find an office store nearby and get that WAV file uploaded to the cloud. He could also e-mail it to himself, to his father (Carl Storm still used an AOL address), and to Heat, so other copies would be safely nestled on secure servers. Then they could proceed to the field office.

Another step. Derrick was reaching for the keys to unlock the rental car. He was perhaps five steps away from the sanctuary of all that steel and shatterproof glass.

Then he did a double take. Across the street was a blue Mazda sedan. Was he being ridiculous, or was that the same car that had been following them on the Grand Central Parkway?

As he was attempting to answer that, something else flashed in the corner of his eye. A Toyota 4Runner was parked a little farther down.

A three-car follow required training, timing, and discipline . . . But that didn't make it impossible.

The ambush was coming any second. He felt it. His hand went toward where he usually kept Dirty Harry, except the gun wasn't there. He had been on an airplane that morning and he hadn't taken the time to get rearmed.

"Dad, r—"

But before the rest of the word *run* could get out of his mouth, Al Gorithem opened the front door to his house.

"They're coming for you!" he yelped. "They're coming for you!"

Derrick turned toward him in time to see Gorithem briefly before he slammed the front door shut.

Then two armed men emerged from the side of Gorithem's neighbor's house. From a hiding spot behind the 4Runner came two more. The woman in the hijab, who was calmly wielding an AK-47, was walking around the side of the blue sedan.

"Hands up," ordered one of the men who came from the neighbor's house. "Nothing funny, Storm."

Derrick was just considering what he really wanted to do with his hands when he heard the throaty whine of an engine revving at approximately 3,500 RPMs. The Chrysler 300 came roaring up the street and screeched to a halt to the side of the rental car—effectively blocking it and any path of escape they might have had.

They were outnumbered five to two. They were surrounded. They were unarmed.

The door to the Chrysler 300 opened and closed. A man was walking around from the side of it. He had a cigarette in his mouth. The smell of cloves was already in the air.

"Mr. Storm. How very nice to see you again," Colonel Feng said, his vocal cords as raspy as ever. "I'll take the CD now."

Derrick knew he had no choice. He reached into his jacket, pulled out the only known copy of the audio file that provided definitive evidence of Lindsy Gardner's massive corruption, and handed it over to a man who would use it for the most ill of purposes.

TWENTY-NINE

HEAT

t is such a pleasure to finally meet you, Captain Heat," Lindsy Gardner purred in that distinctive voice of hers.

Gardner rose, came around her desk, then shook Nikki Heat's hand with a firm grasp.

"Likewise, Senator," Heat said, feeling the warmth of the woman's touch.

"Did John give you a nice tour?"

"I told her about the hive and everything," Null said.

"Oh, so you're practically part of the colony already," Gardner said, making a head gesture at Null that he read as his permission to depart.

"Please, have a seat," Gardner said as the door closed.

She pointed to two cushioned chairs that fronted her desk. Heat selected the one nearer the window. It offered a sweeping view of Battery Park, the Statue of Liberty, and the bay beyond it, all the way to the dim outline of Sandy Hook.

"Thank you, Senator," Heat said.

Even though the two had briefly shared a podium at a press conference, that wasn't the same as being face-to-face. Given the chance to really study Gardner, Heat's impression was that the candidate looked younger in person than she did on television. Her cheeks were a healthy red, her eyes a calming blue.

"I'm sorry, I wasn't going to bring this up, but this really is . . . I mean, it's incredible," Gardner said. "I feel like I'm looking at a younger clone of Mrs. Heat. Of Cynthia. Sorry. I guess you've heard that before."

"Many times."

"Well, it's a compliment, believe me," Gardner said. "Your mother really was a beautiful woman."

She still is, Heat thought, though she kept the smile on her face.

"And such a talented woman. I was really quite taken with her. I always thought she had the intelligence to do so much more than teach piano."

Gardner let that dangle out there for a moment, then ended the pause before it became a gap in the conversation. "I'm sorry. I don't mean to make that sound like a backhanded compliment. I realize teaching piano was what she chose to do, and I was grateful she did. She was marvelous at it. I'm just saying she had this aura of competence about her, like she could have done anything with her life she had chosen to do. I always wondered: Did she have another career before she taught piano?"

Does Gardner know? Heat wondered. *Not possible. Not even US senators would have been apprised of the specifics of the Nanny Network. She's just making polite conversation.*

"Well, she was a concert pianist for a short time," Heat said. "Then she decided teaching piano to wealthy families around Europe was a wonderful way to be able to see the world and experience different cultures. When she had me and decided it was time to settle down, I think it was just what she knew and what she liked, so she kept with it. She really enjoyed watching her students progress."

"It was such a tragedy, what happened to her. I remember

being at her memorial service. All the parents of her students knew each other a little bit from the recitals and whatnot. We were all just so stunned. Back then, we thought it was just a random home invasion, of course. None of the business about that Carey Maggs character had come out yet."

Just like none of the business about that Bart Callan character has come out, Heat thought.

"Not that it makes it any less of a shock," Gardner said. "Anyhow, I'll stop. You don't need to hear this."

"It's fine," Heat assured her.

"Yes, of course. So. On to the business at hand. I'm sorry I sort of sprung this Homeland Security thing on you. That's not normally the way I like to make job offers. I think I was just caught up in the moment. Knowing you were Cynthia Heat's daughter and getting that same feeling with you that I had about your mother, like you could handle anything. And then the way you exposed that fraud, Legs Kline—"

"I had a lot of help."

"Well, yes, of course you did. Every leader is only as good as the people who surround them. But when one leader consistently gets results, it's not an accident. Shortly before I got up on that podium yesterday, I was just seized by the feeling I wanted you to play a major role in my administration. Please accept my apology for putting you on the spot like that."

"Absolutely. It's really not a problem. I'm flattered."

"Good. You should be. And I have to tell you, my team has been vetting you for the last twenty-four hours and the report they've handed me on you is . . . Well, there's a lot about you that *First Press* hasn't reported on. And it's all impressive. Very impressive."

"Thank you."

Gardner leaned forward a little, closing the gap between

the two women. "This is a little impertinent of me to say, but I guess . . . Well, I've just seen too much of this bullshit in my career not to be able to recognize it when I see it. It really strikes me that a person who has achieved such a consistent standard of excellence should have perhaps advanced a little further. I'm not trying to denigrate what you've done—first female commander of the Twentieth Precinct and all that—but how come you aren't a more major player down at headquarters? Why aren't you a deputy commissioner or playing a larger role in the chain of command?"

"I'm not sure I can answer that," Heat said.

"Well, I can. It's because you're not a person achieving these things. You're a woman. It's the same in the Senate—really, in any male-dominated institution. If you're a man who is accomplishing a lot, they look to give you more responsibility. If you're a woman doing the same thing, they pat you on the head and then pat themselves on the back and say, 'Isn't it nice we're letting the girl pitch in a little bit? Hope she doesn't freak out the next time she gets her period.'"

Gardner and Heat shared a laugh.

"Well, I have to be candid, Senator. I haven't always sought promotions as aggressively as I could have. To be honest, I resisted even becoming a captain."

"And why is that?"

"Because I like police work, not paperwork."

"See, but that's exactly the attitude I'm looking for in my cabinet," Gardner said, punctuating the word *exactly* with a broad gesture. "I want doers, not bureaucrats. I want people who are naturally impatient, not people who will let themselves get bound up in process. That's why I'm trying to look outside Washington as often as I can. I want my administration to be filled with people who will challenge the status quo. I want fearless, independent thinkers. And, to be perfectly blunt, I want a few women who will go at it knowing that they don't have to worry about the glass ceiling anymore. Because if I can promise one thing about the Lindsy Gardner administration, it's that the glass ceiling has finally been shattered.

"So," she finished. "I know this is sudden. And I know I still have an election to win. But what do you say? Do you want to be my director of Homeland Security?"

Heat realized she was leaning in as well. She could see why Gardner had been so successful in politics. She was personable and persuasive. She was also well prepared. Could Heat see herself working for this woman?

And then she realized it wasn't even a question worth posing. Working for Lindsy Gardner would mean solving the riddle that surrounded her mother.

"Yes. Yes, I do," Heat said. "I would be thrilled to head up Homeland Security for you. And I have to say, I really like your—"

From behind her, the door opened.

"Sorry to interrupt. I'm afraid I have an urgent matter for you, Lindsy."

It was John Null. His face was strangely blank as he crossed the room and rounded behind the desk. He extracted a phone from his pocket.

Heat was sure she was just imagining it, but it looked like *her* phone, the one she had surrendered to the Secret Service. It was the same size and had the same black casing. It was surely a coincidence. There were only so many phones on the market. That black casing was sold at thousands of retail outlets.

Gardner was reading something on the screen. The skin around her blue eyes had squeezed by a millimeter or two.

She looked up at Null and, in the same quiet-but-commanding

librarian's voice, said, "Why don't you clear out the volunteers. We don't need any witnesses."

Witnesses, Heat thought. *Witnesses to what?*

Then Gardner pulled open one of her desk drawers and extracted what Heat recognized immediately as a Walther PPK.

"I'm sorry, Captain Heat," Gardner said. "It appears my administration has had a change of priorities."

THIRTY

STORM

Colonel Feng's last act before leaving was to puncture the left front tire of the Storms' rental car.

"Can't have you following us," he said. "You're just lucky this is too well populated a place to shoot you. Farewell, Derrick Storm."

Then, taking one last drag on his clove cigarette, he flicked it onto Al Gorithem's rocky front lawn. He and his hired thugs loaded into their vehicles—the blue Mazda sedan, the Chrysler 300, and the Toyota 4Runner—and disappeared down the street.

Carl Storm looked at his son. "I can't say that went particularly well for the good guys."

"I'd go even further to say it went quite poorly."

"You got any thoughts on how we can improve the situation?"

"Yeah, I think you should get started changing that tire while I try and get Nikki Heat on the phone. I'm going to have her put out a BOLO on those three vehicles. Every second that passes makes them harder to catch. We can't let them get away."

As Carl Storm made like a slower, more crotchety, more profane version of an Indianapolis 500 pit crew, Derrick dialed Heat's cell phone.

It rang, and rang, and rang some more.

He waited a moment, then tried again. More ringing.

Derrick swore. He couldn't very well call up the local NYPD precinct and explain everything. It would take too long. And it would end with him being laughed off the phone.

At the same time, he couldn't call on Jones. When the CIA was established, its mission was explicitly international. It was actually illegal for the agency to operate domestically. As an independent contractor, Derrick Storm could disregard that prohibition; the agency itself quietly ignored it all the time. Still, there was always that looming threat of a congressional or criminal investigation that kept the agency, even Jones, somewhat honest. As a result, Jones only involved local law enforcement as an absolute last resort.

But if the order came from Heat, it was no problem. He tried her cell again. Same result.

"Something's not right," Derrick said.

"You're damn straight something's not right," Carl said, already breathing heavily. "The bolts on this tire were tightened by goddamn gorilla. Help an old man out, would you?"

"Sure, why don't you get the jack underneath so you can be ready when I'm done?"

Derrick grasped the tire iron and heaved it counterclockwise until, with a squeal of protest, the first bolt gave way. As he repeated the procedure, he thought more about Heat.

She hadn't answered that last text, even though he was explicit about the urgent need for her to call. And now she wasn't answering her phone. There had to be some other way to get ahold of her.

Of course. Her boyfriend. Or, wait, was he a husband by now? Derrick Storm had had a chance meeting with Jameson Rook a few years earlier—the same evening Storm first met Nikki Heat, over the body of a dead currency trader. Storm and

Rook each came away impressed with the other's intelligence and had complimented each other on their rugged good looks. They just hadn't swapped contact information.

But that was an easy enough fix.

"There," Derrick said, loosening the last bolt. "That ought to do it. You good from here? I have another phone call to make."

As Carl grumbled about the ingratitude of his only child, making his old man do all the work, Derrick dialed into the Cubby.

"I need a few phone numbers," he told the first nerd he connected with. "The gentleman's name is Jameson Rook. Home and cell would be great."

Mere seconds later, Derrick was scribbling down a pair of ten-digit numbers. He thanked the nerd, hung up, and dialed the home number first.

"Jameson Rook," a smooth voice said.

"Jameson, it's Derrick Storm."

The two men spent a few moments confirming their mutual admiration, then quickly got down to business.

"Is Nikki with you?" Storm asked.

"No. She's in a meeting."

"With whom?"

"I'm afraid that's not information I can share."

"Well, can you interrupt this meeting? I assure you this matter is of the utmost urgency."

"And why is that?"

"I've heard a recording in which the likely next president of the United States negotiated a fifty-million-dollar payout to deliver a vote on behalf of the Shanghai Seven, and now they're going to use that recording to blackmail her."

For only the third time this millennium, Rook was actually speechless.

"Hello?" Storm asked, looking at his phone to see if the call had disconnected. "You still there? Hello?"

Rook finally managed to squeeze out: "Lindsy Gardner."

"Yeah, what about her?"

"That's who Nikki is meeting with right now."

Derrick drove toward Rook's loft with haste, alacrity, and a complete disregard for the traffic laws of New York—both the city and state.

Along the way, Storm and Rook filled each other in on all they knew—or, in Rook's case, all Heat had told him—about their joint investigation. Rook paced around his loft as he spoke. Thanks to the miracle of Bluetooth, Storm listened to Rook's mellifluous voice piping through his car's speakers.

Rook and Storm's combined genius—when they put their heads together—was a testament to the brilliance of their creator. It didn't take long for them to conclude they needed to recover both pieces of evidence: the CD, on which Gardner had agreed to the payment for the votes she was delivering, and the bills, which proved the payment had actually been made.

Without the bills, Gardner could claim the conversation with one of the Shanghai Seven had been a ruse, some bit of subterfuge she was undertaking to try to make the Communist Party (to which the Shanghai Seven was intimately tied) more eager to sign the deal, in the hopes she could negotiate more favorable terms. She could point out that there was no evidence the exchange had ever taken place.

And, indeed, there was likely no point in going to the authorities to get a search warrant to look for the remaining bills. Rook and Storm decided Gardner had almost certainly destroyed the notes shortly after learning they were fake.

American bills aren't the most flammable of paper products, on account of the linen. But enough lighter fluid could easily take care of that.

At the same time, in the absence of the phone conversation, Gardner could say she had no idea how she came to possess the counterfeit notes that bore her fingerprints, and that she had passed them to her children's piano teacher unwittingly.

The CD and the bills. The case against Gardner would be incomplete without both. And, at the moment, neither Rook nor Storm had any idea where either was.

They assumed Heat would know where the bills were. As for the recording, they supposed the Shanghai Seven had other copies of the WAV file. Therefore, Feng wouldn't feel the need to guard the copy of the CD he now had with any special care. He had merely wanted to get it out of Storm's hands because if the file got out, it would become worthless—you can't blackmail someone with the release of a recording the whole world has already heard.

"The good news is, that CD is going to find Lindsy Gardner sooner rather than later," Rook predicted. "My bet is Feng is on his way there right now."

"Which means we need to find Lindsy Gardner before he does," Storm added.

"Bonus points to you for that, because if we find Lindsy, chances are we find my wife," Rook said.

"Have I mentioned that your intellect is a stunning thing to behold?" Storm asked.

"You have," Rook said. "And I hope you'll permit me to return the compliment by saying—"

"All right, cut it out, you assholes!" boomed Carl Storm. "If I have to hear any more of this crap I'm gonna get carsick."

"Why don't you just drive," Rook suggested. "We'll think of a plan of attack when you get here."

It should have taken the Storms at least twenty-eight minutes to reach Rook's Tribeca loft from Queens.

With Derrick behind the wheel, they completed it in twenty-two. He alleviated the difficulty of finding parking by wedging the rental car in front of a hydrant. Then he and his father ascended in a freight elevator to Rook's loft.

When they entered, they found Rook in front of his computer with the screen split.

One had the Find My iPhone app up. Rook pointed to the green dot on the map, which was zoomed in as far as it would go. It showed the dot in the southwest corner of a building in downtown Manhattan.

"She's been there since I started monitoring her," Rook said. "That's been about twenty-five minutes now."

"That's The Marlowe, isn't it?" Derrick asked.

"Sure is. Gardner campaign headquarters."

"I texted her before I called you, telling her about the recording. If she's checked her phone at all, she knows about the bribe."

"But we don't know if she knows," Rook said.

"That's right. More importantly, we don't know if Gardner knows she knows."

"So it could still be a normal meeting between the presidential front-runner and a future member of her cabinet."

"Or your wife could be a hostage right now," Derrick said.

The men cogitated over that for a moment. Carl pointed to the other side of the screen, to a still shot of a video, where a woman was bound to a chair.

"Who's that?" Carl asked.

"That's Cynthia Heat," Rook told him. "Nikki's mother."

"This may not be the PC thing to say at the moment, but she's gorgeous," Carl observed.

"Yeah, and she's in trouble," Rook said. He turned to Derrick. "Did Nikki mention The Serpent to you?"

Derrick confirmed she had not. Rook quickly brought the Storms up to speed, then played the video for them.

At the end of it, Derrick was the first to speak. "What makes you think she's in trouble?" he asked.

Rook did not immediately share his own doubts about Cynthia's role in the video. Instead, he looked at Derrick curiously. "That's the general assumption people make when they see a woman tied to a chair and hear her life being threatened, isn't it?"

"Yeah, but that's a highwayman's hitch," Derrick said, pointing to the knot that bound her wrists to the chair.

"I don't follow," Rook said.

"A highwayman's hitch. Also known as a bank robber's knot, a getaway hitch or, more prosaically, a quick-release knot. The legend is that it was developed by outlaws who made their getaway on horseback—and wanted to be able to untie their horses real fast. True knot enthusiasts will debate that history, but there's no question she could pull as much as she wanted, or she could tug here or here"—he pointed to two points on Cynthia Heat's wrists—"and it wouldn't go anywhere.

"But," he continued, "you see that little stray piece there?"

"I do," Rook said.

"You pull that end, and the knot comes apart instantly. Just as a highwayman would do as he's making his getaway from a robbery."

"So Cynthia could get out of that knot anytime she wanted?"

"That's right. I don't know what's going on, but that is not a woman being held against her will," Derrick said. "I can go even further and say that she probably produced that video herself, with no outside help. That's why she had to use a knot that looked formidable but was, in fact, easy to release. Hence the highwayman's hitch."

It was then Rook's turn to share his belief that the video had been scripted. With the sound off, he replayed the parts of the video that showed Cynthia leaning forward to anticipate questions.

"This only adds credence to the theory that the video was a one-woman job," Rook said. "She prerecorded the other side of that conversation, then timed out the pauses just right, to make it seem like it was a real conversation. But she knew she only had so much time to deliver her lines. Hence the leaning."

Carl Storm was shaking his head. "She *really* is one heck of a woman."

The other men ignored him.

"Forgive me for stating what seems to be obvious," Derrick said. "But the empty threats . . . the missed potshots . . . the offer of a vacation in exchange for dropping the investigation . . . Add to it that the video is self-produced, and it seems Cynthia Heat *is* The Serpent, am I right?"

"I think so," Rook said. "And there's one way to find out."

He pulled out his phone and added that 646 area code number as a contact. Then he started a new text message to it:

DEAR MRS. HEAT—THIS MAY BE A STRANGE WAY TO HEAR FROM YOUR SON-IN-LAW FOR THE FIRST TIME, BUT NIKKI IS IN TROUBLE. SHE'S IN A MEETING WITH LINDSY GARDNER, AND MAY BE HELD HOSTAGE THERE. COULD YOU PLEASE STOP BEING THE SERPENT AND HELP US GET HER OUT?

Rook pressed SEND.

"Think that'll work?" Derrick asked.

"A writer can only form the words. He cannot control the impact they have on the reader," Rook said.

They went back to staring at the unmoving green dot on the screen for perhaps five seconds. Then Rook's phone alerted them to an incoming text.

Rook read it out loud for the other two:

I'LL BE RIGHT THERE. —CH

THIRTY-ONE

HEAT

I t took time for the buzz from outside to slowly dissipate as the volunteers and staffers were cleared from the building.

Heat didn't know what they were being told. Probably that it was a security matter. Or that they were needed to bolster numbers at a rally that would, for some reason, later fail to materialize.

Lindsy Gardner kept the Walther trained on Heat the whole time. After her initial spurt of outrage—*What are you doing? What is this about? What makes you think you're going to get away with this?*—Heat had been ordered to remain silent and seated.

She spent the time alternating her gaze between Gardner and staring out the window. What would possibly make a presidential candidate pull a gun on an NYPD captain she was trying to hire for a job? And then hold her at gunpoint?

What was she looking to gain? What was her endgame? And what had Heat done to make herself such a threat to this powerful woman who was soon to be even more powerful?

It was baffling. Unless this was some kind of strange test— the most intense, high-pressure job interview of all time. Was she being filmed and evaluated to see how she dealt with stress?

Heat decided all she could do was stay calm and keep her wits about her.

After roughly twenty minutes—which is a long time to have someone brandishing a gun in your face—Null returned to the inner sanctum.

"Okay," he reported. "We've evacuated this floor, and the ones below it and above it as well."

"Excellent," Gardner said. "Now on to business, Captain Heat. I've been informed you have some counterfeit bills in your possession. Hand them over."

As soon as the words "counterfeit bills" came out of Gardner's mouth, it was like a series of pins and tumblers lined up, unlocking the truth:

"*You* gave those bills to my mother," Heat said, some mix of angry and astonished. "Those were *your* fingerprints on them. That's why the results were classified."

"I'm not here to discuss ancient history," Gardner said. "You have no idea how much trouble these have caused for me over the years."

"Caused for *you*," Heat said. "My mother—"

More locks gave way. "Wait, Callan was working for you, wasn't he? That's why he was hell-bent on getting those bills back. You sicced him on me."

"Working for me . . . Threatening me . . . Sleeping with me . . . It was always hard to tell. Bart Callan and I had a complicated relationship," Gardner said, with a look on her face that was between a smile and a sneer. "Though I can't say I was sorry to hear about his death. Now that I finally have the bills, having him gone is like being freed forever from recurring migraine headaches. Now."

She brought the gun up a little higher. "Are you going to hand those bills over, or am I going to have to search your corpse for them?"

"Why does it matter? You're going to kill me anyway," Heat said.

"Possibly," Gardner said, then tilted her head a little and raised the tone of her voice just slightly. "Or, possibly, you can cooperate and become a part of my little circle of trust—along with John here."

Null shot Heat the same smile she had first seen before the press conference. She had thought it was sincere back then. Now she recognized the deeper truth. Sociopaths always had the most genuine smiles. Nothing weighed on their conscience because they didn't truly have consciences the way other people did. They didn't feel the slightest shred of remorse for any of the horrible things they had done or were planning on doing.

"I could use a woman of your abilities helping me on the inside," Gardner continued. "I'm a good boss, really. You can ask John."

Null nodded.

"And beyond that, I've . . . I've done a lot of good as a senator. And I'll be able to do even more good as president. You could be a part of that."

"If you're so good, why are you waiving a gun in my face?" Heat asked.

Gardner actually lowered the gun slightly. "Look, I'm . . . I know you may find this hard to believe, but I'm sorry about this. I'm not . . . I'm not a bad person. I've just . . . I've made mistakes. I readily admit that. And it seems like in this game your mistakes always compound each other. They start as small little pebbles and the next thing you know, they're boulders, rolling down the hill at you."

"Mistakes? What kind of mistakes?" Heat asked, as much to keep her talking as to hear what she might have to confess. She had no intention of working for the woman or becoming a part of any circle she was in.

Gardner got a faraway look then scoffed. "Starting off as a librarian, for one."

"And why is that?"

"Because it means I've been broke my whole life," Gardner said. "At least if I had been a lawyer or an investment banker, I would have had a little bit of padding. But, no, I had to be a public servant, right away. Do you have any idea how expensive it is to be a US senator? And I'm not just talking about the costs to run a campaign. That you can at least grovel and beg your wealthy friends to cover for you. I'm talking about the clothes. The travel you can't get the government to pay for because you're worried about your opponents using it to launch an ethics investigation. The gifts you have to give people who help you, or the people you want to help you. The charitable donations. The expectations are endless.

"Most of my colleagues in the Senate are members of the lucky sperm club. They came from money, then made even more money. A few are self-made, but they almost all have gobs of money. Did you know the average net worth of a US senator is something like twelve million dollars? *Twelve million dollars!* I've never been able to compete with that."

"So you started counterfeiting bills?" Heat asked incredulously as a door behind her opened.

"No," a raspy voice behind Heat said. "*We* did that. She was just the one gullible enough to accept them as a bribe. She delivered us a trade bill in exchange for fifty million dollars, all of it perfect . . . and perfectly fake."

Gardner's face flushed. Feng was dressed in the same cheap clothes he had been when Heat had seen him earlier that morning, though now he had added a knockoff Ralph Lauren jacket. He had a freshly lit clove cigarette in his mouth. He took a long drag, then blew the smoke into the air.

"Oh, excuse me, I didn't realize you had company," he said. "What an unexpected pleasure to see you, Captain Heat. Though it seems you are not here by your own choosing."

"What do you want, Feng?" Gardner said, saying his last name with enough vitriol that it almost sounded like a different kind of F-word.

"You will be pleased to know we are back in possession of the CD," Feng said. "I took it off of Derrick Storm myself a short time ago."

"That's great. But you're too late," Gardner said. "He's already listened to the recording. He knows everything. I thought you said that encryption was solid."

Feng expelled another lungful of smoke. "He seems to have found one of the very few men in the world capable of cracking it. But it's no great concern."

"No concern?" she exploded. "Not to you, perhaps. But what if—"

"Our intelligence indicates the man who decrypted it is a notorious hermit who suffers from a variety of mental illnesses, including extreme paranoia," Feng said. "He never leaves his house. His computers do not connect to the Internet. He does not correspond with the outside world beyond placing weekly grocery orders. He is consumed with solving mathematical theorems that have stumped humanity for a hundred years or more. He is not a concern."

"But what about Storm? Storm knows."

"He knows, yes. But I assure you, he wasn't able to make a copy of it. So what good will it do him? Without the recording, he would just be an obscure man telling wild stories about one of the most beloved women in the world. You can trust the damage has been contained."

"Trust the Shanghai Seven," Gardner scoffed. "Been there. Done that. Won't do it again."

"It is rather unfortunate that you ever discovered those bills came off our printing presses and not from the US Mint," Feng said. "You really should have been able to use them with impunity. I've always been curious: How did you discover their true nature?"

Tipping her head toward Heat, Gardner said, "Her mother was my children's piano teacher. It also turns out that in addition to teaching children how to play 'Hot Cross Buns,' she was a top secret government agent with connections and resources at the highest levels."

Gardner looked at Heat on that woman-to-woman level, like they were two friends out for lunch. "This is what I mean about pebbles turning into boulders, Nikki."

"Ah, so very unfortunate for you," Feng said. "Well, it doesn't matter now, does it? I believe it was an American folksinger who first said, 'All roads lead to where we stand.'"

Feng chuckled at his own cleverness. Then he pulled the CD from out of the pocket of his jacket. "As you can see, we have taken back that which was stolen from us. All copies of your little discussion with my boss are now back in our control. I trust this means we can count on your cooperation when we call on you?"

"Do I have a choice?"

"No. But I assure you, we'll be compensating you well for your cooperation," Feng said. "Would you like to verify that this is the original?"

Gardner looked at Null, who seemed to understand her tacit instructions immediately.

"Come with me, Colonel," Null said, and the men began walking out of the room.

"Oh, and John? Be a dear and come back so you can persuade Captain Heat about what's in her best interest?"

"Of course, Lindsy."

Null pointed the way for Feng, then shut the door behind himself.

Heat waited until they were gone, then gave Gardner the same kind of don't-play-me look that suspects often saw from the woman who had become one of the NYPD's most gifted interrogators.

"So that's what started all this," Heat said. "You took a bribe."

"Yes, I took a bribe," Gardner said. "But it was for a bill that was probably going to pass anyway. And it was a bill that has been beneficial to a lot of people. It's allowed the expansion of countless US businesses into China, letting them make who-knows-how-many billions of dollars. That's money in America's pocket, Nikki. And then there's what it has done to bring two very different countries closer together culturally. I mean, do you want to *really* know why the Chinese would never risk going to war with us? It's not really because we have the world's best-trained and most technologically advanced military. It's because of this."

Gardner pulled her phone out of her pocket. "Wealthy Chinese are addicted to iPhones. They *have* to get their hands on the next model. And they're addicted to Starbucks and Coca-Cola and Marlboro and everything else that comes when we export American capitalism. That all either started or got a huge boost because of *this bill*.

"And, yes, I took a bribe. I shouldn't have. I know that. I just thought, gosh, everyone else is going to make gobs of money off this thing. Why shouldn't I? I was tired of having to run with a bunch of millionaires who didn't think twice about dropping five hundred dollars on dinner while I was sitting there worrying about bouncing checks. And, yeah, if I had left the Senate, I could have used my contacts to cash in, but . . . Well, at that point, I would stop being able to push good legislation and help constituents and do all the things I love being able to do in the Senate."

"So you took a bribe that allowed you to keep doing good work."

"Something like that. It sounds like I'm trying to rationalize totally indefensible behavior, but . . . I'm not a bad person, Nikki. I promise you that. If you come work for me, you'll see that."

Again, Heat had no intention of doing that. But she also recognized that saying otherwise would put her on the short list for a long dirt nap.

Heat channeled every trick she had once learned as an aspiring professional actress and attempted to fully inhabit the role she was about to play: that of the grateful sellout.

"And what . . . what would working for you entail, exactly?" she asked.

"Well, eventually, as my director of Homeland Security, you'd be part of my cabinet, of course. And that would make you an absolutely indispensable voice. More immediately, I'd hope you would join the hive as . . . well, as a kind of second queen, I guess you could say. You would be a powerful voice on the campaign trail. And beyond that, well, I really like you, Nikki. You'd have as much responsibility as you could handle."

"That's nice. But what I really meant is: What would it entail, in light of everything I've just learned?"

"Ah, yes," Gardner said, looking down at her lap for a moment.

It was an act Heat could read as shame. And it could also have been an opening: Heat might have been able to lunge across the desk at the gun and . . .

Then Gardner looked up. "Well, I would need to know that I can trust you a hundred percent. That I can call on you when I need something, no matter what it is. That you won't violate the circle of trust in any way."

"I see," Heat allowed.

"I'm talking total loyalty. I mean, look, it would be in your best interests anyway. The moment you come work for me, we'd be joined at the hip. If I became embroiled in a scandal because certain, ah, indiscretions of mine came to light, you'd be just as tarnished, even if you weren't directly involved."

"I suppose, yes."

"So you'd have to make sure none of this"—she interrupted herself by making a circular motion around her desk—"got out. There might be some immediate damage control that needs to be done. For example, this Derrick Storm fellow who sent you this text. Who is he?"

Heat sensed from the way Gardner asked the question that she really knew nothing about Storm. Feng must not have told her anything. And Heat knew Jedediah Jones went to great lengths to make sure Storm's profile remained low. The nerds further scrubbed Storm's footsteps so that the man's activities left no trace—in the real world, in the virtual world, or anywhere in between.

"He's a private eye," Heat said. "I hired him to help me with this matter."

"Do you think you could come up with a story to . . . assuage his curiosity?" Gardner asked.

"I'm sure I could. I could tell him I had determined

conclusively the recording was a well-done fake, and that he should forget he ever heard it. And . . . I mean, ultimately, he works for me and I'm the one paying his bills. If I tell him there's nothing more to investigate, he'll stop."

"Yes, yes," Gardner said. "That would be excellent. Maybe you should do that now?"

"I would be happy to," the former theater major said.

"You'll let me look at it before you hit SEND?"

"Of course."

Gardner shoved Heat's phone across the desk at her, keeping the gun up the whole time, but in a more casual way than before. Heat was still trying to be mindful of any opening Gardner gave her to attack.

With one eye on Gardner and the other on the screen, Heat tapped out: IT TURNS OUT THE RECORDING IS A HOAX. NOTHING MORE TO INVESTIGATE. THANKS FOR YOUR HELP. PLEASE SEND ME YOUR BILL AS SOON AS POSSIBLE TO MY PRECINCT ADDRESS ON 80TH STREET. IT'S BEEN NICE WORKING WITH YOU!

Heat turned the phone around and shoved it back at Gardner. The candidate nodded, satisfied, then hit SEND.

"Well, that's a good start. Now. Those bills. We really need to destroy them. It won't do anyone any good to have them still circulating around."

"Of course not," Heat said.

She reached into the jacket of her pantsuit, quickly fanned open the envelope, and plucked out four bills. She placed them on the desk.

"Excellent. That was easy, wasn't it?" Gardner said, smiling her best librarian's smile, like Heat was a fifth grader who had just entered her thirtieth book on her summer reading list.

Gardner took out a handkerchief and wiped both sides of

each bill until the fingerprint dust—and the fingerprints they highlighted—were completely gone. Then she dropped the bills into a shredder, which chewed them into oblivion.

As she finished, Null reentered the room. Heat's phone chirped.

"I assume that's Derrick Storm's reply," Gardner said. "Do you mind if I look?"

Gardner had already grabbed the phone.

"Go right ahead," Heat said.

Gardner read Storm's reply aloud: " 'I copy. Good to hear, because that means I can still vote for her and not the other guy. I'll mail you that invoice as soon as I can!' "

Slowly, Gardner lowered the gun to desk level. "Well, that settles everything, doesn't it?"

"Yes," Heat said, feeling like she had just pulled off a Tony Award–worthy performance. "Yes, it does."

"We should shake on it," Gardner said, standing and reaching out her hand. "Then I'll ask John to show you out."

Gardner made another one of those head gestures that only Null seemed to know how to read.

Heat stood and started reaching for Gardner's hand.

Except the moment Heat's body had lifted from the chair, she felt a rope closing around her arms and torso. Then it cinched tight at her back. Null, who held the other end of the rope, yanked with enough force to pull Heat off her feet.

"Is the helicopter prepared?" Gardner asked.

"Gassed up and ready to go," Null said. "Range should be about three hundred and thirty miles."

"Good. Let's take her out beyond the continental shelf and drop her from about five thousand feet. The fall will kill her. The sharks will get whatever is left."

Gardner walked from behind the desk and peered down at Heat. Null was approaching with what Heat recognized as a Taser, all charged up and ready to stun.

"Sorry, Nikki," Gardner said, moments before Null pulled the trigger. "There's only one queen bee in this hive, and it's me."

THIRTY-TWO

STORM

Carl Storm couldn't have been more antsy if he were a five-year-old trapped one room away from the tree on Christmas morning.

"Wait, Cynthia Heat is coming *here*? Now?" he asked.

"Yeah. What's the matter?" Rook asked.

"Do you have mints or a toothbrush I could borrow?" Carl asked.

"I think I might have a can of Binaca," Rook said. "It might be a little old, but—"

"I'll take it," Carl said.

Rook disappeared in the direction of his bathroom. Derrick was looking at his father, appropriately mortified. "Dad, seriously. I don't think fresh breath is at the top of anyone's list of concerns at the moment."

"Speak for yourself, son," Carl said. "My breath smells like a squirrel died in my mouth. I've got to do something about it before she gets here."

Rook returned with the breath spray and tossed it toward Carl, who promptly pumped a big shot into his mouth.

"Thanks," he said. "Here."

Carl went to hand it back, but Rook held up both hands.

"Keep it. In case an emergency arises later."

"Thanks," Carl said.

Just then, the buzzer rang. Rook walked over to it. "Yes?" he said.

"Cynthia Heat here."

Rook pressed the buzzer to allow her entry. "That was fast," he said.

"I keep telling you," Carl said, "she's one heck of a woman."

Derrick didn't have time to process the implications of his father's insta-crush on Nikki Heat's mother. She was already there, ringing the doorbell.

Rook opened the door for her. Then, for a moment, all three men just stared at her.

For Rook and the younger Storm, it wasn't merely that Cynthia's dimensions, features, or coloring were so similar to Nikki's. It was that she inhabited the space in the same way. She breathed the same way. Her small mannerisms were the same. Even the way she carried her weight slightly on the balls of her feet—like she was ready for anything that came at her—was the same. The resemblance went beyond striking and didn't even stop at uncanny on its way to eerie.

For Rook especially, it was like Nikki Heat—a woman he had loved for years, a woman he thought he knew better than any other—had been revealed to him in a new way. Because, for the first time, he understood where she came from.

For the elder Storm, whose square jaw had suddenly gone slack, the interest in studying Cynthia Heat had a somewhat simpler, more primal, genesis.

Cynthia took one step into the apartment and grabbed both of Rook's hands.

"Jameson," she said, in a voice that was ever-so-slightly deeper and more mature-sounding than Nikki's. "It is so wonderful to finally meet you. I don't . . . I don't even know where to start thanking you for the way you've loved and protected my daughter. We have so much lost time to make up for."

"And we will. But first things first . . ."

"Of course," she said. She walked up to the Storm boys.

"You must be Derrick Storm," she said, shaking his hand. "I have to be honest, I've heard so many stories about you, I assumed you were one of those intelligence community myths that comes along every now and then."

"I could say the same of you," Derrick replied. "Some of the coups you pulled off with the Nanny Network are agency legend."

Then she turned to Carl. "And, hello, who is this ruggedly handsome gentleman?"

"Carl Storm, miss," he said. "Nice to meet you."

"Charmed. Very charmed," she said, beaming at him. Then she turned to face the other two.

"So," she said. "What are we dealing with?"

"How about I explain on our way to The Marlowe?" Rook suggested.

"Practicality," Cynthia said. "I like that in a son-in-law."

Derrick looked at Rook. "As long as we're being practical, you don't happen to have any weapons lying around here, do you?"

Rook held aloft a Writers Edition Hemingway Montblanc fountain pen. "I certainly do."

Derrick shook his head in disgust. "That's really not what I'm talking about. Let's just go."

"Hang on," Rook said, then went quickly to a nearby closet. He pulled out a bulletproof vest with JOURNALIST printed on it in bold white letters and emblazoned with a pair of tiny replica Pulitzer Prizes.

"There," he said. "Now I'm ready."

The Storms' rental car was still in front of the hydrant where they'd left it. All four piled in—Derrick and Carl Storm, Cynthia Heat and Jameson Rook, all of them already starting to feel like some kind of big, strange, modern American family.

Derrick drove. The other three alternated between hanging on as he took turns too fast and getting Cynthia up to speed with what they knew. It wasn't difficult. She knew so much of it already. It had been her saga for seventeen years.

They were nearing The Marlowe when Derrick's phone signaled an incoming text.

Derrick handed it to Rook to read out loud.

"'It turns out the recording is a hoax. Nothing more to investigate. Thanks for your help. Please send me your bill as soon as possible to my precinct address on 80th Street. It's been nice working with you!'"

When he was done, Rook didn't hesitate with his analysis. "Okay, there's now no question this is a hostage situation," he said. "She finished it with an exclamation point. I don't think I've *ever* seen that woman use an exclamation point."

"That's because you didn't know her in the third grade," Cynthia said. "Thankfully, she grew out of them in the fourth."

"The '80th Street' is code for something," Derrick said. "The precinct is on 82nd Street."

"That's her telling us she's on the 80th floor," Rook said. "She knows I have the Find My iPhone app installed. But that doesn't do 3-D. So she's giving us that final piece."

"We need to reply," Derrick said as he gunned the engine to swerve around a taxicab.

"Whoever sent that line of hogwash wants us to swallow it whole," Carl said. "So let's do it. We have to assume that Lindsy Gardner, or whoever is holding Nikki hostage, will be the one reading it. We can't risk alerting them that we know Nikki is in trouble. Surprise is pretty much our only advantage right now."

"Handsome *and* intuitive," Cynthia Heat said. "My, my, such a package."

"I agree," Rook said, then clarified: "That is, I agree with Carl that we should play along. I mean, don't get me wrong, I agree with Cynthia, too. But perhaps not as strongly. No offense, Mr. Storm."

"None taken," Carl assured him.

"Okay, so here goes," Rook said, then read his reply out loud as he typed it:

"'I copy. Good to hear, because that means I can still vote for her and not the other guy. I'll mail you that invoice as soon as I can!'"

The others seemed to be in agreement as Rook added, "I trust you could tell from my upturned voice at the end that I finished with an exclamation point. My hope, of course, is that Nikki will view it as a kind of 'message received' acknowledgment. As a writer, I'm particularly sensitive to punctuation, of course. But Nikki has really—"

"Rook! Just hit 'send'!" Cynthia snapped, saying it with the exact timbre, cadence, and timing that Nikki would have.

"Got it," Rook mumbled just as The Marlowe loomed into view.

Derrick zipped the rental car into a loading zone and hit the flashers—the best he could do, under the circumstances.

They hurried into the building, showing their IDs to a bored security officer who had been sending a steady flood of volunteers and staffers up to Gardner campaign headquarters on the eightieth floor for months now. He did not seem to notice or care that these four faces were new.

They huddled near the elevator as they waited for a car to arrive.

"Think they know we're coming?" Rook asked.

"We wouldn't have made it through security that easily if they did," Carl said.

"We're still going to have Secret Service waiting for us when we get out of this elevator, you know," Derrick said. "Standard operating procedure would be for them to have at least three agents manning a metal detector. And we're going to have to take care of them quietly, because there will certainly be others nearby."

"A minor inconvenience," Carl said. "I used to work with those guys from time to time. When they're doing a public event, they're on their game. But when it's just another day, business as usual, they get a little bored."

"Still, we don't have any weapons," Derrick said. "I don't care how bored they are, we won't be able to stultify them to death."

"No, we're going to do this old school," Carl said.

"Oh, God," Derrick said, slapping his forehead. "Here we go again."

"Show some respect around your father," Cynthia scolded. "What did you have in mind, Carl?"

"That depends. How are you at hand-to-hand combat, Cynthia?"

"This Secret Service agent," she said. "Do you want him stunned, unconscious, or dead?"

"Unconscious will do nicely."

"No problem."

Carl grinned. "Okay, then it's settled. Writer boy here is going to fake a heart attack. Do it big and noisy so they'll be good and distracted. The moment he clutches his heart, the other three of us will each pick a man and be ready to put him out of commission. Sound good?"

They agreed. The elevator arrived and they climbed in.

"Why do I have to be the one to fake a heart attack?" Rook asked as they ascended.

"Do you have years of training in how to hit a human being in a manner that causes their brain to fire an overwhelming number of neurotransmitters at the same instant, thus overloading their nervous system and sending them into a state of temporary paralysis?" Carl asked.

"No. But I wrote about it once."

"Then that's why. If we hit them, they'll go down. If you hit them, you'll just piss them off."

"Fair point," Rook said, and continued the ride in silence.

When the doors opened, there were, as Derrick had predicted, three Secret Service agents on duty. And, as Carl predicted, they looked appropriately bored.

Derrick was first off the elevator. "Good day, gentlemen. We're here to volunteer for the Gardner campaign."

"Sorry," one of the agents said. "We've been told no more volunteers for the time being."

The other three had already entered the vestibule. It was clear Derrick was going to take down the agent he was talking to. With only the barest hint of eye contact, Carl and Cynthia assigned themselves to the other two.

"But we've come all the way from Omaha!" Derrick protested. "My family has been so eager to pitch in. These are my parents, Fred and Ginger. And this is my half-brother, Alexander. We're all huge fans of the—"

Rook let out an agonized moan and bent at the waist. The agents all turned to him.

One started to say, "Sir, are you—"

Rook bellowed again, then clutched his heart. The moment

his hand touched his chest, Carl, Derrick, and Cynthia sprang into action.

Cynthia's leg flashed in the air, delivering a kick to the temple that was reminiscent of her daughter's best efforts.

Derrick executed a devastating Marine Corps knife hand to the neck.

Carl, forever old school, punched his man's jaw, landing the hit at the precise point where the bone met the ear.

All three agents dropped heavily.

"Good work," Derrick said. "Take their guns and rip out their communication devices so they can't notify backup when they come to. They're probably expected to report in regularly, but hopefully we have a little time before anyone notices they're not responding. Let's get them handcuffed to the metal detector. That ought to keep them occupied for a while when they wake up."

Rook, now upright again, had fixed Derrick with a dirty look.

"Alexander? Really?" he said.

"What's wrong with Alexander?"

"It's my middle name. And I hate it."

"Fine. What do you want to be next time?"

"Edgar," Rook said definitively.

"Edgar it is."

A few feet away, Carl was staring, dazzled, at Cynthia.

"You really are a heck of a woman," Carl said.

She looked at him with a provocative smile and said, "You have no idea."

Having secured three insentient agents to the metal detector, the four would-be rescuers proceeded, with their newly claimed guns drawn, through the double doors, into Gardner campaign headquarters.

They were immediately confronted by the divider.

"Okay, so where is she?" Derrick asked.

"Still in the southwest corner," said Rook, who had his phone out.

"That's this way," Derrick said, peeling off toward the left. "Let's go."

The other three followed. They immediately entered a large space filled with desks that had been arranged in no recognizable manner.

There were no people sitting in them, or standing near them, or meandering past them, as there clearly should have been. It made the room feel spooky and dead, like a beehive that was nothing but a series of empty honeycomb-shaped holes.

"Where is everyone?" Derrick asked, his weapon still up.

"I've got a bad feeling about this," said Rook, who had remained unarmed but was somehow mollified about his lack of weaponry by his journalist's bulletproof vest.

"Let's keep going," Carl urged. "Nikki is obviously not here. That's what matters."

They proceeded with caution through the room. Derrick led the way, with Rook behind him. Carl and Cynthia brought up the rear.

When they reached the office suite in the corner, Derrick stopped, held a finger to his lips, and listened at the door.

He heard nothing. Slowly, so that anyone on the other side wouldn't notice it, he turned the door handle. Once he was sure the lock mechanism was clear of the jamb, he threw open the door and entered, gun first.

There was no one there. He whirled and confronted any enemy that might have been behind the door. But that spot was also empty.

Carl had already gone in to cover his son. Rook soon joined them, as did Cynthia, who stood near a desk with a computer and a monitor on it. The screen showed several different views of the outside rooms, still empty.

The air reeked of clove cigarettes. Derrick pointed to his nose. Carl nodded, acknowledging the smell and what it meant: Colonel Feng had been there recently.

No one was speaking, mindful that Nikki was likely being held behind the next door, perhaps by Feng. Derrick walked as softly as he could and again listened intently. His concentration was so focused on the door and what might be behind it that he didn't even see the rail-thin male figure rising up from behind the desk until he already had his gun trained at a spot just behind Cynthia Heat's right ear.

"Drop your weapon," a raspy voice barked. "Drop it. Now! Then raise your hands."

Cynthia slowly lowered her weapon, placing it on the desk. Feng swiped it to the floor as she raised her arms.

The three men turned toward Feng, who had moved so that Cynthia was shielding him from the other two who were armed, neither of whom had a clean shot as a result.

"You. You. Drop your weapons," Feng ordered.

"Not a chance, Feng," Derrick said. "If you shoot her, I guarantee you the next bullet that flies will exit my gun and enter your head."

"Drop them," Feng shrieked. "Drop them."

"Not gonna happen," Derrick said, trying to see if he could even get his scope on some sliver of the unctuous Communist. But Feng was small—Cynthia Heat was actually a shade taller—and he used his lack of stature to his advantage. Derrick had nothing to work with.

Feng still had a one-quarter-finished clove cigarette in his mouth. He took a puff from it.

"Then I will tell you what's going to happen, Derrick Storm," Feng hissed. "I have better things to do than kill this woman. But I also have no plans to be killed myself. So I am going to leave the room with this woman as my hostage. You will not pursue me, unless you would like to see her dead. Then I'm going to leave this building. She will return to you safely once I am lost in the streets of lower Manhattan. Do we have a deal?"

Derrick could see the outline of the CD pressing through Feng's cheap jacket. He hated to lose his chance at recapturing it.

But that now struck him as a problem for another time, some future mission that he and Jones could devise. Keeping Cynthia Heat alive mattered more.

"Fine," Derrick said. "But mark my words, if you harm a hair on her head, I will spend the rest of my life hunting you. And I will not rest until you and three generations of your family are in the ground."

"Of course, of course," Feng said. "The American, always so brave in the rescue of his woman. We'll be taking our leave of you now."

Slowly they began inching out of the room, with Feng very careful about his positioning the whole time. They were just about to exit through the door when Carl Storm broke the silence.

"Wait," he said. "I'd like to kiss her good-bye first."

Feng's face squeezed in anger. "You'll do nothing of the sort."

"Sorry, pal," Carl said. "I've been waiting half a lifetime to meet a woman as incredible as this. And I'm not going to let her go without at least one kiss. You can shoot me for trying. But I guarantee if you do, my son here will make sure I'm not the only one who dies today."

Derrick had no idea what his father was up to, but he said, "Sounds reasonable to me, Feng."

"I'll even drop my weapon," Carl volunteered.

"Fine," Feng spat. "Make it quick."

Carl tossed his weapon into the corner.

"Gotta freshen my breath first, if you don't mind," he said, removing the Binaca from his pocket. "Don't want to make a bad first impression."

He pumped a squirt into his mouth. Then he turned to Cynthia.

"Want some?" he asked.

"I probably need it," Cynthia confirmed.

"Open wide," Carl said, walking toward Cynthia with the Binaca up.

And then, at the last moment, he diverted his aim and sprayed it at Feng's face.

One of Binaca's ingredients is SD alcohol 38F. While denatured, it is still highly flammable. And it did not, in this instance, disappoint.

The moment the leading edge of the spray hit the glowing end of Feng's cigarette, it burst into flames, turning into a blowtorch that splattered into Feng's face. The man roared and flailed backward, reflexively bringing his hands to his face to try to wipe away the flames.

Derrick Storm waited until his floundering target was well out of the way of Cynthia, who further helped matters by diving to the side. When he was sure he had a clean shot, Derrick pumped three bullets into the middle of Feng's face.

The man died instantly, slumping against the door. Derrick walked over to him and quickly yanked the CD out of Feng's pocket, stuffing it into his own.

Carl had gone toward Cynthia, helping her up off the ground.

"My hero," she said, then added suggestively, "Are you that resourceful in everything you do?"

Carl waggled his dark eyebrows. "You have no idea."

It was Rook, of all people, who played the role of the sober-minded, mission-focused guy.

He brought the momentary spirit of celebration that had gripped all of them to a halt by saying, "Guys, sorry to throw rain on the picnic, but you know whoever is in that next room now knows we're here."

Carl had taken back possession of his gun. So had Cynthia.

"Well, then let's not pretend we still have the element of surprise," Derrick said.

He strode over to the door he had once tiptoed up to and kicked it down. He entered the next office with his gun up. But a sweep of the room revealed it to be empty.

"Clear!" he shouted.

His eyes fell on a phone in a black case sitting on top of the desk. As the other three came in, he looked at Rook. "Is that your wife's phone?"

"Sure looks that way," Rook said grimly. No one had to bother saying the rest out loud.

Find My iPhone had done its job and found the phone. What it hadn't found was the phone's owner.

"So where is she?" Rook asked, his misery plain on his face.

The reply came from twelve stories farther up, where the unmistakable sound of helicopter rotors beating the air could then be heard.

"I'm sorry to say I think that's her, making an unwanted exit," Derrick said.

They ran over to the window in time to see a Bell 407 helicopter tilting away from the building. It was red, white, and blue and had LINDSY ONE emblazoned on the side.

It was impossible to see who was inside. But it wasn't hard to guess that helicopter held a daughter, a wife, and a friend—all in the person of Nikki Heat.

"Fer Chrissakes," Carl muttered. "Anyone got any good ideas? Because after that Binaca thing, I'm fresh out."

There was a sickly silence as the helicopter floated farther away, pointed in the direction of the mouth of the Hudson River, the Verrazano Bridge, and the ocean that stretched out beyond it.

Then Rook said, "Captain Tyler's Airborne Escapades."

"What's that?" Derrick asked.

"It's a friend who has a seaplane docked at Pier 11."

"That's three blocks away," Cynthia said. "Let's go."

Rook called on the way, alerting Captain Tyler that he would need to redeem his gift certificate in an unexpected—and quite urgent—manner.

Three blocks of sprinting later, they could already hear the six cylinders of a Continental IO-550-N engine roaring. The craft surrounding that engine, a Seawind 300C, was the newest and best seaplane on the market. It seated four adults and, at 100 percent power, reached a top speed of two hundred miles per hour—about twenty miles per hour faster than a Bell 407, which was all that mattered at this point. That the plane had been specially modified for skydiving was just a bonus at the moment.

"Welcome aboard," Captain Tyler shouted over the din as Rook and company clambered on, their breath ragged from the run. "Seat belts on, everyone. I'm going to get us up in the air quickly."

"Thanks, buddy," Rook shouted back. "Did you keep an eye on that helicopter like I asked?"

"Better than that. I got a lock on it on radar. They're heading south-southeast at about one-three-oh."

Rook pounded him on the shoulder. "Good work. I owe you one."

"A feature about Captain Tyler's Airborne Escapades in *First Press* will do nicely," Tyler said.

"You got it. Now let's take off."

"Aye, aye."

The Seawind was soon out on the Hudson River. Once it had the required 1,100 feet of water in front of it, Tyler floored the engines and the plane took flight.

They climbed steadily to five thousand feet. Then Tyler put on the autopilot and turned to his passengers.

"Okay, I'm keeping the throttle against the stops. We're gaining on them, but slowly. And they've got about a seventeen-mile head start. Another fifty minutes or so, and we should be dead even with them."

THIRTY-THREE

HEAT

The Taser had incapacitated Nikki Heat in at least two respects.

First there had been that initial jolt: fifty thousand volts of brain-frying fury that separated her from the ability to control either her mind or her body.

Then there was what it had allowed John Null to quickly do to her. With Heat unable to resist, the campaign manager had trussed her up like an eight-point buck he planned to toss on the hood of his pickup truck, securing her feet at the ankles and her hands at the wrist, then tying the two of those constraints together so that her body was bent into a parabola.

He dumped her into a mail cart borrowed from the seventy-ninth floor, like she was nothing more than a load of campaign junk mail, then took her for a ride in the elevator that was so disorienting she couldn't tell if they were going up or down.

Then they emerged on the roof, and Heat heard the beating of the helicopter rotors that would deliver her to a watery demise.

Heat was slightly more functional at that point, enough that she could at least twist herself into a position where she could see the blue sky above her. She felt the downdraft from the blades pressing against her face as Null wheeled her toward the chopper.

The cart stopped. Then Heat felt herself being lifted and

tilted until she slid out of the cart and landed roughly on the floor of the aircraft. The cargo door slammed behind her, then she heard two other doors opening, both of them at the front of the aircraft.

"Are you in?" Null yelled over the roar of the engines.

"Yeah, let's get out of here," Lindsy Gardner replied.

The whine of the turbines grew louder, then Heat felt herself being pressed downward. They were airborne.

Heat's range of motion, there on the chopper floor, was limited. She could roll left or right, not that it helped her much.

When she was on her left side, she could see into the cockpit, where Null was at the controls and Gardner was belted into the copilot's seat. On her right side, she could only see the underside of the rear seats.

She tugged against her constraints, which were made of thick twine. But that only made its scratchy burrs dig deeper into her skin. Likewise, working her fingers to try and get a grip on the ropes or something else useful didn't accomplish anything.

Heat studied her immediate surroundings, looking for something sharp that she could rub her ropes against. If she could get even one hand free, it might make a difference. But all she could see were the rounded rectangles of the stainless steel chair legs, which had been bolted into the floor.

A panic rose in Heat as she felt the chopper gain altitude. She had been in some tight spots in her life. But they usually had emergency exits, however small.

There was no getting out of this one. She had only the vague hope that Storm might properly interpret that text as a distress call.

But then what? Of all the vessels in the sky at any moment in the New York metropolitan area, how would he figure out which she was in? And then what could he do about it?

The minutes passed like hours. Heat couldn't help wondering if they were among the last she would ever experience. Hitting water after a five-thousand-foot drop would be like hitting concrete. Her body would shatter on impact.

Even if, by some absurd miracle, she survived the fall—which was incredibly unlikely—it sounded like she would be in the ocean, more than a hundred miles from land, out where there would be very few boats to come along, and without the use of her hands or feet.

She might be able to do a dead man's float. But, realistically, how long would she last out there? The Atlantic Ocean in October was probably no more than fifty-five degrees. The human body cools twenty-five times faster in water than in air. She had seen those charts of survival times in water. At that temperature, hypothermia would set in within an hour or two. At some point, she would fall unconscious. Then it would be all over.

Macabre thoughts flooded Heat's mind. She imagined Rook, Raley, and Ochoa tirelessly probing every aspect of her disappearance until, slowly, and with great agony, they came to recognize they were really investigating her death. Would they be able to pin it on Gardner in any meaningful way?

Probably not. The Gardner campaign would surely spin the whole thing as Nikki Heat mysteriously disappearing. A great tragedy, Gardner's spokesman would say. But, ultimately, it had nothing to do with the candidate.

Officially, Nikki Heat would be a missing person until, at some point in the future, the city would issue a death certificate. Would they even have a funeral? Would they bury an empty box? Would her mother come to the ceremony in disguise? That would be some kind of irony.

Heat jolted herself back to the present. There had to be some way she could give herself a chance of survival. She searched the underside of the backseat until she found a slim glimmer of hope. A screw had come slightly loose. If she scooted herself in just the right position, might she be able to rub the rope against it and get it to fray just a little?

It might not accomplish anything. But it was better than nothing.

Heat began working as furiously as her constraints would allow—which was not much. Her range of motion was small. She couldn't really get a lot of leverage. She plugged away all the same.

There had been no conversation from the front of the helicopter, at least not until they had been in the air for about forty minutes. Then:

"We're being followed," Null yelled.

"What are you talking about?" Gardner demanded.

"There's been a blip on the radar screen that has been shadowing our exact course. It's getting steadily closer."

"What is it?"

"Couldn't tell you. I don't think it's a helicopter. It's moving too fast."

"How long until we're over the deep water?"

"Another five minutes or so."

"Should we just drop her now?" Gardner asked.

"We could," Null said. "But there would be a better chance her body would be found. It could float and then be swept in on the tide."

"Then keep flying," Gardner said. "They'll probably veer off."

Heat felt a surge of panic that had her rubbing the ropes even faster. They had warmed from the friction she was generating. Now and then, the screw would catch just right and another small hair of the twine would fray.

If she had another half an hour, she was sure she could work free. But she didn't have that kind of time. She rubbed anyway.

"They're not veering off," Null said two minutes later. "We've got maybe four or five minutes until they intercept us."

"Change course," Gardner ordered. "See if they follow."

"You got it," he said.

Heat felt the chopper bank then even out again. She was still rubbing the ropes, even as her muscles ached from the effort. She reminded herself sore muscles wouldn't be a bother when she was dead.

Every now and then, she would test her bonds. They were as firm as ever.

Two minutes later, Null said, "They changed course with us. They'll be on us any moment now."

"What is that thing?" Gardner asked. Heat could see she was craning her neck by the window, having made visual contact with their pursuers.

"There's no landing gear. It's some kind of seaplane."

"Do you think they know about our extra passenger?"

"Maybe they do. Maybe they don't. Either way, what are we going to do about it?" Null asked.

"Get rid of the evidence, of course. Do you think the water is deep enough?"

"Yeah. It changed color about a minute or two back. We're definitely off the shelf now. It drops off quickly after that. But wait."

"What?" Gardner asked.

"Won't they see us?"

Gardner paused over this. "Put us into a hover. I'll wait until just after they pass us. Unless their plane is equipped with rearview mirrors, they won't be able to see the body falling."

"But they'll certainly know this is the campaign's chopper."

"We'll say someone stole it, took it for a joyride."

"Are you sure?"

"Yes. Put us into a hover."

The helicopter's forward movement slowly came to a halt. The aircraft was now floating in midair. Heat abandoned her efforts with the ropes and flopped her body in the direction of the front, just in time to see Gardner un-belting herself from the seat.

The senator contorted herself so she could pass through the narrow opening between the pilot's and copilot's seats. She knelt over Heat for a moment.

"It's really nothing personal," Gardner said. "You would have made a fine director of Homeland Security."

Heat didn't give her the pleasure of a response.

Gardner stood, grabbed the length of rope that bound Heat's hands to her feet, and slid Heat's body along the floor. Then Gardner opened the cargo door.

The terror was even more real now. The wind whipped into the cabin of the helicopter. Heat could see the ocean spread out far below them, looking flat and blue and endless in all directions until it bent over the horizon.

Gardner had switched sides and was now shoving her from behind, ever closer to the edge.

Heat's feet and hands went out the door first. Another shove and her arms and legs were out, too. There was nothing Heat could do to stop what was about to happen.

"Is it time?" Gardner yelled.

"They're about to pass directly overhead," Null replied. "I'll give you a countdown."

For a few sickening seconds, Heat was perched on the edge, feeling the abyss underneath her. She thought perhaps her life would be passing in front of her eyes. Instead, all she could see was the helicopter's fuselage.

She strained impotently against her restraints one last time.

Then Null said, "Okay, here goes. Three . . . two . . . one."

Gardner pushed. Heat felt her body tip over the edge.

She was falling. And there was nothing but cool October air between her and the ocean, five thousand feet below.

THIRTY-FOUR

STORM

For most of the flight, there had been little discussion aboard the Seawind 300C.

Captain Tyler was concentrating on getting every last bit of speed he could churn out of the aircraft. The passengers were alone with their thoughts.

The Bell helicopter, which had at first only been a blip on the radar, eventually came into sight. At first, it was little more than a pinprick of darkness against the blue sky. Then, slowly, it grew larger as the Seawind gained on it.

It was still a mile or so off when Derrick Storm broke the silence.

"I feel like a dog who is chasing a car," he said. "I don't know what I'm going to do once I catch it."

"I just assumed we were going to follow them and improvise once we figure out where they're going," Cynthia Heat said.

"Yeah, but why are they going so far out to sea?" Rook asked. "I don't know the range of a bird that size, but there's nothing out here to land on. If they go too much farther, they won't have the gas to get back to land. What are they even doing out here?"

This was met with silence until Carl Storm spoke up.

"They're heading for deep water," he said. "Then they're going to drop Nikki out of the helicopter."

Cynthia Heat gasped. Rook blanched.

Derrick didn't miss a beat. "Dad's right. If you toss a body in shallow water, it sinks at first, but then floats to the top as the decomposition gasses begin to build up. And then there's no telling where it goes. In deeper, colder water, decomposition is much slower. The body goes down and stays down."

This was too much for Nikki Heat's mother and husband.

"How long until we've passed the continental shelf?" Derrick said, pointing the question toward Captain Tyler.

"Not far now," Tyler said. "Probably around the time we catch up to them, actually. They changed course about two minutes ago, so I changed course with them. Another two or three minutes and we'll be over top of them."

"So what are they thinking right now?" Derrick said, again looking at his father. "How are they going to do it?"

"Well, they have to know we're following them at this point. They changed course and we changed course. Besides, there's really nothing else out here in this airspace, especially at this altitude. It's not like we can hide in the clouds, Red Baron–style, and then swoop down on them."

"So they know we're onto them," Derrick continued. "Which means they're going to wait to drop the body when they think we can't see it."

"And that happens right as we pass over them. They're in our blind spot at that point. That's about as good a time as there would be."

"Well, then," Derrick said. "It seems like I need to be ready to go after her. Captain Tyler, show me to your skydiving equipment."

Carl grinned. "I guess maybe it's good you're into that action-adventure hero crap after all."

Captain Tyler verbally directed Derrick to a compartment

in the back of the plane that contained a full complement of top-of-the-line skydiving equipment. Derrick selected a Javelin Odyssey, which had a large enough chute to handle a tandem jump, and quickly shrugged himself into it. He checked it over. Twice. Everything seemed to be in order.

He pulled the CD out of his pocket and thrust it at Rook. "Do me a favor and hang on to this. I've gone through too much trouble to get it to go jumping out of a plane with it."

"Of course," Rook said.

Then Derrick turned to Captain Tyler. "I hope pickup is part of this package if I end up in the drink."

"That'll be extra, actually," Tyler said, grinning. "I usually don't tell customers about the up-charge until they're already wet."

"Bill it to Jedediah Jones."

"You got it," Tyler said.

They flew in silence for another few moments. The tension inside the cabin was palpable. It was still entirely possible the *Lindsy One* was simply choosing a very roundabout way to get to, say, Delaware.

Then came evidence the craft and its operators had a more pernicious plan after all.

"They're slowing down," Tyler called out.

"Because they're getting ready to do the drop," Carl said.

"Okay. Get that jump door open, Captain," Derrick said.

"Hang on, everyone," Tyler called out. "It's going to get windy in here."

Tyler pushed a button, and the door on the port side of the plane slid open. As promised, a rush of air poured forcefully into the plane, which lurched a little until Tyler compensated for the change in aerodynamics.

Derrick gripped the straps near the door and leaned out. He

could see the chopper lose its forward tilt and go into a hover.

He quickly brought his head inside the cabin. "Okay, Captain. I want you to pass over them with as little room to spare as you can. Make them feel like you're buzzing them, trying to harass them. But do it just to the right. I want a good view of what's happening out my side of the plane."

"Yes, sir," Tyler called.

Derrick returned to his spot by the door, grabbed a strap, and hung himself perilously out. He had to squint against the rush of air, but he could see that the plane was approaching the now stationary helicopter very quickly. Ominously, he noted that the cargo door—which was on the helicopter's starboard side, in plain view—was now open.

His father had been right. They were going to throw Heat out of the vessel.

As the Seawind passed directly overhead, no more than a hundred feet above—an eyelash in the world of aviation—Derrick kept his attention squarely on the chopper's cargo door. He could see someone's arms and legs already dangling out.

Derrick leaned even farther out the door once the Seawind passed by, giving him a good view as the arms and legs suddenly tilted down, falling out the side of the helicopter. Then the body—Nikki Heat's body—followed.

Without a moment's hesitation, Storm leapt after her.

There are all kinds of physics involved in a free fall from five thousand feet.

Start with the mass of the falling object. For whatever Galileo may have thought about the matter, heavier objects really do fall faster—because gravity acts on them more.

Advantage Storm: a two-hundred-twenty-pound man falls

faster than a one-hundred-forty-pound woman.

On the other side, there are things that can slow the object down, like its surface area and drag coefficient. A skydiver who spreads out her body reaches a terminal velocity of about one hundred twenty miles per hour. A skydiver who assumes a smaller profile can reach two hundred miles per hour or more.

Again, advantage Storm: he went headfirst, pinning his arms to his sides and pointing his toes to minimize wind resistance as he plunged toward the earth.

Except, to his horror, he realized it might not be enough of an advantage. He quickly located Heat, roughly one hundred twenty feet below him. Had she assumed the classic spread-eagle skydiving position, he would have caught up to her in no time.

But Heat was more like a parabola. She was falling butt-first, with her arms and legs pointed skyward, almost like a diver in pike position. Her surface area, mostly her back, was only barely greater than Storm's.

Which meant this was going to be close.

Storm remained as coolheaded as was possible under the circumstances. He was a veteran of many jumps, from training to some of the most difficult operational conditions imaginable. The old joke in skydiving was that if something went wrong, you had the rest of your life to fix it.

But that still meant, even during a plunge from the relatively low height of five thousand feet, you had *some* time to make things right.

Storm set a timer in his head. He had roughly fourteen seconds before they reached one thousand feet—the lowest he dared go before pulling the rip cord. If he didn't deploy his chute at that point, the chances of survival began diminishing greatly. At five hundred feet, they would be very small. Any lower, they would be nil.

After three seconds, they had reached 50 percent of their terminal velocity. But they were accelerating quickly—Isaac Newton's 9.8 meters per second squared never feels so fast as when it's working against your interests.

Storm could feel the air tearing at him. He steered himself so he was directly over Heat, so he would literally fall on top of her if he managed to reach her in time. He could now see why she was falling in such a strange position: Her hands and feet were bound together.

There was nothing Storm could do about that now. He willed himself to go faster, flattening himself even further. He was gaining on her. Some. But he was starting to have real doubts about whether it would be enough.

After eight seconds, they were at 90 percent terminal velocity, closing in on top speed very fast. Heat was still sixty or seventy feet away.

At nine seconds, Storm realized he wasn't going to get there in time. He was too far off. She was falling too fast.

At ten seconds, he began the debate: Did he just pull the rip cord? Or did he die trying to save her?

He didn't bother looking at his altimeter. He had done enough jumps that he had a feel for where the one-thousand-foot ceiling was. And he was closing in on it altogether too quickly. Decision time was coming.

Eleven seconds. He couldn't bring himself to give up. And yet . . . continuing the free fall would be madness. He was still at least thirty feet away. Close enough that he could see the terror on Heat's face, far enough that he knew he simply wasn't going to make it in time.

Twelve seconds. They were nearing 99 percent of terminal velocity. Two hundred miles an hour. Hitting water at that speed would quickly lead to another kind of terminal.

And then, during the thirteenth second, Heat's countenance changed. It went from fear to determination to . . . pain?

She had ripped one arm away from her restraints, dislocating her thumb and tearing a good chunk of skin off her hand in the process.

But it changed everything. The amount of surface area she was able to present doubled. The drag coefficient increased accordingly. The physics were suddenly on their side.

She slowed to perhaps one hundred fifty miles per hour. It was still fast, but not compared to Storm's speed. He was suddenly falling a full seventy feet per second faster.

That meant it took Storm less than half a second to close the gap between them. They collided with a heavy thud, but it enabled Storm to koala bear hug her with two legs and two arms.

The timer in Storm's head had just hit fourteen seconds.

"Pull the cord!" he yelled at Heat.

With her one free hand, she reached for his shoulder and yanked.

The drogue deployed smoothly, followed by the main chute. They were soon floating down toward the water at a leisurely ten miles an hour.

"Sorry to just drop in on you like that," Storm said.

"You know, when you did that at my apartment the other day, I have to admit I was a little put out," Heat said. "This time I don't mind so much."

THIRTY-FIVE

HEAT/STORM
ONE WEEK LATER

A s experienced, decorated, high-level employees of two of America's elite paramilitary organizations, Nikki Heat and Derrick Storm had been subjected to extreme duress on many occasions.

Physical agony. Psychological warfare. The threat of imminent death. They had been through that and more. In Heat's case, it had happened in every borough. In Storm's case, it had happened on every continent.

But nothing—either in their training or during the crucible test of live ops—had quite prepared them for this.

The uncertainty. The torment. The wait.

Interminable.

The hour had grown late. Dangerously late. And still, nothing. No contact.

"How much longer do you think?" Heat asked.

"At this point, there's no telling," Rook said.

"Try the phones again," Storm said.

"We tried three times already," Rook said. "Two rings, then voice mail, every time."

"We have to be able to establish communications somehow," Storm said. "Without that, we're lost."

"I'm afraid it's hopeless," Rook said.

They settled into an aggrieved silence. How had they gotten there? Where had they gone wrong? They were questions that had been asked—but not answered—many times already.

"Should we try the police?" Storm suggested.

"I *am* the police," Heat reminded him.

"Should we try police who can actually do something?" Storm asked.

"Not at this point," Rook said. "They're not an option. We have to rely on our own resources."

"Limited though they are," Storm said.

More waiting. The hour grew even later. All seemed lost.

The previous week had been a hectic one. A compact disc containing evidence that Lindsy Gardner had accepted a fifty-million-dollar bribe from Chinese criminals had been given to the Offices of the US Attorneys. Heat had given them a counterfeit bill with Gardner's fingerprints on it—the one she had managed to keep in her pocket, trusting that Lindsy Gardner had long forgotten she paid Cynthia Heat a hundred dollars every two weeks for piano lessons, not eighty.

Indictments had come quick and sure. The evidence was overwhelming. Gardner's defense had been so inadequate a judge had refused to set a bond, given the defendant's ability to flee.

The scorched body of a Chinese national, found in Gardner campaign headquarters, had only added to the confusion, though it appeared no charges could be brought from that. The bullets that killed him had been fired by a weapon belonging to a Secret Service agent, who had no memory of how he had wound up chained to a metal detector, separated from his service weapon.

The story had exploded across the media like a huge ratings-producing bomb. There had been much speculation—most of it wrong, as usual—though rumors had surfaced that Jameson Rook was set to release an article in *First Press* that would set the record straight. Another Pulitzer was surely in the offing.

None of which helped the situation at hand.

"This isn't like them," Heat said. And not for the first time.

"So irresponsible," Storm confirmed.

"And so selfish," Heat said.

"It's like they aren't even thinking about us at all," Rook declared.

They waited some more. Finally, the door handle to Rook's Tribeca loft turned downward, and the two outlaws entered.

"Oh," Cynthia Heat said. "You shouldn't have waited up."

"Fer Chrissakes," Carl Storm said.

Nikki stood with her hands on her hips.

"*Where* have you two *been*?" she asked.

"Do you have *any* idea what time it is?" Derrick asked.

"We were worried sick about you," Rook said. "You could have been bleeding in a ditch somewhere. Or, worse, you could have been stuck watching reality TV."

"There is going to be some serious punishment, young man. Serious," Derrick said.

"You have a lot of explaining to do," Nikki said.

Then Cynthia, her face aglow, thrust out her left hand. On her ring finger was a glittering 2.4-carat diamond ring.

The air momentarily left the room.

When it returned, Nikki gasped. "Oh, Mom," was all she managed to say.

Derrick was looking at his father, unable to form the question that was on his mind. Carl sensed it all the same.

"Your mother and I used to joke that if one of us died, the other should be in proper mourning until the funeral," Carl said.

"Then, once the body was lowered into the ground, we should dry our tears, then look up to see who might be available."

He laughed. "Just took me thirty years to dry my tears, is all."

"We went to The Players Club first," Cynthia said. "George got Carl's drink order wrong three times, wouldn't you know."

"I decided not to drink the fourth version," Carl said. "I worried at that point it might have been Drano."

"Then," Cynthia said, "he took me to the Empire State Building and told me he had a surprise waiting for me there. *Well . . .*"

"I decided if it was till death do us part, that isn't as far away as it used to be," Carl said. "I figured we'd better get to it."

The two beamed at each other for a moment.

"Are we too old to ask for anyone's blessing?" Cynthia asked.

"Oh, Mom," Nikki said again, and squeezed her mother with enough force to almost knock the wind out of her.

Then Derrick hugged his dad twice as hard.

"There's only one thing more beautiful than two young kids in love," Rook declared. "And that's two old kids in love."

"Yeah, and speaking of kids," Cynthia said, "when am I going to get a grandchild?"

"And speaking of mothers," Rook said, "I think I hear mine calling me right now."

But no. Not quite.

Instead, Rook opened a bottle of Krug Brut.

"I've been saving this for my third Pulitzer," he said. "But this occasion is more than worthy of it."

They toasted the Heat-Storm engagement. They toasted the new family that was forming. They toasted all the things they had to be thankful for.

Someone watching might have thought any group of people with that much to celebrate was coming to some long-awaited conclusion of a great chain of events—like a television show going through its series finale.

But, truly, this was not the end for Heat and Storm.

This was only the beginning.